This is a work of fiction. Names, characters, and places are products of the author's imagination.

Formatting by M. H. Woodscourt

Cover design by Luisa Galstyan

Interior maps and illustrations by Annamarie Dunne.

Published by Yarrow Leaf Press

ISBN: 979-8-9850208-0-9

www.wordsinmyblood.com

FIRES OF FREEDOM

BOOK TWO OF TALES OF SEA & SKIES

BRIGITTE CROMEY

YARROW LEAF PRESS

To Amy. See, I caught the White Whale after all!!

CONTENTS

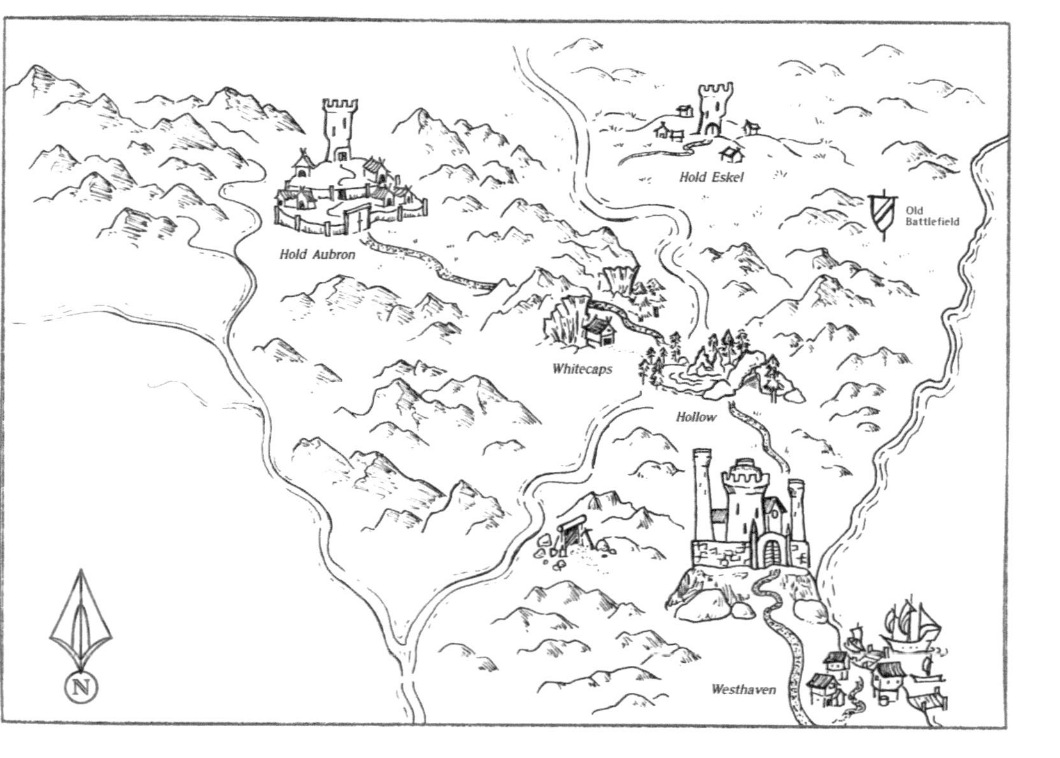

Hold Aubron
Hold Eskel
Old Battlefield
Whitecaps
Hollow
Westhaven
N

FIRES OF FREEDOM

1
CORONATION DAY

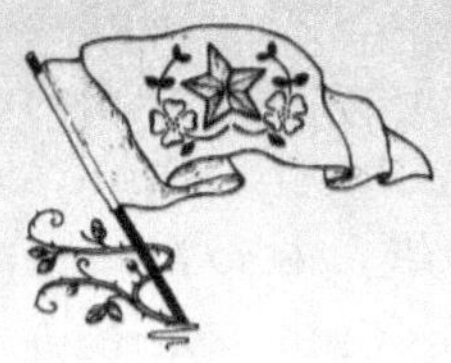

Water stood for new birth. The priest poured a trickle down the new queen's forehead, errant drops beading on her raven-black hair like morning dew. Setting the bowl aside, he beckoned to a little girl standing to the side of the dais. Her soft footsteps could barely be heard in the vast room, as she approached with a silver filigree crown on a scarlet pillow. The priest's solemn words filled the hall with whispers of bravery, legacy, and duty as he lifted the crown.

"Kneel, my child."

RosE's heartbeat thudded in her ears as she knelt on the steps of the dais. They had been unsuccessful in finding a carpet to temper the early spring chill, and the edges of the steps pressed coldly into her shins. Overhead, she could feel the weight of the buttressed roof, as if all of the history of Illyn was contained in the stones of the hall.

The priest intoned, "By right of blood and birth, I crown

you Brielle Thinar, Queen of Illyn." He raised the crown for all to see before fitting it carefully on her head. The hours of practice helped steady her nerves as he commanded, "May your reign be as steadfast as the seasons and as long-lived as the mountains."

Rose could sense the support of all who had gathered to witness the coronation, filling the hall behind her as the priest began the blessing prayer. Even with the number of onlookers, it was still cold. Dreadfully cold.

Brielle Thinar. It still feels so foreign to me. She closed her eyes through the blessing, warning herself to keep her doubts outside where they belonged. *I've come a long way, becoming the person I was born to be. To falter now would be disastrous.* The first rays of the rising sun illuminated the hall through the open doors, kissing the back of her neck. Warmth spread through her chilly limbs. *It'll be all right. I've already come so far.*

The priest finished his prayer before her knees had the chance to go stiff. With a reassuring smile, he offered her a hand up. His words carried to her ears alone.

"Long live the queen."

2
EARLY WINTER

A hawk spiraled above the cliffs, sending a shrill cry into coastal air laced by sea spray and the crashing of waves. Many feet below, a number of riders waited in anticipation for its kill, the brown of their horses and rich colors of their clothes contrasting the bleakness of the late autumn landscape. One young woman bore a simple circlet on her head, intertwined gold and silver bands glimmering in her dark hair. She sat comfortably on her black mare, the hood of her cloak framing a pale, delicate face. A shriek split the sky as the hawk descended, a sea bird clutched in its talons.

With the hunt concluded, the hunting party urged their horses back towards the castle, perched on a rise overlooking the sea. Ships dotted the harbor below, a growing town sprawling beyond old fortifications to embrace the sea's edge. From above, the sounds of wind and water erased the noise of town life, punctuated by the greetings of sentries atop the walls. Once inside the formidable gates, the hunters dismounted, dusting off their clothing and making for the keep as hostlers came to collect their horses.

. . .

Amid chatter and laughter, Rose fell in step alongside one of her guests, a man with sleek black hair and tilted eyes. "Did you find the outing enjoyable?"

The Kittai Isles ambassador gave her a slight smile. "Very interesting, Your Majesty. Your methods of hawking differ from our own, and I found it most intriguing."

"Just as intriguing as we found your people's swordsmanship," Rose offered politely. "It seems there is much we can learn from each other." She shivered in the late-autumn air. Although this was her second autumn in Illyn, the wind still bit right through her cloak. "May I invite you to join us for hot beverages, Your Highness? These afternoons are getting a little cold for my taste."

The prince bowed graciously. "Thank you, Your Majesty, but I must respectfully decline your generous offer." His forehead wrinkled in a brief frown. "This morning, I received a parcel of communications from my own monarch, and I must do my duty in examining it before the dinner this evening."

"I understand." Rose raised her voice as they stepped inside the shelter of the keep. "Cedric? Will you show the prince and his companions back up to their rooms?"

One of the guards stepped from his post to escort the Kittai Islanders towards the guest quarters. As they departed, Rose followed the rest of her party to a smaller room just off the hall, where a fire crackled merrily on the hearth. Taking off her scarf, she stretched both hands out to the fire gratefully.

"Cold, Milady?" one of the servants asked.

Before Rose could answer, one of the soldiers spoke up,

shrugging his shoulders free from a cloak to reveal a navy uniform over a mail shirt. Crimson chevrons on his shoulders indicated a high rank, and an armband emblazoned with a diving hawk circled his left bicep. "The queen is an Illyn native," he said, quirking his brows over eyes brighter blue than the sky at midsummer. "Why should she ever find it cold?"

"Well, this Illyn native spent most of her childhood in a more pleasant climate." Rose shivered eloquently. "It wasn't nearly this cold in the woods during autumn."

"And it's only going to get colder." The Shona commander Erven looked worried as he adjusted his sword belt over his shoulder. "I've been watching the mountains since this morning. I'm afraid we're getting our first bad storm early. It might change when the Kittai Islanders are able to leave."

Rose withdrew her hands from the fire reluctantly. "It's going to be that bad?"

Her first ally in Illyn—now twenty-one to her eighteen years—nodded. "I can't say for certain, but it's brewing to be a strong one."

"Hmph." Rose pulled off her cloak and handed it to one of the menservants. "Maybe it's just as well we have the formal dinner tonight, and not tomorrow."

Erven grinned, his eyes full of mischief. "Just enough time for us to deal with guild heads and village leaders once more before winter sets in."

Rose made a face. "I know it's all part of the role, but I hate these." She shook her head, gathering up her scarf as Erven laughed. "I'll see you in a bit."

· · ·

EVEN WITH THE promise of snow looming, most of the invited guests managed to make their way to the dinner that evening. Uncomfortable in her ceremonial crown and best dress, Rose presided over a table filled with influential guild heads and villager leaders. It was just like other formal events—the whirlpool of small talk, introductions, and conversations plunged her deep into the persona of the person who wore the crown until she wasn't sure where she left off and it began.

At last, the dignitaries retired to their rooms, the guests departed, and the kitchen workers appeared to begin clearing up the remains of the meal. Rose stood at the foot of the dais, bidding a final goodbye to the High Magistrate. Once the cantankerous old fellow had left the hall, she sagged and let out an exhausted sigh.

"Tired, dear?" Her friend Violet sidled up to squeeze her hand.

Rose pulled the shorter girl closer, grateful for the several inches of height difference that made Violet the perfect size for hugging. "I didn't realize how tired I was until now." She let go of Violet to adjust her braids under the crown, a headache starting where the metal put pressure on her skull.

"I thought you mightn't." Violet tucked a lock of mousy brown hair behind her ear. "Willow noticed you didn't eat much, either."

The reminder made Rose's stomach growl in protest. "I suppose not." She frowned. "Where *is* Willow, anyhow?"

"Upstairs. A message came, and she jumped at the chance to slip away." Violet tilted her head to the side, quiet blue eyes sparkling with amusement. "She *also* says that if one more person gives you an underhanded compliment that's really a critique on how you run your country, she'll drop an anvil on their heads."

Rose laughed, the tension easing around her temples. "You sounded exactly like her just then!"

"Well," Violet said, linking her arm through Rose's and leading her towards a door in the side of the hall. "I felt the same way, but it's not very becoming of a healer to wish harm on anyone." She pushed open the stairwell door, winding steps illuminated by the occasional flaring lantern. "We got together a few things for a nice late supper in the council room, if you're feeling up to it."

"That does sound nice," Rose agreed. "Let me change out of these clothes first." She flattened a hand against her stomach. "I can hardly breathe with how tightly Arielle laced me into this."

"All right," Violet said. She stopped at a landing and added, "I think I'll do the same and join the rest of you. The others can take care of the tidying up for tonight."

AFTER CHANGING INTO COMFORTABLE CLOTHES, Rose gently pushed on the council room door. It creaked open to let out a brilliant glow of firelight and the sounds of merriment.

"Aye, an' I told him so, too!" Willow was saying. "I said if he had any complaints, he could stuff 'em right up his nose." Rose's friend—two years older and much more confident—emphatically dropped a wooden bowl of berry sauce on the table, straightening a dove-grey shirt under a soft leather vest with a precise tug.

"I could think of a few other places he might take complaints," Heather suggested from a chair tilted against the wall. She twitched an eyebrow towards the third girl in the room. "What do you think, Ducky?"

"I hear the pigs are in need of a new caretaker," Clover agreed with a pert smile. The youngest of the three brushed a lock of dark brown hair from a permanently tanned forehead. Heather and Clover teetered on the cusp of informality even on the most solemn occasions, and had obviously taken the first opportunity to disappear from the public eye.

Rose leaned against the arched doorway, quietly enjoying her friends' banter. After their father had returned to their home village, far south in the Gaillen Woods, the three sisters had stayed in Illyn to make themselves useful— or useless in just the right way, as Willow often remarked with a sarcastic twist to her mouth.

Heather noticed Rose's presence first. "Here she is!" She sprang up to make an elaborate bow before Rose, chestnut curls fighting loose from their pins to bounce around her face. "Your Majesty! We were starting to take bets on how long it'd take Violet to retrieve you."

"Let it be known, I was the closest," Willow announced, sweeping a pile of hazelnuts from in front of Clover to join a heap on her side of the table. The fire gleamed off her blonde hair, tinting it the color of sun shining through honey as she greeted Rose. "Hello, dearest. I'm glad you finally managed to get away." She pulled out the corner chair, gesturing at the dishes spread across the table. "Sit down, and let's eat in peace."

Rose settled gratefully into the seat, happy it wasn't at the head of the table. Reaching for an apple cake, she asked, "Is anyone else coming?"

"Mmhmm..." Clover swallowed a mouthful of food.

"Erven said he just needed to check something with the night watch, and then he'd be up. Arielle, perhaps?"

"She said maybe." Heather leaned her chair against the wall again. "You never know when something will come up in the infirmary to delay her. Her, Violet, Lena," she counted on her fingers. "All of them are so difficult to pin down."

"That's what happens when most of your friends are healers." Willow raised an eyebrow ironically. "Terrible planning on your part, Rose."

"Please, no more comments about my planning." Rose set the apple cake down on her plate, eyeing it with a somewhat diminished appetite. "I can't take any more of that this evening."

"Well, if anyone grumbles, we have some excellent suggestions for where they can take complaints!"

"Heather!"

Violet's admonition dissolved into laughter as the door opened to admit her, Erven, and several of their other friends. As snow began to fall outside, the evening that had begun in frenetic formality ended in a sweet, comfortable gathering, filled with the laughter of old friends.

3
WINTER'S ADVENT

The storm Erven had predicted came that night, the wind whistling around the towers and sapping the warmth from everyone unlucky enough to be on midnight watch. The trees creaked under heavy loads of snow, sending many crashing to the ground in the middle of the night. By morning, snow thickly covered the ground, and the leaden sky proclaimed more to come. Amid hurried pleasantries, the Kittai Isles delegation bade their farewells and made their ship ready to sail.

Rose firmly closed the shutters on the weather the morning the foreign diplomats left, returning to her work with mixed feelings. Snow had never been her favorite, and her bed called to her with promises of warmth and safety. Ignoring the urge to sleep in, she paid a visit to the chapel with Willow for morning prayer, crossing the courtyard back to the keep just as Erven returned from an early patrol around the wall tops. All of them shook snow from their clothes just inside the hall, already grown chilly after the festivities a few nights before.

Willow unwrapped yards of scarf from her head and neck, face still reddened by the cold when it emerged. "Is this rotten weather going to slow down Violet and Lena on their way home?"

"I hope not." Erven tugged his insignia band higher on his arm. "Lena's been packing and repacking her bag every night, she's that excited. It makes me a little less worried, seeing how happy she is to go with Violet."

The reminder of the healers' imminent departure made Rose frown. After almost two years, Violet was returning to their old home to take her place as the Yarrow Leaf tribe's healer. She wasn't expecting her voice to catch as she said, "I —I need to make sure I have all the things together that I want to send with them." Rose cleared her throat. "Did you have anything for your family, Willow?"

Willow nodded, her stormy blue eyes preoccupied. "I do, but not just for Mum. I got something from Ethan that needs t'be passed on to Da. Can I give it to you now?"

"By all means." Rose thought of the pile of documents awaiting her attention upstairs. "I'll probably also write a letter of my own to them, if I have time."

"I'll see you both at dinner." Erven saluted her cheerfully as he went towards the stairs. "I have work to get done as well."

Rose and Willow followed him, taking the stairs at a slower pace. Halfway up, Rose asked, "The letter from Ethan...is there trouble?"

"Not exactly, no." Willow wrapped her scarf around her shoulders. "But we're always keeping our ears open for anything that could endanger Da and the others."

Rose nodded. One of the many surprises in the last several years had been the revelation of Willow's father as a former Sea Wanderer naval commander and tactician. While a surprise, the information made sense, given Alder's mannerisms and no-nonsense attitude towards people who behaved foolishly. In that respect, he and his oldest daughter were very similar. "Is something simmering I need to know about?"

"That's doubtful." Willow carefully opened the door to their adjoining studies, letting out a wash of warm air and the smells of ink and paper. "I'd just rather keep Da informed so he can make decisions if he chooses to. A few of the enemy commanders knew he was here, and I just hope they're too stupid to realize he's not actually *living* in Illyn."

"You're still on about that, Old Thing?" Heather asked, looking up from a long table covered in stacks of slates, several books, and a lockbox. In the time since their victory, Willow's eighteen-year-old sister had grown into her gangly limbs and madcap energy. She and Willow typically shared responsibilities as administrative assistants, doing more to ensure things ran smoothly than anyone but Rose—and possibly Erven—suspected.

Willow lobbed her scarf at her sister's head. "Yes, I'm still 'on about that'. So would you be, if you *read* any of the reports Ethan sent." She squinted at the table. "Where'd you put it?"

Heather's curls bounced on the shoulders of her thickly knit sweater, eccentrically worn over a battered pair of boots, grey wool dress, and highland patterned tunic. "You know I can't read that cipher the two of you use." She flicked a document tube with a practiced finger, sending it spinning across the table to her sister. "There y'go. Also, something came urgently from the Shona earlier." Sharp intelligence flickered in Heather's cloudy blue eyes as she commented, "I didn't know new plots were brewin'."

"Thank you. I'll give you a hand in just a moment. We'll see if we can clear this lot before dinner." Willow raised a cynical eyebrow at the messy table. "Though, if your work habits were just a bit tidier... I left you alone for what, an hour?"

Rose laughed as Willow turned her attention back to their previous conversation. "Plots, I can handle. If we can stay ahead of them, they're less troublesome. I'd just hate for Da to wake up one morning in the hands of Iorcan bounty hunters. Here you are." She handed Rose the document tube. "There's also a letter for Mum and our brother in there."

"Thank you," Rose said. Peeking through the connecting door, she could just see the edge of her own desk, currently scattered with documents that needed reviewing. "Can you two try to intercept any visitors or questions for today?" Guilt tugged at her stomach as she explained, "I'd like to take care of all this so I can enjoy Violet's last few evenings here."

"Right," Willow replied from behind a slate, clearly already distracted with her own tasks. "Close your door. If anyone comes lookin' for you, we'll tell 'em you're dead."

ERVEN PULLED his hood farther over his head as he exited the keep. The wind howled around him, sending snow into his face with a stinging wetness that made him blink hard. He'd planned on taking a quick walk after a morning filled with administrative work, but the sound of children's laughter made him change his course towards a building sitting in the shadow of the walls.

Once a slave barracks, the building had been re-roofed and every crack battened. Banners hung from the steeply pitched roof, chief amongst them a brightly colored kerchief hanging from a javelin over the door. They snapped in the furious wind, brilliant colors a foil for the bleak sky. Under the kerchief swung a hand-painted sign, proclaiming the edifice to be 'Her Majesty's Rogue School of Underage Minions'.

Warmth washed Erven's face as stepped inside the snug building, the rows of beds covered in worn, brightly colored quilts. Inside, he found the source of the laughter, as Willow and Heather's younger sister Clover tumbled to the ground under a pile of wriggling, shrieking children.

"Hoy, hoy, hoy, stooooop!" the sixteen-year-old yelped, as a pair of little boys and a small girl started tickling her ribs. Her hazel-green eyes met Erven's. "Haallp!!"

Erven laughed and dove into the fray, hauling one boy off Clover by the belt and hoisting another around the waist. The child squirmed and yelped, flailing his elbows into Erven's ribs. The rest of the children scattered with shrieks and laughter as he offered Clover his free hand. "Good morning!"

"Morning!" Clover greeted him enthusiastically as she gained her feet. Straightening her apron, she eyed the boy still trapped under his arm. "Let that be a lesson to you, laddie. Never mess with the Shona commander."

Erven set the boy down before his ribs took more damage. "Busy morning?"

Clover retrieved a large, floppy-brimmed hat from the floor and jammed it on her head. Different useful items rattled and spun on a chain strung from her belt as she explained, "We've been dealing with insurrections all day. I didn't realize how much this lot needs to get outside and play."

"I wouldn't think of it, either," Erven confessed as one boy took a flying leap from one bed to another. "How do you manage?"

Clover's face turned thoughtful as she scanned the crowd of children, all orphans cared for by the Crown. "Merald and Tora took as many as they could into the nursery—Oy!" With the speed of long practice, she caught a girl just as she tripped over the edge of the rug. "Well, we manage, anyway."

His ears beginning to ring, Erven decided to check in on the nursery. Abandoning the chaos, he brushed through a curtained doorway to the room where babies and toddlers slept. The light from lamps and candles flickered around the room, holding its own against the light from a screened-off hearth. Most of the babies were already on their first nap of the day, swaddled in their cots in a dark corner.

Their caregiver Tora sat near the hearth, one child on her lap and several others playing on the rush mat. Although she'd been a fierce fighter, then a brilliant healer, Tora had gladly accepted the job of caring for the most delicate children in the Rogue School. Erven could see the difference even as he approached the cozy circle. The littlies' innocence had gone a long way towards softening the rough edges on a woman who'd spent her entire youth as a Shona resistance fighter.

"Erven!"

Occupied as they were, the littlies quickly noticed Erven

and swarmed him, begging in squeaky voices to be picked up and carried.

"Up? Up?"

"Can we go for a ride?!"

One little girl had never been known to speak. She tugged on the edge of his tunic, reaching up with open palms. He scooped her up, glad that he'd chosen not to wear chainmail under his uniform that morning. "Noisy bunch, aren't they?" he asked, pointing towards the other room.

She nodded contentedly as Tora laughed. "I might suggest that Clover let them outside, even just for a little bit. Well, the older ones, anyway. We'll just stay in here for today." The child on her lap began coughing, and she rubbed his back soothingly. "It's far too cold for these lungs, eh?"

"Too cold for me, too."

Erven peered around the side of the cupboards next to the door. Tora's husband Merald sat with his back to the wall, weaving a darning needle through the heel of a worn-out sock. Even though Violet and the other healers had done their best with the horrendous wounds he'd received fighting Lord Kuma, they'd eventually had to acknowledge that Merald was lucky to have survived at all. He didn't say much, but Erven suspected he was in constant pain after the morning star strike that had driven chain mail links deep into his side.

To everyone's delight, romance had blossomed between him and Tora in the months he'd spent recovering under her care—romance that had soon developed to a strong commitment and marriage. It made Erven's heart happy to see them together, first during Merald's long recovery, then working side by side with the children.

Erven sat down next to Merald, settling the little girl in his lap. "It looks like you've been busy."

Merald bit the yarn off and tossed the sock into a basket of others. Picking up a new one, he said, "I'm hoping this one only goes for a day." He shook his head. "It's just a warning of what's ahead, I'm afraid."

Erven rubbed his side, which hadn't stopped aching since the previous night. "I hope we're wrong, but it does feel that way."

Tora ran a hand through her short hair, tucking flyaway strands back behind her ears. "You get this sense after enough winters to know when one's going to be bad." She snuggled the child on her lap closer. "Don't worry, we'll be all right."

"I'm sure of it." Erven bounced his knees, making the girl on his lap break into a dimpled smile. "Cold and snow for you, eh?"

She made a delighted noise, punctuated with each bounce. Merald grinned at her before saying, "Violet was by, earlier." He scrambled to his feet with a grunt, picking up a basket piled with clean rags. "Since she and Lena have had to postpone leaving, she did a clear-out of the infirmary supplies."

Erven frowned at the basket as the girl scrambled off his lap and began running in circles with a few of the other toddlers. "And you're using them for..."

"New quilts," Tora said brightly. "Once we re-dye them, they'll be perfect. A few of these rascals are about to outgrow this room, and they need something of their own. Oof—Anneli," she exclaimed as the little girl smacked into her. "Easy!"

Erven was on the verge of asking more questions when one of the babies began shrieking in its cot.

Merald broke into sympathetic laughter. "Spontaneous woe!" He scooped up the infant and cradled her against his shoulder. The baby calmed, nuzzling into his shoulder with hungry whimpers. "Oh, that's what you want." He began carrying the baby towards a door at the back of the room. "Thanks for stopping in. I'll see you later."

Erven and Tora exchanged a significant glance as the door closed behind Merald. "He's still not up for much, is he?" Erven asked.

Tora shook her head, bending to swing Anneli to her hip. The little girl laughed as Tora tweaked her nose. "I've tried getting him to go spend time with you or the others after the littlies are asleep, but he always says he's happy staying here." She sighed deeply. "I know he's capable of more than he believes."

Erven hugged her around the shoulders. "I'll see if there's anything I can do that will help." He opened the door to leave. Reluctant as he was to leave, the work up in the keep called to him louder than the storm outside. "Will either of you be at dinner tonight? Lena and Violet are leaving as soon as the weather clears, and we're trying to make it a little special for them."

Tora brushed a wisp of dark hair from Anneli's face. "I'll make sure Merald comes," she promised. "It'll be good for him to get some time away from this lot."

His paperwork finished, Erven joined the others that evening in the council room. Heather formally christened dinner a

'Winter's Advent' party, and as the snow whirled around the castle, she proposed a toast.

"To snowstorms!" Heather cheered, raising her cup of mulled wine to Violet. "May they always keep our friends close."

"Friends close, and enemies distant." Erven tapped the rim of his glass against Heather's with a grin.

"Here's to keeping enemies distant, anyway," Violet said, raising her glass in half-hearted agreement. Though the healer hadn't said much, her disappointment at the delay was apparent.

Beside him, Erven's younger sister Lena betrayed no such disappointment. Instead, the delay had only increased her enthusiasm for the journey. Erven found his apprehension for her departure lessening as she and Violet shared their plans for what they hoped to accomplish upon reaching the Yarrow Leaf tribe's village.

With his mind set at rest, Erven noticed that Rose had not engaged much with her friends. Instead, she sat quietly in the corner, crumbling a piece of oatbread onto her plate. The conversation went on around them as he joined her. "You seem quieter than usual tonight."

The young queen startled from contemplating crumbs on her plate. "What?" As he repeated himself, she gave a wan smile. "Sorry, I was thinking." A businesslike look appeared in her eyes as she said, "I've finally heard back from the Sea Wanderers. They're sending another ambassador and a Council representative sometime after Wintermorn. We'll be able to finalize that trade agreement we've been working on for so long."

"That does solve some of our problems," he agreed. Across the table, Heather and Clover began rehashing an old, humorous story. Although Rose smiled fondly, she didn't engage with her old friends like she ordinarily would. "There's something else too, isn't there?" he asked. "Something else is bothering you."

Rose sighed. "I always forget how observant you are."

"Do you want to step out so we can talk?" Erven gestured at the door. "I'm sure no one will mind."

After a moment's hesitation, Rose nodded. As they left the warm, cheerful room for the dimly lit, chilly corridor, she stopped to whisper something in Violet's ear. The healer nodded and pressed Rose's hand caringly before resuming her conversation with Merald.

"Let's go up to the study," Rose suggested, crossing the ends of her shawl over her dress with a shiver. "There should still be a fire, and it'll be warmer."

As they climbed the flight of stairs, she asked, "Do you have any idea how long this storm will last?"

"Early winter storms don't typically last more than a day," Erven answered confidently. "Just like the ones we had last year. It'll be over by tomorrow morning—agh." He stopped halfway up the stairs, wincing at the pain in his left side.

"What's wrong?"

Erven waved her off, taking the last few steps two at a time to join her on the landing. "I'll be fine. It's just the old injury... it always aches when it gets really cold." He grinned. "Violet says I make a good weather guesser."

Rose nodded sympathetically as she unlocked her office door. It was warmer than it had been in the stairwell, and it grew even more comfortable once he'd stirred up the fire. He sat on the rug in front of the hearth, the pain in his side finally subsiding as the warmth seeped through his tunic. "So, what's wrong?"

Rose dragged her chair from behind her desk to sit in front of the fire. She huddled in her shawl for a long moment before finally confessing, "The Shona sent us some worrying news about the highland tribes. It seems they're getting more discontent with the changes I've been making."""

Erven scooted to lean against the woodbox. "They'd be discontent with anything that goes against tradition, even if it were their own grannies making the changes."

Rose bit her lower lip. "I know, but this is getting closer to home now." With her face illuminated by the firelight, she looked younger than her eighteen years. "The report I got this afternoon said a few of the tribes have formed a coalition to govern themselves. The Free Holdmasters, they call it." Her voice dropped to an ashamed whisper. "And the Thinar have joined them."

"The Thinar?! Your own clan?" Erven clenched his hands on his knee. "You're sure?"

He knew from past experience that Rose rarely cried, but her eyes reflected the fire with a glassy sheen. With an irritated huff, she grabbed a thick notebook from the desk and handed it to him. "Read it yourself."

The silence stretched out as Erven inspected the entry, written in Willow's large, looping handwriting. He took a moment to compose himself before looking back up at Rose. "I'm sorry for doubting you." He handed the book back. "I can't believe they'd do something like this! They fought with us!"

"I know." Rose pulled her necklace from under her shawl, clutching the silver aspen leaf pendant that had once belonged to her royal mother. There had once been a gold star that hung alongside the silver pendant, but Rose hadn't worn both necklaces in some time. "I mean, they're my father's family. I thought they'd be the last ones to ever turn on me."

Erven readjusted his posture against the woodbox, flexing his hand as his wrist twinged. After being broken in battle two years previous, it still ached at the most inopportune times. "If this spreads farther, we could have a rebellion from within." He got up to pace in front of the fireplace. "I'll take a patrol of my own to look into this."

"That's what I was hoping for." Rose smoothed the notebook pages in her lap. "If the tribes are so concerned about my rule, I need to know why. Maybe we can reason with them."

"Once this storm's over," he promised. "We'll find out what's going on."

4
FOUL TIDINGS

Sunlight was a welcome change from the howling winds and swirling snow of a few days previous. Rose hugged herself tighter in her cloak as she stood on the steps of the hall, shading her eyes to look up at the sky beyond the tower. The sky remained clear, and she trusted her judgement enough after two years in Illyn to assume that the storms had faded, for now.

"It's a beautiful morning," Violet said from behind her, shifting a bag over her shoulder as she came to lean against Rose.

"It is." Rose lowered her hand to place it around Violet's shoulders, sharply aware that it would be the last time in—

Don't think about that. You knew she couldn't stay forever.

"Here." She slipped her arm from around Violet to dig in an inner pocket of her cloak. A soft leather pouch met her fingers, and she closed her hand tightly around it before her fingers started shaking. "I meant to give you this last night, but things kept coming up." She held out the pouch to

Violet, wrapping her friend's hands around it as the silver inside clinked dully.

"Ah, yes." By the look in Violet's eyes, she knew exactly what 'things' had come up. They'd spent their last evening around the fire in Rose's room, playing games and talking with Willow and her sisters until late into the night. "You know, you don't need to…"

"Please let me," Rose begged, scrubbing a hand across her face to banish the tears threatening to fall. "Take—" she cleared her throat. "Take it home and use it to spoil your little brothers rotten." She looked away with a lump in her throat. "I'm counting on you to take care of them, just like you've taken care of me."

Violet followed her gaze to Erven, just now hugging his sister Lena at the foot of the steps. The Shona commander carried a pack over travelling clothes, his patrol waiting impatiently at the gatehouse. "I'll take care of her, too," Violet said quietly. "Don't worry. They're all in good hands." She seized Rose in a hug stronger than anyone would have expected from such a small person.

Rose bent her head to bury it in Violet's shoulder, taking in the healer's smell of lavender, mint, and rosemary one last time. Her breath came out in a ragged gasp, choked by tears she refused to let fall.

"Easy, now." Violet gently pushed Rose upright, straightening her own shoulders to match. "It'll be all right. You've come so far, and you're doing splendidly. You *can* do this." Violet's eyes reflected the same color as the cloudless sky as she put her hand over Rose's heart. "Remember, take care of yourself here, no matter what. You're the queen, but you must remember where you come from. Don't lock yourself up in your own head."

Something settled in Rose's heart, and she straightened her shoulders with a nod.

"Don't worry about her." Willow slipped from behind the heavy doors to join them on the steps. Her eyes held a steely glint that suggested she was close to tears, but her movements remained purposeful as she handed over a pair of document cases. "I'll mind her. Go take care of our people." She raised a cynical eyebrow. "And make sure the Council of Elders minds you."

Violet gave a hiccupy laugh, the sound breaking Rose's urge to cry. "I'll do my best." She looked up at them fondly as the hostlers brought her and Lena's horses towards the steps. "Goodbye, dears. I love you both so, so much."

Rose watched from the steps, hands clenched tightly together as the small party of healers and guardsmen disappeared through the gates. Erven's patrol departed on their heels, Erven turning back and saluting before following the road in the opposite direction from his sister.

Papers and reports called to her from her office, but Rose turned her steps towards the tower. Leaning her elbows against the battlements, she watched until the figures of Violet, Lena, and their guardsmen vanished into the horizon. A chilly breeze rustled her skirts as she turned back, the peaks to the northwest standing starkly against the blue sky.

One of Willow's old phrases came back to her mind as Rose watched the sun gleaming off the fresh snow. *Shoulders back. Chin up. It's going to be all right.* She shivered as the breeze freshened.

I hope.

THE WARMTH in the kitchen was a welcome change from Willow's chilly office. With her blonde hair tucked securely under a cap, she briskly moved from one task to the other—stirring stew, cutting dumpling dough, and keeping an eye on pots of simmering stock. Across the table, a stone mortar and pestle made a rhythmic thumping noise as Heather aggressively pounded hazelnuts for dessert.

"Needs more... something..." Willow muttered, tasting a spoonful of the stew. Winter was difficult in many ways, but fresh meat came easier as animals roamed in search of food. She set down the spoon and looked around for someone to give a second opinion.

"Hoy!"

"Whaat?" Heather looked up from the mortar and pestle.

Willow held another spoon out to her sister. "What does this need?"

Heather bounced around the worktable, dodged one of the other kitchen workers, and took the spoon from Willow. After sticking it in her mouth, she closed her eyes thoughtfully. The clatter of normal kitchen life swirled and settled as Willow tapped her fingers on the table. "Well?"

Heather opened her eyes. "One bite wasn't enough." She snatched the test bowl and dug the spoon in again. "Needs further testing."

"All right, all right," Willow laughed. "Let me know when you're done, eh?"

The dumplings had just joined their fellows in pots of simmering water when a draft alerted Willow that someone had just opened the door to the hall. It was Rose, unexpectedly appearing from where Willow had last seen her elbow-deep in papers. After seeing Violet off two days previous, the shadows around the young queen's eyes had deepened. Willow herself had felt their friend's absence acutely, but she hadn't thought of the effect it would have on Rose.

"Why aren't you upstairs?" Rose asked.

Willow brushed flour off her cutting board. "Good afternoon to you too."

"I needed you or Heather. Or someone." Rose huffed. "And when I checked, neither of you were there!"

Willow had an even temper most of the time, but hearing the tone in her old friend's voice set her on edge. "You know if I stay up there too long, I'm useless." She set her knife back on a tray alongside others. "If you want me t'do things differently, you know you just need to say something." She sighed and untied her apron. "What's the matter?"

Rose slapped a piece of parchment on the table. "I just got this. One of your scouts brought it to Clover when they couldn't find you."

"I'll see if she remembers who," Willow mused. "*Then* I'll take them to the laundry. They know better than t'hand things to just anyone."

She examined the parchment. It had the look of something that had been scraped clean and overwritten many times, and the ink had faded beyond her ability to make out. With a sigh, she shoved the parchment towards Heather, who'd been studiously *not* looking in their direction. "Read this, please."

With a wrinkled nose, Heather began, "It's... Ah. It's a notice. Must've been circulating around the foothills. 'The Crown's taxes and policies, being not beneficial to the interests of... Hmm." She frowned. "It's encouraging the smallholders to 'express their loyalty to the ones who'll keep their best interests in mind—" She looked suddenly at Rose with worry. "The Free Holdmasters?!"

"They're behind this?" Willow pulled the parchment from Heather's hand to peer at the seal along the bottom edge. Even to her eyesight, a tower stood in relief against the edge of the parchment, identical to the one on the previous report. "Oh, fish. I didn't think they cared about anything except the highlands. Rose, I think I forgive you for being so upset."

"Thank you," Rose answered distractedly. "I'm sorry for snapping. If you can leave, I need you."

Willow looked wistfully at the pots of dumplings. Heather decided for her by handing her the test bowl of stew, empty. "Needs some vinegar." Her sister patted her shoulder as she went past with a swish of curls. "You do your best thinking down here, anyhow. I'll see you in a bit."

***

THE WIND WAS PICKING UP. Erven eyed the patches of sky visible through the trees and waved a gloved hand to hurry the patrol onward. Even though he knew this portion of the foothills as well as his own bedroom, some part of him felt unsettled and jumpy. He pulled his hood farther over his head as the wind sharpened. As the clouds dropped lower, causing the already short afternoon to take on the cast of evening, the patrol finally sighted the towers of home in the distance.

The town below—Westhaven—had grown since Rose's coronation, houses and businesses spreading farther around the harbor with each season. From the rise, Erven could see fewer ships in the harbor than there would normally be for this time of year. Evidently, the sea captains could read the skies as easily as he had. His side ached as they skirted town to take the sloping road up to the castle. Behind the walls, smoke wafted from the kitchens and outbuildings, getting caught in the wind and shredding in the air. The flags over the gatehouse snapped briskly, gold star and red roses shining proudly against a navy field.

They barely made it through the gates before the sentries closed them for the night. Amid greetings and hails, Erven dismissed his patrol and made for his room in the barracks.

Merald greeted him from the hearth, just then pushing another piece of wood into a newly lit fire. "Welcome back!"

"Thanks for getting a fire going," Erven answered gratefully. "This cold gets into your bones like nothing else." He handed Merald his sword belt and eased the kinks out of his shoulders. "It's going to storm again. We raced it all the way back from Hollow." He squirmed out of his quilted jacket and knelt before the fire.

"How's the garrison there?" Merald leaned the sword against Erven's bed and joined him.

"They've insulated the roof, and most of it is below the level of the ground anyhow. They're good hunters, and the lake's not frozen all the way." Erven stretched out his hands, rotating and flexing his bad wrist as the warmth hit it. "I'll have the chance to check back in on them soon, if Rose has anything to say about it."

"I *wondered* why you were back so soon." Merald sat back on his heels. "Willow said she wasn't expecting you for another week."

"We didn't need to go all the way into the highlands," Erven explained as he stood from the fire. He opened the small chest by his bed pulling out a clean shirt and tunic. "We found out what we needed just from going up to Whitecaps and back—they'll be all right, too, in case you were wondering."

"Tora has lots of friends that stayed with the Shona," Merald said. "She asks after them whenever someone's been up that way." He stood up with a grunt of pain, steadying himself against the wall.

"Are you all right?" Erven pulled his shirt off over his head. "Have the littlies been climbing on you again?"

Merald waved him off. "They have, but that's not bad." A shadow crossed his face, and he sat on the edge of Erven's bed. His broad shoulders slumped dejectedly. "They keep telling me I'm lucky to be alive. I keep hoping it'll get better, but it's been two years. With as much as this hurts every day, I wish the healers had let me go."

"I understand," Erven said. He shivered as a draft hit the scar running across his left side. "When I ended up surviving, I was devastated."

"I think that's one of the only times I've seen you scared," Merald agreed.

Erven thought back as he finished dressing. The injury he'd received saving his sister Lena had been severe enough that he hadn't expected to survive more than a few hours. The timely intervention of fortress healers had saved his life, but also preserved it for future interrogation. "There've been other times, but you're right." He did up the clasps on his tunic before reaching again for his jacket. "I *was* scared. Surviving after that became a question of whose will would break first."

"I remember." Merald's brow creased with frustration. "But this isn't like that."

"Well, think of it this way," Erven offered Merald a hand up. His friend shook his head and stood on his own. Erven ducked his head through his sword belt instead. "That wound wants to break your will. You're worth much more to all of us than just the things it won't let you do."

"If you say so," Merald sighed. He donned his own cloak and followed Erven into the hallway, raising his voice over the wind as they left the barracks. "Why *did* you come back so soon?"

Erven glanced up at the sky. Even with the storm, he could tell it was close to dinnertime. "Other than the weather? Things are worse than we thought. If Tora can spare you, I'd like you to be there when I tell Rose and the others. I expect it'll be after dinner in the council room."

He caught a glimpse of relief in Merald's face as his friend said, "I'll check with her. Some of the babies are having a hard time, but I think I can make it." He gave Erven a slight salute before turning back towards the Rogue School.

"See you in a bit!" Erven shouted after him before turning his steps towards the keep. The hall, as usual, was freezing, but the kitchens and dining hall were warm. He apologetically collected his meal early from the kitchen workers and ate by the ovens, dodging the questions of those who knew he'd returned. After asking one of the serv-ingmen to start a fire in the council room, he took the steps two at a time to his office, across the hall from Willow and Heather's.

He'd only had time to sort through a handful of the reports stacked neatly on his desk when the door creaked open. Heather's curls appeared around the edge as she intoned, "Sir Erven, your presence is required."

He set down a slate tablet. "I take it they found out I'm back?"

"Willow heard you coming up the stairs. Her eyesight may not be so good, but there's nothing wrong with her ears." Heather pushed the door farther open and leaned against the door frame. "The news isn't good, I take it?"

"No, it's not." He set down his work and crossed the hallway, both Heather and Willow's body language spelling the stress of the last few days as he stepped into the office. "Though, I'm guessing mine won't have been the only bad news you've heard this week."

"It's not," Willow said without looking up. Piles of slate tablets, map cases, and papers lay scattered over her usually tidy desk, wisps of hair standing out around her hairline like a ruffled owl's feathers. "Things've gone from 'troubling' to 'bad' while you've been gone."

"Erven?" Rose appeared from around her office door. Despite the week she'd apparently been having, Rose's dress and hair were still immaculately neat. "I thought I heard your voice. How long have you been back?"

"Just long enough to change and eat." He crossed his arms. "I told everyone you'd want to see them in the council room after dinner."

"The news is that bad?"

Erven sighed. "It's that bad. The Whitecaps Shona told us two more tribes have joined the Free Holdmasters. The Thinar are part of it, like you knew—but they're not just along for the jaunt, they're one of the prime instigators."

Rose's dark blue eyes narrowed. "I shouldn't be surprised, but I am. What else?"

"It's hard to tell." Erven uncrossed his arms and rubbed his thumb on the pommel of his sword. "They don't seem ready to take up arms or do anything violent. From what Whitecaps told us, they're still settling into the idea of being opposed to your rule. But they're getting organized."

"That I could've told you," Willow groused. "Look at this." She reached over the desk to hand him a slate tablet, transcribed in chalk. "This is the basics of what they're saying—it's being distributed all around the foothills. Happened just after you left."

"Read it while we go," Rose commanded. She reemerged from her office with her shawl around her shoulders. "If the others are going to the council room, we should as well."

Erven quietly absorbed the contents of the tablet while he followed the others down the stairs. He caught Willow's sleeve before she went into the room, shaking his head in disgust. "I knew it was bad, but *this* is what they're saying?"

"They've taken this beyond complaints to open opposition." Willow's jaw muscles tensed as she said, "They're claiming that by being raised outside of Illyn, Rose's blood has been compromised and she's not one of them. They're saying she's not fit to wear the crown."

5
THE COUNCIL'S DECISION

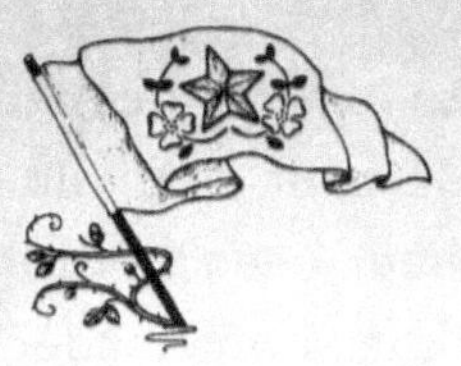

The response from Rose's advisors closely resembled Erven's reaction. Amid the swearing and exclamations, Arielle's voice cut through to Merald's ears. He sat between Heather and Arielle, listening without much surprise as she explained, "The highlanders don't like change and never have. More than that, they like to be left alone, to do as they please." The last few years had seen new wrinkles form around the older woman's eyes and put silver streaks in her hair, but more than age lent wisdom to her words. "While Rose spoke words their ears liked, they followed her without question."

"Aye, like 'warlords must die'." Heather propped her chin in her hand, scowling. "But the moment you expect them t'actually contribute to something that doesn't benefit them…"

"And that's the point," Arielle smoothly agreed. "If we'd accepted their help in battle, bade them farewell, and never interfered in their business again, they'd have no trouble with us."

"Apparently, stirring up trouble is an outsider's trick," Rose said wryly. "I expected resistance from those who *liked* Lord Kuma, not from those who fought alongside us."

"Not everyone fought with us," Merald reminded her. "A majority, but several tribes didn't."

"Lord Kuma had trouble with the highlanders throughout his rule."

Everyone turned to look at the man sitting in the corner of the room. The last of the old castle officers left, Commander Ricar had been indirectly responsible for Erven's survival after the Shona leader's capture. Now over-seer of several garrisons surrounding the capital, he rarely attended council meetings. His presence now indicated how seriously everyone was taking the new threat.

Erven laughed briefly as he corrected, "Lord Kuma *intended* to have trouble with the highlanders, but the Shona kept stopping him."

The burly soldier chuckled. "And quite the burr in his blankets, you were." He shook his head. "We had other run-ins with the highlanders that you may not have known about. Kuma knew they'd never accept his rule, even under right of conquest, until he could prove he'd wiped out the Thinar line."

"Which he didn't." Arielle inclined her head towards Rose. "And once the highlanders saw that, they pledged their support."

"That's the past now." Willow had been taking notes, the tip of her pen scratching as she wrote in a looping cipher. "What can we do *now*, now they've decided breaking oaths of fealty is the course they're setting?"

"We need to talk with them, and as soon as we can." Rose's circlet reflected the lamplight as she sat straighter in her chair at the head of the table. "Before winter really sets in. If there's a chance we can reason with them, we have to try. The last thing I want is to assume they're bent on hostility. This country's seen enough wars."

The conversation lasted late into the night as the snowstorm outside thickened. After two hours, Merald had stopped paying attention. As the sand trickled through their hourglass a third time, he struggled to keep his eyes open.

"Merald?"

He snapped to attention as Heather nudged him. "Yes?"

"I can tell you're falling asleep." Erven smiled. "If you want, you can go. We'll talk more tomorrow."

Surprised and a bit relieved, Merald excused himself from the council chambers. He pulled his hood close around his head and hurried across the courtyard to the Rogue School, feeling a stab of pity for the sentries on night watch. The lamps inside had been extinguished, but a thin line of light shone under the nursery door. He stuck in his head to see Clover sitting in Tora's usual chair amid the rows of cots, cradling one of the babies against her chest and rocking softly.

"Everything all right?" he asked quietly.

Clover nodded. "Are they done talking?"

He shook his head. "They're still going. Erven turned me loose."

Clover's hazel eyes betrayed disappointment as she confessed, "Willow asked if I could come up too, but by that point I was too deep in here to leave."

Merald nodded sympathetically. "And now you're stuck under a sleeping baby."

"This part I don't mind," Clover whispered, kissing the

top of the infant's head. "It's peaceful. Are you looking for Tora?"

He nodded. "I couldn't remember if she had night rotation."

"She doesn't tonight." Clover nodded towards the corner of the room, and Merald noticed one of the cots stood empty. "Anneli was having a hard time, though. She's with Tora."

"I'll check our room, then."

Merald put his cloak back on for the brief walk from one building to the other, stopping in the common area of the building where many other Rogue School workers lived. He walked down the hall to the room he and Tora shared, opening the door quietly.

Tora was still awake, her arm curled around Anneli. The sleeping toddler's face bore traces of tears, and a bruise was forming on her forehead. "Looks like someone took a tumble," he said softly.

"She tripped on a blanket someone left on the floor," his wife explained. "She was too upset to fall asleep on her own, so I said we'd take her."

"Did you tell anyone we were planning on making that permanent?" Merald looked affectionately at the toddler. Her oversized nightgown made her seem even smaller than usual.

Tora carefully slid her arm out from under Anneli and got up. The little girl stayed asleep, putting her thumb in her mouth before rolling over and giving a contented sigh. "I told Violet before she left. I'm not sure who else needs to know."

"Arielle, perhaps. I don't know if Rose has her taking over all of Violet's responsibilities." Merald sat down on one of their two chairs, staring into the lamplight. "I don't know how else to make things official."

"There's a ceremony the priest can do," Tora said, stifling a yawn. She began folding a washcloth from a basket on the table. "Maybe during Wintermorn... there's no better time to start a new family than with the return of the sun." She smiled at the toddler sleeping in their bed. "Will you be able to spend some time with her tomorrow?"

"I hope so." He rubbed his side gingerly. Cold weather always made things ache more, in addition to the pain that always lurked in the background. "I don't know if there'll be more meetings."

"What's happening so far?"

Merald smiled sheepishly. "I stopped paying attention after a while. I think they're going to send someone to try and talk with the Holdmasters. Rose wants to make sure of their intentions before assuming they're hostile."

"Oh?" Tora stopped mid-fold. "That bad?"

"It could be." He took one of the washcloths from her and began twisting it around his hand absent-mindedly. "If they're already set on rebellion, it'll take a lot to change their minds."

Tora took the washcloth from him. "We'll talk sense into them. I just hope they decide to see reason."

Merald raised an eyebrow. "That makes two of us." He laid his hand on hers. "It shouldn't be that bad. Don't worry."

Tora squeezed his hand. "I won't." She went back to folding. "Are you going to bed soon?"

He shook his head. "It's not that late, yet. I'll go out so you can sleep, though."

Tora stifled another yawn. "Thank you, my love."

Merald bent over to kiss Anneli. Their future daughter had turned on her side, hugging her rag doll tightly. "Sleep well, little one." He gave Tora a last kiss. "I'll be in in a bit."

In the common room, a fire was lit with a pot of cider warming over the flames. A handful of the other servants and Rogue School workers lounged around the room, playing quiet games of dice or talking. Amid the conversations and laughter, Merald found a place to sit, out of the draft from the door. No sooner had he gotten settled when the storm door rattled open to admit Erven, who joined him after thumping the snow from his boots.

"You're finished already?" Merald got another mug of cider and handed it to Erven. "I thought the meeting would go on for another hour."

"We were all getting tired." Erven hunched over the table, staring into his cup. "Can you be there again tomorrow?"

"I suppose." Merald took another sip of his drink. "I can't see what use I'll be, but I told Tora you might still want me there."

Erven glanced around as one of the groups broke into boisterous laughter. "Rose asked me to take another patrol up to try and talk with the Holdmasters. We just need to figure out some of the details." He returned his gaze to his cider cup, twisting it around and around on the table. "I suggested you come with, and she agreed."

Merald accidentally inhaled a mouthful of cider. He coughed as Erven pounded him on the back. After recovering his powers of speech, he sputtered, "Why?"

"You're one of the Aubron tribe." Erven propped an elbow on the table. "The Holdmasters have their knickers in a tangle about honor and the respect due to the clans, so we have a better chance getting them to listen with you along."

"My parents were exiled," Merald protested. "They're not going to care what I say."

"Exiled, perhaps, but by men who are now dead themselves," Erven reminded him. "And even with that, you more than earned respect in battle."

"But what about Tora? And Anneli?" Merald frowned, thinking back to the conversation he'd just had with his wife. "They need me."

Erven smiled sympathetically. "It's not going to be months. Besides, I think Tora will understand. If this was a Shona problem, she'd probably volunteer."

Merald sighed. "She would, at that." Pain battered at the back of his mind, and he had to force himself to ignore it before asking, "Are you sure you want *me?* I don't even know if I'll be able to keep up."

"I know you can do this." Erven's gaze was stern. "And I want you along badly enough that I'm willing to risk travelling slower."

"All right, all right." Merald set his drink down. "Just when were you planning on leaving?"

Erven shrugged. "As soon as the weather clears and I'm able to clear the backlog of things I have on my desk. We have to work out details, but everyone agreed we need to move quickly."

Merald sighed. "All right, I'll do it. But I'll need to find someone to cover my shifts with the Rogue School."

"Clover's happy to take care of things. There are plenty of people who can help."

Merald gave him a flat look. "You knew all along I'd say yes!"

"Well, I wasn't sure." Erven's bright blue eyes held a hint of mischief. "Call it an educated guess."

"Well, now that you've manipulated me into agreeing, I'm going to break the news to Tora. And then I'm going to bed." Merald stood up. "Talk to you tomorrow." He headed back towards his room, Erven's amused laughter following him.

THE PATROL CONSISTED of veterans from the previous conflict, former Shona mixing in with men from the castle garrison. Rose could hear their boisterous talk from inside the hall, where she and the rest of her advisers were finishing a quick final meeting. She adjusted the brooch holding her cloak closed at her chest and shivered in the draft from the open doors. "It's times like this I wish we had messenger birds like the Sea Wanderers."

Heather nodded, stuffing her hands deep in the pockets of her sweater. "Someday, once we figure out a way to breed ones that can take the cold." She grinned. "Those little tropical ones wouldn't last a week in the winter."

"Ethan's still able to send me messages," Willow said. "He seems to have no end of ways to communicate.

Heather winked. "Aye, I wonder why someone as high ranked in Sea Wanderer intelligence as him would prioritize communication with Illyn. And, ah, *how* long was his last letter?"

"It was business, I swear!" Willow's cheeks had turned pink. "We don't use *all* our time writing personal notes."

"I wish I had half the cunning he has," Erven commented, a hint of a smile on his face. "He seems to know everything that's happened across the whole Sea Wanderer territory within days of it happening." His cloak shifted aside to reveal leather armor over his travel clothes. "I'm with Rose. It'd be wonderful to know what's going on in the highlands without having to go all the way up there."

"The sooner we have an accurate picture of what the Holdmasters are doing, the better we can make our plans to counter them." Commander Ricar had been recalled to the castle to take over the garrison in Erven's absence. The burly soldier had donned mail under his uniform, the single chevron on his shoulders newly stitched.

As the others filtered outside or off to their respective duties, Rose caught Erven's eye. "One moment, please?"

He stopped near the door to let Commander Ricar pass. "What's wrong?"

Rose shook her head. "Nothing, really. I saw you're wearing armor."

Erven ran a hand over the wing design on his arm guards. "If there's a chance of trouble, I want to be prepared. I know you're hoping this is a big misunderstanding, but I'm afraid we may need to prepare for the worst." He tapped his fingers on his sword hilt. "Commander Ricar is going to recall some of the men from the outlying garrisons to boost our numbers here. And we'll be spending a night at Hollow. I'm going to ask the Shona there and at Thunderhead and Whitecaps to step up patrols."

Rose's chest felt tight. "*Quietly*," she insisted. "I don't want the people to think I'm getting paranoid. They're just starting to get used to being out from under Lord Kuma's rule."

"It's not paranoid to want to stay safe," Erven reminded her. "We're being discreet. I don't want to be caught off guard any more than you do."

"Well, thank you for thinking of it." Rose stepped outside, squinting against the glare of sunlight on snow. "I'm glad I have you to think of these things before I know they need thinking of."

Erven followed, pulling up his hood to cast his face into shadow. "That's what we're here for." He bowed his head briefly, the gesture more indicative of farewell between friends than deference to a superior. "And we'll be back with good information, so we can plan our next move."

Rose swallowed hard. "Stay safe, please. And return as soon as you can."

"Don't worry, we'll be back before anyone knows we've gone." Erven strode to join his men, sunlight gleaming off his sword hilt.

More than the cold sent shivers into her stomach as the patrol disappeared through the gates. *He says he's not cunning, but he's always anticipated our enemies' moves. I hope he can do it again. Otherwise, we're all in deep trouble.*

6

HOLD AUBRON

Although they had prepared for cold weather, the patrol had to stay an extra day at the Whitecaps Shona outpost before leaving for the high mountains. Snowshoes would be needed for traversing higher elevations, and they needed warmer gear for spending nights in the open. Erven took the opportunity to iron out some plans with the outpost command for increased patrols. Although he didn't specify why, he knew they were more than acquainted with the threat the Free Holdmasters presented.

Well into the third day of their journey from Whitecaps, everyone was keeping their eyes open for a good campsite for the night. Based on how fast they'd been able to cover ground, Erven suspected they were nearing Hold Aubron, the home of Merald's tribe. Examining Merald's gait with a practiced eye, Erven was relieved they were so close to their destination. Though Merald hadn't said anything, it was apparent how quickly his friend was tiring.

They came out of a narrow valley and into the stretch of

forest between several rises. The ground had opened out, leafless aspen thickets studding the landscape between the taller pines. Ahead, one of the older men sounded a path with a branch across a frozen creek. As they waited, one of the Shona asked, "Good spot? Or should we try farther upstream?"

Erven looked at the sky. They still had another hour or two until nightfall. He pulled down the scarf over his mouth so everyone could hear him. "Let's try farther up. If we can get into thicker cover, I'd feel better."

As they picked their way across the stream and continued following it west, Erven fell into step near Merald. "Doing all right?"

"I'm all right." Merald rubbed his forehead. "I won't say no when we decide to stop, though."

"Good man." Erven clapped him on the shoulder. "Hang in there; we'll be stopping soon." Commotion a few hundred feet away caught his eye, and he looked up as the men scouting ahead came scrambling towards them. "What's going on?"

One of the scouts slid to a halt. "Just around the corner, a war party."

Erven swore and loosed his sword, shaking his shoulders free from his pack. Around him, the others also dropped their packs. "Did they see you?"

The scout shook his head. "I don't think so. We—arrg!" He clutched frantically at the arrowhead that suddenly jutted from his throat before dropping with a gurgle. Behind him, the other scout toppled as well, several shafts buried in his back.

"Find cover!" Erven shouted.

The patrol scattered as their enemies appeared from around the rocks. Wielding axes and swords, the highlanders were armed heavier than a hunting excursion would warrant. Goldenrod paint etched curving designs on their shields, and several wore tunics of blue shot through with gold. The arrows cut down another of his men as Erven scrambled to get behind a rock.

Merald was already there, gasping for breath. "An ambush. How'd they know we were coming?"

"I don't think they did," Erven answered grimly. "But I don't think they want to talk, either." He pulled a whistle out of his jacket and blew a signal that echoed sharply across the forest.

The men with him had all been trained with Shona commands. They counterattacked fiercely, packs discarded and blades shining in their rush against the enemy tribesmen. Erven's sword clattered against a shield, and he cursed as the man followed up with a blow from a short axe—a blow that Erven only narrowly caught on his own blade. The haft of the axe splintered, and he finished the man with a thrust through the lungs. His sword bloodied, he hurtled over a fallen man to parry another blow about to land on one of his men. The attacker backed up, eyeing the pair of them before turning to run back into the trees.

Settling into a fighting stance, Erven took the opportunity to scan the battlefield. Most of his men still fought, but several lay unmoving on the ground. Others swore as blows from the highlanders found their marks. With a sick feeling in his stomach, Erven knew they were outmatched.

Something thudded against his chest—an arrow, flight mostly spent. Immensely thankful for the decision he'd made to wear armor, Erven ducked behind a tree as another arrow plunged into the snow near him. He heard Merald yell, followed by a crashing, splashing sound.

The creek had widened into a stream, and several of his men had retreated up to its bank. Merald sprawled in the frigid water, struggling to his feet as another man engaged his attacker.

"Soldiers of the Crown, surrender!" one of the highlanders shouted. He held a longbow drawn; an arrow leveled at the men near the creek. "We don't have any quarrel with you. Lay down your weapons and surrender peacefully."

Erven cast a frantic look around the creekside. Several of his men favored injured limbs, and Merald's movements were beginning to slow. He lowered his sword and stepped out from behind the tree. "Don't hurt them!"

"Commander?" one of the men exclaimed, lowering his sword before raising it again at a stern glare from one of the others.

"Cedric, put it down," Erven commanded. "Put them down and check on the wounded." He knelt to clean the blood off his own sword before sheathing it and laying it on the snowy ground. Under his breastplate, the spot where the arrow had struck ached deep in the muscle. He left the weapon where it lay, going over to Merald. His friend's lips were already turning color, and he was shivering.

"What happened?"

"Caught me behind the knee with his spear haft," Merald muttered. "I didn't even know the stream was there until I fell in it." He eyed their attackers, gathering the weapons as the other men laid them down. "We're in for it, now."

Erven helped him over to a log, dropping to one knee to switch Merald's soaked scarf for his own. "Rest as long as they'll let you." He straightened back up, giving the enemy spokesman a withering look. "Move around if you start getting sleepy. I've got to find out what they're going to do with us."

After collecting the weapons into bundles and tying their captives into a string, the highlanders marched them along a trail that eventually turned into a well-trodden path. Erven walked at the back of the column, supporting Merald whenever he stumbled. After almost an hour, in which the western sky grew brilliantly colored before fading to dusk, pinpricks of light appeared out of the gloom. Their captors ushered them through a village, terraced stone and timber buildings glowing as the day's work ended and fires were stoked. At the crown of the hill, a stone tower loomed over the terraces, banners flapping from its walls.

Erven couldn't hear the discussion between their guards and the sentries outside the Hold. As they neared the tower, Merald kept missing his footsteps and losing his balance. By the time they were inside, Erven supported most of his friend's weight, the ropes around his wrists chafing with the extra strain. After leading them to a disused storeroom, the Aubron leader freed their hands and warned, "If you try to escape or attack anyone, you'll face dire consequences. Don't try us."

"Look," Erven said as one of the men untied his hands. "Some of us are injured." He gestured at Merald, leaning lethargically against the wall. "He's soaked and freezing. We've lost friends and comrades, and we still don't know why." His pulse thumped in his throat. At least two of the men who'd died had been Shona. "We need a healer, and dry clothes and food." He looked the highlander square in the face, wondering if he'd fought alongside him two years before. "I'm their commander—if there's any fault here, it's mine."

The man nodded curtly. "We know who you are, and we know why you were here." He announced, "One of the healers will come tend to your wounded, but you may not leave this room. Food will be brought shortly." The door clanged shut behind him, and Erven could hear the sound of a bar being lowered on the other side.

He turned to face the others, trying to keep the worry out of his voice. "Well, at least they're going to send healers. I'm sorry, everyone. I'll do what I can to make sure you're all right."

"It's not your fault," Merald mumbled through blue lips. "They didn't even stop to ask why we were here before attacking."

"Aye," one of the others agreed. "There's nothing we could've done. At least we're still alive."

Erven surveyed his men, trying to gauge who was the worst wounded. "Let's see what we can do for ourselves. Some of you, get Merald out of those wet clothes. Between all of us, we might have enough extras to get him dry."

"I'm all right," Merald insisted, his words starting to slur as two of the men went over and crouched around him. "'m fine."

Cedric, one of the castle guards, pushed him back as he tried to get up. "Steady there, soldier. If we don't get you warmed up, you'll be chatting with your ancestors soon."

"And your wife will kill us," the other man added, unbuttoning his jacket. "Let us help."

Seeing Merald in good hands, Erven checked on the others. His own bruises ached as he finished, reassured that the injured would recover in time. After a while, a silent healer came to clean and bandage wounds and hand Merald a bowl of warm tea. Erven didn't bother seeking attention for his own injuries, his chest tightening at the thought of an unfamiliar healer tending to him. Someone else brought food and blankets while the healer worked, the woman glancing his way with something like respect. Both highlanders left without saying a word, and everyone heard the bar slot across the door outside.

"All right." Erven gestured to the others to gather in the corner farthest from the door. The men drew closer together, as much for comfort as for information. "I'd assume the Aubron Tribe have joined the Free Holdmasters. Any disagreement?"

"The war party had more than just Aubron fighters," Merald said, wrapped in blankets from head to toe. "I saw Thinar and Westin colors on some of the shields, too."

"Did it seem to anyone else that they're not sure if they wanted violence?" Cedric asked. "They attacked first, but they didn't seem dead set on killing all of us." He raised an eyebrow at the storeroom ceiling. "And they *have* treated us better than I expected."

"If there are multiple tribes involved here, there might've been some kind of disagreement about whose orders to follow." Merald's lips were starting to regain color, but he was still shivering. "If they're disagreeing, there's a chance we can turn it to our advantage."

"Well, one thing's certain," Erven rubbed his forehead as

he counted how many men had survived the attack. Out of the fifteen men they'd left the capital with, only ten were alive now. "Whoever ordered this attack won't get away with it." He looked over at one of the uninjured Shona and asked, "Did they let you do anything for our dead?"

The boy nodded grimly, slanted eyes filled with grief under crow-black hair. "Aye, Sir. The four we lost; they're laid out apart from those traitorous murderers."

"Four?" Erven blinked, certain he hadn't miscounted. "Who's missing?"

"Arrick, Sir," Cedric answered. "Just as they attacked, I saw him bolt into the wood."

Erven felt a stir of hope. "Arrick's a good woodsman. If he's smart, he'll get back to Whitecaps and from there to Her Majesty. I don't know what the Crown's response will be, but we ought to keep our heads down and watch for any opportunity to escape." He leaned against the wall, pondering the new information. "Better get all the rest you can. Let me know if we need anything, and I'll try to negotiate with them in the morning."

As the men dispersed to sleep in the corners of the room, Erven went to sit next to Merald. "How are you feeling?"

"Cold," Merald answered, crossing his arms to tuck the blankets tighter. "And angry. I'd hoped we'd find a different welcome here."

"I can't say I was hoping for this, either," Erven agreed, shivering under his quilted jacket. Merald's eyes looked heavy, and Erven hoped their efforts to counteract the icy water had been effective. "I don't know why they decided capturing us was better than an outright massacre."

"It's not us they're interested in," Merald said drowsily. "It's you. You're the person the queen relies on most."

Erven swore under his breath. He looked across at the rest of the men, now falling asleep in the dim light from a single lamp. *Even if Arrick manages to get back, they won't be able to rescue us for months.* "I'm sorry, mate. I'll do everything I can to get us out of this."

7

THE CALAMITY LIST

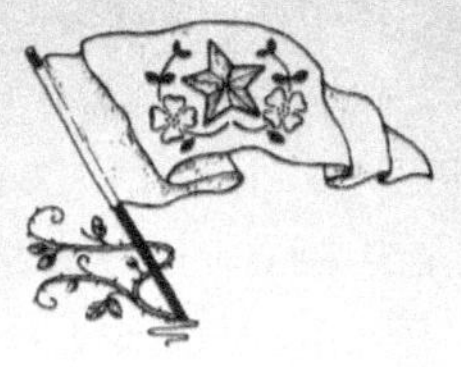

Raindrops never come alone, Willow reminded herself as she pored over a report from one of her informants in Westhaven. *Petty crime on the rise, silver mines suffering sabotage, gangs of mercenaries terrorizing locals...*

"Bah!" A cloud of ashes flew from the hearth as she hurled the crumpled report into the flames.

"You're not a sheep, Old Thing." Heather said. "What's wrong?"

"Everything," Willow snapped as she closed her notebook. Erven had been gone for almost a week. Even though the likelihood of news so early was slim, she was still disappointed by the dismal reports flooding in. "I'm sick of everything being bad news. I'm sick of being cold. I'm sick of sitting around waiting for the Sea Wanderer ambassadors so we can just sign that *stinking* trade deal. I'm sick of feeling on edge around everyone. I'm sick of—"

"If you keep on like that, you *will* be sick," Heather interrupted. "Have you talked to Rose?"

Willow shook her head. Rose had been distracted to the

point of bad temper in the last few days, and no one liked being snapped at. "She's been so off since Erven left; I haven't wanted to bother her."

Heather threw a paper pellet at her. "Where's your sense of duty gone? Get your backside in there, Old Thing, before I boot it."

"All right, all right." Willow seized a list off her desk and stomped off towards the connecting door to Rose's office. She knocked, and at Rose's answering 'come in', opened the door briskly. Rose sat at her desk, but the neatly piled documents and dry inkwell told Willow that the queen hadn't been able to accomplish much work.

"Did I hear Heather out there? Why are both of you working today?"

Surely, she should know why. Willow crossed the office in several quick strides to slap the list down on Rose's unnaturally tidy desk. "*That's* why, Your Majesty. While you're brooding in here, Illyn's about to go to bits around our ears."

"What?" Rose bent her head to scrutinize the list. "What's this?"

Willow leaned against Rose's desk, crossing her arms over her work clothes. "That, Your Majesty, is a list of all the people who're currently angry enough at your reign to do something about it." She ran her finger down the list, compiled over the last two weeks and growing with every new report she received. "And I'll thank you to notice that the Holdmasters and their grievances don't even appear here."

Rose bit her lip as she looked over the list. As she read over each article, her insides twisted into tighter and tighter knots. "Why didn't I know about this sooner? I mean, any one of these is problematic enough," she admitted, "but how have all of them gotten so bad so quickly?"

"Many of them have gone from 'insubstantial' to very 'troublesome' in a remarkably short amount of time." Willow shifted so she was sitting on the corner of the desk. She ran her fingers through her hair, currying flyaway bits back into her bun. "Most of it isn't even related to the Holdmasters, either." She tapped a line written in somewhat faded ink. "Example, here. The Silversmiths' Guild is getting their knickers in a tangle on account of us not asking for their help at the Thunderhead mine."

"It only became productive last month!" Rose protested, "It's barely been any time at all!"

"Time enough for them to stew on it," Willow said sinisterly. "And as for the rest, I wouldn't have brought it to you all at once if it weren't necessary. I'm sorry."

"I suppose it's good to know about everything at once," Rose said with a grimace. "In your opinion, what's the most pressing?"

"They're all connected," Willow said. "Across all of the complaints is this common thread of disliking your rule." She winked, and despite herself Rose had to laugh. "Take the merchants, for example." She got up and stirred the fire, sending a puff of ashes swirling up the flue. "Under Lord Kuma, some of them got rich profiting from others. When he fell, they saw all their custom vanish."

"And I'm glad it has," Rose said darkly. "I'm guessing some of the loudest are the ones who supplied the workers for the castle."

As one of the first acts of her rule, Rose had sent the army to put a stop to the continued purchasing of slaves from pirates. While she didn't regret the decision, she now understood the powerful enemies she'd made as a result. "What about this other one? Mercenaries? Didn't we get rid of the last of them?"

"Apparently not," Willow sighed. "I thought most of them left with the Iorca when they retreated from the battlefield, but it seems I was wrong." She added another piece of firewood and nudged it backwards with the poker. "When they weren't getting paid any more, some decided to take matters into their own hands. Ethan says the Sea Wanderers've been having trouble with raiders along their northern border waters, so at least the problem's not just here." As Willow mentioned the country her father hailed from, her voice took on a hint of the Sea Wanderer accent. "Farms along th'foothills are saying there're a few gangs roaming around, both Iorcan and local toughs. They're doing th'usual—demanding food an' supplies, extortion, roughing up anyone who doesn't comply..."

Rose made a disgusted face. "We had so much trouble with that in the first year. How quickly everyone's forgotten this used to be an every-day occurrence."

"I'd prefer to think of it as Illyn gettin' used to being free again," Willow leaned back against the desk. "Now that the people've had a few years of remembering what freedom feels like, they're more ready to complain about the smaller things that would've gone unnoticed in the past." She quirked an eyebrow. "And the Holdmasters know that. That's why they've decided to incite things now."

Rose propped her forehead in her hand, circlet digging into her palm. "We've got to get some of these cleaned up before the Sea Wanderer envoys get here. If they arrive now, they'll be certain they're supporting a lost cause."

"Easy now," Willow's voice was stern, but her words filled Rose with reassurance. "You've come such a long way since the beginning. We'll handle this just like we've handled everything else—together, and with lots of tea for the nights when we can't stop worrying."

Trying to make up for time she didn't even realize had been lost, Rose disappeared into a planning haze for over two days. She met with the magistrates, reviewed grievance reports, assigned Commander Ricar to hunt down and bring to justice the renegade soldiers, and sent another message to the Sea Wanderers asking about the increased raiding.

Finally, Willow declared it was time for planning to be replaced by action. "Your guards are waiting downstairs with the horses, Your Majesty," Willow announced, closing Rose's notebook with a brisk snap. "I have shopping to do. And your people need to be reminded there's a face under that crown."

As they rode down the hill into Westhaven, Rose took a deep breath of the crisp air. Above the town, the smoke and cooking smells had yet to reach them, and the forest nearby lent a hint of pine and damp wood to the breeze. Looking ahead, she saw a few townsfolk trundling a handcart filled to the brim with rowan and holly berries. "Are they preparing for Wintermorn already?"

"You've had your head too deep in your own troubles," Willow said in her characteristically blunt way. "Yes, they're getting ready for Wintermorn. It's only about a fortnight off."

"I didn't realize," Rose said softly, looking around with renewed interest as they slowed their horses to a walk, the guardsmen trailing behind at a respectful distance. Around them was plenty of evidence that people were preparing for the winter holiday. Many of the homes bore pine and spruce wreaths on doors, while others had simply tacked the branches on the lintels.

She slid down from her saddle, taking care to brush horse hair and wrinkles from her skirt before following the snow packed street deeper into town. "What shopping did you need to do?" Rose shaded her eyes to look up as Willow consulted a list, messily inked on the inside of her wrist.

"Well, the kitchen wants rowan, and haws." Willow squinted towards one of the houses, eyeing the tufted bundles of juniper and holly over its windows. "Or maybe the Steward wanted the rowans for decoration." She slid to walk beside Rose, holding her horse's reins in an ungloved hand. "We need dulse for dinner."

"Seaweed again?" Heather moaned from behind them. "Old Thing, you've got to stop feeding us that stuff."

"It's good for you. And it grows free, so it's cheap. I don't care *how* deep our pockets are, it's better to economize." Willow winked at Rose and said in an undertone, "And I like it, so there."

Heather eyed the bag dangling from Willow's belt. "I like the cider they make for Wintermorn. Will there be enough money for that, oh mighty keeper of the purse?"

"I think that's why we need the haws...?" Rose asked.

"That's why." Willow confirmed. "Frogs and toads. I've gone and smeared it now." She held out an inky wrist. "Does that say 'cloudberry', or 'clawberry'?"

Rose frowned at the letters. Willow's handwriting was difficult to read at best, but smeared ink made it almost impossible. "It can't be cloudberries. They're only ripe in the summer."

"Clawberries, then." Willow frowned. "I hope Tora didn't make a mistake."

The reminder of Merald's wife sent a pall over Rose's enjoyment of the sunny morning. Although handling her husband's absence better than any of them had expected, Tora betrayed her nervousness by hardly ever leaving the Rogue School. Rose curled her hands into fists inside her fur-lined mittens. "I haven't checked on her recently. Just one more way I've been stuck in my own head."

"It's not just your fault," Willow said, pulling her sleeve down over her wrist. "We've all been wrapped up in our own problems." She tipped her face to the sun. "That's why we're out here."

Enough activity hummed through the marketplace that their arrival went unnoticed, though Rose was glad she'd dismounted in the outskirts of town. A bonfire was under construction in the center square, broken crates, stools, and wood shavings amidst the jumble. "Seems a waste of fuel, during a cold time of year," Rose commented as she followed Willow towards the docks.

"When things are darkest and coldest, people need to feel warmth and light. No matter how much it costs." Willow stopped outside a building with baskets of holly and rowan branches by the door. A wicker basket dangled from its handle outside one of the shuttered windows. "Let's see if they have extra, or if we can order some."

"I'll go see about that cider, Old Thing." Heather patted her tunic pocket, making something jingle. "And I have a few other things I want t'check on."

Rose followed Willow into the shop after tying their

reins to a fence rail outside. The basket shop was the front room of a home, the open space of floor taken up with heaps of pine, spruce, and fir branches. Inside, a pair of women—one middle-aged, the other much older—looked up from tying evergreen boughs into wreaths. The older woman's face lit up. "Your Majesty!"

As the women dropped their work to curtsey, Rose implored, "Please, don't be uneasy. We're just here to… umm." She made a pleading face in Willow's direction. "What were we here for?"

Willow smirked at her. "Rowan berries, Your Majesty." She turned to address the younger of the two women. "Though I suspect we'll need more than what I saw outside…"

Staying by the door as Willow and the other woman negotiated prices, Rose watched, entranced, as the older woman deftly overlapped and tied evergreen branches to form a wreath. Seeing Rose watching, she asked, "Would Milady like to try it?"

"I hate to be a bother…" Rose said, embarrassed to have been caught watching.

"It's no trouble." The woman pulled a spool of twine from the basket at her feet as a boy came through the back door with another armful of pine boughs. Upon noticing Rose, he shot her a look of dislike and mistrust.

Dropping his armful next to the older woman, he whispered, "You're selling to *her?* She don't deserve your work, let alone your respect." The words were loud enough that Rose heard from the other side of the shop. Heat flared in her cheeks, and she looked hard at the floor.

The older woman—probably his grandmother, Rose thought—swatted the boy's hand with one of the fir branches. He yelped as she commanded, "Put a courteous tongue in your head, or I'll warm your backside." She pointed at the door he'd entered through. "Go put tea on, sharpish."

As he departed, rubbing his arm and giving Rose a venomous look, the old woman apologized, "Please don't take offense, Milady. He's full of blood and fire, and nothing stirs it up like a wrong idea planted in a willing heart." She extended a wrinkled hand to point to a stool. "Please, sit."

Rose obeyed, watching the woman's precise movements as she layered new spruce and pine boughs to cover a bare twig circle. "And if you want, you add the holly and rowan for luck at the end, see?" The artisan held up the finished wreath triumphantly before laying a fresh circle in Rose's lap. "Let's see how you do, then."

Feeling like she had grown a second pair of thumbs, Rose attempted to copy the motions she'd seen the weaver use. As her fourth branch slipped loose from the twine, she apologized, "I'm sorry. I'm really useless at this. It's nothing like sewing or embroidery."

"Aye, an' your embroidery was trash when you started." Willow pointed out with a laugh. "You always expect to be perfect at everything you try."

"No one's perfect their first time," the middle-aged woman agreed.

"It's all practice, like most of life." The white-haired woman gestured to the back door, where her grandson showed a sullen face around the doorpost. "I think tea's about ready. Will you do us the honor of joining us?"

Willow winked at Rose before handing several heavy silver coins to the younger woman. "Her Majesty would love to, but I'm afraid my errands can't wait." Rose gave her a panicked look as Willow waved cheekily. "Scream if you need the guards, and I'll be back in a bit. Have fun!"

"Ah, now that wasn't very kind of her." The white-haired woman laughed as the door closed behind Willow. "Don't worry, Milady, you're safe with us."

Feeling flustered, Rose stood up to follow the women back to where beds lined the walls of a narrow room. The boy was just setting pottery cups on a solid wood table, swinging a kettle from the fire before departing the room with a scowl.

"I'm sorry about Kit," the younger woman apologized, looking at the doorway where her son had disappeared. "If only his father were here..."

"What happened?" Rose asked, her ears still echoing with the sound of the door slamming.

A flicker of worry passed between the two women before the younger one finally said, "M-my husband joined the army at Hold Eskel. He didn't survive."

"Oh." Rose looked at the floor, not sure what to say. "No wonder he's willing to hate me."

"He doesn't understand," the woman said with a heavy sigh. "If Raul hadn't left us, he would have been conscripted by Milord's recruiters. He might've died anyway, and it wouldn't have been fighting for our freedom." She shook her head. "Kit doesn't understand that."

"He'll come around as he gets older." The older basket-weaver urged Rose to a seat near the fire and pressed a cup into her hands. "Don't mind him."

The tea smelled like winter—fir needles and spices that hadn't been available in Illyn before trading with the Sea Wanderers. Rose sipped gingerly, reminding herself that making polite conversation wasn't the worst way to spend a morning.

Just be yourself. Violet's voice from months ago sounded in her head. *You're a quick study, and you read people well.*

"Thank you for the tea." She warmed her hands around the pottery. "It's wonderful."

"It's the spice." The white-haired woman pushed over a plate of cookies, their tops studded with dried berries. "Some of those foreign spices are a bit much, but these'ns are nice."

The women gave her their names—Carine and Mari—and filled her ears with talk of holiday preparations, family, and winter. Rose suspected their talk was partially to cover the nerves of serving tea to the queen, but the stream of family details and business dealings was comforting in its own way. By the time the tea had been drunk and a cookie politely eaten, she felt warmer than she had in months.

"Hallo?" a voice called from the front shop room. "Anyone in?"

Rose brushed a few crumbs from her dress. "That's Heather. I'm afraid I have to go."

Mari, the older basket maker, kissed her hand as if bestowing a blessing. "It was our pleasure." She winked. "Come back again, and we'll see if practice gives you a better result on your second wreath."

8

ICE CRACKING

Riding back to the castle, the others noticed Rose was quieter than usual. Willow nudged her horse closer to Rose's black mare. "Even songbirds share their thoughts."

"Sorry, I was thinking."

"We noticed."

"Heather," Willow warned. A chill breeze blew right through her sweater sleeves as she asked, "Thinking on what?"

Rose rubbed her horse's mane. "We used to do this all the time, before it got cold." She straightened with a perturbed look on her face. "I want to do this more—go walking in the city, and get to know the people better. If more of them can say they've met me and found me normal, they'll be less likely to believe the things the Holdmasters say."

"I'd say it's a lovely idea," Willow agreed. "But next time, I think I'll send a few more guards with. Disguised, like. Just in case the nice townsfolk try to put something sharp in your tea."

Rose laughed. "I'd have to be very unobservant to not notice something like that, but if you think it's a good idea…"

"I do," Willow answered firmly. "But yes, it'll be good for you to get out in the air again. And until we get more news from the highlands, this's a good way to build up the people's opinion."

Back at the castle, the three of them swung down from their horses and handed them off to be groomed and watered. Rose brushed her skirts. "I'd better get back upstairs. I don't know what could've happened in the last few hours, but I'm sure *something* has."

"I'll come with you," Willow said, handing the remaining silver over to Heather. "Will you give that to the Steward, and tell him we're expecting delivery of lots and lots of decorations today or tomorrow?"

"I'll tell him," Heather replied absently, looking across the courtyard at the Rogue School. A new banner was floating amidst the hodgepodge of decorations, the ruffled edge looking suspiciously like a nightgown. "In a bit, though. Seems a certain group of Underage Minions has been in my drawers…"

Leaving Heather to her detective work, Willow linked her arm through Rose's as they cut through the kitchens on their way towards the stairwell. "Did your new friends feed you?"

"A cookie," Rose said as they passed a worktable where one of the kitchen workers stood peeling parsnips.

"You need more than a cookie if you're going to be actually using your brains." Willow glanced around the kitchen. "And we missed lunch, too." She went over to one of the storage cupboards and began rummaging through the shelves. "You go on, I'll be there in a moment. Just going to collect some things."

Rose departed to her office to continue working. The morning outing and conversation had given her several ideas of how to reach the people she was tasked with leading. *The connection of one person to another is more important than any number of new policies or notices. If I can reach past the people's grievances to their hearts, I'll be able to lead them in a way they won't resent.* Dipping her pen, she began writing with renewed urgency, scarcely noticing that time was passing without the reappearance of Willow. Only when her stomach started growling did she look up, wondering why her friend hadn't rejoined her.

No sooner had the thought crossed her mind than Willow herself burst into the office. "Rose!"

"Oh, there you are!" Rose greeted her. "I was wondering where you'd gotten to. I've been working on something that I wanted to run by you—what's wrong?"

Willow's cheeks were flushed as she shifted from foot to foot in the doorway. "You'd better come downstairs. Some of the Shona just turned up, and they look like they've seen their own ghosts."

"What?" Rose bolted from her chair, running down the stairs behind Willow. "Did they just get here?"

"Yes, just now," Willow said. "A few other things wanted tending before they arrived, that's why I was late coming up." She shoved open the door to the hall at the foot of the stairs.

The air in the hall was bitingly cold, reminding Rose why they rarely used the huge room during the winter. The

Shona patrol clustered around the dais, looking as if they'd been traveling hard. *And they must have.* Rose thought, calculating the distance from Hollow to the castle. *It's barely afternoon now. They must've left Hollow right at sunrise.*

"Lady Queen!" Annika—the original leader of Whitecaps, now the Hollow commander—looked grim and worried beyond her years. "There's no easy way to put this. Something's happened to the Commander's patrol."

"They were ambushed by the highlanders, Lady Queen," one of the others chimed in. "Arrick managed to make it back to Whitecaps yesterday." The boy kept a hand clenched around his knife hilt as he explained, "He says they didn't even give them time to explain, they just attacked."

Annika's silvery eyes hollowed with grief as she added, "Domin and Kendric are dead, and maybe more. Arrick couldn't tell for sure."

Rose's spine crawled. Shaking off the feeling, she asked a question that didn't quite match the one thrumming in her bones. "Did anyone survive?"

"Aye, Milady." Tension showed in every line of Annika's shoulders. "The highlanders captured all the survivors, including Commander Erven."

Rose felt Willow stiffen next to her. "Not again."

Annika nodded helplessly. "We have a good idea of where they've been taken, but we didn't want to endanger anyone else by looking further."

"No, you did the right thing." Rose turned away numbly. "You're all dismissed. Make sure you get some food. I need some time to think—I'll send for you shortly."

"As you command, Lady Queen."

Rose strode back into the tower, hearing the squad disbanding with low conversation and mumbled questions. She could hear Willow and Annika talking behind her, their voices low and urgent. Once inside the stairwell, she abandoned all pretense of control, running up the twisting stairs to slam the door of her room behind her. She placed her hands flat against the door, trying to control her breathing.

"Not again!"

The last time Erven had been captured, he had barely escaped with his life. Since then, his importance to the Crown had only increased. *They couldn't have taken a better target.*

"This can't be happening again! Not again!" she shouted, pounding a fist against the door. Her shouts turned to sobs, and she sank to her knees. "I can't do this again!"

Willow disbanded the Shona, telling Annika to join them in a few hours once they'd had time to collect Rose's advisors. She made for her office and scrawled a note to Commander Ricar, who'd left that morning to deal with the mercenaries plaguing farmers to the south. Skirts flying, she went back downstairs to pass the note to one of the guardsmen. The guard, a former Shona, had evidently heard the news of Erven's capture. He saluted briskly and took off running towards the stables.

On her way back to the keep, Willow caught sight of her sisters outside the Rogue School. Embroiled deep in an argument, they stopped in shock as Willow yanked them apart. "The Holdmasters attacked Erven's patrol," she snapped. "He's been captured, and several are dead. Finish anything that can't wait and meet us in the council room." Leaving her sisters sputtering questions, Willow left to give the same message to Arielle in the infirmary before navigating the stairs one last time.

Out of breath and with quivering legs, she knocked on Rose's door. When no answer came, she poked her head through the doorway. "Rose?"

A chilly wind blew through the room, swirling ashes across the hearth and stirring the curtains on the bed. Outside the open window, dark clouds rapidly gathered to obscure the sky. Another storm was coming.

Rose stood leaning against the windowsill, looking out at the sea. "Please go away."

Her voice sounded shaky, and Willow wondered if she had been crying. If that were the case, it would be one of only a few times in their long friendship.

"No." Willow briskly crossed the room and wrapped her arms around Rose's waist. "Whatever happens, we're getting through it together."

"This is my fault." Rose's chest heaved. "I told him he was the only one I trusted to find out the truth." She pushed Willow's arms away and turned around with fury in her face. "If something happens to him, I'll never forgive myself."

Willow took a step back. She'd never known Rose to look this way before. "Steady on. If something happens, it won't be your fault."

"Everything ends up being my fault."

"That's not true, and you know it here." Willow tapped her breastbone. "This has nothing to do with you."

Rose ducked her head. "You just don't understand."

Her temper flaring, Willow grabbed her friend's shoulders. "Look at me!" she yelled. "Look in my eyes, Brielle Thinar!"

Surprisingly, Rose did, with the wide-eyed look of someone who'd just been slapped unexpectedly.

"Your royal responsibilities do not—and have never—made you responsible for the actions of others! Mercenaries attacking innocents isn't your fault. Merchants getting upset over a loss of profit isn't your fault. The Holdmasters resisting your rule is *not your fault!*" She shook Rose's shoulders. "*None* of this is your fault! You heard Annika—they attacked without any warning. Thinking like this only makes you second-guess every decision, and uncertainty is a luxury we can't afford." Willow let her voice soften. "And I won't stand by to let you get all icy inside. We both know it's not good for you."

At this, Rose's eyes filled with tears and her posture sagged. She buried her face in Willow's shoulder, her circlet cold against Willow's neck. Willow quietly rubbed Rose's back until the tears died down to occasional sniffs.

Barring the shutters of the open window, Willow pulled her friend to sit on the foot of the bed. She dragged a blanket over and wrapped it around Rose's shoulders. "There, that's nice and warm." They sat quietly for long minutes until the young queen's shoulders relaxed. "Do you feel better?"

Rose wiped her nose with the edge of the blanket. "I won't lie and say yes." She shuddered. "It's terrible news."

"Yes, and I'm shaken too," Willow agreed. "It's a hard blow they've dealt."

Rose sighed. "It would be hard enough if it was just a patrol they ambushed. But..." She pulled the blanket tighter around her shoulders. "I can't lose him again. When I first got here—when the Thunderhead Shona rescued us from the caravan—Erven was my first ally. He's risked himself so many times for my sake, and I wouldn't be where I am now without him."

"Interesting…" Willow said, wondering if Rose had any idea how affectionate her words sounded. "I'm glad you have someone you can talk to, other than Violet and myself."

"Sometimes, I wish it wasn't that way." Rose shivered, frustration tingeing her voice. "My reliance on him is such a weakness."

"If it's a weakness, it's a necessary one," Willow reassured her. "You need strong people around you." She squeezed Rose's shoulder. "And speaking of strong people, several are waiting downstairs for you. Let's go see if we can make headway against this latest catastrophe."

"WE'VE GOT TO DO SOMETHING."

"We can't," Commander Ricar insisted. "Listen to that wind."

The keep shuddered as the storm broke outside. Rose buried her face in her hands, forgetting the dignity befitting a queen. "You don't understand."

"Your Majesty," the soldier said, his voice gentle despite the hoarseness brought on by years of shouting. "I know it's hard to face. But winter's set in, and it won't loosen its grip easily."

"I hate to say it, but he's right." The hours had barely eased the worry in Annika's face. "It was risky sending Erven to the highlands in the first place, but now it would be stupid to try sending anyone else. We'd be half frozen, exhausted, and in no shape to fight by the time we reached Hold Aubron in this weather."

"We can't leave them." Rose closed her fists around the

edge of her shawl. "We have no idea of what could be happening to them up there." *Almighty, help us. He must be so scared.*

"I know you're afraid." Arielle's voice was soft, but no less strong than Commander Ricar's had been. "Erven means so much to all of us. But of anyone, he's the best possible person to have been in command of that patrol."

"She's right." Commander Ricar leaned an elbow on the table. "Commander Erven is experienced, determined, and resourceful." Rose could see the years of hard-earned wisdom in his eyes as he said, "Milady, it's something every leader must learn; trust in one's subordinates. As hard as it is, you need to trust that he'll do whatever he can to keep himself and his men safe, even if rescue must be delayed."

"What about Whitecaps, then?" Rose insisted. "They're closer to where the highlanders attacked. Can't they get close enough to attempt a rescue?"

"They could..." Annika said. "But Whitecaps is our smallest outpost. Given how hostile this attack was, there's a chance the highlanders could take any intrusion as a threat. We can't afford to take that chance."

"I think we need to trust him, Your Majesty."

The sound of her title coming from Willow's lips sent a jolt of surprise through Rose's chest. She looked up at Willow, sitting in her usual spot taking notes.

"He's proven himself time and time over." Willow balanced the end of her pen on the lip of the inkwell. "Until the time is right for a proper rescue, we have to trust that he'll be able to keep his men safe." She smoothed a page in her notebook thoughtfully. "And as terrible as this news is, I'm not so certain he's in any mortal danger."

"You really think so?" Rose asked tentatively, unwilling to acknowledge the sudden pounding in her heart.

"I think so." Willow's stormy eyes narrowed. "The highlanders were clearly interested in taking him alive. I'd give a lot to know why."

ERVEN TWISTED his wrist free from the highlander holding it. "Let me go. I'm not going to run."

The man grunted and released him with a shove, forcing Erven to catch his balance quickly as he stumbled to the center of the room. The meeting room was high-ceilinged and heavy-beamed, with a large hearth and sturdy furniture. Torches flared in sconces, and braziers sat in the corners to provide warmth. The Holdmasters—almost a score of men—sat in a semicircle, allowing space in the center for speakers to address the group. As he regained his footing, Erven recognized the patterns and colors of at least six of the highland tribes. *More than fought with us at Hold Eskel.*

"Commander, thank you for joining us." The man speaking looked old enough to have been in power before Lord Kuma's attack, eighteen years previous. Erven could see a slight resemblance to Rose in the man's face, reminding him of the distant relationship as the Thinar chief added, "I hope your men are well."

"As well as to be expected." Erven chose his words carefully, aware of every eye in the room. "But I still have to protest your treatment. Your people attacked us without warning, and now several good men are dead."

"We apologize. There were certain... misunderstandings

in our encounter with your men." The leader of Hold Aubron glared at one of the other men seated near him. "You can be sure that won't happen again."

"It shouldn't have happened at all," Erven retorted. He squared his shoulders and stared down the three men seated in the places of highest honor—the leaders of Holds Aubron, Thinar, and Westin. "We entered these mountains trying to end this conflict *before* it became violent."

"We're seeking a satisfactory end to this hostility as well." The Westin spokesman spread his hands. "What more would you ask of us?"

"Let my men go. Your issue with the Crown shouldn't include punishing men whose only crime was stepping wrong in territory they didn't know was hostile."

The men shifted under his gaze, and one of them commented, "Your devotion to your men is admirable, Commander, and well in keeping with your reputation." He looked around at his fellows. "At this time, we're not willing to release any of you, but your needs will be entirely met. If you're lacking in anything beyond what we've already provided, you have only to ask."

Erven blinked in surprise. "I'll pass that information to my men, and will supply a list of requests for your consideration." He paused, thinking of Merald. After his dunking in the freezing river, Merald had developed a cold. They were trying to keep him warm and comfortable, but Erven couldn't shake his worry every time his friend coughed. "For the time being, can a healer be sent to attend to one of my men? He's become ill."

The Aubron leader nodded gravely. "One will be sent." He raised a bushy eyebrow. "Anything else?"

Suspicious now, Erven shook his head. "I'll provide a

more detailed list once I've had a chance to speak with the others." He realized he'd been standing in parade rest, a habit he supposed he'd picked up from the career soldiers in the castle guard. He crossed his arms sternly. "Your generosity is much appreciated, but the fact still remains that we're being held here against our will. Why?"

"Commander," the Westin chief adjusted the drape of a grey and black cloak against his shoulder. "It seems to us that there's an opportunity here that can't be passed up. Up to this point, we'd been considering our options for negotiations with the Crown. With you here, though, a new path has opened up for us."

"What are you talking about?"

"The fact is this," the Thinar leader said, his eyes dark over a black beard. "When Her Majesty called the tribes to her at Hold Eskel, we came. We fought to free Illyn, but haven't seen a return to strength and prosperity. Many of us feel it to be a result of the queen's lack of understanding and respect for our ways."

"Aye, it's been two years," one of the other men chimed in from the back row. "We fought alongside the Shona and those foreigners she recruited, spilled our blood, and for what?" He made a dismissive gesture. "She accepted our service and repaid us by completely flouting Illyn custom and values. It's time we take matters into our own hands."

"The highlands would have no ability to take things into their own hands, were it not for Brielle Thinar's courage." Erven countered, "If Her Majesty had not chosen to pursue the throne, there would be no freedom in Illyn."

"In the old days, each man had to prove himself worthy in combat before being trusted with leadership." This man didn't rise from his seat in the corner, his voice cold as he said, "Too long has Illyn been governed by those who would seek security over strength." His dark eyes pierced Erven's heart as he said, "It's time for the Thinar line of rulers to end."

Erven struggled to keep his voice level. "You'd lean on ancient traditions to overthrow the woman responsible for your freedom?" He scowled at the rest of the coalition. "Do you all feel this way?"

A shiver went up his spine at the Aubron leader's next words. "Returning Illyn to the old ways of succession by combat is best for all of us, and there's no better person to do it than you." The coalition rumbled with agreement as the man added, "You killed the warlord in single combat. You have a valid claim. But more than that, you have the people's trust. With you on the throne, Illyn can grow strong once more."

"It's despicable," Erven spat. "You swore—you *all* swore —to defend and protect the Crown. This is treason, plain and simple." His foot slid back into a fighting stance. "I won't support traitors."

SHORTLY AFTER, the storeroom door crashed open and Erven hit the floor with a grunt. The others were quick to respond, shouting insults and outraged questions before the door slammed shut. He shook off their hands and stood on his own.

"What happened?" Cedric asked. "Keep an ear to the door, someone."

Erven gingerly touched the bruise forming on his cheekbone. "I'm fine." He shook his head. "They want me to overthrow Rose."

"I hope you told them where they could put that recommendation," one of the others spat.

"Trust me," Erven said, "I made my distaste for it quite clear. When I said no, and kept saying no, one of them lost their temper and punched me."

Ansel, one of the Shona who had joined them at Whitecaps, handed him a kerchief dipped in water. "Here, put that on it. Did you learn anything else?"

Erven held the wet cloth to the bruise, wincing at the cold. "I don't think all of them are completely committed to this course of action." He thought back to the expressions on some of the quieter members of the coalition. "In fact, I'd say it's taken so long to summon me because they've been arguing amongst themselves."

"It's one thing to follow along with big talkers, but I guess open rebellion takes more stomach," Cedric agreed.

"I *was* able to talk a bit with them," Erven said as he sat down on his bedroll. "They told me I could make a list of requests, and they'll try their best to honor them."

"Well, that's a relief," one of the others admitted. "I'm sure they're just trying to get on your good side, but perhaps they'll let us have the rest of our things back."

"Were you able to hear anything while I was gone?" Erven asked, looking at the barred door.

Ansel shrugged, his slanted black eyes unreadable. "The guard changed over once. A healer came to look at Merald, but she didn't say anything other than to try and keep him resting."

Erven glanced over at Merald, who slept despite the commotion around him. "I wish she'd been able to do more for him. He's not strong enough to take a long illness."

"Well, don't tell him that." Cedric laughed. "He'll try and

prove you wrong and end up sick for longer." He shook his head. "Other than the healer, it was just people going back and forth with supplies and things."

Erven nodded. "We should keep our ears open. If we can escape, they won't have any kind of leverage over Her Majesty." The bruises from a few days previous ached, and he shifted to a more comfortable position against the wall.

"Are you all right, Sir?" Ansel asked, "We could try to get the healer back again."

Erven shook his head warily, side aching. "Better not let them see they've hurt me." He didn't explain the terror that had swept over him at the thought. *If it weren't for Arielle and Violet, I don't think I'd ever want to see a healer again.* He sighed. "Try and figure out what else we want to ask for, and I'll say something once I get the chance."

"Will do," Ansel agreed before going back over to sit at Merald's side.

Erven spent the rest of that day and evening deep in thought. The others understood, and left him alone. The conversation with the Holdmasters had revealed more than he had hoped for. With their new plan emerging, it was becoming apparent which tribes actually held grievances, and which were merely following along with the others. Still, the suggestion that he seek the throne in place of Rose was enough to make his head swim.

I can't imagine how they believe this will work. Surely, they knew I wouldn't agree.

Long after the others had blown out the lamps and settled down for the night, he found himself unable to sleep. As the tower stones vibrated under the onslaught of another storm, he caught himself thinking back to the morning in Hollow when he'd first met Rose. Though she'd been years younger than him, dressed in cast-off clothes and clearly out of her environment, he had still been impressed by the unnatural calm that radiated from her that morning—and after, as they'd worked side by side to organize the new Illyn government.

The longer I'm here, the more they'll try to use me as leverage against her. We have to get away from here.

9
DETERMINATION

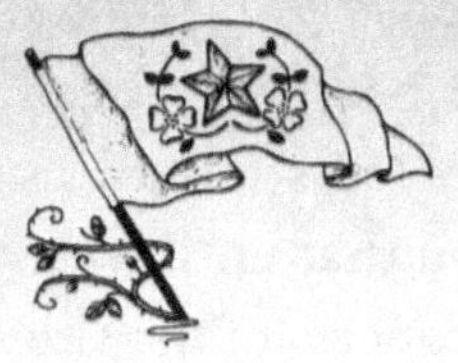

One storm after another pounded Illyn over the days following Erven's capture. Even Rose had to admit that any rescue attempt would have to wait until the wave of inclement weather ended. The constant worry kept her awake at night, eroding her confidence until she felt like a shell of herself. It was only with a supreme effort of will that she continued to press on with the other crises from the 'calamity list', a copy of which now dwelt in large letters on a smooth slate in her office.

Even with Wintermorn rapidly approaching, Westhaven felt grey and gloomy as she attempted to reconcile yet another conflict. The Silversmiths' Guild was a tall, well-insulated building on a prosperous street adjoining the harbor. As she and Heather met with the elder guildsman, she was relieved to discover that handling this challenge no longer terrified her as much as it had previously.

"Under Lord Kuma, our guild saw our handiwork seized, or traded for at prices several times worse than fair value. Since his demise, we've been able to open a few new mines of our own, but the possibility of competition with the Crown makes us uneasy." The elder guildsman steepled thin fingers over a solid desk bearing a set of scales and several ledgers. "By opening its own mines in the area formerly known as Thunderhead, we fear that the Crown is circumventing the privileges granted to the guild and seeking to undercut our livelihoods."

"That is not and has never been my intention." Rose hoped her tone conveyed strength as well as cordiality. "I would also remind you that until recently, *all* silver mined in Illyn used to be the property of the Crown."

"Under your predecessor, yes," the guildsman said, sliding the scales over and dropping a lead weight into one of the pans. "But without the expertise of our miners and artisans, the Crown will see only mediocre returns from what we would consider a good vein." He twisted a heavy silver signet from his finger, the band etched around with a hammer and crucible motif. He dropped the signet into the opposite pan of the balance. The scale tipped, the silver side hitting his desk with a dull clank. "If you would see Illyn prosper, it does not do to alienate those with the most expertise in this matter."

"I understand," Rose said slowly. In a split moment, she decided it would be better to heed his suggestion. "As I'm sure you know, we've discovered what seems to be a good vein in the Thunderhead mine. It's productive, to be sure, but we've been having tremendous difficulty telling where best to dig."

The man's eyes lit up with the enthusiasm of the passionate. "If the Crown is willing to allow the Silversmiths' Guild free access and first rights to the refining and trade of the silver produced, I know our guildsmen will be able to double or even triple the yield."

"Without any of it walking," Heather commented.

Rose raised a warning eyebrow at her friend, but Heather ignored her. Instead, she addressed the guildsman, "If your artisans are involved in the entire process, from mining to casting, we can be better assured that less silver will be diverted into others' pockets." She raised an eyebrow at the silversmith. "I'm assuming your guild already has procedures in place for just such a safeguard."

The man returned her smile, telling Rose, "You've got a sharp advisor, Majesty." He picked up his signet and the weights from the balance and rolled them between his fingers. "Yes, the guild has rigid protocols in place to ensure that no silver leaves our possession without bearing our stamp of approval."

Rose took a deep breath. "In exchange for the guild's assistance in acquiring and refining the raw silver from the Crown mine, I'm prepared to remand a portion back to you." She smiled. "We'd make it worth your while."

The guildsman's face creased around a smile. "I'll bring things before our guild heads."

"I realize it's Wintermorn in a few days," Rose said as she stood, Heather joining her. "Please feel free to bring any questions to my attention quickly, so we can settle things before the solstice."

"It would be my pleasure, Milady." The silversmith bowed, ushering them out of the building. "I'll assemble our guild heads this afternoon, and you may expect our representatives as soon as possible."

As they left the guild building and walked over to the

guardsmen and horses, Heather breathed a sigh of relief. "I hate meetings. They make my tripes go all funny."

Rose laughed and reached up to adjust her circlet, even though it didn't feel out of place. "Mine too, and it's not getting any easier the more I do it." She gratefully accepted help mounting her horse before noticing Heather had stayed on the ground. "Are you coming?"

"Erm, no." Heather gave her a shifty look. "I have… things I need t'attend to."

Rose raised an eyebrow. "Things?"

"Yes." Heather's cloudy blue eyes were elusive. "Things."

"All right…" Rose gave a small wave as the guardsmen mounted their horses. "Enjoy yourself!"

Heather tipped her a salute as she walked off in the direction of the harbor. Rose watched her go, wondering how much it would be worth to try and pin down her mischievous friend on the nature of 'things'. *I'm sure she's just going to collect reports from Willow's informants. Though, knowing her, she could also be planning a prank.*

"Ready, Your Majesty?"

Shaken from her thoughts, Rose nodded. "I think I'd better forego the ride today. Let's swing around the edge of town on the way back, though."

They men agreed with quiet words, moving their horses behind hers as they left the shelter of the tall market buildings and into the outskirts of Westhaven. Deep in thought as they rounded a corner, Rose didn't see the wad of refuse hurtling towards her. The shouts of the guardsmen startled her, and she lost her balance. The snow—melted, mixed with dirt, and refrozen—felt as hard as any flagstone as she slipped from her horse.

"Milady, duck!" one of the two guards yelled as more

refuse hailed down on them. As Rose grabbed her horse's reins and ran for the road towards the castle, she was glad the dung heaps had been frozen for weeks. Her boots slipped on the icy ground as she ran between two rows of shops with small gardens in the backs, the shouts from her assailants echoing off the pitched roofs.

As she ran, she risked a glance backward. The shrill voices suddenly made sense. The people throwing muck were much younger than she had originally thought.

I'm not running from children throwing manure. Rose dropped her horse's reins, trusting that it wouldn't wander far. As she slithered and slipped back towards her guards, she saw they'd laid hold of a boy. Several other youths were backing uneasily into a closed alleyway as a suddenly alert passerby menaced them with a long knife.

"HALT!" The voice she'd had to perfect in the months of leading the Shona served just as well to resound between buildings.

"Milady?"

"I said, halt," she insisted, crossing her arms. "They're children."

"Scoundrels, more like." The guard shook the boy he held by the collar. As the child looked up with a tear-streaked face, Rose saw it was the boy she'd seen in the basket weavers' shop.

"Let him go," Rose commanded. She glanced over at the passerby, who she now recognized as another guardsmen. "And the others as well."

The men eyed each other suspiciously before obeying. She took hold of the boy's collar as the guard released him. The other boys in the alleyway took to their heels, pushing and shoving in their hurry to be away.

The child under her hand sniffed, wiping tears away with a filthy hand.

"I know you're angry," Rose told him. "But this is the wrong way to approach things." She gave his collar a shake, picturing a mother dog shaking a puppy. "Go back to your mum and grandmum. If you're lucky, I won't tell them why your collar's ripped." She let go, giving him a push towards the street. "And think about this the next time you want to throw muck at people."

As the boy scrambled away, the guardsmen turned to her with equal parts surprise and concern in their faces. "Milady, are you all right?"

"Of course I'm all right." Rose went to catch her horse. "They were just children. If I can't handle children on my own, it's a problem."

Later that evening, Heather knocked on her door. "I heard you've been spankin' unruly boys."

"That's what they're saying?" Rose dipped her pen in the inkwell, shaking off an excess drop.

Heather stuffed both hands into her sweater pockets. "Well, I can't say for sure. After all, I was *nowhere near* the marketplace when a pack of boys came running past, looking like puppies with their tails b'tween their legs." She eyed a loose stitch in her sleeve and poked it back into the weave with a grimace. "And I *certainly* didn't spread about the idea that the queen had handled such unruly children just like any mother would."

"Thank you." Rose smiled. "I didn't realize I needed to appear maternal."

"People respect their mothers." Heather's shrug was almost lost in her bulky sweater. She turned back to her own office. "I'll get back to work now, Your Majesty." She popped her head back around the lintel, curls bouncing into her eyes. "Or should that be 'Mum'?"

BETWEEN MORE BAD WEATHER, another frustrating summons to the coalition leaders, and monotonous hours spent planning, Erven had learned the highlanders' patterns. That afternoon, he and the remaining men from his patrol rested as much as possible, counting down the hours until the evening change-of-watch bells. Sure enough, soon afterwards they heard the unmistakable tramp of feet down the hall towards their prison. Within a few seconds, the door creaked open to admit the unfortunate highland guard in charge of emptying the slop bucket.

"Now!"

The two burliest men from the patrol—stationed in combat stances just outside the door's radius—dove onto the unsuspecting highlander. Erven was the first through the door, smashing a knee into the other door guard's stomach. The man doubled over with a groan, Erven's fist slamming into his jaw and sending him to the floor unconscious. Erven winced at the shock through his bad wrist, feeling the loss of his arm guards most acutely as the others pulled the guard backwards into the storeroom.

"Better hurry," he said, looking back along the corridor. "I don't know if anyone heard that noise."

One of the castle guards grunted as he tied the highlanders' limbs with twisted ropes of torn bedding. "You were fast, Sir. I don't know as they heard."

"Heard or not, let's make sure these two are well secured." Erven crouched to retrieve the dagger from one of the guards' belts, sliding the sheath onto his own belt and checking the edge. "And keep them in opposite corners from each other."

"Will do." The man dragged the first guard off into a far corner as the remainder of the patrol swung their packs to their shoulders.

Merald came to stand alongside Erven. Even with the days of rest, his eyes still carried the cast of illness. Anxiety clawed at Erven's heart as his friend muttered, "There should be a storehouse down by the wall. We can get supplies and skis there, if they haven't changed everything in twelve years."

Erven took a deep breath and let it out slowly as the rest of the patrol joined them at the door, pulling on hoods and scarves. "We'll have to chance it. Let's go."

They made it unnoticed through the Hold, emerging into the clear, cold night with hushed whispers and hurried rearranging of cloaks to cover exposed limbs and faces. Just as Erven's boots crunched on the snowy ramp leading to the next terrace down from the Hold, a shout came from the tower behind them.

"Halt!"

"Move!" Erven commanded, drawing the dagger from his belt and running for the ramp.

The men broke into a run around him, Shona and castle guards alike readying the makeshift weapons they'd grabbed on the way out of the Hold. Even as they reached the next terrace, new footsteps and voices sounded all around them. The ramp opened out into a small square, abandoned marketplace stalls crusted with snow and glistening silver in the moonlight. Erven looked sharply around the square as they dodged behind a stall, counting to see that—miraculously—all his men had made it out of the Hold.

He'd scarcely drawn breath to give orders when the first arrow sliced down into the square. One of his men dropped with a gasp, hands clamped frantically around a shaft jutting from his eye.

This can't be happening. "Take cover!"

Bowstrings snapped from the terrace overhead as armed highlanders rushed into the square, a few appearing from the doors of the building just below the ramp. Another man screamed and fell as several arrows pierced his stomach and chest, his thrashing growing weaker with every passing moment.

Panic colder than ice and hotter than fire burned in Erven's veins as one of the Shona hit the ground—tripped by a highlander head and shoulders taller than him. A cry of pain broke the night air as the highlander raised his club for another strike.

Erven's feet moved unbidden, and he caught the strike on his upraised dagger. The small knife wrenched out of his hand, and he turned to catch the remainder of the blow on his shoulder. Staggering forward, he was just in time to see panic and fear on Ansel's face before another blow caught the back of his head, sending him into blackness.

Something struck his ribs, and fierce pain exploded through his side. He clamped his lips shut as someone said, "You don't have anything to gain by this! We'll find them, with or without you."

The pain in his side never lessened as another blow landed, then another. From behind closed eyelids, the world narrowed down to just the next breath.

. . .

"Commander, we told you not to try anything foolish."

Erven swam back through darkness to find himself lying on the snow just outside the Hold. Overhead, the stars shimmered faintly against the sky, points of hope swallowed up in darkness. He groaned and ducked his head closer to his chest as one of the highlanders' boots thudded against his lower back. *Just hold on. It'll be over soon.*

One breath after another had stretched into hours. Strong hands held his shoulder in a crushing grip, his ligaments threatening to crack under the strain. "Just give them up. What are they to you, anyway?"

He answered in the best way he could muster—spitting blood straight into the face of the guard holding him.

It'll be over soon. Won't it?

Erven wondered if his prayers were even reaching the Almighty as another boot slammed into the base of his neck. His jaw ached with the strain of keeping silent as the highlanders egged each other on, blow after blow landing on his limbs and back.

"That's enough."

The clear, cold voice was one he recognized, and Erven peered cautiously past protective arms to see the man who had occupied the corner seat in the Holdmasters' council.

"Interesting..." The fellow crouched a few feet away,

examining Erven with eyes as dark and unfeeling as smoke-blackened stones. "You don't care what we do to you. No wonder we've gotten nowhere." He looked up at the other highlanders. "Haven't you learned anything from his reputation? As fun as this is, it's only going to make him more determined." He straightened with a curt order, "Put him back in with the others. Seeing the pain his men are in might change his mind faster than this."

It's over. Dizzy with relief, Erven let himself be pulled to his feet and helped along the corridor to the storeroom. The surviving members of his patrol were all there, most nursing bruised heads and wrenched arms. After grimly assuring them he was all right, Erven curled up in his bedroll and tried to piece together what had just happened. As painful as the last quarter hour had been, it paled in comparison to what the dark-eyed man had insinuated.

He knows I'll never give into their demands when I'm the one they're threatening. And after this, there's little chance another escape attempt will succeed.

"Mate? Are you sure you're all right?" Merald knelt alongside him, stifling a cough in his shirt sleeve.

Erven sighed and sat up. "I'll be fine."

"You look terrible."

As badly as he felt, Erven had to smile. "It's not like this is the first time."

Merald shook his head. "At this point, I'm not sure which is going to kill you first; your stubbornness or your loyalty."

"I hope neither." He looked across at the rest of the men. "Did they say anything when they threw you back in here?"

"Not really. They weren't too interested in us. Just you." Merald shifted uncomfortably. "I hate to say it, but I think our plans might've put us in a worse spot than before. A different man was giving the orders, this time around." He coughed again. "He felt dangerous. Cold."

Fear wormed through the back of Erven's mind. "That's not good."

"I'm sorry, Mate." Merald stood back up. "I just wanted to be sure you were all right. I'll let you rest."

Erven winced as he lay back down, bruises already beginning to ache deep against his bones. *Power may have shifted in the coalition. I don't know what they'll do to us, now that they're angry.* His mind drifted as exhaustion set in, rendering productive thought all but impossible. Just as he was about to surrender to sleep, a new thought shattered his concentration with heartbreaking clarity.

Suppose Rose had never arrived, and the Shona had to take back Illyn? Could I have led our people?

He pushed the thought away with disgust before shutting his eyes. *She trusts me. I can't do that to her.*

THAT NIGHT, Erven's dreams were plagued with the faces of those he'd witnessed die over the years, Shona and highlanders alike calling to him for help. When the nightmares finally subsided, the thought remained, skewering through his mind in a way he'd never acknowledge had he been awake.

I could have done it.

If it was to save others from suffering, I could have done it.

10

RAISED STAKES

Willow breathed a sigh of relief as the head of the Silversmiths' Guild affixed his seal to their copy of the agreement. She examined the seal for patency before passing the heavy document over to Rose. There wasn't exactly applause as the queen placed her seal beneath the hammer and scales, but it was apparent from the smiles and jovial handshakes that all present were pleased with the outcome.

Willow carefully rolled up the agreement and cleared away the inkwells and pens as the other dignitaries went to join Rose and Arielle for a celebratory dinner. Humming under her breath, she carried the document to the Steward's office, where several clerks worked under his expert supervision. Passing through the antechamber, the air thick with the smells of ink, paper, and dust, she returned the clerks' greetings with a smile.

"Is it finished?" one of the women asked as Willow knocked on the Steward's door.

"It's signed!" Willow announced, displaying the document with a flourish. She smiled at the clerks, ranging from a boy in his late teens to a pair of women old enough to be her aunts. "Thank you all for your hard work. We couldn't have finished before Wintermorn without your help."

The Steward—a weathered old fellow who had served the Crown under Rose's father—greeted her enthusiastically. "Congratulations, Lady Willow!"

Willow passed the document to him, stuffing her hands in her pockets with a sense of satisfaction. "It feels wonderful to have things signed and done with. I was worried they'd find some reason to delay signing until after Wintermorn, and we'd be stuck trying to hammer things out before the Sea Wanderers' envoys arrive next week."

The Steward perused the signatures at the bottom of the official agreement, whistling softly. "What did she say to them? I know there must have been significant debate over this, yet so many of the senior guildsmen signed it."

"Debate or not, no one can claim they were coerced," Willow told him, setting the ink and pens on a narrow shelf next to the door. "I don't know if you want to make copies of the exact agreement, or come up with something different for the town heads to distribute." She pursed her lips, thinking hard. "Come to think of it, we'd better make sure whatever we say portrays Her Majesty in the best light possible. Let's try to emphasize how this agreement will bring in new jobs at the silver mines, funding for repairs to the roads, and new stocks of food and supplies over winter."

"At rates better than what most merchants would charge," reminded one of the clerks, his eyes bright behind an abacus. "No one will want to argue against that!"

"I'll have these layabouts knock something together and

bring it to you to look over," the Steward promised with a wink. "Now all of us can look forward to the holiday with clear consciences!"

Willow trotted out to the hall just as Tait came bursting in. The Shona captain's eyes were red-rimmed, and his hair mussed. "Where's Rose?"

"She's upstairs..." Willow dropped her gaze to the edge of his cloak, which was stained a deep red color that no dye could possibly replicate. "Oh no."

"I'm sorry, Willow." Tait rubbed a hand through his hair helplessly. "Some of the Hollow lot wasn't content with Her Majesty's order to stay away from the highlands. A handful of them made it almost all the way to Hold Aubron, but the highlanders got to them before we did." He looked at her with haunted eyes. "I don't know what's gotten into them. Time was, they'd *never* have attacked without warning."

"It's hard to tell, now." Willow said. "What's become of the Shona who left—oh." She bit her lip at Tait's stricken expression. "That bad?"

"That bad." Tait shook his head. "Only one made it back to Hollow, and she died soon after. Whoever did this wasn't playing. They want us to stay far, far away from Hold Aubron until *they're* ready to talk."

"They're raising the stakes, that's for certain." Willow rubbed her eyes, wondering how her heart was still beating after so much bad news. "They'll have a lot to answer for."

ERVEN GROANED and rubbed his eyes, yanked from a dream of Hollow as the highland guards shoved the door open.

"Commander, the Holdmasters require your presence."

The guard stood impatiently at the door, outlined in a rectangle of light from outside.

He clambered out of his bedroll, trying to gather his thoughts. The bruises from the failed escape attempt throbbed in his limbs as he carefully straightened. The rest of the men watched worriedly as the highland guard clamped a hand around his shoulder and pulled him out of the room. His head still clearing, he had to allow the man to lead him to the room where all the previous meetings had occurred.

Like before, representatives from the rebel clans crowded the room. The atmosphere felt decided and intense, in marked contrast to the previous days. The man from before sat in his seat in the corner, giving Erven a chilly gaze as the Hold Aubron leader addressed him. "Commander, your actions last night were completely unnecessary. We've been exceedingly accommodating to you and your men, and you've repaid us by injuring our clanmates."

Erven shook his head. "You can't expect those wrongfully imprisoned to stay happily in their cells."

"We'd hoped you would have taken this time to consider our proposal further."

Erven didn't see the man who'd said it, so he directed his answer to the whole coalition. He hoped his voice was even. "I told you, my loyalty isn't so easily broken." He swallowed hard. *I could be stating my own death sentence.* "You've stated you want me to challenge Queen Brielle Thinar for the throne that is hers by blood. But surely you know my history. The Shona fought hard to put her on the throne, and they'll fight hard to keep her there. If I were you, I'd approach Her Majesty directly. You're not going to get the answer you want from me, no matter what."

The change in the faces of the three ringleaders was remarkable, and surprising. Respect mingled with regret as the man in the corner spoke up. "You must think we're children. We aren't going to be manipulated that easily." The force in his words conveyed a cold, calculating intelligence, guided by a temperament stubborn enough to start a fight and see it through to its end, no matter the loss. "The patience of this coalition has run out."

He snapped his fingers at the door, which opened behind Erven. Not daring to look around, he heard scuffling behind him as the guards dragged someone else through the door.

"You speak well, and your loyalty is admirable," the Hold Aubron leader said. The man had seemed conflicted, but new determination resounded through his voice as he added, "But your men bear no such loyalty."

Erven turned with dread to see a pair of guards holding Merald between them. He was gagged, his hair disheveled. Their eyes met, and Erven felt a pang of guilt at the trust in his friend's face.

"We wanted to make sure you understood how seriously we're taking this," the Thinar chief said before gesturing abruptly at the guards. One of them swung a short club into Merald's stomach as the other kicked him down.

Merald hit the floor with a muffled groan, curling to protect his head as the highlanders swung their clubs again and again. Erven didn't realize another highlander was behind him until he tried to run to his friend's side. Fighting the strong arms holding him back, Erven yelled, "This is an outrage! He's one of you!"

The Thinar leader raised a hand. "Enough."

Mercifully, the highlanders stepped back, leaving Merald curled on the floor.

Driving an elbow back into his captor's ribs, Erven slipped free and fell on his knees next to Merald. His friend was barely conscious, his face creased with pain around the gag. An unspoken question passed between them, and Erven saw his own defiance mirrored in Merald's eyes.

He shook off the guards as they pulled him away, getting to his feet with his heartbeat pounding in his ears. "A few years ago, we fought together to free Illyn, and now you're responding like this!?"

"We do what we must," one of the men said grimly as the guards hauled Merald out of the room. "Hopefully now you'll see reason."

"I know what you're hoping to gain by this, but it *won't work*." Erven gritted his teeth on the last two words, wondering how true they really were. "All of us took oaths to serve the queen with our lives—oaths that *you* swore as well." He forced back the fury threatening his composure. "Unlike you, we won't break our word."

"Brave words, Commander." One of the men behind the ringleaders shifted in his seat, his face troubled. "It makes me regret not fighting with the Shona when we had the chance. If we'd joined forces long before this, we could have routed the warlord on our own and saved ourselves this problem now."

"I'd been saying that for years, Sir. The highlanders hid in the mountains, biding your time while Shona blood bought your safety," Erven answered, trying to keep the shaking out of his voice. "But for all your strength, it took a girl who wasn't even raised here—an *outsider*—to reignite Illyn's fires. Who does that make stronger?"

This time, he expected the blow that knocked him to the floor.

11
WINTERMORN

Not for the first time, Rose found herself appreciative of her servants' attention to detail. As Wintermorn dawned, her maids greeted her with a traditional breakfast rattling on a tray—smoked fish and cheese, rolls dusted with poppy seeds, and a tiny bowl of precious cloudberry jam. As she finished breakfast, Greta brushed her hair and carefully twined it into intricate braids, wrapping them around Rose's head and securing them with silver pins.

"Milady will want to wear the crown today, yes?" Greta lifted the lid on the box where Rose's coronation crown rested, tilting it so Rose could see inside.

Rose bit her lower lip at the sight of her father's star necklace, curled inside the crown. *I can't wear that any more. Not with our tribe rebelling against me.* She shook her head. "Everyone knows who I am. Let's just keep the circlet for today."

"All right, Majesty." The cool metal squeezed her temples as Greta fitted it over her braids, pulling them to fit around the circlet. "What about a lovely dress, at least?" the girl asked, smoothing a strand of hair back from Rose's forehead. For a moment, Rose was reminded of Violet's calm, insistent voice.

"It *is* a holiday, after all." Rose sighed. She turned to look Greta appreciatively in the eye. "Thank you for making sure I don't bring it to gloom with my own troubles." She felt a thread of optimism begin, and—as Heather might have reminded her—decided to 'tug on it'. "Are there any pretty ones I don't ordinarily wear?"

"There's this one, Milady." Hilda, the older of the two maids, had cleared away the breakfast dishes and was rustling in a trunk under one of the windows, now shuttered against the cold air outside. She lifted out Rose's burgundy and gold coronation gown.

Rose ran loving fingers down the embroidered panels on the sides of the bodice, the colorful designs comforting under her hand. She hadn't known the women who'd done the painstaking work, but learning the craft had made her appreciate it all the more. "Yes, let's do this one." She smiled. "Though it might be a bit cold for it?"

"You'll have a warm shift beneath." Hilda's face crinkled into smile lines as she laid the dress on Rose's bed and smoothed out the wrinkles. "And no one says you can't wear your warmest woolens under." She reached up and cupped Rose's cheek in one hand. "Winter's hard, but the sun will return. Wear the pretty dress, Majesty."

Going down the steps to the hall, warmed over the last few days by the ever-attentive staff, Rose was glad she'd put forth the effort to feel cheery. The older children of the Rogue School bustled across the cut-stone floor, setting out benches and chairs. Others stretched red tablecloths along the tabletops, layering the ends and hiding the edges with bundles of rowan berries. Most impressive of all, some inventive person had managed to stretch garlands of evergreens and holly across the hall, the ropes holding them tied high along the buttressed roof.

"Lovely dress, Your Majesty," Willow commented as she went past with another basket of table decorations.

Rose instinctively brushed a hand across the embroidery on her bodice. "Thank you. Beautiful decorations, too!" She gestured up at the garlands. "I can't believe you managed to find places to tie them off!"

Willow still wore work clothes, her Sea Wanderer-style trousers tucked into her boots and sleeves pushed up under a short-sleeved tunic. She set the basket on the floor and brushed flyaway hair out of her eyes. "It took some doing, and a bit of cleverness with our tallest ladders, but we managed. Clover's really the one you ought t'thank, though. She suggested employing the Underage Minions to do the decorations." She winked. "Though, I suspect it has more to do with her hoping they'll sleep easily tonight after the bonfire."

"I don't think I can blame her," Rose laughed, feeling her optimistic mood expanding despite the ever-present list of worries in her mind. "Where's Heather?"

Willow hooked a thumb towards the kitchen as she bent to pick up the basket once more. "Helping the kitchen lot finish up the food. I understand they're a bit behind making the apple pancakes. Last I checked, they had a vat of batter big enough to bathe the entire Rogue School."

"Anything else?"

"Hmmm." Willow shifted the basket to her other hip. "We've arranged for a nice dinner to be sent over to the infirmary."

Rose frowned at the reminder. "I'd better go down, just to be sure they're doing all right."

"Aye, good idea." Willow nodded. "We've made sure there's a little bag of sweets for each of the Underage Minions. And a good pot of cider for the watch." She frowned. "I can't think of anything else."

"I didn't think of any of those things." Rose hugged Willow around the shoulders. "I feel so bad when I forget the details; I'm glad you and Heather are there to pick up the bits I drop."

"We're good at that," Willow remarked, shimmying out of Rose's arm and giving her a flick of a salute. "I'm going to go make sure these get put out, then I'll go see where the kitchens are with the rest of dinner."

"Thank you!" Rose called after Willow. The bustle of decorating and preparing swirled around her as she helped several of the children spread the last few tablecloths. That done, she made her way towards the side door, intending to go check on the few patients in the infirmary.

A gust of cold air flew in the moment she opened the door, and she immediately shut it again. Pretty as her coronation dress was, she didn't think it equal to the wintery weather outside. Gathering the skirt in both hands, she returned to her room for a cloak. "We'll have to see about connecting the buildings through the storeroom levels..." she mused as she fastened her cloak at her neck. "Or at the very least, putting walkways in between."

Returning downstairs, she paid her visit to the infirmary. Relieved to see the healers comfortably engaged in keeping their patients company, she returned to decorating the hall, signed some supply orders, had a very late lunch with Arielle, and had barely finished reading Willow's condensed report from yesterday when the light from outside began fading.

"Coming?" she asked at the connecting door to Willow and Heather's side of the office.

"Coming, yes." Willow briskly stacked documents into a pile, dropping it all into a wooden box marked 'later' along the side in sloping letters. She locked the box, then the office door, stowing both keys on a string around her neck.

Rose accompanied her friend down the spiral stairs to the hall. The dinner that followed was better than any she remembered having in Illyn, as she presided over a head table filled with her friends and advisors. Farther down the hall, the Rogue School had several tables all to themselves, the children keeping their caregivers busy with their antics. Guardsmen, laundry and kitchen workers, maids, and scribes all crowded the other tables, sharing food and drink under the evergreen garlands.

As the meal ended, Rose caught herself thinking how unlike her coronation it had been. Then, visiting dignitaries and tribal leaders had taken up her attention and time, and she had concluded the meal with tense nerves and ears that could bear no more noise.

Finishing the last bite of her rice pudding, she set her spoon down with a sigh. Down at the other end of the hall, Clover and Tora were herding the youngest Underage Minions towards the door, undoubtedly intent on getting them to bed before the bonfire was lit. As Tora carried Anneli out the door by her pinafore straps, a pang went through Rose's stomach that had nothing to do with the food.

If I hadn't sent them, Merald would be here right now. She folded her napkin into a tighter and tighter square, her happy mood fading with each face she recalled was missing.

"Everything all right?"

Rose looked up at Arielle as the older woman sat down in Willow's vacated seat beside her. "I'm all right." She nodded at the end of the hall. "Just, Merald didn't deserve to miss Wintermorn with his family."

"Nor Erven," Arielle sighed, her expression downcast. "I miss him. Watching him dump Lena into the snow every Wintermorn is one of my better memories of his childhood."

"I know you've mentioned him as a child in the past," Rose said, wondering why she hadn't asked sooner. "When did you meet him?"

"He was six, I think," Arielle said. "Lord Kuma had been in power for about three years, and many children were homeless. I came across him and Lena in a ruined building. They were with a gang of older children—scavengers and suchlike." The lines in her face softened as she said, "Even though he was younger than most of the others, he was the one hanging onto Lena, and her just a tiny baby."

"You took them both in?"

"In a sense. Erven was so independent, he didn't want to stay in the village," Arielle said. "He ran away to join the Shona when they first started making trouble for the soldiers. I suppose he was... oh, eleven or so. He'd be in and out, gone for months and back again to see Lena. After a few years, he took her with him."

Rose took a drink of her cider, the dregs long gone cold. "But you seem so close now." She tried to picture Erven as a headstrong boy, the image totally at odds with the capable leader she'd met several years previous.

"Once he took command, he asked for my help. The

Shona needed to become more organized, or the soldiers would've wiped them out." Arielle laughed softly, her eyes faraway. "By then, Erven was ready to listen."

"When was that?" Rose asked. "How old was he when he took command?"

"He was fifteen. A little younger than you were when you took his place." Arielle's voice warmed at the memory. "For him, responsibility came early."

ARIELLE'S ANSWER left Rose quiet and thoughtful long after the healer had been called away. The elderly Steward found her an hour later, being brushed aside after trying to help clear the tables.

"Everything is ready, Your Majesty." The Steward had served under her parents before the invasion, and his face showed his age. His voice, on the other hand, was still strong, tinged with the good humor and resilience that had seen him through the occupation. He handed her a long taper with an oil-soaked piece of fabric tied around the tip. "All who are able are gathering outside, for Your Majesty to light the bonfire."

Rose took the taper gratefully as the kitchen workers disappeared with the last of the leftover food. "Thank you."

She made for the door before pausing and turning back to him. "You and the others have put so much effort into everything—won't you light the fire?" Rose held the taper back out to him. "I know I wear the crown, but I'd be nowhere without people like you."

With a hesitant look that quickly grew into a wrinkled smile, the man bowed and took the taper with an arthritic hand. "It's our pleasure, Your Majesty." He winked. "But it is nice to be remembered."

They joined the others around the bonfire, where the Steward lit the taper from a brazier hidden in the lee of a buttress. As a gust of wind kicked up, Rose knew she had made the right decision in asking the experienced elder to start the fire. *That wind would have certainly put out any fires I tried lighting.*

The Steward touched the end of his taper to several others in the hands of guardsmen before holding it carefully to the prepared kindling. "To light!"

The roar came back from every throat present. "To light!"

The bonfire caught, melting the packed snow and warming their faces. As cider was passed around, Clover and Heather caught Rose up in a hopping dance around its perimeter. Laughing uproariously, the incorrigible pair snagged Willow as well, who whooped with surprise as Heather grabbed her.

The dance eventually ended as Clover's shoe caught on the hem of Rose's cloak, tumbling all but Willow into a heap on the steps leading into the hall. As they disentangled themselves, Heather gave her older sister a resentful look, "Why didn't you fall?!"

Willow smirked, offering Rose a hand up. "Just lucky, I suppose."

Rose put a hand to her ribs. "Well, I need a rest after that." She sat on the damp steps, Willow joining her. After brushing off snow, Heather and Clover joined them, the four of them sitting shoulder to shoulder in front of the bonfire.

"It's different from home, but I think I like it," Heather said.

"Me as well," Clover agreed. She dug in her apron pocket and handed each of them a cloth-wrapped package. "Happy, happy Wintermorn, girls."

"Oh, lovely!" Heather exclaimed, holding up a woven-cording bracelet strung with tiny beads.

Rose undid the string on her package to see a similar bracelet to Heather's, hers carefully braided embroidery silk in vibrant red. "It's beautiful, Ducky," she said, holding out her wrist for Clover to tie it on.

"Thank you." Clover's worn-roughened fingers were gentle as she smoothed the bracelet across the bones in Rose's wrist. "I know it's not tradition here, but I thought we might do just a *little* something like we used to at home."

Willow ran her fingers over her own bracelet. "I like it."

"It's good to keep in our minds where we've come from." Rose said, unsure if the warmth came from the fire or from the closeness of her friends.

"Remember the past while we look to the future." Willow stood up, pulling Rose with her. "And tonight, you'd best not ruin the happiness with worrying. Let's dance, girls!"

Rose tried to do what Willow had said. As the dancing continued around the fire, the thought remained that Erven and the others were still imprisoned somewhere high above Whitecaps, helpless and possibly suffering.

Stay safe until we can get you back, she thought as Willow grasped one hand and Heather the other. She looked across the fire at Arielle, laughing and talking with one of the guard captains. *There are more people than just me who want to see you return safely.*

OUTSIDE THE STOREROOM, Erven and the others could hear the chorus of 'to light' as the Aubron tribe lit the Wintermorn bonfire. Erven was taking his turn on watch, leaning against the heavy door of their prison as the others rested. As the holiday evening passed, the faint sounds of dancing, drunken songs, and stories filtered through to his ear, pressed close to the rough wood.

As jubilant as the highland celebrations sounded, Erven preferred the Shona's way of celebrating with a snowball fight. Every year, he made it a point to sneak up on his sister Lena and toss her into the deepest snowdrift he could find. They'd always ended the evening piled together around the biggest fire their secrecy could allow, telling stories until the youngest fell asleep.

He rubbed his eyes in an effort to pull himself back to the present. The attack on Merald at his last meeting with the Holdmasters had only been the beginning of a new tactic to force his submission. Over the last few days, the door would open unexpectedly at any hour of day or night, and the highland guards would drag one of their number out. Only after a maddeningly inconsistent interval would they return, throwing the badly beaten hostage to the floor before barring the door once again.

It had not escaped Erven's notice that the Holdmasters were explicitly avoiding him in their assaults. He'd taken to staying as close to the door as possible, hoping with each altercation that their captors would choose him instead of one of his men. No matter how loudly he shouted, they acted deaf to his demands. He could only try to reassure the others and wait anxiously until the door opened again.

Merald coughed across the room. Erven pulled his ear away from the door to listen for the sounds of his friend's breathing. *I shouldn't have brought him. It's my fault he's hurt.* He clenched a fist against the floor at the memory of Merald's eyes, blurred with pain over the gag. *I wish there could be some way to get them out of here. Then I could outlast as long as I needed to.* He shifted to press his ear back against the door as Merald coughed again. *I never thought I'd consider giving in to our enemies, but I always expected I'd be facing them alone.*

As if in response to his worried thoughts, he caught the sounds of several people coming along the corridor towards their prison. "Look alive," he warned as he scrambled away from the door. "They're coming back."

Those awake enough to hear him responded with muttered curses.

"Rot their eyes."

"On a holiday?"

Erven crouched beside Cedric, helping him sit up. The soldier had been the Holdmasters' target the previous day, and still complained of dizziness and a blinding headache. "All right?"

Cedric blinked hard and nodded. "All right." He looked with unfocused eyes at the door as it opened, letting in a blast of cold air and the brilliance of torchlight. "Here they come," he whispered.

12
WILLOW'S GRAND NIGHT OUT

"Frogs and toads." Willow barely caught a jug of milk as it tipped over the edge of the table. Her wrist aching at the sudden weight, she shoved it to sit next to a bowl of eggs on the worktable.

"What's th'matter?" Heather asked as she slid a pile of chopped dried apples to the side of her cutting board.

"Nothing." Willow began cracking eggs into a bowl of flour. Too many days of papers and reports over the week after Wintermorn had given her a grumpy disposition and tired eyes. As if to add insult to injury, the morning's meeting—another frustrating planning session with the Shona on how to best rescue Erven and his patrol—had ignited a disturbing thought.

After this long, I would've expected some kind of communication from the highlands. A ransom demand, or another attack, or something. They're planning something; I'll bet my life on it. But we have no idea what, and there's no way to get close enough without everyone we sent dying, just like those Shona.

She hissed and picked a broken piece of shell out of the bowl. The Shona who'd perished in the failed attempt hadn't been good friends, but their faces still rang sharply against her mind. *Even if we could get close enough without getting attacked, how can we rescue them without causing an all-out war between highlands and lowlands?*

She smacked the next egg against the bowl much more forcefully than she'd meant to. *And there's the sabotage at the mine, and the storms keep delaying the ships with supplies, and that town governor of Hillholm who says he's not going to pay homage to a foreigner, and...*

She belatedly realized that Heather had said something. "What?"

"I said," Heather scraped apples into her bowl of batter. "If it's nothing, I'll boil my shoe and eat it." She set the cutting board down with a slap. "Cooking is supposed to give you a minute to breathe, Old Thing, not make things worse."

"I know." Willow dropped the last eggshell into a trash bucket and began stirring milk into the batter. "I can't get away from it. No sooner do we take care of one thing, when another comes up."

"Go outside." Heather lifted the spoon out of Willow's hands. "You're going to turn into a mushroom."

The courtyard snow had gone from fluffy to packed hard and streaked with mud and dirt. Willow could hear children's voices as she neared the Rogue School, but it took several minutes of looking between the different outbuildings before she found the source of the noise. A bizarre conglomeration of firewood, splintered timbers, and ancient bed linens sat wedged between the Rogue School and a barracks. Clover waved from a hole in the mass. "Hey, Willow! Come on!"

Willow waved back. "That thing looks like it'll fall on my head the moment I go in. I'm all right here."

"Awwww," Clover pouted, brushing the brim of her giant hat out of her face. "She doesn't want to join. Everyone! Willow doesn't want to play with us!"

A flood of children poured from the doors, windows, and sundry holes towards Willow. She held up her hands in self-defense, laughing, "Stop, stop! I don't want to—"

Her breath left her lungs in a whoosh as the first pair of children crashed into her legs. She could hear Clover laughing as the little Rogues piled on top of her.

"Hahaha, stop! Stop! Stopstopstopstopstop!" She whooped as someone began drumming their feet on her ribcage.

"Oy, get off her!" Clover yelled. As the children piled off Willow, Clover offered a hand up. Most of her chestnut-brown hair stood on end as she declared, "Nothing clears the air like a good squabble. They'll sleep well tonight!"

"I'm glad to hear it," Willow said, brushing away the melting snow. "They seem to have a lot of energy."

"Care to stay and help me run it off them?" Clover offered hopefully.

Willow was on the verge of agreeing when she noticed someone in brightly colored clothes walking through the main gates. "I would love to, Ducky, but I think I'm about to be called away."

Clover sighed and waved a hand. "Go on, then. I'll see you at dinner."

"Good luck!" Willow called as she left the alley. As she

wound between carts of supplies and soldiers drilling, she found the person who had originally caught her attention. It was a Sea Wanderer some years younger than her, his clothes spattered with salt rime. He whooped when he saw her, and his enthusiastic hug almost bowled her over into the snow.

"Tiren!" Willow squeaked as she extricated herself. "I wasn't expecting them to send you!" She looked up at the young man, stretching to her fullest height. Her head barely reached the top of his shoulder. "You've gotten taller again!"

Her friend brushed messy brown curls off a sun-bronzed forehead. "My mother can't believe it, either. She always said I'd be taller'n either of them."

"I understand that. The last letter I got from home said my brother's already taller than my mother." Willow peered past the gates towards Westhaven. "I hope you're here to tell us the envoys have arrived."

Tiren stuffed his hands in his pockets. "That they have. They sent me up t'tell Her Majesty they'll present themselves 'at her convenience'."

Willow snorted. "That means they're going to be formal about it, eh? Come on, then. I need to find the Steward. We'll have t'warm up the hall again." She looked back over her shoulder at him. "We've barely used it since it got cold."

"It gets cold here?" Tiren hunched his shoulders, making his face disappear into his jacket. "I'd no idea."

"Rascal." Willow kicked a spray of snow in his direction. "Let's get you some food, and we'll tell Rose she's got an audience." She pulled open a side door to the kitchens. "Hopefully, she'll be happy about the news. She's been on edge ever since the reports from the highlands turned sour."

"That reminds me," Tiren said. He unbuttoned a pocket

in the lining of his jacket and pulled out a scrap of paper. "That's for you. I was told you'd know what t'do with it."

Willow stopped next to a table where rolls for dinner were cooling, scrutinizing the tiny, ciphered message. "Ethan's here?" She felt her face flush at the thought of the Sea Wanderer intelligence agent. "And when were you planning on giving me this?!"

Tiren's warm brown eyes filled with amusement as he juggled a roll between his fingertips. "I knew you'd wonder who the Sea Wanderer Council sent. He's at the inn by the harbor... errr, the Lazy Duck, I think it is?"

"The Sleeping Goose, you goose!" Willow laughed.

Tiren winked. "Said there'd be dinner too, if y'cared t'join him."

He dodged a flying roll as Willow ran to go find Heather. As she pounded up the stairs, Willow mentally went over the last few letters she had received from Ethan, wondering if there'd been hints about a visit that she'd missed.

"What's got you like a cat that's et a hedgehog?" Heather demanded as Willow plunged into their room and began ransacking their chest.

Willow found the dress she'd been looking for and held it up triumphantly. "The Sea Wanderer envoys are here! Tiren's downstairs right now!" She pulled her work-day dress off and hauled the new one over her shift.

"That's wonderful!" Heather agreed. She set down her sketchbook to help Willow lace up the sides of the rich blue overdress. "But generally speaking, Tiren being here means you're more likely t'fill someone's socks with sand, not blush and change into your best dress."

Willow craned her neck to fasten the brooches at the

shoulders of her dress. "Care to guess who *else* the Sea Wanderers sent?"

"Ahhh..." Heather did up the other brooch and gave it a professional polish with the cuff of her sweater. "Might I guess a certain representative of Council Intelligence is here as well?"

Willow knew she was smiling foolishly as she grabbed her hairbrush. "He's at an inn near the harbor, and he's asked me to meet him for dinner. I'm so nervous; I haven't seen him in so long. Oh—" She stopped brushing her hair. "Rose doesn't even know they're here yet. They're doing the right thing and waiting on her to summon them for an audience. We need to make sure the Steward can get the hall presentable and warmed up."

"I'll tell Arielle and we'll arrange things," Heather reassured her. She opened a box from her chest and pulled out a carved-wood headband. Smoothing back Willow's hair, she settled the headband gently. "You go have a lovely evening, Old Thing." She raised an eyebrow. "You'll owe me later, of course."

"Of course," Willow answered affectionately. "Thank you, love."

THE SLEEPING GOOSE was a strange setting for a first evening after being reunited, but Willow didn't mind. The tavern's dining room was warm against the chilly wind coming off the harbor, and the room quiet for a work-day evening. She hummed happily at her first bite of noodles, making Ethan laugh across the table.

"All that venison leaving a bad taste in your mouth?" The Sea Wanderer hadn't lost any of the exuberance that had endeared him previously. Even with the cold, he didn't wear a hat to cover hair blonder than hers, and his ice blue eyes snapped with the keen intelligence that had seen his appointment to a Council seat at a very young age. A crooked eyetooth made his smile equal parts mischievous and cheerful as he said, "I'd have sworn you'd've gone mad long ago, not bein' able t'cook as often as you'd like."

She laughed, feeling the awkwardness of their initial meeting melt away. "I still have the chance when I feel like it. But Illyn food does lack a certain something that Sea Wanderers have perfected."

"I think the word you're lookin' for is 'flavor'."

"There's something to be said for spices," she agreed. "The few months I spent with Tiren's family have altered my tastes forever."

Their conversation drifted from food, to weather, to discussing the contents of their most recent correspondence. Eventually, the discussion drifted towards the reason Ethan had been sent to Illyn, and Willow's good humor began to evaporate.

"I'm glad the Council still decided to send you, with winter here and all. Continued trade between us means so much to Illyn's fortunes, and we could use something going right for once."

"It wouldn't hurt, that's for certain." The intelligence agent set his knife down and flicked the handle with fingers traced by scars from years of weapons practice. "I heard about th'highlands makin' trouble. An' what's this about them attackin' unprovoked?"

Willow pushed her bowl away. "They attacked Erven's patrol when Rose sent him to try and talk with them, and the one rescue mission that made any headway ended with everyone dying."

Ethan winced. "He's Rose's right hand. They couldn't've chosen a better target."

"Oh, believe me, she knows," Willow's chest tightened at the memory of Rose's tear-stained face. "And I'm not sure she realizes how much she relies on him as more than an ally."

"Let's hope th'Holdmasters don't realize it either." Ethan sent the knife spinning again. "Has a ransom demand come yet?"

"No, and that worries me more than anything." Willow glanced around the common room, grateful that it was a quiet evening. "They clearly have plans for him, but we haven't any idea what." She sighed. "And just between us, we don't know how to rescue him without starting another war."

Ethan leaned back and crossed his arms, watching as the knife juddered to a stop. "If it were me, I'd say they're buildin' up towards some kind of move that'll place them in power."

"What move, though?" Willow asked. "We've been trying to address each conflict as it comes up, but more keep coming." She shook her head. "It's like fighting a fire in a haystack."

"How many tribes've joined this coalition?"

She planted her chin in her hand and tried to think. "At least two we know of, plus several that we don't. That's based on what the one man who escaped the attack said." She folded her napkin and set it on the table next to her bowl. "We didn't realize it at the time, but not everyone came to fight for Rose when the tribes gathered to Hold

Eskel. There've always been some disinclined t'accept her leadership."

"Including her own clan, er..." Ethan searched the ceiling with his eyes before snapping his fingers. "The Thinar?"

"How d'you know these things?" She raised a hand as Ethan opened his mouth. "Don't tell me, it'll only frustrate me more. The Thinar fought for Rose because of her parents. Now they've taken back their support." Willow sighed. "With Rose's connection to the Gaillen Woods, they're anxious to paint her as an outsider, someone who never should've ascended the throne in the first place."

Ethan raised his eyebrows. "That bad?"

Willow nodded wearily. "Luckily, some of the tribes still recognize the right of blood over the right of conquest. Otherwise, the Holdmasters would've had enough backing to overthrow her already."

Ethan's gaze sharpened. "There's a right of conquest?" He clarified, "They'll allow succession if the previous ruler was defeated by the current one?"

"Apparently," Willow sighed. "Some of the really bizarre report's I've heard have said Lord Kuma was the legitimate ruler, because he defeated King Alaber in battle."

"Ah, there it is. *That's* why no ultimatum has come yet." Ethan swiped his knife off the table, sheathing it and standing in the same movement. "I've got t'see Rose immediately, an' protocol be hanged."

"What? Why?"

The chilly night air swirled around them as they left by a side door. Once outside, the intelligence agent's eyes glimmered in the dim light as he scanned the buildings around them. He grabbed her elbow and pulled her several paces down the street before explaining, "If the tribes're looking for a way t'take control of Illyn, they'll have t'find some way that satisfies tribal honor *and* goes over well with th'rest of the people, yes?"

"Y-yes," Willow stammered, scrambling to wrap her scarf properly. "That's about the size of it."

Ethan's next words came as rapidly as his footsteps. "They've ruled out Rose's claim based on th'idea that her blood's tainted, or even that her bloodline's right t'the throne ended in Lord Kuma's conquest. Well, answer me this, Willow." Ethan stopped in the entrance to an alleyway, dropping his voice despite the empty street. "If right of conquest rules here, who'll the tribes consider t'be next in line for th'Illyn throne? Who killed Lord Kuma?"

"Erven." As Willow answered, dread pulsed through her blood.

"Exactly." Ethan quickened his pace again, boots crunching against the icy ground. "It's bad enough they've removed Rose's strongest ally, but now there's a chance they could turn him against her."

They crested the hill long after the gates had been shut for the night. When an inspection of the office and a quick trip upstairs revealed the queen had already gone to bed, Willow returned to the ground floor to give Ethan the bad news.

"That's not ideal," he said. "But I suppose she couldn't do anything until morning, anyhow."

Willow crossed her arms as he brushed past her. "*You* shouldn't be taking this much interest. Aren't you supposed to be motivated by what's best for the Sea Wanderers?"

"What's best for th'Sea Wanderers is strong allies an' profitable trade. Would th'Council like my methods t'ensure those things?" Ethan shrugged eloquently. "Possibly not, but they knew I was shifty when they appointed me. And," he took her hand and gently kissed it. Willow blushed as he continued, "I've got other reasons t'see Illyn prosper. The sooner things're settled here, the sooner someone dear t'me will be able t'come visiting."

"You're full of beechmast," Willow informed him. "Focus on why you're here, and leave courting for after."

"If you insist." Ethan tipped her a nonchalant salute. "We'll doubtless speak tomorrow. Sleep well!"

Still shaking her head, Willow returned to her own room. Despite the late hour, her sisters were still up.

"Sitting up waiting, were you?"

Heather gave her a haughty look, the severity of which was lessened significantly by her floppy nightshirt. "Of course not." She waved at a game spread across their table. "We were *obviously* playing Sails and Shores."

Clover propped her chin in her hand. "And as you can see, Heather's winning." She nudged a bowl of honey-soaked chestnuts, the majority pushed to Heather's side. "I'm not so good at this game."

"It's all right, Ducky," Willow reassured her sister, sitting down next to her. "Tiren says it's always more fun to make up your own rules, anyway."

"Right..." Clover examined the board with a quirked eyebrow. Seizing one of the carved-wood ships, she plowed it across the table into Heather's amassed navy. "My flag-ship just made a contract with the kraken," she announced. "What do you have to say to that?"

Heather rummaged in the game box. "I say—" She slammed a model dragon in the center of Clover's fleet, tipping a cup full of dice onto the table. "—my admiral and his dragon sister think your boats are tasty."

Pieces flew everywhere as Clover dumped the board into her sister's lap. While they tussled back and forth, Willow stole out a hand and commandeered the bowl of chestnuts. Both of her sisters' heads popped up.

"Oy!"

"Those were *mine!* And honestly won, I might add!"

Licking her fingers, Willow handed Heather the bowl. With a sad gaze, Heather extricated the last few sweets and shared them with Clover. "So, Old Thing, how was your romantic evening?"

"And here I thought you were just staying up playing a game." Willow shook her head. "It *was* lovely, until we started talking about things."

"Things..." Clover encouraged.

"You know," Willow waved a hand vaguely in the direction of Rose's room as she got up to get ready for bed. "Things."

"Oh," Heather said, clearly disappointed. "Pity. I was enjoying a nice evening not thinking about *things.*"

"So was I." Willow hopped around on one foot, trading fine stockings for thick socks. "But life has a way of ruining nice evenings." She sat on the corner of their bed as her sisters put the game away. "Ethan had some rather frightening thoughts about where the Holdmasters could be taking their opposition of Rose."

"The pigpen. We talked about this," Heather said.

"No." Willow balled up one of her stockings and threw it at her sister. "Pipe down and listen, would you? This affects all of us."

"All right," Heather conceded. She perched on the bed

next to Willow, her cloudy blue eyes curious. "What's the master of intrigue come up with this time?"

Saying it out loud felt wrong. "You know—Ducky, you may not—there's the whole disagreement with the highlanders of Rose's claim being invalidated by Lord Kuma defeating King Alaber in battle."

"Birthright versus battle right, if you will," Heather helpfully added. "Not that it makes any sense," she added as Clover nodded silently, "so don't feel so bad if you don't understand." She sighed. "I don't understand their logic, but something tells me they're not interested in logic anymore. They've just decided to dislike Rose, for some reason."

"They're all lying, scheming, *stupid* nitwits, but it's the argument they're presenting." Willow sighed. "And they've got Erven in their claws—the man who killed Lord Kuma in battle, which, depending on who you ask, gives him a valid, traditional claim to the throne." Comprehension dawned on both girls' faces as Willow said, "Ethan's worried he'll take the opportunity to declare that claim."

"It doesn't sound to me like something he'd do." Clover ran her fingers through her hair, making it stand out like the corona of a sunflower.

"Not to me, neither," Heather agreed, a little more hesitant than Clover. "You're sure Ethan hasn't been a spy for too long? Suspectin' everyone now?"

"I don't know," Willow conceded. "He does have a slippery turn of the mind, but it's served him well many times over. I'm inclined to trust him. Or, well," she added, "I'm inclined to follow this line of questioning until I find a conclusion."

"Well, let's suppose we pull on this thread and see what

unravels." Heather pulled her knees up to sit cross-legged in her nightgown. "What will we tell Rose?"

"And when?" Clover added. "Does she know yet?

"No, she was already in bed when I got back." Willow pressed her lips together worriedly. "I'll tell her tomorrow. She won't be happy, but she needs to know."

13
A DANGEROUS CHOICE

Merald woke from a dream of his family to the unyielding stone walls of the storeroom. Confused for a long moment, he blinked hard in the dim light of what passed for nighttime in their prison. As his head cleared, he realized the noise had come from Erven, curled under his blanket near the wall.

"Mate, you awake?"

Erven twitched back and forth under his blanket, his brow furrowed and his breathing harsh as Merald shook his shoulder. "Erven, wake up!"

Erven's eyes popped open. He shrank back in his bedroll as Merald let go of his shoulder. "They're coming again!"

Merald jumped, looking over his shoulder. The doorway remained silent and dark across the storeroom. Finally, he ventured, "I think you were dreaming."

Erven sighed, pushing himself up to his elbows. "It's getting to where I can't tell what's real and what's not." He rubbed a shirtsleeve across his face. "I can't do this anymore."

Merald followed his gaze across the room to Ansel, sleeping in the corner. The attacks had lessened since Wintermorn, but the highlanders still remained unpredictable and ruthless. After being hauled away by the guards two days earlier, the young Shona had returned semiconscious, massive bruises making their presence known in rainbow hues across his ribs and back.

"We don't expect you to be able to protect all of us," Merald reassured Erven. "We talked about it, one of the times you were gone."

"I know." Erven sat up to lean against the wall, tipping his face towards the ceiling. He was quiet for a long time, the barest flicker of movement behind closed eyelids the only indication that he was still awake. Finally, he whispered, "When the warlord's men captured me, my choice was easy—death from my injuries or torture, and then it would be all over." He wrapped an arm around his torso, the muscles in his hand tensing in the dim light.

Merald bit his lip and looked away as Erven's voice broke. "I've lived it so many times in my dreams, over and over again." He clutched his free hand in a fist. "It didn't matter what they did to me. I could take it, because it was just me paying the price."

"You were alone, then," Merald said, understanding finally dawning.

"Yes. But the longer I outlast the Holdmasters, the more danger I'm putting all of you in." A single tear ran down Erven's cheek, and he shook his head fiercely. "The next time they summon me, I'm going to agree to their terms."

Merald nodded silently. The timbers across the ceiling groaned, and a flurry of pain ran through his side. He looked up at the ceiling as Erven gingerly moved his own hand from the site of his old injury. "Is another storm coming?"

"I think so." Erven pulled a knee up and wrapped his arms around it with a deep breath. "I've thought it over backwards and forwards. There's no way a rescue attempt would succeed, but I might be able to negotiate releasing the rest of you."

"And you'll be able to undermine them from inside," Merald agreed. "Good plan." A disturbing thought stirred in his mind as Erven refused to meet his eyes. "Sea and skies, are you actually going to side with them?"

Erven buried his face in his knee. "I keep telling myself Rose is the right one to lead Illyn, and the Holdmasters are wrong and treasonous."

"But...?"

"But there's that voice in my head that says I *could* lead our people." Erven's eyes were haunted as he looked up. "That I could take the crown in her place."

Alarm sparked through Merald's mind, driving away the last few bits of sleepiness. "Mate, you've got to fight it! That thought's more dangerous than any wound you've ever taken."

"I know!" Erven rubbed his fists into his eyes. "I wish I could get rid of it, but it's there every single time they try to convince me. I've tried and tried, but it won't go away. And they'll leave you alone if I promise to do what they want." His voice faded from anger to desperation. "I can't let you die for a choice I'm making."

Merald wanted to contradict, but he knew Erven was right. He looked at the sleeping figures of the others, huddled in their blankets around the room. "If you think this is the only way to ensure our safety, then do what you think is best." He gripped Erven's shoulder. "But you need to fight. You've got a stronger will than anyone I know—don't let your own head be the thing that breaks it."

"I'll do my best." Erven leaned his head back against the wall again, exhaustion settling across his features.

"Are you going to tell the others?"

Erven shook his head. "If the Holdmasters are going to be convinced to release you, the reactions from the others need to be real." His blue eyes went as hard as chips of ice. "And they might have a right to be angry."

AFTER THE BRIEF reprieve Wintermorn had offered, the calamity list had swallowed Rose once more. That morning, she could practically hear her duties calling to her from the office downstairs. The wind whistled outside, and the shutters rattled against the storm as her maids moved around the room, quietly warming her clothes and stoking the fire.

"Ready, Your Majesty?" Greta pointed her towards a plate of breakfast and held up Rose's hairbrush.

Rose ran her hand through her hair, wincing as her fingers caught in a snarl. Her night's sleep had been uneasy, and the tangles bore testament to the hours of tossing and turning. "Thank you, yes." Rose wriggled her feet into the slippers waiting on the floor and tightened the belt of her dressing gown snugly around her waist.

Even with the draft coming from outside, the fire cast enough warmth that Rose could feel it against her face as she sat down to breakfast. The tea in her mug steamed against her face, sending soothing aromas of fir and spice into the air. Greta hummed softly as she carefully brushed Rose's hair and began plaiting it.

The peace was interrupted by someone rapping on the door. Rose hastily swallowed a bite of bread as Hilda went to answer.

"Her Majesty's still waking up. You can speak with her in a bit."

Willow's voice came from outside. "It's important, and it can't wait." The door creaked in protest. "Rose, I'm sorry, but we need to talk."

Rose sighed. "It's all right, Hilda. Willow's one of the only people who can come in at any time." She looked up at Greta, who had just finished putting the last hairpin in the knot of braids at the back of her head. "Thank you for your help. I can finish getting ready on my own."

"Yes, Milady." The maids gave half-curtsies as they left, closing the door behind them.

Willow leaned against the closed door, stuffing her hands into her pockets. "Sorry to bother you so early."

"Don't worry." Rose went to her dressing table, picking up her circlet and fitting it around her brow. After the warmth from the fire, the cold metal came as a momentary shock. *Time to be queen.* "Did you enjoy your evening with Ethan yesterday?" She smiled at her friend. "I assume you went to the embassy as soon as you heard he was part of the delegation."

The note in Willow's voice—and that she didn't respond to the teasing about her personal life—made the cozy morning come to an abrupt halt. "I saw him for dinner. We were talking some things out, and he had a really frightening thought. I came to tell you as soon as I could, but you'd already gone to bed."

"I was tired." Rose wondered if she should feel as defensive as she did. "I went to bed early, not that it helped." She undid the belt of her dressing gown. "What's the matter? If it's more bad news, I'd rather hear it when it's new, and not once it's built to the point of engulfing us all."

"It's bad." Willow pointed in the direction of the council room. "He's waiting downstairs."

Once Rose had hastily dressed, she took the lamp from her table and hurried to the meeting room. The newly laid fire crackled happily as it ate up the kindling, casting flickery light around the room. Ethan greeted her from the shadows as Willow lit the rest of the lamps, dropping to one knee and bowing his head. "Your Majesty. I'm sorry our meeting couldn't've waited for th'proper time."

Rose extended her hand for him to kiss, a gesture she still felt very silly making. "Willow says you needed to talk to me urgently?"

Ethan stood up, the lamplight chasing shadows away from his face. "I do, Your Majesty." He eyed the end of the table closest to the fire. "May we sit?"

"Please do. I'm sorry I wasn't available last night," she apologized as they sat. "I went to bed early. What's the matter?"

Willow and Ethan exchanged concerned looks before Ethan explained, "While Willow and I were at dinner, she was tellin' me about th'challenges you're facing with the Holdmasters an' all."

"I'm sure that was wonderfully light dinner conversation," Rose remarked. "It's certainly taken away my appetite over the last few weeks."

"We did talk about other things first, and that was quite pleasant." Willow gave Rose a sympathetic look before patting Ethan's arm. "Go on."

"Right." Ethan lowered his voice, even though it was only the three of them in the room. "Willow explained that some are questioning the legitimacy of your claim to the throne, yes?"

"You could call it that, I suppose," Rose said. "They're saying my blood is so tainted by my upbringing that I might as well not be from Illyn at all." She sighed. "They want someone else sitting on this throne."

Ethan winced. "If that's what they want, they're crazy *and* ungrateful. Unfortunately, there's someone else in Illyn who'll suit their ideals." He ducked his head, as if not wanting to meet her eyes. "If my guess's correct, th'Holdmasters'll take any opportunity t'rally around someone who'll fit their ideal of rule by combat...and Erven's a perfect-made match."

Rose closed her eyes and counted three deep breaths before opening them. *No wonder they haven't tried to ransom him.* "I'm so stupid, not to have seen this possibility."

"That's squirrel scat, and you know it." Willow's voice sounded exactly like her father's. "No one expects you to be able t'predict every event throughout your reign."

Rose rubbed her temples. "No, but this one I should have seen coming. What was I thinking?" She looked sharply at Ethan. "You just put this together last night, yes?"

Ethan drummed his fingertips on the table, blade scars white against his knuckles. "I did some research of my own overnight."

"I gave him the most recent calamity list," Willow told her, tapping a slate tablet at her elbow.

"It was enough to give me an idea of what's going on." Ethan looked directly at her with eyes the same color as midwinter ice. "It makes me wonder what will happen if he actually *does* take their side." Rose's heart began pounding in her ears as he added, "I know it's a lot t'imply, but I can't look at this situation without at least *considering* th'possibility of him deciding he'd make a better king than you make a queen."

"He doesn't—wouldn't. Hasn't ever!" Rose winced at the sound of her voice, high-pitched with disbelief. "Erven's been the strongest ally I've had since I arrived here. They tried to beat the locations of the Shona outposts out of him, and Commander Ricar says he never made a sound." She locked eyes with the Sea Wanderer agent. "If you knew him any better, you wouldn't even dream of questioning his loyalty."

"Rose," Willow softly said. "We know Erven's history just like you do. We're not saying any of this is frozen into the ice. People *can* change, and the draw of power can make anyone do funny things." She stood from the table, taking one of the lamps with her. "I was afraid to even mention it, especially knowing how much you rely on him, but you needed to know."

"I suppose I should thank you." Rose grimaced before softening her words. "I mean, thank you. Will you give me some time to think while you find the others?" She rubbed her eyes, already dreading the conference ahead. "Arielle needs to know for certain. And Commander Ricar should be at the Headwind Garrison today. I'd like a messenger sent as fast as possible."

"Have you looked outdoors today?" A draft whistled in the fireplace, stirring the flames as Willow said, "It's storming again. Even if the snow doesn't stick, it's blowing sideways."

"I had difficulty gettin' here from the embassy this morning," Ethan said, running a hand over his blond hair. "I'm *still* damp. I don't know if the commander will be able to leave his garrison."

Rose groaned. "We still need him. He has more experience with military things than any of us."

"I'll send a messenger, but it'll take a long while for him t'get here," Willow warned. "Would you rather wait until everyone can be here?"

"I want everyone's input." Rose crossed her arms. "Send the messenger, and impress on him how urgent it is."

"Right…" Willow pulled over her slate, erased it with a sweep of her sleeve, and began writing. "We need someone from the Shona." Willow pursed her lips. "Erven left Tait in charge here while he's gone, and Tora's always here."

Rose nodded, wondering how the Shona would take to the news. "Yes, both of them. And if we can get Annika from Hollow, we'd better try."

"That'll certainly be tomorrow, then," Willow said. "Even if it weren't storming, it'll take a whole day for someone to get here from Hollow."

"Tomorrow, then," Rose conceded. "As soon as everyone can get here."

"Arielle and I will notify everyone who's here. And I'll get started on those messages." Willow picked up her tablet, tugging Ethan's sleeve. "Come on, Lord Suspicion. Let's give Her Majesty some time to think."

Ethan bowed briefly to Rose. "I'm sorry, Your Majesty. This wasn't how I wanted our mission here t'start. Be assured, none of what we've spoken here will leave my lips."

A twisted eyetooth gave his smile a conspiratorial edge. "The Sea Wanderer Council trusts me t'act in their best interest, but I'm allowed leeway of my own."

The lamp flickered in the draft as he and Willow departed, leaving Rose alone in the council room. With no witnesses, she let her head drop to the table. *Just when I thought things were already as bad as they were going to get. How can this be happening?*

14
FORGIVE ME

Even with their quick action, it took until the next day to assemble everyone—a very restless night that passed like a year for Rose. After spending too long with her mind going in circles, it was a relief to finally discuss the problem out loud with others. Just as she had expected, the Shona were the hardest to convince.

"He wouldn't!" Tait insisted. The years had not dulled the Shona captain's jittery nature, and his gaze roved constantly around the room from a seat in the corner. "He's been her strongest defender since she arrived. How dare you question his loyalty?!"

"I'm not exactly doubtin' him on that account," Ethan said. He fiddled with a stick of charcoal as he suggested, "I'm just saying, *is* there a chance he could decide he'd make a better ruler than Her Majesty?"

"It doesn't seem likely. He's loyal to a fault, in some opinions." Willow sat at the end of the table with her sisters. She carefully sharpened another charcoal stick as she added, "And most of the time he makes his predictions right, but there've been a time or two where it's gotten him into trouble—"

"And saved hundreds of lives in the process," Rose said, surprising herself with the defense. *What happened to looking at this logically?*

"Last time he was taken by the enemy, he was alone," Annika said, fiddling with the hilt of her dagger as she leaned back in her chair. Her clothing was still creased and speckled with damp spots, witness to her hurried journey from Hollow. "Now, he has the patrol with him."

"Ahh..." Rose clamped her lips tightly on the exclamation. "You think they'd threaten the others?"

"Leverage." Tait began tracing the grain lines on the table. His mouth twisted in disgust.

"But you think it could be enough to make him turn?" Rose frowned. "That doesn't sound like him."

"It doesn't," Commander Ricar agreed. "Every experience I've had with him implies a will stronger than iron." Like Annika's clothes, his uniform was marred with the signs of a hard ride from the Headwind Garrison. He rested an elbow on the table tiredly. "Even when he was imprisoned here two years ago, he resisted Lord Kuma's attempts to pry the location of the Shona bases out of him, and that was no small feat."

"True, but with his men at risk, it wouldn't necessarily be the same. And it wouldn't be the first time a Shona leader took protection too far," Tait said reluctantly, brushing dark hair away from his eyes.

"You remember what happened with Soren," Annika reminded them.

Rose sighed. The former leader of the Thunderhead outpost had rescued her and Violet, but refused to acknowledge her leadership after she'd taken command of the Shona. Upon the clan's discovery that he'd allowed safe passage to soldiers through Thunderhead territory—and the rejection that came with the exposure—he'd attacked her and been killed in turn by Willow and Heather's father. "Someone told me he's what Erven could have been if things had gone differently."

"Soren was so protective of Thunderhead that he refused to accept help or lend it, lest they get hurt in the process." Tait's eyes were cautious as he warned, "He and Erven weren't so different, really."

"I understand." Rose grimaced. "And I understand how he could easily let the balance tip too far." Her temples ached under her circlet as she looked over at Arielle. "You know him better than all the rest of us. Do *you* think there's a chance of him rebelling?"

"It's difficult to say..." Arielle began slowly.

Rose hadn't been expecting the hesitation. She and Willow exchanged a single startled look as the healer continued, "If the Holdmasters want to bring Illyn back to the old ways, part of it could involve leadership decided in combat rather than by birthright. It's always been an acceptable means of changing leadership within a clan, but it could become a way to remove Rose from the throne." Arielle looked at her lap. "Being the man who killed Lord Kuma lends Erven significant credibility."

"That's a plain way of saying it, yes." Willow shook out her writing hand as she exchanged a filled slate for a blank one. "But given how long you've known him, what would you predict?"

The thin lines around Arielle's eyes and mouth deepened. Finally, she said, "I expect we'll hear that the Holdmasters have a new leader, and soon. Now wait," she held up a hand to forestall the exclamations, "I didn't say it'll be with willingness on his part. They control all the information coming out of the highlands, and they'll be able to twist things to suit themselves."

"Well, we can't wait until news reaches us," Clover said unexpectedly from her seat between her sisters. "Tora had her hands full, but she was very firm about that." She rubbed her upper arm absently. "For a woman who spends most of her time hefting babies, she's still got a strong grip." Though younger than Rose by almost three years, Clover maintained an air of urgency that Rose wished she could match. "Those men have families counting on us to make sure they're safe."

"We're doing what we can," Annika reassured Clover. "But we might *have* to wait. They attacked without a single word of warning, and we don't want to risk more lives unnecessarily."

"We *will* eventually need to open communication with them—or with Erven, if he does what Ethan's concerned about," Arielle warned, her eyes hard as flint.

"It's the dead of winter," Commander Ricar objected. "There's no way anyone will be able to travel in numbers until spring."

"Spring, then," Rose said. "As things are now, we can't go after them with force. I don't want to risk them doing something nasty to their prisoners. And the weather's too unpredictable to chance a large diplomatic meeting." She rubbed her forehead tiredly. "Even with this new complication, we're still where we were a fortnight ago."

Clover's chair screeched across the floor. "I hate winter." She stomped out of the room, slamming the door behind her. The rest of the council sat silently as the reverberations died out, Rose secretly feeling the same way as her younger friend.

"She's right—I hate winter too." Willow's charcoal scraped against her slate as she set them both down.

"And this winter's being peculiarly nasty. To everyone." Rose sighed. "Whatever it throws at us, and whatever other bad news we hear, we have to remember it's still our people we're dealing with."

"Nice thoughts," Ethan said. He planted his elbows on the table. "And you're right, Milady. You *can* keep abreast o' all this, an' the winter's lending you a helpin' hand by slowing th'Holdmasters plans as much as it's slowed yours. But, if I may?" His icy blue eyes pinned hers with the experience of many years. "Prepare for th'worst, while you're hoping for th'best. If Erven *does* decide that Illyn's best off with a new ruler, all the progress you've made towards reconcilin' your people will disappear in an instant." His normally cheerful face was serious as he admonished, "If I were you, Your Majesty, I'd begin puttin' my thoughts towards how you'll end the whole thing."

Sometime after the morning bells had rung, the storeroom door burst open. The highland guards menaced them with spear hafts and clubs as their leader commanded, "Keep them back, except the Commander." With a curt look at Erven, the man added, "Pick whomever you like after we leave."

Erven had bolted to his feet the moment the door opened, adrenaline coursing through his body. The others were also on their feet, Cedric helping Ansel up. If he'd been uncertain of his course of action, the terrified looks on his men's faces decided for him. In the span of a second, fear turned to determination.

"Don't hurt them!" he yelled, holding out his hands. "I'll do what you want; just don't hurt them!"

He could hear exclamations of outrage from the others as the highlanders dragged him from the room. Outside, Erven dug in his feet and twisted himself free. "I'm not going anywhere until you call them out of there. Once your masters hear what I have to tell them, there won't be a need to hurt anyone."

The highlander gave him a long, searching look before banging on the door again. Only once he had counted as many guards leaving as had entered did Erven say, "All right. Let's go talk to them."

The guards let Erven walk down the chilly corridor unencumbered, stopping to open the council room door and allowing him to walk in on his own. Fewer Holdmasters were present this time, but Erven recognized the handful of men as the more influential leaders of the coalition.

"All right." He tried to emulate Commander Ricar's tone when addressing insubordinate soldiers. "I'm not going to let you take my men apart piece by piece until you get the right answer from me." Erven took a deep breath. *Forgive me.* "What exactly do you want me to do?"

The Holdmasters looked in shock and disbelief at him—and each other—for a long moment. The Aubron chief leaned forward. "You're accepting our offer?"

"Not willingly. You can be completely clear about that. If it had been just myself you captured, you can be assured I'd die before giving in. But—" Erven let the distress of the previous few days slip into his voice. "My pride isn't worth the pain my men are going through."

"It's about time you saw reason." The Westin leader looked relieved. "Do we have your word you won't try any tricks?"

Erven answered bitterly, "I'm joining your cause against the Crown. You'd better take that as your assurance of my trustworthiness." He crossed his arms. "Do I have *your* word that my men will be unharmed?"

The Holdmasters looked at each other, nodding assent. The Thinar leader cleared his throat. "They'll be unharmed. You have our word." He gestured towards the door while eyeing one of his subordinates. As the young man left, the Thinar leader turned his attention back to Erven. "Now that you've come around, we can get down to business." He leaned forward and steepled his fingers. "The coalition of the Free Holdmasters has no intention of allowing Illyn to be governed by someone ignorant of our ways."

Erven bit back a retort as the man continued, "When the people see your loyalty to tradition, they'll quickly return to us, and the girl will have to concede the throne to its rightful owner."

"I *know* all that," Erven answered tightly. "I told you, I'll do what I have to." He hardly trusted the words to come out of his mouth. "The people *might* be more willing to follow someone they know over someone who's still a relative stranger. I'll take that responsibility, if it means that Illyn can be led by someone with her best interest in mind."

"I'm pleased you've begun to see our perspective," the Thinar chief said. "It'll be a relief to work with you, not against you."

Erven crossed his arms. "Once the Shona hear about this

betrayal, they'll disown me. You won't have any hope of winning their loyalty."

"Somehow, I doubt that," the man in the corner commented. "You're a legend to them—and most of the highlands. You single-handedly saved your clan, defied the warlord's interrogation, escaped with your life, and tied things off by killing him in single combat." He leaned back in his chair, eyeing Erven as a pickpocket might eye a heavy purse. "Your reputation will speak for itself. With you on our side, she'll have no choice but to leave the throne in the hands of those who deserve it. Just do exactly what we tell you, and no one else needs to get hurt. Understand?"

I've been so distracted by the wolves, I missed the snake in the room. "I understand." Dread coiled in Erven's stomach. "My word doesn't mean much anymore. But you have my word —I'll do my best to guard and guide Illyn towards prosperity. It's the best way to protect the people I love." *And if I have to, I'll take the reins you give me and choke you with them.*

ERVEN HADN'T EXPECTED the Holdmasters to let him return to his comrades, and his suspicions were confirmed after the meeting ended. The guards—now somewhat less gruff than they had been—ushered him to a small room in a barracks, on a terrace just below the main Hold.

One of the guards kicked aside an empty crate. Light flared from a pottery lamp on a rickety table as he said, "Your home for now, Sir. Someone'll bring your things over from the Hold." The highlander gave him a stern look. "Stay put. Any of us see you lurking around where you're not allowed, there'll be hell to pay."

Erven nodded numbly and sat down on the narrow bed.

The straw mattress crackled as he lay back, barely caring about the passage of time. Several bells rang over the course of as many hours, breaking up the wind whistling around the eaves of the building. One of the highlanders came and went without saying anything, leaving a bowl of vaguely steaming food on the upturned crate.

Staring at the timber ceiling, he found himself missing the storeroom prison. Confining as it was, he knew his friends were passing the time telling stories and talking. *I didn't expect to be lonely, but at least now they're safe.* His old injuries ached as the storm outside built in fury, and the straw in the mattress stabbed his back as he rolled over into a ball. *How appropriate,* he thought bitterly.

Erven closed his eyes, a tear escaping down his cheek. Of all the nightmares that interrupted his sleep, the least common was the one in which he screamed acquiescence in the middle of interrogation. *Even in my nightmares, I didn't think I'd turn on anyone.*

He angrily wiped the tears away. *This has to be done, if all of us are going to survive.* With that thought in mind, he sat up to examine the room. At some point—he supposed when they had left the now cold food—someone had brought his belongings. His bedding had come unbound, tumbling aside to reveal not only his quilted jacket, but his pack as well. *Someone's deciding to trust me.* He slid off the bed and emptied the bag onto the packed-earth floor.

Almost all of his belongings were still there. Shivering in the cold, he slid out of his dirty clothes and into the spare set he'd brought. Pulling his navy jacket over his tunic and doing up the clasps, he felt a boost of optimism. The many-layered jacket was thick enough to dull both cold and some weapons, and he often used it as extra protection under his armor. He glanced around, disappointed but not surprised that the Holdmasters had not returned the leather chest piece he'd been wearing when captured. *They don't trust me enough to assume I won't try to escape.*

Gloom overtook the optimism from before. *Even if I had an opportunity, it would be the stupidest thing I could do. They'd kill the others in an instant if I left.*

Erven paused as he picked up a faded pink handkerchief. Smoothing the fabric over his knees, he could clearly picture his sixteen-year-old sister tucking it into his hand before leaving for the woods. A somewhat blobby depiction of forget-me-nots adorned the corner; her first project when the girls had taken up embroidery in the evenings. Erven tucked the handkerchief into his belt pouch before packing the remainder of his belongings away.

I never thought I'd be so glad she went with Violet. Hopefully, by the time she hears about this, it'll be all over.

He ate the cold food, choking down the lumps of gristle in what he supposed was mutton. Stomach filled, he glanced out the door. No guards could be seen in the corridor. The few people around the common area paid him no attention as he passed through the storm room and into the open air.

Outside, the wind tore at his clothes, making the ends of his cloak whip around and snow sting his face. It was difficult to tell time with the sky obscured by thick clouds, but he estimated it was nearing sundown. Nestled into the side of the hill, the steeply pitched roofs of Hold Aubron sloped away beneath him, terraced rows disappearing into the snowstorm. From what he recalled, the village had no outer walls other than a rammed-earth embankment near the edge of the pinewoods. On the hill above him, the banners outside the Hold snapped in the wind, the colors much less vibrant from a distance.

More clans have gathered to the Holdmasters than rallied us at Hold Eskel. I don't know how we didn't realize it then, how few really believed Rose could unite the highlands. It was growing rapidly darker, and he realized it was much closer to nightfall than he'd originally assumed. *I'd better get back before anyone realizes I'm gone.* As the end of watch bells rang, he ducked back inside the barracks and shook the snow from his cloak and boots. Just as he exited the storm room, the hallway door flew open.

The guard from earlier barged across the common area, one hand on his club. "What are you doing out here? I told you no sneaking around."

Pleased it had taken them so long to notice his absence, Erven addressed the guard sternly. "I stepped out for a moment. Don't you realize how long it's been since I've seen the sky?" He walked through the common area, ignoring the man's spluttered objections. "Don't worry; I'm not about to disappear into the snow."

Erven stopped in the hall, seeing another Aubron man outside the door to his room. "And there's no need to put a guard on me at all hours of day and night. Tell your masters that if they want me to cooperate, they need to give me a little freedom."

He closed his door firmly in their faces, sitting down and leaning against it with a heavy heart. The brief journey outside had stirred a longing for home, so powerful he had to force himself to think about anything else. As if waiting for the opportunity, the Holdmasters' words came back to his mind unbidden, whispering the words he had been fighting for days. *Rose never united the highlands after all. You could do just as well as her, and better.*

Guilt and grief warred in his mind as the storm roared outside. By morning, he knew the paths to and from the Hold would be choked with deep snow. *Even if they had a plan to rescue us, no one could get up here unseen. It's up to me to keep everyone safe. No matter what.*

That night, the nightmares returned.

15

LIKE A LEGEND RETURNED

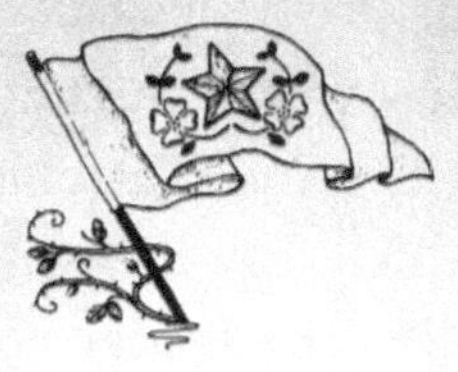

Between guilt and restless nights, Erven found himself in a mood reminiscent of a bear woken too early from hibernation. Fortunately, the Holdmasters mistook his mood for an air of command. Another chair had appeared in the council room, and the atmosphere was reasonably cordial as the leaders of the coalition greeted him that morning, almost a week after his agreement.

"Your men were outside my room again last night," Erven snapped as he took his seat. "If you want me to act like the leader you're hoping for, you can't keep treating me like a prisoner."

"We apologize for the oversight," the Aubron leader said. "You'll forgive us for assuming caution was necessary."

"I'll swear on whatever you want me to," Erven insisted. He looked up at the heavy beams in the ceiling. "I'm not trying to escape. I've spent more time outside than inside most of my life, and being cooped up is driving me insane."

The appeal did what it needed to. The Hold Aubron chief nodded agreement. "We'll relax the guard on your quarters.

You may have freedom to move around the Hold, so long as you remain inside the earth walls."

"Thank you, sir," Erven said, with every bit of gratitude he could muster.

"Now that that's out of the way," the Thinar leader dismissed Erven's escort with a wave before leaning forward and clapping his hands, "to business."

"Aye, business," the Westin chief agreed. He crossed one knee over the other with a thoughtful look. "The other clans will need to be told which way the wind is blowing. And we need to present you like the leader you are." He narrowed one eye appraisingly. "Armor, to start with. And you'll have to get rid of those colors, too. I'll see about getting some proper clan patterns for you."

"You've thought this out, haven't you?" Erven didn't care that he sounded unreasonable.

The man tugged at his beard sheepishly. "My old mum would laugh, but it's in Illyn's best interest to have a ruler in whom people can put their trust without ever hearing you speak."

"You killed Lord Kuma..." one of the others said, rubbing a stubbly chin. "Did you claim hunter's bands for that?"

Erven shook his head with annoyance. In highland tradition, warriors could choose to add a band to a tattoo for killing a strong adversary in combat. It was an honor he'd never sought, though some of the other Shona had sported them. "It wasn't important to me."

"Consider it important," the man in the corner said. Erven had finally learned his name—Torvald—and that he hailed from one of the holds destroyed in Lord Kuma's conquest. The knowledge hadn't brought him to like or trust the man. "If you're to win the hearts of the remaining tribes, you need to look *and* behave the part." From the directness of his gaze, it was apparent Torvald barely believed Erven's change of loyalties. "Unless you want to return to our previous means of negotiation?"

"I'm aware of the other options," Erven said irritably. "I'll play the role you need me to. But even if I look and speak like a legend returned, it'll do us no good if the clans still decide Brielle Thinar's blood claim outweighs my killing Lord Kuma." He crossed his arms. "As legitimate as the right of combat is within a tribal dispute, Her Majesty *is* the hereditary heir of the Thinar Line." He tried to keep the sarcasm out of his voice as he added, "The last time I checked, more than a few of the clans still recognized her as the rightful ruler."

"We'll call a moot. The clans will decide for themselves, and the majority will have its way. You'd know this," Torvald glanced dismissively at Erven, "if you'd been born in a clan yourself."

Erven raised an eyebrow. "I couldn't choose my parents, any more than Brielle could." He couldn't keep a bitter edge out of his voice as he added, "If either of us could have, we wouldn't be having this discussion now."

"We'll need to send messages to the others," one of the Holdmasters said, glancing around as the others nodded.

"Passes will be blocked for months yet," one of the other men put in. He shook his head. "It'll be spring before a full moot can assemble."

"Will Her Majesty be allowed representation?" Not for the first time, Erven wished he'd paid more attention to Arielle's stories about the days before the occupation. "Or is this a highlands decision only?"

One of the more reserved men shook his head. "We have

our differences, but she *is* still the child of the Thinar clan. She deserves the right to convince the moot on her own merits."

Erven frowned. "If we're going to convince the Crown to send representatives, we'll need to extend some gesture of goodwill. There's no way Her Majesty will attend or send representatives into danger without some kind of assurance from us."

The Holdmasters looked at each other with varying degrees of suspicion. Finally, the Thinar leader asked, "What are you suggesting?"

For the men left in the storeroom prison, the week had passed slowly. After Erven's departure, everyone fell into a slump of depressed recovery, wounded spirits lasting far longer than physical injuries.

Merald was quietly talking with Cedric when Ansel, leaning against the wall by the door, sat up suddenly. "Shh! Listen!"

Outside, they could hear the Holdmaster who'd been directing the guards' attacks. Merald glanced across the room at one of the Shona, who had been slower than the rest of them to recover from his injuries. The boy lay staring with glazed-over eyes at the opposite wall, oblivious to the commotion as Merald joined the others near the door.

"I think I hear Erven," Ansel said, his slanted eyes wide with fear.

"Aye, that's him," one of the others commented.

As they crowded around the door, they could hear the conversation in the corridor.

"—agreed we'd release all of them!" Erven's voice

sounded hot with anger. "How do you expect me to lead this country if you keep countermanding everything I say?"

The voice answering him was clear and cold as the outside air. "I'll risk anything to make sure our goals are achieved." The air hummed with malice as the man said, "You have the others well and truly fooled, but I don't trust you any more than I'd trust an untrained falcon to stay its talons. Open it!"

They scrambled away from the door as the bar slid away. It opened to reveal Erven standing beside one of the Holdmasters. He was wearing his armor, polished until it gleamed, over a tunic in the gold and green Aubron colors.

They're doing their best to make him look like one of them, even if we have no idea what clan he's from. Merald belatedly remembered he was supposed to be angry, not concerned, as the others reacted with shouts of derision.

"Traitor!"

"You'll lose your head for this!"

The Holdmaster shook his head before walking into the room, the guards flanking him. Erven followed a pace behind, looking shaken as the man yelled, "Quiet! Quiet, or I'll make sure of it." He crossed his arms disdainfully as the guards menaced them.

While the others reluctantly quieted, Merald examined Erven's expression. Lines traced the corners of his mouth, and he shifted from foot to foot uneasily as the Holdmaster declared, "The Free Holdmasters have a message for Queen Brielle. With winter still holding us in the ice, we're unwilling to risk our own men. We have agreed to allow you your freedom in exchange for bearing our message to the Crown." Merald's heart pounded suddenly as the man gave Erven a thin smile. "Two stay here. Choose, Commander."

Erven's eyes widened, darting from man to man. "Let the castle men go," he finally said. "If you're so insistent on someone staying, let it be the Shona."

Merald felt a cough coming too late to be stifled. The action of trying sent a stab of pain through his side, and he had to steady himself against the wall. As he did, he caught a flash of concern on Erven's face.

Unfortunately, the Holdmaster saw as well. The man smirked. "I think not." He eyed Merald before moving his stony gaze to Cedric. "You there, help your friend. And sit down, both of you. The rest of you, collect your belongings and prepare to march. No funny business."

The Holdmaster turned to leave, Erven following with a backward glance. Merald's heart ached at the stricken look on his friend's face. *He was hoping they'd let all of us go.*

Merald and Cedric watched in silence as the other men finished assembling their belongings, Ansel helping the injured Shona to his feet. The door closed behind them and the guards with a final thud that sent a shudder through Merald's stomach.

"So that's it, then." Cedric shook his head, his deep voice somber. "I don't know what I was expecting, but it wasn't this."

"He was hoping they'd release all of us." Merald said. "*I* was hoping they'd release all of us." He sighed. "This was not how I wanted to spend my return home."

"That's right, you grew up here." Cedric looked at him with new interest. "You know the area?"

"Yes..." Merald answered, the memories so far away that it took a moment to dredge them up. "But we were exiled when I was eight. That's almost a dozen years ago; I can't imagine everything'll be the same."

"Well, some knowledge is better than none," Cedric answered. He stood up and started pacing the confines of the storeroom. "If we can escape on our own, they'll have nothing to hold over Erven's head."

"*If* we both manage to get away." Merald coughed again, the knotted scar in his side sending dull stabs of pain through his ribs. "You have a chance to make it all the way back to Whitecaps on your own, but not me. I'm practically as weak as a newborn."

"It's not exactly your fault," Cedric argued. "I mean, you're—"

"—lucky to be alive. I know. You don't need to remind me." Merald shook his head. "I need to regain strength before I'll be useful for anything."

"Well, there's not much else we can do at the moment except train and be ready for an opportunity." Cedric clapped his hands. "Push-ups, mate. You've been hefting toddlers around, and they're not light—I'll bet you can do more than me."

───

ILLYN'S WINTER had continued confounding Rose's plans, as the Steward informed her that an icy cold reception hall would not present the right image to the Sea Wanderer delegation. Fuming at the delay and resenting the distraction, she ordered the hall warmed again and set a day for the audience.

Finally, the distinguished guests were able to struggle uphill through yet another storm, presenting themselves with all required formality. Although she managed to preside effectively over the initial audience and subsequent social events, Rose could feel herself growing dangerously inattentive. She could only hope the Sea Wanderers wouldn't notice their host's distraction.

I can't give them any opportunity to break ties with us. We need their help.

Finally, an opportunity came for Rose to clear her head. The financial expert in the foreign party had expressed an interest in seeing the Thunderhead silver mine, and preparations were made for a brisk ride. With Westhaven disappearing behind the foothills, Ethan reined his horse over next to hers. "Mornin', your Majesty. Sleep well?"

She eyed the Sea Wanderer, who had been absent from yesterday's gathering before reappearing with ink staining his left shirt cuff. "You know the answer to that, Milord. I'm sure Willow tells you everything."

"You can leave off th'title." Ethan brushed snow off his horse's mane. "Sea Wanderers don't use them." He looked ahead of them, then behind, his hair gleaming gold in the sunlight. "Willow didn' say anything," he reassured her, dropping his voice to a level unlikely to be overheard by any of their companions. "I wouldn't've slept a wink either, if I'd received a shock like you have. I fought alongside Erven at th'ridge, remember?"

"I'd forgotten." Rose pursed her lips in frustration, wondering how the detail had slipped her mind. With the Illyn lines under heavy bombardment, the intelligence agent had worked with Erven to sabotage the catapults, earning a reprieve that lasted long enough for their reinforcements to arrive. "You're worried about him, too?"

"Anyone would be." Ethan ducked under a low-hanging pine branch with such ease that Rose wondered how much riding the Sea Wanderer had done. "My comrades know what's been happening, but they're not deterred." He gestured back at the other Sea Wanderer envoys, riding at a slower pace alongside Arielle. "We've all agreed it's best th'trade agreement get signed quickly, though."

"Willow took it to the magistrates today." Rose tilted her face to the sun, enjoying its faint warmth. "She wanted to be here, but she didn't think they'd let her get away in time. They're that particular about legal things."

She thought Ethan was about to ask something else when the Sea Wanderer suddenly kneed his horse aside, dodging a snowball aimed between his shoulders. His shout of laughter fell on Rose's ears like balm on a bruise as he dove off the horse to pelt towards Tiren and Heather. Rose had barely enough time to shout a warning before Ethan dove on Heather, dragging her down into the snow. Heather's surprised yowl vanished into a tangle of jackets, sweater, and snow, and the scuffle devolved into a full snowball fight.

"Your Majesty!" Clover held the reins of her and Heather's horses in one hand, brushing her hat brim out of her eyes to look up cheekily at Rose. "Permission to engage?"

Rose laughed. "Permission granted!"

"Will you join us?" Clover winked. "I hardly think our honored guests would mind."

"I don't know…" Rose hesitated. "It's not really becoming of a queen to play snowballs." A shout of laughter interrupted her protest as Ethan hurled a handful of snow into the face of one of the other Sea Wanderers.

"Please?" Clover looked over her shoulder at the mayhem, a dimple showing in her cheek. "I think they've been dying to do something like this."

Rose laughed. "All right, Ducky."

Most of the guests were reluctant to throw snow at their host. Certain other members of the party had no such hesitancy. Within seconds, Rose was dripping and freezing, victim of a well-aimed volley from Heather. She couldn't help but laugh as the snow flew into the air, glittering in the sunlight. For a moment, the worry melted away and Rose could relax, caught up in the simple joy of a snowball fight.

"Evening, Your Majesty!" Willow hailed her as Rose came through the kitchen door. "Enjoy your ride?"

Rose sank down on a stool, watching Willow crimp dough around the edges of a pie. "It was really wonderful," she said. "I forget how easy it is to get people to talk when they're doing something other than sitting in a council room." The Sea Wanderers had been full of praise for the Thunderhead mine, and the ride back became filled with discussion on how to better foster the relationship between Sea Wanderer and Illyn silversmiths. "They said our guild's methods are more advanced than anything they have in their islands."

"Well, I suppose it's hard to mine anything when you're trying to keep the sea from invading." Willow set the pie with several others. "Glad you found some way to keep your time occupied. I left the contract with Milord High Magistrate and came back here to make pies."

"What kind of pies?"

"Chicken." Willow pointed with her rolling pin towards a steaming pot. Once Rose's attention had been drawn there, she could smell sage and onions. "I would have done something more interesting, but a wildcat got into the coop, and we needed to salvage the meat."

Rose shook her head. "Between predators on one side and children on the other, it's a wonder we ever get eggs." She recalled the one time a fox had gotten into her foster parents' pigeon cote. The resultant argument over who had left the door ajar had lasted long enough that she'd ended up sleeping in the haystack. "What did the magistrate think?"

"He said there are some things that want changing and renegotiating." Willow stirred the pot of filling. "I know it's for all of our benefits, but I can't help but wish he was a little less... I don't know, persnickety?"

Rose sighed. "He is that. At least he's on our side."

"Did you eat dinner?"

"The Sea Wanderers offered, but I declined." Rose smiled as she added, "Arielle and your sisters accepted on my behalf, though. I thought Heather and Clover could be a handful, but adding Tiren makes them unstoppable."

"Luckily, they know how to stop being ridiculous when they need to." Willow flopped the pie crust into a long, narrow tin. "If you want to get changed and warm, I'll bring up some dinner of some kind."

"Thank you." Rose slid off the stool, feeling more optimistic as she went up the stairs than she had in quite some time.

16

NEWS OF THE MOOT

"...And when the enemies finally broke through, all they found was a cloud of autumn leaves settling to the floor."

A few nights later, Willow leaned against the doorpost of the dormitory in the Rogue School, listening to Clover putting her own twist on an old Yarrow Leaf tale. As the story finished, the quiet disappeared into lively chatter. Anneli toddled beside Tora, clutching her foster mother's skirt in one chubby hand as they made their way back to the nursery. Willow watched them leave, struck by longing. For the first time in many months, she found herself wishing that circumstances hadn't forced her and Ethan apart. *If things were different, and we lived closer.*

Clover joined her for the walk across to the keep. They trudged wearily across the courtyard, their shoes crunching on icy bits. A gust of wind sent a swirl of glittering snow into their faces, the flakes so cold they stung against Willow's cheeks. Clover yawned, pulling a knit cap farther over her eyebrows.

Willow smiled at her younger sister. "Early bedtime tonight, Ducky?"

"Dinner first, then early bedtime," Clover corrected. "It's hard enough to get those squirrels to eat, let alone get a bite in myself." She blew snow away from her face, her breath appearing in a cloud of vapor. "Does the wind feel odd to you?"

Willow squinted at the sky. It was still clear, but the wind *was* picking up. "I didn't think we'd get another storm so soon after the last one."

"Hopefully, it won't be bad enough to keep us indoors too long," Clover said as they shook the snow off their feet in the storm room. "But if it does, I suppose we'll manage."

They had dinner off leftover soup in the kitchens, Willow making sure the kettles of cracked oats, hazelnuts, and dried berries were the proper distance from the fire to be ready for breakfast in the morning. Her legs and feet ached as they sat down to eat. The fact was confusing until she recalled she'd spent the day taking inventory of supplies. "I need to train more, if just that makes me tired," she commented to Clover.

Clover flexed a bicep. "You just need to let the littlies climb all over you! That'll give you muscles!"

Willow laughed. "If I get desperate, I'll come to you." She shook her head. "I'll ask Tora for some help. I notice she's kept in fighting shape, even after leaving the Shona."

"She'd probably welcome the distraction." Clover shoved her empty soup bowl across the table and rested her head in the spot where it had sat. "Let's go to bed."

"Agreed." Willow dropped their empty bowls off in the scullery before following Clover up to their room.

"Evening, Ducky. Old Thing." Heather sat sideways in

their chair before the fire, already dressed in her nightgown. She brushed a curl away from her face, leaving a smudge of charcoal across her freckled nose. "The Underage Minions finally let you escape?"

"Finally." Clover flopped diagonally across their bed.

Willow pulled off her shoes and set them in the rack near the door to dry. Wriggling her toes out of a sock, she began getting ready for bed. "I spent the day counting supplies and moving bins of turnips."

"How're we doing?" Heather closed her sketchbook and set it on the table.

"Not too badly," Willow admitted. "It'll be tight if the storms keep the traders from delivering their loads, but we'll manage."

"No more seaweed for dinner?"

Willow made a face. "I won't promise that. Besides, it's —"

"—good for us, I know." Heather crossed her eyes. "I'm only joking, Old Thing. You do a good job making sure everything's tucked in and sewn up."

Willow pulled on her own nightgown, shivering as the cold fabric hit her skin. "Thank you. I do try."

They put a pot of tea to warm on the fire, settling around it to share the last of a box of dried apples and work on their respective projects. Willow, inspired by Rose's forays into embroidery, was carefully picking out a pattern of oak leaves and acorns around the bottom hem of her riding dress. Heather, having assured her that the symbolism of strength would be very appropriate, idly drew a stylized version of the front of the Rogue School building. Clover fell asleep outside the bedcovers after regaling her sisters with stories of her day. She was snoring, and Willow and Heather on the dregs of their tea, when a knock came at the door.

"This had better be important," Willow muttered as she got up, dumping dress and embroidery hoop onto her chair. She pulled open the door to see Greta, the younger of Rose's two maids, standing there in a nightgown and shawl. "What's wrong?"

"Her Majesty and Lady Arielle sent me to get you. Captain Arrick's here from Hollow."

"That can't be good," Willow said. She shook her head, trying to reassure the younger girl. "I mean, thank you. If no one else has already, please go find Tait and ask him to come as well. I'll be right there."

"Surely, they know a storm's on its way," Heather said as the door closed, concern etching her face.

"Something's happened. Something urgent enough that it couldn't wait." Willow yanked her nightgown off and bolted into a shirt, trousers, and tunic. Heather did likewise, both of them glancing halfheartedly at the remains of their quiet evening as they closed the door.

"Just for once, I wish it was good news," Heather said as they clattered downstairs.

Willow was trying to keep their lamp from going out. The light cast eerie shadows as she clenched her jaw. "At this point, I'm afraid nothing coming out of the highlands is good news."

THE KITCHENS WERE dark and quiet, the early-rising kitchen workers long gone to bed. "Are the others all right?" Rose asked, her skin prickling under the tension in the room as Willow brought a plate of toast and cheese over to the table.

Ansel and Arrick leaned against a sideboard where bowls of bread dough were rising, both of the newcomers looking windblown and damp after the trek from Hollow. Neither met her eye as Arrick explained, "They're not as used to travel in the high country. They're resting another day at Hollow, and Ansel and I came on ahead. We agreed it would be best for you to hear the news as fast as possible."

"And miserable news it is, too." Willow handed the document they'd brought to Rose. "Heather went to go check something, but I think I know what she'll find."

Rose smoothed the document on the worn tabletop. The seal across the bottom displayed the tower she'd come to recognize as the Holdmasters' insignia, now crossed with a pair of bird's wings. With a sinking feeling, she recognized the design, just as Heather's boots clattered on the flagstone floor.

"It took a bit to find it, but you were right, Old Thing." Heather brushed curls out of her face before laying the object she'd gone to retrieve on the table. "It's a match, or I'll eat my boot."

Rose steeled herself and picked up the object—a carved-bone ring, one of several seals that Erven had used when signing official documents. "Hawk wings," she sighed. "Now I remember—his arm guards are the same design."

"They gave us that right before throwing us out of Hold Aubron." Ansel slumped into a seat as Arielle handed him a mug of tea. At the other end of the table, Willow produced a sack of hazelnuts and began methodically cracking the shells to drop the nutmeats into a bowl. "Said it was a message for you, Milady."

"They've gone to the trouble of making a new seal..." Arielle commented as she joined them at the table. Her brow furrowed as she added, "I'd give a lot to know how that change in loyalties went."

The door closed on a gust of wind as Tait entered, pulling a snow-dusted hood back from his shaggy hair. "I just came off watch." He waved away the salutes from the other two Shona. "I heard you had to leave Nels up at Whitecaps."

Rose frowned. She recognized the name, but couldn't reconcile it with the memories of a boy younger than her. "What happened?" The expressions on the Shona's faces told her everything she feared. "He's dead?"

Arrick's face was tense. "Dead, or he will be soon."

"We still don't know what they did to him, but he barely had strength left to get out of Hold Aubron." Ansel's slanted eyes filled with helplessness and fear. "Right before we made it to Whitecaps, he collapsed."

Tait cursed softly. "Nels was my trainee, years ago at Hollow." He shook his head. "Always thought he was invulnerable."

"Why?" Rose asked, a knot of ice forming under her breastbone. "Why him?"

Ansel pushed up his sleeve. "They had a few goes at Erven, first. When he didn't give in, they decided to take it out on us." Rose stifled a gasp at the sight of tawny skin covered in livid bruises.

"Monsters." Willow swept nutshells into a trash bucket. Beside her, Heather emphatically smashed a hazelnut with a mallet. "What happened once they started that?"

"It took a week before they broke him." Ansel buried his head in his hands. The boy's voice echoed against the tabletop. "He was so desperate, the day he finally agreed. He told them he'd do whatever they wanted, if they'd leave us alone."

The defeat in his words drove the ice deeper in Rose's chest. "D-do you—" she stopped and took a deep breath. "Do you think he actually switched sides?"

The silence stretched as the three Shona exchanged worried glances. Finally, Ansel said, "Knowing what he was going through, it's difficult to say. But the day they let us go, he looked just like one of them—and I don't just mean the tribal colors. He didn't seem like himself anymore."

Heather smashed another hazelnut and began picking through the shells. "So, he's either been manipulated, or he's the best actor this side of the woods."

"And now they're summoning us to a moot, to let the people decide between us." Rose sighed and eased her circlet around her head. "Will the passes be open, then?"

"I think so." Arielle set a bowl of steaming water beside Ansel, soaking a folded cloth and holding it to his bruised arm. "The lower ones are free all winter, but the higher reaches will be sealed till then." Her mouth gave a wry twist. "That's assuming there isn't a freak storm. Sheep-killers, we called them. Just when you thought it was safe to let your flock out to pasture, you'd have a storm wipe out all the lambs that'd already been born."

"Let's hope that doesn't happen." Rose twisted the edge of her shawl around her finger. "At least we can finish negotiating the treaty with the Sea Wanderers."

"Not that Milord High Magistrate is making it easy," Willow muttered as she tied the sack of hazelnuts shut. "Old Seagull."

Rose barely managed a smile at the description of the official, her chest tightening with pain.

Arielle slid Ansel's sleeve up to reveal more bruises, her voice distracted. "Once the treaty is settled, I'll take our answer to the highlands under a truce flag. The letter they sent made it sound like they're expecting our response."

"They've given us until spring." Heather propped her mallet against a pickling crock, voice uncommonly serious. "We've time enough before you have to face them yourself, Your Majesty."

"Face him," Rose corrected. The ice curled around her heart. "And if he's so willing to betray us, he'll see I'm willing to let him go just as easily."

WILLOW CAUGHT up to Rose in the stairwell. "I just wanted to be sure you're all right."

"I'm all right." Rose tugged on her circlet, wishing she could yank it off and send it tumbling down the stairs. "I can't afford not to be."

"Hmm. That's not true." Willow crossed her arms and leaned against the curving outer wall of the stairs, blocking her path. "The moment you try to carry all this on your own is the moment you—all of us—will lose everything."

"I have to," Rose whispered. Her hands skittered nervously across the hem of her shawl before she forced herself to be still. "If I'm to rule, I have to be able to do it by myself. That's what Arielle said, once, and she's right."

"What about us, then?" Willow asked. "None of us expect you to lead this country alone, because *no one* is meant to do anything this big without help."

Loss haunted Rose's heart as she said, "Maybe not. But if I hadn't trusted Erven so deeply, his betrayal wouldn't hurt this much." She brushed past Willow's shoulder to continue up the stairs. "I can't let that happen again—not with anyone."

---

*P*AIN *WAS the first thing to shock him back to consciousness. Pain, tempered by terror, both growing as he realized what had happened. Hands fell on his limbs, stomach, chest, forcing his head back and pinning him to the table. Robbed of the ability to fight, he could only scream as something pierced his skin once more.*

"Sir?" one of the highlanders relaxed his grip on Erven's shoulder. "Are you all right?"

Erven took a shuddering breath. The words came out miraculously steady. "I'm fine. Don't worry."

"Hold still if you can." The artisan said behind him. "I'm almost finished, but it'll hurt more if you move."

Erven gritted his teeth against pain both real and remembered. Finally, the highlanders released him.

"I can't believe you never claimed them before," one of them said, looking with admiration at the parallel black bands that now circled Erven's right arm just above the bicep. "If I'd made a kill like that, I'd want the world to know."

He took a measured breath, then another. The words *I didn't want them* were on his tongue, but he bit off the explanation with a sour taste in his mouth. *If I imply it wasn't a choice, it makes the Holdmasters look bad. I can't seem anything except enthusiastic, or they might get the wrong idea.*

"I can't say it was pleasant, but you did a wonderful job." He clasped hands with the artisan, who was carefully cleaning his tools and setting them aside. "Thank you."

"My pleasure." The man wound a length of bandage around his arm. "I've done this many times, but never for a hero. Congratulations, Sir."

Erven's arm burned under his sleeve as he took his seat in the council room that evening. The other Holdmasters had duly congratulated him on his new status symbol, and he bitterly acknowledged the truth that he now appeared to be 'one of them'. The atmosphere that night was more relaxed than it had been in days, enough that the door slamming open was highly unexpected.

"Damn those Shona!"

Erven looked up in surprise, as did most of the others. "Say that again?"

The man made a half-hearted apology, his face red. "Sorry, Sir. It's Whitecaps—they're pushing further into the pass. It's like they mean to come all the way to our gates."

I'd do the same, if I was in their position. "They're angry. Or worried." Erven shifted to face the rest of the Holdmasters. "Whitecaps is the first place the men we released would've gone to. Depending on what was said, they'll be on edge."

"That, or the queen ordered them to spy on us. Again." Erven hadn't even noticed the door opening before Torvald spoke.

"They're angry at me for betraying them." Erven kept the frustration out of his voice as he faced his adversary. "They don't realize I'm doing this for the good of everyone."

"Oh?" Torvald took his usual seat in the corner. His dark eyes revealed no emotion, but his words held contempt as he asked, "So, what would you suggest?"

Erven leaned on the arm of his chair, propping an elbow up and trying to keep his voice nonchalant. "At the moment, nothing. They're angry, but there's no real threat they could present for now."

"Are you sure?" the man who'd reported the incursion asked. "They've been patrolling so deep into the pass there's no way they're making it out and back in a day."

Erven snorted. "That's *normal*." He tugged his sword belt flat against his shoulder, grateful his uneasy allies had finally seen fit to return it. "Long patrols take a day going out, spend the night in the open, then return the following day."

"Even in the dead of winter?" Torvald smirked. "Or are you saying they're treating all of this as business as usual?"

"I didn't say that—"

"The Shona are loyal to Queen Brielle, not to highland tradition," one of the other men cut in. "Even if she doesn't have a hand in these incursions, the Shona will have to be reckoned with."

"Aye, we need to send them a clear message."

If I can't control this situation, they could attack and slaughter everyone. "I think we're being a little quick to charge in," Erven warned. "They're not doing anything out of the ordinary, and certainly nothing threatening. If we're going to succeed in uniting the highlands, the Shona have to be dealt with like—well, as if they were another clan."

The Hold Aubron leader rubbed his beard thoughtfully. "We'll let them be, for now." He frowned. "But if they keep pushing their noses in where they're not welcome, there'll be a price to pay."

"And that's when I'll be willing to think about some kind of action. Trust me," Erven said, the words heavy in his heart. "I won't let the Shona or anyone else get in the way of our goals for Illyn. You have my word on that."

17
THE WATCHMEN

Rose sat beside Mari on the basket-weavers' stoop, Mari weaving and Rose stripping the bark from a new supply of vines. What had started with the chance meeting at Wintermorn had become a weekly routine; one that Rose stubbornly insisted on, even as Willow and Heather muttered darkly about security.

"Your Majesty isn't yourself today," Mari commented. Her hands never stopped threading strands of vine into the basket on her lap as she squinted at Rose.

Rose brushed bark scraps off her lap. Even with the familiar cold inside her chest, the sunlight made the morning feel warm. "I've heard a lot of bad news lately."

"I heard news, myself," Mari said conversationally. She plucked another vine from the tub beside her, holding it between her teeth and speaking around it. "The call to moot, what's not been made in almost twenty years. And they're saying that lovely man's taken sides against you." She snorted. "They must be mad, thinking he can do a better job with this basket of wildcats than you've been."

Rose fumbled her knife and bent to pick it up with stiff fingers. The icy feeling from a week ago was fading to a bitter ache each time she thought of Erven. "Sometimes, I think they're right. He understands the people better."

Before Mari had a chance to answer, Carine approached along the street, walking beside a tall man. Between them, they towed a handcart of willow wythes. "Well, will you look at that." Mari set down her work. "About time you got back! I'm working myself into an early grave without you."

"Sorry, Mum." Carine was all smiles as she turned to the man. He wore a dark quilted jacket under a leather vest and arm guards, and the pouches and dagger at his belt were both sturdy and well-used. "Thank you for your help."

"No trouble." The man bowed to Carine, then to Rose. "Your Majesty. You're here for another lesson?"

Rose smiled sheepishly. "I've been sent back to start at the very beginning, I'm afraid."

"We were about to have tea," Mari cut in. "Will you stop and join us?"

The man scanned the street up and down, and suddenly his attire—and the short baton at his side—made sense to Rose. In the wake of a rise in petty crimes, the magistrates had recommended instating a standing police force. "I've a few minutes. If we stay outside, I'll happily accept."

Carine vanished into the house, Mari setting down her work to follow. Rose began to get up, but the older woman winked at her. "Better not, dearie." She nodded towards the guardsmen on either side of the street. "I'd hate to make your shadows nervous with you out of sight."

As Mari disappeared, Rose looked back up at the Watchman. Now, she saw his face bore several recent cuts and bruises over a carefully trimmed beard. "Has there been trouble?"

"What?" The man asked. "Oh." His hand traced one of the cuts. "Nothing, really. Just the usual."

"I'm interested in 'the usual'," Rose assured him. "What happened? Does the garrison have healers to look at those?"

"We do," he answered cautiously. "Just, not every day. And this really *is* nothing. It was just a tavern brawl." He shrugged, eyes continuing to rove across the street. "Some wharf rats got into it with a few of the Sea Wanderer sailors."

Rose rolled her eyes. "If you don't mind my asking, who started the fight?"

The Watchman snorted. "The wharf rats. Tavern owner said they'd been getting drunk over the evening and kept insulting the Wanderers."

"Oh, dear." Rose rubbed her forehead. "Did it take too long to clear them out?"

He shook his head, tapping his fingers on his baton. "It really was nothing. Just part of the job."

"Teatime!" Mari announced, coming out of the house with a pair of steaming mugs.

"I'm sorry, I can't stay after all." Rose brushed her skirts clean as she stood, bending to kiss Mari on the cheek. "Thank you for the lesson."

"Come back soon, Milady." Mari warned, "You'll never learn without practice."

"I'll try," Rose said. She nodded to the Watchman. "Thank you, as well. I know to you it's nothing, but I rest easier knowing someone is keeping the peace."

"It's an honor, Majesty." He stayed standing as she

walked across the street to her horse, tethered outside one of the other shops.

"Milady?" One of the guardsmen came over. "Is everything all right?"

Rose shook her head. "Did you know about a fight between some harbor workers and the Sea Wanderers?"

By the confused look on his face, she guessed he hadn't. "Sorry, Milady."

"I want to find out what happened," she said as he helped her mount. "Let's make for their embassy."

The ride across town to the Sea Wanderer embassy lay through the dockyard. Unfriendly stares prickled against Rose's skin as they passed fishermen mending nets, piers crowded with coils of rope and lined with skiffs, and workers moving cargo from ship to shore.

She shivered despite the sun. *You'd think I'd be used to stares by this point.*

Soon, the buildings changed from dockside warehouses to the tall, grand buildings of the tradesmen's district. Here, a sea-green flag flew from the balcony of what had once been a guild hall. Bearing a scallop between two crashing breakers, it signified the nationality of the inhabitants. Rose dismounted in the snow packed street with a sigh of relief, leaving the guards to tether the horses while she approached the imposing doors.

The Watchman's account of a fight had been accurate. The door guard's dark skin did little to conceal a spreading bruise across his cheekbone and eye, and he slumped against the wall as he watched the street.

"Good morning! Are the ambassadors here?"

The guard jumped to attention at the sight of her circlet. "Your Majesty!" He shouldered his spear and opened the door, ushering her into the comforting warmth of a wealthy nation's embassy. "They're here, but—hoy!" He caught the attention of a maid. "Go tell th'mighty ones Her Majesty's here t'see them."

The maid disappeared up the stairs with gratifying swiftness as Rose's guards joined her in the hall. It wasn't her first time in the embassy, but she never got tired of looking at the intricate carvings on the pillars holding up the second story balcony. Woodcarving still sent a pang of loss through her stomach, a reminder of the foster father who'd preferred his tools to his wife and daughter.

Presently, Rose heard a door overhead open, and one of the Sea Wanderer ambassadors came to the edge of the balcony. "Your Majesty! What a pleasant surprise!" He hurried down the stairs to kiss her hand. "We weren't expecting t'see you till t'morrow. What brings you here?"

Rose withdrew her hand, wishing she could dispense with that custom. "I heard an interesting story from one of the magistrate's Watchmen." She waved a hand towards the door, now closed against the elements. "And I see it wasn't exaggerated."

"Ah, yes." The Sea Wanderer clasped his hands awkwardly. "There *was* a fight between some of our men and th'locals." As a maid opened a door on the ground floor, he bowed fractionally and offered, "Will you take some refreshment?"

"Thank you." Rose turned to her guards. "Stay here, please."

"Milady..."

Ethan's boots clattered on the steps as he hurried down, fastening the cuff on a brightly colored sleeve. "It's all right, lads." He bowed graciously and offered her his hand. "May I escort you, Majesty?"

Rose had to stop herself from rolling her eyes as Ethan ushered her into the side room—a dining room, if memory served. As the door closed behind them, she asked, "Does Willow know about this side of you?"

"Which? The courtly side?" Ethan said innocently. "She knows I'm nobility, or as close as we get to nobility. Rest assured, I have no intention of tryin' t'get her to play th'noble for anyone." He laughed, "She'd either burst into tears or slap me."

"Your Majesty?" Ethan's comrade offered her a finely worked silver cup filled with dark wine.

Ethan pulled out a chair for her, before sitting down himself. "I take it y'heard about th'fight?"

"I heard, yes." Rose set her cup on the table. "I wanted to hear from you what happened."

"I wasn't there," the other man said apologetically. He took a sip from his glass before saying, "But the report from th'Watch was that th'locals started it."

"Oh, I hope you don't think I'm here to take you to task," Rose said. "I'd just hate for your men to take injury because of the bad behavior of my people."

"Beggin' your pardon, but I *was* there." Ethan had pulled a slender dagger from his boot and was spinning it on the table. "An' if it weren't for th'specific insults, I'd swear I'd been in any tavern back home." He snorted. "Th'dock workers kept making comments about foreigners, an' how we ought t'go back t'the sharks instead of puttin' our fingers in where we're not wanted."

"More of this," Rose sighed. "You'd think they'd

forgotten who helped get rid of all the foreign mercenaries the warlord hired."

"Change always takes longer than you hope it will," the Sea Wanderer ambassador said. "Though, for everyone's sake—" He coughed and made a face. "We should—"

"Are you all right?" Rose asked.

The man's face was going pale, and the veins in his neck bulged as he coughed again. Both she and Ethan shot to their feet as he toppled to the floor.

"Milady, stay back," Ethan warned. He shoved the chairs away as his comrade began thrashing. "Stefan! What's going on, man?!"

Rose backed up to the wall. She could see the ambassador's eyes, rolling back as another convulsion shook his limbs. "I'm getting help!" The door slammed open under her palms, and her guards leapt to their feet with hands to sword hilts. "Help! Someone help!"

One of the guards bolted for the front door, the other pushing past her. "Run for a healer!" Rose yelled at the maids they'd been joking with. "Hurry!"

She only had time to draw a quick breath before a strong pair of hands seized her shoulders, pulling her backwards. She yelped, an elbow flying to clip Ethan across the side of the head.

"Easy, Your Majesty!" The intelligence agent seemed used to being smacked unexpectedly. "Don't go outside," he warned, "I don't know who's responsible for this, but we can't rule it out bein' directed at you, instead of us."

"What?" They were the same height, and she looked over his shoulder to see the other Sea Wanderer lying very still beyond the table. The stillness of his limbs and wide, unseeing eyes informed her mind of what had occurred. Her guardsman knelt beside him, checking the man's pulse. "He's dead?"

The man nodded, pulling a glove back on. He dipped his head towards Ethan. "Much obliged, Milord, for your care towards Her Majesty."

"It's no trouble." Ethan released her, saying, "We'd best stay here till more help arrives." He stepped around her, drawing a finger through the spilled wine on the table and sniffing it. "Ha. I can't smell anything through all the honey an' spice in this." He wiped his fingertips on his vest.

"I sent for a healer," Rose said, numbness reaching all the way to her toes. "I don't know where the closest one lives, though."

"Don't th'Watchmen have a healer?" Ethan looked out the door of the dining room as the other guardsman reentered the building. "There's a sub-post down by the docks."

One of the door guards was dispatched. He returned after a gratifyingly short interval in the company of two Watchmen, one with a band of blue cloth around his upper arm. Rose was relieved to recognize the other as the same man she'd met earlier. As his comrade knelt to examine the deceased ambassador, the Watchman bowed in her direction. "Your Majesty."

"Thank you for coming so quickly." Rose was beginning to feel like she could breathe again. "I'm sorry, I didn't hear your name earlier."

The man smiled a bit under his beard. "It's Gregor, Milady." He shifted to a rest position, one hand never far from his baton. "I'm sorry about this, Majesty. We'll do whatever we can to get to the bottom of what happened."

"Well, poison, obviously." The Watchman wearing healers' colors sat back on his heels, looking up at them.

"Damn." He sighed, pulling gloves back over work-roughened hands. "Was this sealed when you received it?"

Even with the tragedy, Rose had to smile at Ethan's affronted face. "If I trusted unknown hands with my life, I'd've been dead fifty times over." He crossed his arms irritably and leaned back against the sideboard. "Yes, it was sealed. Yes, we bought it here. No, I've not had eyes on it from th'moment of opening till now, which's why *I* didn't drink any of it." An edge of anger came into his voice as he glanced at his dead comrade. "An' no, I don't expect this was an accident." He turned back to the healer. "You've no idea what type of poison it was?"

"I'm *barely* a healer, Sea Wanderer. I clean and sew up wounds, and that's the extent of my knowledge." The man crossed his arms, mirroring Ethan's posture. "And I'm no hand with poisons. You'd do better askin' *him*." He pointed at Gregor, and Rose barely caught a flash of frustration on the bearded Watchman's face.

"Can you help?" she asked.

He pulled off his gloves, tucking them into his belt with a deep sigh. "I'll look, but no promises."

Rose clutched her hands together as—like Ethan had done—Gregor drew a fingertip through the wine left in the glass. Everyone watched anxiously as he first smelled the residue, then touched a bit to his tongue. He made a face and immediately spat back into the cup.

"What is it?" Rose asked, almost in the same heartbeat as Ethan did. "Are you all right?"

Gregor pulled a kerchief out of one of his belt pouches and scrubbed his fingertips with it. "You said he only took a sip or two?"

Ethan nodded. "He sat down after the two of us did."

"And I'll bet he started choking right after."

Rose and Ethan exchanged a curious look. "Yes," Rose answered. "Does that mean you know what this is?"

Gregor carefully folded the kerchief and tucked it away. "I were a huntsman, before. Some winters, you get wolves what get too settled with the idea of making meals off sheep and the like. They're fast, so you tip your arrows so's you don't have to shoot them more'n once." He looked solemnly at the dead man. "You've seen the pretty purple flowers growing in spikes out in the meadows, during the summer?"

Rose nodded silently, wishing she could immediately recall what plants looked like. *Violet would know.* She fiercely shoved the thought of her absent friend into a far corner of her mind. *I can't afford to think of that now.*

"Wolfsbane, we call it." Gregor rubbed his mouth. "Or Killer's Hood, for reasons like this. I'd know that tingle anywhere, but that's after too many brushes with it while tipping arrows." He gestured at the spilled wine on the table. "With all the honey in that stuff, you'd never know it were filled with enough wolfsbane for a whole pack."

"It's assassination, pure and simple," Willow spat as lamplight danced across the office walls. "An' even if they weren't targeting you, someone's going to have t'pay for this."

"I know." Rose wished she had kept wearing her circlet after returning to her office. It would have given her the confidence to face her friend's formidable temper. "The Watchmen are looking into it, and Ethan says he'll also investigate. I thought you'd be pleased with that."

"It's a start, but it's not enough!" Willow threw up her

hands. "Can this agreement even go forward, now there's only one Sea Wanderer Council representative here t'sign it? If it falls through, we're not going to have a tadpole's chance against a pike to get them to agree to another one."

"I hope so." Rose thought back to the initial drafts of the trade agreement. "Ethan said he thought his signature would suffice, with the captain who brought him here to witness."

"It'll have to do." Willow went back to writing in hurried cipher on a scrap of paper. "If ambassadors are getting killed right an' left an' up the street, no one will want to *sniff* at trading with us, let alone send their people here!"

"I *know*," Rose said. Upsetting as it was, she couldn't help but feel frustrated at Willow's reaction. "Believe me, I know. I can't change other nations' perspectives of us, but I'm working on making sure Illyn's a safe place for everyone. That's the best I can hope for right now, especially now that news of the moot is spreading through the lowlands."

Willow dashed blotting sand across the paper, shaking away the excess angrily. "If we don't find the person responsible for this, the Holdmasters won't have to rely on the moot to get rid of you. You have to be more careful!"

"Willow," Rose asked impatiently, "Why are you so upset?" She held her arms out. "Look! I'm all right. I'm scared, but I'm all right. Given how hostile some people are towards the Wanderers, you can't even say this comes as a surprise. What's the matter?"

Willow slammed the shaker of sand down, making Rose jump. "How do you think it feels, hearing there's been a death without knowing who died?" she demanded, her voice going ragged. "How do you think it feels, not knowing if the person you can't imagine life without is alive or dead?"

"I imagine it's similar to learning your strongest ally has just been captured by your enemies. Which, if you'll remember, has happened twice now." Rose's words came out effortlessly cold. "Only this time, imagine that same person stabbing you through the back as well. How do you think *that* feels?"

She slammed the door on Willow's shocked expression. Outside, the wind whistled across the parapet at the top of the tower, and clouds were beginning to rise over the mountains. Safe from prying eyes, and with the cold in her bones seeping out to match the cold in the wind, Rose sank down against the battlements and wept.

18

A NEW DEFINITION OF HOME

Erven hadn't been lying about the effects of being inside for too long. As the weeks passed, he kept finding reasons to be outdoors, walking around Hold Aubron for hours regardless of the weather. In between storms, the sun bathed the snowy peaks around them in glittering white light, warming the air despite the freezing wind. At first, the walks were a good time to think—and stew—but eventually the villagers grew accustomed enough to stop and talk with him. Over the weeks, Erven grew more acquainted with the shepherds and hunters, woodworkers and herb women, coopers and weavers—who had never left the mountains they were born in.

"No need to," an old codger told him between strokes of a plane. "We have all we need right here." He spat in the sawdust. "It's the right proper way, keepin' to ourselves, an' no outsiders to tell us what to do."

"I'll leave, then," Erven laughed. The sunlight in the enclosed woodworkers' yard felt good on the back of his neck, but he slid off the crate he'd been sitting on and prepared to go.

The craftsman waved a gnarled hand. "Ah, stay. Talking makes the work go lighter." He squinted at Erven's tunic, green and gold visible under the hem of his jacket. "Besides, you're no outsider. You're one of us."

The sentiments were similar to the ones expressed by the others—ignorance of life outside the mountains, distrust of foreigners, and general acceptance of him as the Holdmasters' choice to lead Illyn. *They talk so dismissively about the lowlanders, it's like they don't care how many lost everything during the occupation. You'd think they've forgotten how many lives were lost to ensure their freedom.*

The evening bells were only just ringing as he sank into a seat in the council room. Not all the Holdmasters were there, the storms having subsided enough that most had returned to their own holds. Only a handful of men assembled that evening, their mannerisms suggesting more old friends gathering around the tavern than of the leaders of a treasonous coalition.

The Aubron chief dragged his chair across the floor and crashed into it. "Wind's picking up again." He took a deep drink from a flask of mead—now that formality had relaxed, most evenings included drinking while plotting. "We'll be lucky if the passes open at all this spring." He laughed at the concern on Erven's face. "Don't worry, Commander. The clans know better than to ignore the call to moot. They'll be there."

"I wasn't worried," Erven lied. "But just in case things go badly, I'd like to be in better training than I am right now." He shifted in his chair, wondering how far his new authority would stretch. "I know winter's not exactly the best time to learn new fighting skills, but I'd still like to train with my men. The two that didn't return to the queen are some of the better fighters I know, and they're doing us no good rotting in a storeroom."

"One of those 'fighters' is the child of a disgraced family." The Hold Aubron leader snorted, and Erven briefly saw the resemblance between him and Merald.

"He happens to have saved my life, two years ago," Erven retorted. "And according to him, everyone responsible for that exile is long dead."

"I don't think we can let you do that," Torvald insisted with a glance at the others.

Erven stood up angrily. "This is getting ridiculous. It's been over a month, and I've done every single thing you've demanded. If you want me to rule—really rule—you have to trust me."

Torvald still glared, but the other Holdmasters gave each other amenable looks as Erven continued, "My reputation is built on my fighting skills, but we're sunk if someone challenges me and I lose." He tapped his sword hilt, the cool metal reassuring under his fingers. "I need to be able to train. And it's absurd to leave two innocent men imprisoned because of who they chose to follow."

The following day, Erven stood outside of the storeroom door as the guards pulled away the bar. As long as he lived, he would never forget the expressions on his friends' faces as he stepped into the doorway—distrust, caution, and fear, all mixed with relief. "They finally trust me. I'm here to get you out."

. . .

MERALD blinked in the dazzling sunlight. He stumbled against Cedric, catching his balance as they stepped out of the Hold and into the open air.

"Fresh air," the soldier muttered. "I didn't realize how much I'd missed it."

"That's because you're a castle boy," Erven said from the other side of Cedric. His voice had gained an edge that hadn't been there several weeks ago. "I can't go a day without being outside."

His vision finally clearing, Merald looked around Cedric's broad shoulders to Erven. "Are we free to go?"

Erven shook his head. "I tried. They're still not convinced of my loyalty, and they want to keep you as insurance against my good behavior." He started down the path from the Hold to the terrace below, gesturing for them to follow. "I convinced them to let you have some freedom within the village. So long as you don't go outside the earth wall, you don't have to be locked up anymore."

"I'm assuming they'll be watching." Merald glanced back at the Hold as they left, his suspicions confirmed as two highlanders sidled after them.

"It was the only way they'd let you out." Erven stopped at the storm entrance of a long building, built against the terrace wall. "Your room won't be locked, but there'll be guards everywhere. And it's safe to say they'll be watching your every move." His eyes shifted up to the Hold. "They've certainly been watching me, and I'm on their side."

Merald and Cedric exchanged a cautious look before following Erven into the narrow hallway, lined with the doors to individual rooms. Looking down the hall, Merald caught sight of another door, no doubt to a common area beyond the living quarters.

Just like home. The thought of Tora and Anneli clutched at his heart. *She's got to be so worried.*

Erven pushed open one of the doors, striking a light to reveal a room furnished with two narrow beds, a chest, and a weapons rack. Upset as he was, Merald had to stifle a laugh as he looked at Cedric. The castle guard was taller than either him or Erven, and the beds seemed too small even for a man of normal stature.

"Here's your room. I'll see about getting food brought down. And I'll have to show you around the village, as well." Erven drummed his fingers on his sword hilt. "They let you out because I told them I need sparring partners, so I'll be ready if anyone challenges me."

"What are we supposed to do until then? Just sit here?"

"Settle in," Erven said. "Try to stay put. I'll get food and reassure them that you didn't try to run away or attack, and I'll be back." The sun gleamed off his sword hilt and armor before the storm door closed behind him.

"This isn't much better than the storeroom," Cedric muttered, setting down his pack. He inspected the straw mattress. "I'm not even going to fit on this thing, and I think there might be mice."

"Probably." Merald set down his own belongings on the other bed. "Did he seem different to you?" It had been over a week since they'd last caught a glimpse of Erven, though they'd heard his voice in the corridor several times.

"Something's different," Cedric agreed.

"I wonder if he's afraid to talk too much," Merald surmised. "If they're keeping as close an eye on him as he made it sound..."

"Or he's afraid of what we'll do to him, now that he's thrown in his lot with the coalition." Cedric sat down on his bed, broad shoulders slumped. "Didn't you see how close those highlanders were following us?"

"I saw," Merald answered. "He's obviously enough on their side that they don't need to hold our safety over his head anymore."

Cedric's feet stuck over the end of the bed as he laid down. "See, I knew it wouldn't be big enough." With an irritated grunt, he sat back up. "How far do you think he's taken this? D—do you think he's actually turned over?"

"I have no idea." Merald thought back over his friend's mannerisms. "Ordinarily, I wouldn't believe it. But now?" He sighed. "He might have."

* * *

THE HIGH MAGISTRATE always reminded Willow of a seagull. It was a silly resemblance, really, but there was something in the angle of his head, the pitch of his voice, and the way he picked apart inconsistencies that reminded her of the aggressive, quarrelsome birds frequenting the harbor. She shivered as a draft wound across the back of her neck. Even though they'd put their best efforts towards warming the hall again for the signing, the urgency of their efforts had left the place much colder than her blood preferred.

At the other end of the table, Ethan gave her a slight smile. She couldn't help but smile back with relief as the magistrate finished imprinting his seal across the bottom of the document. She knew she'd never be able to forget the chill that had spread across her heart at hearing the news of a death in the Sea Wanderer embassy, nor the shocking relief at hearing Ethan was safe after all.

I didn't realize how much he meant to me. Now, when I think of my future, I can't picture it without him.

With the agreement safely signed by Rose and Ethan, witnessed by Arielle and the Sea Wanderer captain, and applauded by the guild heads and other dignitaries, the party retreated to a celebratory dinner. The guests were courteous enough not to comment on the increased number of guards in the hall, or the conspicuous absence of certain beverages. Even with their precautions, Willow barely ate, and her muscles pulled tighter and tighter as she watched Rose and Ethan's every bite with trepidation.

As the evening finally concluded, Willow felt as worn out as a washrag. Rose looked similarly tired, and only gave her the briefest of smiles before retreating towards her room. Willow watched her go, wondering if it was worth trying to talk to her friend. Their conversations over the last week and a half had been stiff, and punctuated with cold, frustrated barbs when one or both of them grew too hurt.

I overreacted, Willow thought, collecting napkins into a basket for the laundry maids. *We just didn't know anything at the time.* The Watchmen had been diligent in approaching and questioning anyone who might've had a connection to the ambassador's death, but so far had come up empty of answers. It seemed wolfsbane was commonly enough used against pests that every farmer and hunter knew how to purify it into deadly form, and the local herbwives grew it in quantity for just such a use. *I overreacted, and she overreacted, but neither of us wants to try and fix things. What's the matter with us, anyway?*

As the kitchen workers finished clearing up the remains of the meal, Willow sank down on the dais with her chin in her hands, debating once more if she should try and reconcile things. *If she wants to talk, I'm sure she'll come find me. I don't want to be frozen out again. Not tonight.* Willow looked back towards the stairwell and her room, where her sisters and Tiren had retreated at the earliest socially acceptable moment. She had just decided to join them when Ethan sauntered back into the hall.

"What are you still doing here?" Willow asked, in a tone much more irritable than intended. "You're supposed to be going back with the others. And where are your bodyguards?"

"You don't think I c'n take care of myself?" Ethan asked, patting his sword hilt. "I told th'others I'd catch up. Besides, isn't Tiren still here?"

"He's upstairs." Willow quirked an eyebrow. "My sisters wanted to see if he approves of their new 'house rules' for Sails and Shores."

Ethan chuckled. "I'm sure his head's spinning, if that's what they're up to."

Willow stood up, crossing to secure the big doors at the end of the hall. "I was planning on offering him guest lodging tonight. Will you need it as well?"

Ethan lifted the other end of the sturdy bar, and together they slotted it into place. "We'll see how long th'game lasts." He looked around the hall, dimly lit by the banked fires. "I wanted t'talk to you, but now I'm not so sure this's a good time or place."

"Well, I was going to go help the kitchen clear up," Willow said, even as the idea occurred to her. "If you come, we can talk while we work. Unless what you have to say can't be overheard."

"Actually…"

"Ah." Willow went back to sit on the dais steps. Ethan joined her, a dagger hilt sticking out over his boot top. "What's wrong? If it's more bad news, can't it wait for morning?"

"Well, there is news. Good or bad or irrelevant, it remains t'be seen." Ethan pulled a scrap of parchment from his pocket and handed it to her. "Found that t'day, when we —ahm—approached one of the leaders of a local gang of toughs. I think I've figured out who planted th'idea t'murder foreign dignitaries in their heads."

Willow's spirits sank at the sight of the now-familiar tower crossed by wings. "Them again." She shook her head, her timidly optimistic mood from the treaty signing evaporating. "I'd *never* have thought it of him."

"We trust until it becomes too dangerous," Ethan reminded her, propping his elbows on his knees. "Then we guard our backs."

"I need to tell Rose." Willow's stomach flopped over at the thought of yet another chilly conversation with the already tense queen.

"That might be best for after we've gone," Ethan suggested. "We don't have any evidence that they were targeting her—just us. Once we leave, the threat'll be lessened."

"I suppose…" Willow pulled her knees to her chest and wrapped her arms around her skirts. With the hall dark and the noise of dinner gone, the tension in her shoulders finally started releasing. "I know it's safest for you to leave as soon as you can." She laughed halfheartedly. "Actually, I'm impressed you were able to stay as long as you did."

"I'd a very compelling reason." Ethan gently took her hand. She could feel his pulse thumping through his fingers as he said, "I know the concerns of rulers make for bad courting."

"And assassinations don't help," Willow agreed tartly, pulling her hand back. "But it is what it is."

"It *does* make y'rethink what's important." Ethan pushed the dagger back down into his boot. "An' I know I shouldn't ask, but I've only got so long t'be with you face t'face."

"Ethan—"

"Please, just let me finish," he pleaded, the tone so uncharacteristic that Willow found herself with no desire to interrupt. "You've got a job here, and there's no one better'n you t'do it. But someday, when Rose rules unchallenged, an' th'highlanders kneel before her as one, an' she's got someone unshakeable t'watch her back—when all this is settled, will you come home?"

Home. The word reverberated strangely in Willow's mind. She craned her neck to look up at the buttresses holding the roof.

Home should mean the woods, she thought, picturing the mighty trees guarding the thatch-roofed cottages of her childhood. *I always thought I'd return there, once the work was done.* She looked over at Ethan, waiting patiently for her answer. His crimson shirt brought back memories of the taste of mangoes, warm air caressing her face, and the sun glimmering off the waters of an infinite sea.

"I thought I'd always consider the woods home," Willow said, wiping away tears she didn't remember crying. "But now, they wouldn't be home without you." She sniffled. "I wish I could give you a more definite yes. I'd love to come back with you now, but I can't."

"I know it won't be for a long while. An' a million things might happen b'tween now and then. But I'm glad t'have that assurance, at least." Ethan dug in his pocket and handed her a packet wrapped in teal silk. "Here."

The wrapping fell away to reveal a delicately worked bracelet of polished agates set in silver. "Oh..." Willow looked up to see Ethan smiling. "How long have you had this?"

"It's been a fair bit," he admitted. "Long b'fore the assassination, just so you know." He helped her clasp the bracelet around her wrist. "I remembered you hadn't any jewelry, an' I thought this'd be less intimidating than a ring or something."

Willow held her wrist so the stones caught the faint light from the hearth. "It's beautiful."

"Not as beautiful as you." Ethan said, the corner of his mouth twitching.

"You can't even say that with a straight face," Willow accused. "You're just lucky things've happened the way they did. As a romantic, you're terrible." She stood up briskly, brushing the wrinkles from her skirts.

"Terrible, am I?" Ethan grinned. She yelped as he caught her up in a swirling dance, his laugh surrounding her. Finally, their feet slowed. "I didn't know you danced so well."

"I don't often," Willow admitted. "Only when there's someone worth dancing with." She wrapped her arms around him and gazed into his clear blue eyes, just a few inches higher than her own. "I'm glad you're not vastly taller than me."

"Me too," Ethan agreed thoughtfully. "Makes it easier t'do this." He softly kissed her lips, sending a chill right down through her feet.

"I take it back," Willow squeaked, certain she was blushing. "You're very romantic." She stepped back awkwardly, keeping hold of his hand. "Come on, let's go see if my sisters have made Tiren's head explode with their house rules."

19
UNDER TRUCE

Arielle took a deep breath of the crisp, pine-scented air. The Whitecaps buildings, built of pine logs banked with sod, hunkered in the glade around a single stone-and-wood building. Around her, the patrol finished their preparations; checking snowshoes, coiling bowstrings, and settling packs. She glanced at the sky, hoping the weather would hold long enough for them to conduct whatever negotiations the Holdmasters would allow. While the business with the Sea Wanderers had been critical, the anxious parts of her heart were growing impatient to see this mission completed.

She reached up and touched one of the spruce tips. "I miss living this high in the mountains. There's something so clean about the air." Arielle smiled wistfully. "No matter how long you're away, the mountains always call you home."

Arrick, the Shona who had first brought word of Erven's capture, frowned at the trees surrounding them. "I don't know, Lady Arielle. They don't feel right to me anymore." He shifted his bow to his shoulder. "In the old days, the Shona were the ambushers, not the ambushed."

Arielle was about to answer when their patrol leader joined them. "We'd better make sure we're all ready to go." Tait said, coming out of the main building with the White-caps commander, a young woman with a face scarred from cheekbone to temple. "Lady Arielle?"

Arielle pulled her hood over her head. "Ready." She gave the Whitecaps commander a warm hug. "Carina, thank you for your hospitality. Keep your guard up while we're gone."

The young woman smiled, her good eye glinting ice blue in the shadows of her hood. "We'll be patrolling extra. Good luck go with you."

By the second day, the patrol had settled into an uneasy rhythm. They moved forward cautiously, keeping their pace deliberate as they passed the spot where Erven had lost four men. Tait glanced around the clearing, commenting, "I don't see any graves. They must've burned our dead along with theirs."

"They deserved better," one of the other Shona remarked. "But at least they weren't left for the scavengers."

"A small mercy," Arielle agreed.

"We're inside the range of their patrols." Tait pulled out a green square of cloth and began tying it to his javelin point. "If anyone thinks to attack us, they'll know it's under a flag of truce."

Arielle rummaged in her belt pouch and handed him a pennant patterned in charcoal and rust colors. "Tie that under it." She smiled. "That'll give them second thoughts about attacking."

"Let's just hope they have their heads properly fastened

on, this time," Ansel muttered, quietly enough that only Arielle and Tait heard him.

"Steady, lad," Arielle reassured him. "All of us are nervous, too."

One of the men yelled a warning, making all three of them jump. "Someone's coming!"

The patrol scrambled to draw weapons and find cover in the trees. Tait pushed Arielle behind him, the Shona captain pointing to a depression behind a boulder as he readied his javelin. "Get behind there and stay down."

Arielle obeyed, ducking behind the rock as the Shona readied their weapons. An arrow plunged into the snow nearby with a hiss, the sound followed by Tait shouting, "Truce! Truce!"

"Don't loose! We just want to talk!" Arrick shouted.

Arielle strained her ears to hear anything from the other side of the rock. Finally, someone called, "Stay where you are! Don't make any sudden moves. Do you come in peace?"

"Yes, in peace!" Arrick said. "We're here on the queen's business."

Scuffling came from the other side of the rock, and Tait reappeared to beckon her forward. "Lady Arielle, I think you'll need to talk to them."

Arielle hurried forward, shielding her face from the glare of the afternoon sun. The highlanders had emerged from the shadows of the woods, swords drawn and arrows leveled at the Shona. Their curiosity and suspicion as she approached confirmed that some had already connected the colors on the pennant with her presence. Arielle banished the nerves from her voice and peered past her raised hand to address the highland spokesman. "I am Arielle of Hold Brynjar. By the bloodright that is due to me, I would speak with your masters."

The highlanders looked at each other with varying degrees of amazement and trepidation. Arielle understood their uncertainty. As far as she knew, not many of her clan— the few survivors of what had once been the farthest east Hold in the mountains—claimed any affiliation with the highlands after being wiped out in Lord Kuma's invasion.

The spokesman lowered his spear. "We weren't expecting outsiders. Are you here about the moot?"

"I've brought Her Majesty's regards," Arielle said. "The lowlands have heard the call to moot, and I've come with Her Majesty's response. Will you conduct us safely?"

The man waved a gloved hand, and the men began slowly advancing to surround them. "Don't make any sudden moves. If you don't incite anything, you won't be harmed."

The Shona shifted uneasily as the highlanders surrounded them, but their weapons remained sheathed. "Lady? Can we trust them?" one of the younger ones asked in an undertone.

"We have to," Arielle reminded him as they started up the trail. "This is what Her Majesty sent us here to do. Just keep your wits about you, and remember everything you see." They emerged from the trees to see Hold Aubron rising in the distance, forbidding and grey against a backdrop of snowy peaks. "Something tells me we'll need every bit of information we can get."

RAYS of late afternoon sunlight filtered through the doorway, casting golden lines across the dusty floor. The shadow of a guard outside the door fell across Erven's face as he and Cedric circled each other, both of them breathing hard and shaking sweat out of their eyes. Their practice sessions had been lasting longer over the last few days, and this afternoon had been tiring for all of them. As Cedric shifted his grip around his sword hilt, Erven lunged. His practice sword thumped against Cedric's hip, making the soldier swear and flinch. Their blades met in a series of blocks and strikes before Erven finally twisted his sword free of Cedric's, the weighted practice weapon flicking up to tap his older friend's collarbone.

"Dead!"

Cedric sighed and lowered his sword. "I'm getting tired. You shouldn't have gotten me that easily."

"It's all right. You've gotten me twice today." Erven set his sword down on the hay bales around their practice arena and flexed his hand. "I just got lucky." He glanced at the doorway, trying to gauge the hour by the sunlight. "All right if we're done for today? I have to be in council again tonight."

Merald nodded and stood up slowly, pushing himself up with a hand against the wall. "I thought I'd built up muscle last month, but this week's proving me wrong. I don't think I've held a sword so much in a year."

Erven laughed, "Honestly, I haven't either. I wasn't lying when I said I'd gotten out of practice."

"You're doing well enough, I'd say." Cedric said, pulling his tunic on. "It's a good day for me if I beat you more than once in a session."

"I'm just happy if I'm able to finish a match." Merald laughed shortly. "I don't care if I win."

"It's good to be actually practicing again." Erven slid out

of his sweaty shirt. From inside the fabric, he heard Cedric exclaim something.

"Hunter's bands?" Cedric said with astonishment as Erven's head emerged. "When did you get those?"

Erven sighed. "Right before they let you out of prison." He examined the twin black bands encircling his arm. "They're trying to capitalize on my reputation."

Cedric whistled. "You have to admit, you earned those the hard way."

"Aye, and now you certainly look the part." Merald said, picking up his practice sword.

Erven made a face at the reminder. "I tried to protest. I said it wasn't really single combat, because I had you with me."

Merald shook his head. "I was unconscious with chain mail stuck in my side. You killed him all on your own. That's one thing they're right about—you *did* earn those."

Erven gingerly rubbed his arm. "I was happy without everyone knowing." He didn't bother adding that even after weeks of healing, the memories of receiving the hunter's bands still made his skin crawl. "And it worries me that they wouldn't let me decide such a silly thing for myself. I'm not in this to be led around like a baby."

He knew he'd said something that hit a nerve. Neither Merald or Cedric said anything more as they collected their things. The sun had just dipped behind the western peaks, casting a final glow of gold over the Hold as they exited the practice arena.

Erven tugged his sword belt straight and gave the others a brief salute as their guard approached. "Tomorrow morning?" he said as cheerfully as he could.

Merald nodded halfheartedly. "Tomorrow."

"Assuming you're up for it." Cedric's smile seemed forced. "Unless you're afraid I'll beat you again."

"I'm not afraid," Erven said. He turned to go, calling back over his shoulder, "See you tomorrow!"

Collecting a hasty dinner from the kitchen in the Hold and dodging Torvald as the man left one of the meeting rooms, Erven returned to the barracks. Going over his armor with an oiled cloth, he reflected on what he'd said to Merald and Cedric. Even with the Holdmasters giving him more leeway, he couldn't shake the feeling that he was being penned in on every side.

Did you expect anything different? He set aside his chest piece and began working on his arm guards, carefully buffing dirt and scratches out of the wing designs. *You're lucky you've managed it this far with no one else dead. For that, you can deal with the discomfort and humiliation.*

"It would be nice to remind them I don't take their orders," he muttered, setting aside the armor and inspecting his sword belt and scabbard. "I still have teeth, after all."

A sound from outside jarred him from his mutinous reflections. *A bell?* He'd been about to put away his sword and armor, but decided to put them on instead. *It's not the change of watch yet. The sun's barely down.* A chilly feeling swept through his chest. *Could the Shona be attacking? If they decided to kill me, I wouldn't blame them.*

Erven had just tugged the side strap on his armor tight when Torvald shoved his door open. "You're wanted uphill. Let's go."

Irritated and confused, Erven snapped, "Politeness wouldn't go amiss, highlander." He yanked the remaining straps on his armor and stuffed his hands through his arm guards before following Torvald. "What's going on?"

Torvald ignored his protest, hustling him past Merald and Cedric's room. Once outside, he finally explained, "Your rival's sent envoys. A whole patrol of Shona, armed to the teeth. And here I thought you weren't concerned about them."

Erven steadied himself against a wall as he rounded a corner behind Torvald. *She wouldn't have sent the Shona on their own.* "Are they escorting someone?"

"There's the interesting part." Torvald's tone revealed a hint of curiosity. "The woman they're guarding approached us under the colors of Hold Brynjar. She's claiming to be their leader."

Deep inside, something stirred in Erven's chest. As the last bits of light faded in the western sky, a tiny voice sounded in the back of his head. It grew stronger as he hurried towards the Hold, and some of the cold inside burned away.

You wanted a way to push back. Here's your chance.

Arielle's breath formed clouds of vapor as the highlanders escorted them to the Hold. They'd passed the night uneasily in lodgings provided by the village's public house, Arielle unsuccessfully trying to rest while formulating her plans for the morning. The tavern owner had already met Erven, and seemed happy with him as the choice for a new ruler.

"He's personable," the man had said, rubbing a hand through his beard while topping up her glass. "Makes you feel like your problems mean something to him." He set his jug off to the side. "I've never met the queen, so I don't know if that's what all royals are like. Could be it's just him."

It was food for thought, and gave Arielle plenty to mull over as she retired.

The next morning, the Holdmasters allowed her only two guards. Flanked by Tait and Ansel, Arielle held her head high as they passed through the doors of the Hold. Their escort stopped outside a heavy door, behind which she could hear the rumble of many voices.

"Wait here." The man disappeared inside, and the rumbling gradually decreased before he reemerged. "Lady Brynjar. They're ready for you."

ERVEN HELD his breath as the council room door swung open. They'd arranged the chairs in an arrangement similar to what had greeted him upon his first introduction to the coalition. Now, however, he sat at the head of the semi-circle, facing an empty chair at the open end. He stood with the others as the Crown's representative entered the room, flanked by two of the Shona. At the sight of Arielle's calm, stern face, his heartbeat steadied. *Thank the Almighty, she sent Arielle. This is my only chance.*

ARIELLE TOOK in the room and its contents in a heartbeat. Her attention immediately went to Erven, standing at the head of the semi-circle. His armor had been polished until the battered leather glowed, and he still wore the same sword she remembered him carrying as the Hollow commander. The expression on his face, however, made her pause in her curtsey before the Holdmasters. Gone were the easy mannerisms of the Shona commander she'd watched grow up. Hard edges etched his face, his shoulders level under his armor. While his eyes still held the same blue intensity she knew of old, they carried no hint of affection or sentiment towards her.

It wasn't the first time she and Erven had been in a delicate situation, but the man she was facing held little resemblance to the boy she had raised. *Can I have misjudged him that much?*

Their eyes locked as she rose from her curtsey, and a hush spread across the room. Later, she would realize that the Holdmasters had been looking not at the man they'd thrown their fortunes behind, but at her—the leader of a long-lost tribe. In that brief moment, Erven's gaze softened and his eyes dropped. One hand curled into a deliberate fist at his side.

Relief and adrenaline shot through Arielle's veins.

THE CAPTAIN HURRIED her towards the stairs leading to the dungeons. "Milord ordered the interrogation hours ago. I've told them to make sure he'll still be able to talk, but I don't know how much good it'll have done." An undercurrent of pleading ran through his voice as he said, "I've held this post for years, but I'm through with letting innocents get hurt while on my watch."

He heaved the door open. Erven lay crumpled on the floor of an open cage, bloodied and unconscious. The guards jumped to attention as the captain roared, "Enough!" He pushed his way through the men as they shook off their bloodlust. "It's not working. Let the healer look at him."

Arielle shook off fear as she knelt at Erven's side. Deep purple bruises surrounded his eyes, and she wondered what other injuries were hidden where she couldn't see. Shaking his shoulder, she called, "Wake up, boy!"

Erven's eyes slid open briefly. She caught a glimpse of blue and a spark of recognition before they closed again. A tiny bit of hope flared. It took no acting for her to snap at the lieutenant commander, "Officer, you've gone too far."

As the lieutenant began blustering, she took advantage of the commotion to bend her head over Erven's. She wasn't certain if he would be able to respond as she whispered, "Erven, if you can hear me, make a fist."

She caught her breath with relief as his hand closed into a tight fist.

"Follow my lead. This is your only chance."

THANK THE ALMIGHTY, Arielle thought as Erven met her eyes knowingly.

20

NO CONTEST BETWEEN US

"My Lords," Arielle addressed the Holdmasters. "Brothers. Thank you for your courtesy and hospitality. I am Arielle, Crown healer and the mistress of Hold Brynjar."

"I don't remember Hold Brynjar ever being held by a woman." The man addressing her had eyes as hard as midwinter stones.

"I was born the daughter of our greatest chief," Arielle answered evenly. "I am the sister of our last queen, and bound by marriage to your own people." She glanced aside at the Thinar leader, the distant resemblance to her dead brother-in-law fueling the anger pulsing through her blood. "I earned my right twice over when the warlord razed our Hold and massacred our people. You claim the right to leadership lies in combat." She returned her gaze to the man who'd challenged her. "Anyone who claims that the spilling of blood is of more consequence than the saving of it has no place among us."

She gracefully swept her skirts aside to sit in the chair at the mouth of the semi-circle. "I'm here on behalf of my kin, Brielle Thinar, to extend her greetings." She placed her hands demurely in her lap, keeping her back straight and her voice level. "Even though the behavior of this coalition has been contemptible and dishonorable, Her Majesty declines to respond with military force. She is disheartened that such a rift exists between the highlands and the Crown, and it is her hope that an open and honest exchange of information will go a long way towards healing that wound."

The Holdmasters looked at each other hesitantly before the man wearing Aubron colors answered her, "Lady Brynjar, we know your dedication to the Thinar Line. Your connection with the royal house is understandable, and your loyalty admirable." He rubbed a scruffy grey beard wearily. "Had the queen taken note of our grievances earlier, and tried to rectify them by demonstrating loyalty to Illyn tradition, this could have been a conflict avoided. But as time has worn on, our tolerance wears thin."

Arielle couldn't keep the disdain out of her voice. "And rather than voicing your concerns, supporting Her Majesty and helping her learn our ways, or behaving in any other honorable way, you've chosen to express your discontent through breaking your oaths and open rebellion."

"The consensus we've reached is that there *is* no way for this rift to be mended without the removal of Brielle Thinar from the throne." Arielle noticed the man with the dark eyes glance sharply at Erven as the Thinar leader spoke.

"Yes, and I understand you've already selected your chosen one to assume the throne. There really is no contest, is there, between a war hero and an unknown woman?" Arielle tried to keep her voice level as she addressed Erven.

"I'd be very interested in hearing what *you* have to say. There was a time when I thought your devotion to Her Majesty was greater than anyone else's."

"My loyalty lies with my people," Erven answered, standing to address the group with an expression she had only seen once, when he'd challenged dissenters among the Shona. "We did have some misunderstandings at first, but those have been rectified. More than that, I believe the high-lands have legitimate grievances that must be addressed." He glanced at the Holdmasters on either side of him, and Arielle could have sworn she saw a hint of fear in his face. "With Lord Kuma's death, there is potential for us to restore Illyn to its former glory. If the highlands are united under a ruler who satisfies honor *and* tradition, there can once again be peace—without reliance on outsiders to fight on our behalf. They've chosen me, and I can't shy away from that duty to my people."

A subtle smile caught at the corner of his mouth as he added, "The other highland clans have pledged to present themselves at Hold Eskel at the appointed time. With the call to moot, we are free to let the people of Illyn decide who will rule. Like Her Majesty, this coalition is bound by the traditions we hold most dear. If she's willing to accept the moot's ruling, we're prepared to do the same. Like you said..." His hand tightened, and a thread of fervency crept through his clearly enunciated words. "Between her and I, there's no contest."

Sooner than Erven had expected, the audience was over. As the door closed on Arielle and her escorts, Torvald spun him around with an abrupt hand to his shoulder. "What was that about!"

"Nothing!" Erven insisted. He'd been clenching his hand so hard it was spasming, and he tried to shake the cramp out inconspicuously. "We've known the entire time that the moot would have to decide between us. I'm entirely within my rights to let them know that as well."

"There's rights, and there's discretion," the Hold Aubron leader reminded him sternly. "And you might have considered using a bit more of it just then."

"I'm not a child," Erven said. "If you want me to rule, you can't tell me what I should or shouldn't say." He yanked his shoulder free from Torvald's grasp. "You *have* to trust me. I know how Brielle and her advisors think, and they'd never believe us if I came out of this meeting looking like some kind of horse led along by the reins. Besides," he added, stepping out of grabbing range. "It's dishonorable to challenge someone to a fight without making them aware of the terms."

"So you say," Torvald said quietly, in the type of voice that sank through to Erven's bones. "But if you're not careful, some people could see your willingness to accommodate as a sign of weakness." His tone shifted from threatening to mocking as he added, "I don't know what would have to happen in order to prove your loyalty, were that the case."

Erven's stomach churned at the thought. "It's not disloyal or weak to try to stop unnecessary bloodshed. You know that, that's why you decided to force my hand the way you did." He made a decisive gesture, his other hand ready to undo the catch on his scabbard. "Stop these games and let me lead our people."

He turned on his heel and left the room, aware that one

of the guards had left his post to follow. As he left the Hold, he could hear the faint sounds of an argument starting behind him. *If I try to talk to Arielle, they'll know something's wrong. I'll have to trust that she saw the signal.*

Opening the storm door into the barracks, he saw the guards still outside Merald and Cedric's room. Steeling himself, he commanded, "The envoys are on their way back to their quarters. You can stand down."

The men exchanged wary looks before one of them tightened his hand on his spear haft. "I don't know if I can let you in there, Sir."

"Really?" Erven put as much confidence into his words as he could. "On whose authority? The last time I checked, I had just as much power as any of the others." *That's not true, but maybe they'll believe me.* "Let me in."

"Just do it," the other guard told his comrade. "Nothing's going to happen."

With a final uneasy look at Erven, the man blocking the door stepped aside. "All right, Sir. Best make sure none of you leave the building, though."

"We're not going anywhere," Erven promised as he opened the door.

Merald and Cedric looked up in surprise as he came in. Their room was barely larger than his, the floor crowded with their belongings.

"What's going on?" Merald asked.

"Her Majesty sent Arielle and some of the Shona up to accept the terms of the moot." Finding nothing large enough to brace the door, Erven settled for wedging a practice sword diagonally between the door and the adjacent wall.

"That's interesting news," Cedric said, sitting up from

the too-small bed with a groan. "But why exactly are you here? I thought you had kingish things to do."

Erven hadn't missed the sarcasm in his friend's voice. "I *thought* I was supposed to—well, accept their acceptance—but apparently I was expected to just stay quiet and look impressive. I'm worried they'll hurt you two in order to remind me where my loyalties ought to lie." He sat down with his back against the door, tipping his head to look up at both of them. "You'd think they'd be done with that sort of thing by now, but I don't trust Torvald from here to the door."

"You're *sitting* against the door," Merald pointed out. "You trust him that little?"

The realization made Erven laugh, for the first time in what seemed like days. "Yes, I trust him that little, and like him even less." He leaned his head back against the door. "He keeps baiting me... I think he's just waiting for me to do something suspicious or violent. Then he can say I'm a liability and they might as well just declare full-on war instead of going with the moot."

"That's what the alternative is?" Cedric whistled softly. "I'd go with a moot as well, if that was my option."

"So, is it all right if I stay here?" Erven asked. "I don't want to say you need protection, exactly—"

"We'll take it," Merald said quickly. "And if they know you're here, they're not afraid you're plotting against them with the queen's envoys."

"I don't imagine they'll be here much longer, anyway." Erven unbuckled his sword belt, laying the weapon where he could reach it. "The Holdmasters don't want to give anyone time to act against them."

• • •

Their pace back to the public house was swift. Both Arielle and the Shona were quiet, each processing what they had seen and heard. As they came back into the public house, the others stopped their games and conversations to look up with curiosity and apprehension. Arielle held off the tide of questions, making instead for the private meeting room off the common area. Once the door had closed behind them, she let out a sigh of relief. "I'm glad that's over. Thank the Almighty."

Ansel's face darkened. "I don't see what there is to be thankful over. He's playing right into their hands." Beside him, Tait shifted from foot to foot as he nodded.

"No, he's not," Arielle said. "Trust me, there was more there than met the eye."

Just as she was about to explain, the meeting room door rattled as Arrick burst in. "What happened? Everyone's swarming out there."

"Erven *did* speak on the Holdmasters' behalf." Arielle closed the door behind him and wedged a stool under the latch. Giving it a shake to make sure it was well settled, she observed, "But I suspect they're now regretting giving him such a public opportunity to speak his mind."

Arrick spat on the floor. "Traitor."

"Hold on." Tait put a hand on his friend's shoulder. "Lady Arielle thinks there might be something else than just what we heard."

All three of them looked expectantly at her as she explained, "It's something from a long time ago; a signal we used once when things were really dire, and I needed him to follow my lead. He used it in there just now. *And* what he said effectively backed the Holdmasters into a corner." She had to smile at the memory. "He openly stated that they'll abide by the ruling of the moot—no matter what it is. He also implied he doesn't really want to challenge Rose at all."

The silence in the room stretched out as the men contemplated her words. Finally, Ansel said, "He didn't seem like himself to me."

"I know," Arielle agreed. "He's clearly been under a lot of strain. But I know him, and I know what I saw."

Ansel shook his head, his shoulders slumped. "I just didn't expect it." The young Shona clenched one hand around the hilt of his hunting knife—the only weapon they'd been allowed in the meeting. "Seeing him like that— all king-like."

"It *is* a bit of a shock," Arielle agreed.

"That's just it, it's not," Tait said. He glanced at the door before lowering his voice. "Look, my loyalties will always lie with Rose. She managed to keep the Shona together when we all thought he was dead." The other two nodded in agreement as he said, "But after today, I think I understand why the Holdmasters put their support behind Erven. He's always had the qualities of a great leader, but today I really *saw* it." Tait dropped his voice ashamedly. "If things were different, I'd have followed him all the way to the throne."

Arielle patted his shoulder. "I understand. I saw it too." She sighed. "This will be difficult, to say the least. If *we* think he'd be a good king, I'm certain the rest of the highlands will feel the same."

The door rattled under someone knocking. "Lady Arielle?"

Outside, she could hear commands being given. Setting her shoulders firmly, Arielle pulled the stool from under the latch and stepped out with the others behind her. A collection of highland guards stood around the room, flanking the man with harsh eyes who'd originally challenged her in the meeting. He nodded to her curtly. "We're not so stupid as to allow you to spread dissension among our people. Collect your belongings and prepare to march."

"This is outrageous," she insisted. "We've been travelling hard to get here, and you're casting us out with no time to resupply or rest."

"That's your outlook, not ours." The man gestured at the door. "Get your things and leave. You've overstayed your welcome."

21

BURNING COLD

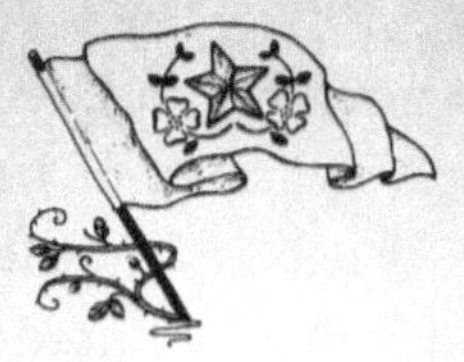

Nights had become clear and cold. Long after midnight, Rose sat up in a huff. Try as she might, sleep was eluding her once again. Wrapping her dressing gown over her shift and pulling a blanket around her shoulders, she sought the refuge of the tower battlements. Below, the sea stretched out to the eastern horizon, waves breaking soundlessly on the rocks far below. Overhead, the stars continued a chilly dance, pale bands twisting in light across the night sky. She sat down with her back to the battlements, gazing up into the stars.

Signing the trade agreement had lifted some of the weight from her mind, and the Sea Wanderers' departure the previous week had helped life resume its ordinary rhythms. For Rose, 'normal' meant resuming her daily rides around the city; facing the alternately sympathetic and hostile attitudes of the people and desperately reaching out for connection. She'd also added combat training sessions with Tora, the Shona woman guiding her towards skills she hoped would never need to be used.

A shooting star streaked across the sky, disappearing behind the snow-capped peaks to the northwest. *New birth,* Rose thought automatically. *That's what they say a dancing star means.* She watched as others followed, leaving brief flashes of light across the insides of her eyelids with each blink. *Erven said he didn't believe it, but it's still a charming thought.*

Rose wrapped her arms around her knees, looking up at the sky from inside the warmth of her blanket. Since the assassination a few weeks back, her interactions with Willow had remained stilted, limited to dealing with the day-to-day crises that kept Illyn on the cusp of boiling over. *I wondered why leaders were usually solitary,* she thought. *Now, I think I understand. Given enough time, we'll push away everyone around us.*

Far below, a high-pitched call cut through the night. Getting to her feet and looking down into the courtyard, she saw bobbing torches approaching from the road leading into the mountains. A momentary flash of fear froze her hands to the battlements before her reason took over. *If we were being attacked, they wouldn't use Shona signals, and they wouldn't betray their position with torches. It must be Arielle.*

She stopped in her room long enough to pull a work dress over her shift and cram her circlet over her braid before running down the stairs as fast as she could. She reached the hall just as Arielle came inside, the older woman's clothing creased and travel-worn and an exhausted expression on her face. She dropped her pack and opened her arms at seeing Rose. "Your Majesty."

Rose forgot about the dignity suited to a queen and ran the last few steps into Arielle's arms. "You're back."

"You're awake." Arielle wrapped a hand around the back

of her head, gently smoothing her hair. "It's long past midnight."

"I couldn't sleep." Admitting it to Arielle felt safe. "When I lie down, it only gives me more time to think about all the ways I could do better."

"I understand." Arielle let Rose go, bending to pick up her pack. "I suppose I'm glad you're still up. Do you want to hear how our mission went, or would you prefer to wait until tomorrow?"

Rose made sure the big doors were still barred before following Arielle towards the stairs. "If you're not too tired, I'd like to hear."

As they stopped in front of Arielle's room, the older woman explained, "Tait's back at Hollow, and I left Ansel at Whitecaps with a handful of the others. Hopefully, they won't be needed."

The door next to Arielle's creaked open. "What's going on?" Willow asked sleepily.

"Oh, good. You're awake." Arielle couldn't have missed the expression on Rose's face as she turned to see Willow. "Give me a moment to change."

The door closed behind her, leaving Rose and Willow alone in the corridor. "Did you go to bed at all?" Willow asked, yawning widely and rubbing bleary eyes.

"Couldn't sleep," Rose answered curtly. She folded her arms over her work clothes and turned to face Arielle's door.

"This can't wait until morning?"

Rose knew Willow was never at her best when woken abruptly, but the knowledge didn't make her soften her words. "*I* didn't call you. If you want to wait until morning, you can."

"Something tells me it's not news you need to hear alone."

"Alone or not, I'll be the one it impacts the most," Rose said, looking back over her shoulder. "Go back to bed."

Willow's sleepy face filled with hurt. "All right, then." She opened the door to her room. "But when you decide you're through shutting all of us out, I'll be here."

The door clicked behind her, leaving Rose alone in the corridor. After a moment, Arielle reemerged from her own room. "What was all that? I thought you'd have made up by this point."

"No," Rose answered defensively. "I've had to keep my mind on staying abreast of everything. And I'd rather hear what you have to say by myself."

"All right," Arielle sighed as she wrapped her shawl around her nightgown. "But let's make it brief? I'd still like to get some sleep tonight." She held the door open in a gesture sharply reminiscent of their first meeting, when the wisewoman had welcomed Rose and Violet into her foothills cottage.

Rose pulled two chairs over to face the newly lit fire, where a woven rag rug softened the stones nearest the hearth. "How did it go? Were you able to talk with them?"

Arielle nodded wearily. "They intercepted us under the truce flag, near where they ambushed Erven. I suspect that's the outer limit of their regular patrols, or they just keep a watch on that specific path." She pulled her braid over her shoulder and began undoing it, silver streaks catching the firelight. "We were right—there are as many clans siding with the Holdmasters as rallied to you at Hold Eskel. Only a few of their leaders were at the meeting, but I suspect that had more to do with our visit surprising them than anything else." Arielle absent-mindedly undid a snarl in her hair before continuing. "The Thinar clan heads were still at Hold Aubron, but that's not a surprise. Your family's Hold is deep in the mountains, and I'm sure the storms have well and truly sealed them off until spring."

"Who did you speak with, then?" Rose wished she'd brought her notebook. *Willow would have been taking notes this whole time.* She scooted closer to the fire, wondering why it didn't seem to be warming the room like it should. "Did —" she stopped to clear her throat. "—did you see him?" *What's the matter with me? What does it matter if she saw him?*

"I did see Erven." Arielle picked up a hairbrush from the table, examining it for a long, silent moment before saying, "I don't know how to describe it any other way, but he looked absolutely confident in his authority. He spoke with the attitude of someone who knows their orders will be followed."

Something I've never managed to learn. Rose swallowed hard. "So, he really has betrayed us." She balanced her chin in her hand, fingers cold against her cheek. "I suppose I shouldn't be surprised, not after everything we've heard."

"I wouldn't give him up so easily," Arielle warned. She began pulling the brush through her hair. "That's not all I saw."

Rose looked up, a spark of hope jittering along her veins. "Did you see something none of us would have noticed?"

The spark grew as Arielle nodded. "During the war, when he was imprisoned here... did he ever tell you what happened?" As Rose shook her head, Arielle explained, "When Lord Kuma found out Soren could no longer pass him information, he decided to question Erven. Commander —well, Captain at the time—Commander Ricar sent Merald to find me. When I reached the dungeon, they'd been interrogating Erven for hours."

A strange feeling forced its way through Rose's heart. She shivered, cold fighting against the new warmth as she said, "I knew about that, but I didn't realize he outlasted them for so long."

Arielle had set down the hairbrush and was gazing into the fire. "He was barely conscious when I got here. I think Commander Ricar was just as angry as I was, but he had more authority. While he was yelling at them, Erven woke up enough to recognize me." Her voice went quiet, and Rose had to strain to hear her words. "I told him to make a fist if he could hear me, and he did. He was aware enough to follow my lead. Between the two of us, we were able to make the guards believe what we needed them to believe in order for him to get out alive."

She looked back at Rose with tears in her eyes. "I've always known how strong-willed he is, but he keeps surprising me. In the meeting with the Holdmasters, he signaled me again the same way." Arielle's voice strengthened as she said, "There were shadows in his eyes, but he was still the Erven I know. He phrased their official response in such a way that the Holdmasters will *have* to abide by the moot's ruling, even if it's not in their favor. No matter what they've said, or rumors we've heard, I'm certain he hasn't betrayed us."

Rose shivered again as she sat back in her chair, trying to process Arielle's story. After a long time, she asked, "You're sure?"

"I know what I saw." Arielle wiped tears away with the corner of her shawl. "And I know what I felt. He's still fighting them, Rose."

Rose let her head sink to the table beside her. *Shadows. How far have those shadows taken him?* The firelight danced bravely across her closed eyelids. *A good ruler wouldn't even be considering this. The evidence of everything is so against him. If I was a good queen, I'd be ordering his assassination right now.*

As her thoughts settled, she returned to the conversation she'd had with Erven soon after his escape from the castle. She'd expected criticism for her clumsy leadership of the clan he'd been willing to die for. Instead, his words had placed confidence in her heart. The truth fell into her mind, just as the words from that afternoon returned to memory.

"I expect to die before I betray you," Rose whispered. The bitter knot under her breastbone flared and disappeared, replaced with certainty—and longing. She took a shuddering breath.

I hope he's all right. I miss him.

THE NEXT MORNING, Willow was elbow deep in bread dough when Rose approached her work table. The hurt from the night before hadn't left as she snapped, "I'll be back to the office in a few hours, Your Royal Majesty. Go away."

"I'm here to apologize, you goose." Rose said impatiently.

"Fine, lovely. I accept." Willow thumped the dough back into the bowl. "I told you, I'll be upstairs in a bit. Now, if you need anything else?"

"Willow, please."

The change in Rose's voice made Willow look up in a hurry. She didn't *think* her friend was crying, but something else felt off. Reluctantly, she swallowed back the harsh words piled up behind her tongue. "Is there something else bothering you?"

"No, just, I really am sorry." Rose leaned an elbow on the table. "All this with Erven, the Holdmasters, the guilds, the assassination…" Her words halted as she pressed a hand to her temple, before coming out all in a rush. "I've been letting my own worries cut me off from you and the others. You said it's not good for either of us, and you're right. I'm sorry."

"It's all right—I forgive you, and properly this time." Willow shook the last of the dough from her hands, grabbing a rag to remove the remnants. Between Rose's bearing and the unfamiliar note in her voice, Willow's irritation quickly faded to worry. "How much did you sleep last night?"

"I don't know. A few hours, maybe?" Rose's hand still hadn't moved from her temple, and her slump against the table spelled exhaustion beyond lack of sleep.

Willow frowned as she finished scrubbing her hands. "Hold still." She held her damp wrist against Rose's forehead. Heat radiated off Rose's skin, and even the circlet felt warm. "How are you feeling?"

"Cold, actually." Rose laughed tiredly. "I was out watching the stars again last night, and I just haven't been able to get warm since."

Willow sighed. "Lovely." She threw the towel over her bread dough and reached back to untie her apron. "You're getting sick, my love."

"No, I can't be." Rose looked at her with alarm. "There's still so much I need to finish."

"Bed. Now." Willow put an arm around her friend and led her out of the kitchen towards the stairs. As they went up the twisting stair, Rose's footsteps grew slower and slower. By the time they reached Rose's bedroom door, Willow's arm had moved from comfort to support. Opening the door with her free hand, she ushered Rose over to the bed, calling, "Greta? Are you here?"

"Here," the maid replied, coming out from the side room. "What—oh dear."

"I'm fine."

"Quiet, Your Majesty." Willow could feel the heat of Rose's torso through her dress as she asked Greta, "Would you get Arielle, please?"

The maid hurried out the door. Rose sat down on the edge of her bed with a defeated sigh. "Maybe you're right."

"Of course, I'm right." Willow held out her hand. "Crown, please."

With a tired smile, Rose acquiesced, pulling hairpins free and letting her long braid fall against her collarbone. "I *am* tired."

Once she'd tucked Rose's circlet away in its box, Willow helped her friend out of her overdress and under the covers.

"I don't understand why this is happening," Rose said from behind her. Now that she was sitting in bed, the young queen seemed to have resigned herself to being ill.

"I can tell you exactly why." Willow cast about until she found Rose's teapot. "You don't sleep. I don't remember the last time I saw you eat with the rest of us. You act like every single thing that happens in this country is your fault. And you're scared to let yourself be close to us, because you're afraid we'll betray you too." She set the teapot on the table with a decisive thump as Arielle came in.

"I'll agree with all that," Arielle said. She set a basket on the table and took out a glazed pottery flask. "Though, why now?" Pouring dark liquid into a tiny cup, she handed it to Rose. "Drink that," she admonished. "It'll make you sleep, but I daresay that's what you need. You've had a month of uphill and down, and your mind was just put to rest regarding the person you care most about." She snorted. "I can't say I'm surprised you'd take ill."

Willow stopped ladling steaming water into the teapot. "Sorry, did something happen I don't know about?"

Rose made a disgusted face as she swallowed the medicine. "Arielle thinks Erven might still be fighting the Holdmasters." She handed the cup back to Arielle, a tired smile creeping across her face. "I knew he wouldn't really betray us."

Willow raised her eyebrows at Arielle. The healer nodded, and Willow saw the same emotion in her face. "I think we've been right about him all along."

"Well, that *is* good to hear." Willow peered into the basket and retrieved a cloth bag of tea. Shaking it into the teapot, she said, "I'll finish this, then go back downstairs. You'll stay with her, yes?"

Arielle nodded. "Don't worry. We'll be all right."

Willow busied herself the rest of the day going through the documents in Rose's box, sending messages to follow up on most of them, and organizing the rest so she could attack them the following day.

"Hallo, Old Thing." Heather breezed in just as she locked up. "Have you decided t'subsist off air like our beloved monarch?"

Willow looked at the shuttered window, where no bits

of daylight could be seen. "I just kept telling myself, 'I'll finish this last little bit…'"

"That's when you *know* it's time to stop." Heather hooked her elbow through Willow's and hauled her up. "Down the stairs with you."

"Steady on!" Willow only had time to grab the key out of the box before being towed towards the stairs.

"So, what's happened this time that's got you all asweat?" Heather asked, her curls bouncing with each step.

"Rose is sick, and I was trying t'clear her desk," Willow explained.

"Hmph." Heather didn't sound at all surprised. "Honestly, I expected it before now. What's finally set her over?"

Willow slowed as they approached the last turn on the stairs. "Don't tell anyone about this, all right?"

Heather pulled herself up short to spit on her hand. "My lips're sealed."

Willow sat down on the second-to-last step. "Somehow, Erven managed to signal Arielle during the meeting in the highlands. Now she—and Rose—believe he's remained loyal this entire time."

Heather sat with a bump next to her. "That's an awf'ly slim hunch to pin all our hopes on. Not to mention a reversal of what the Holdmasters have led us all to believe. What d'you think?"

Willow rested her chin in her hand, fixing her gaze on the stones at the foot of the stairs. "I don't know what to think. On the one hand, he's only ever been loyal. On the other hand, he might take that loyalty to strange places in order to preserve lives." Willow looked up at her sister. Even slouching, Heather was still taller than her. "But then on the other hand—"

"You've only got two hands, Old Thing," Heather reminded her. "Unless you've gone octopus when I wasn't looking."

"On the *other* hand," Willow continued with a smile, "Rose was so relieved to hear the news. I'd hate to make her doubt her own judgement." She turned the bracelet Ethan had given her around and around on her wrist. "She's been so worried about him, and so hurt by all this, it's almost like..." She fell silent, watching the light play over the gemstones.

"Like...?" Heather prompted after a long moment.

Willow pressed her lips together. "I'd hate to put my odds on something that might not be there."

"I'll fill it in for you, then," Heather suggested. "She's actin' the same way you were when Ethan left last week. She's pining."

Willow snorted. "Rose doesn't pine. I'm not even sure she knows what that is."

"Fine, then. Not pining, but she's not really settled since Erven's been gone." Heather wriggled her eyebrows. "I didn't think queens felt that way about their right-hand men unless something else was there."

Willow looked at Heather with new respect. "You're better at reading people than I give you credit for."

Heather burrowed her face into the collar of her beloved sweater. "Thanks, Old Thing. Now what?"

"I think she's gotten sick because her mind's not fighting her heart anymore." Willow got to her feet and offered her sister a hand up. "If she's mistaken, I don't want to be the one to mention it to her. Doubtless, all of us will find out rapidly if she's wrong."

. . .

IN THE WEE hours of the morning, someone hammered on Willow and her sisters' door. Shaken out of sound sleep, Willow grabbed her work knife from where it lay on the bedside table. It took a long, confused second for her to recognize the voice as belonging to one of the kitchen workers.

Wrenching the door open, she demanded, "What in sea and sky is going on?!"

The boy's eyes were wide over a face streaked with charcoal. "Someone's here from the Shona, Milady. Whitecaps was attacked!"

Willow drew back from the door in shock, her sisters' exclamations echoing behind her.

Someone's made a terrible mistake.

22

CROSSING THE LINE

"Aren't you going to tell her?" Heather exclaimed, her long legs easily overtaking Willow as she crossed the courtyard. Overhead, the sky was still dark, the barest hint of grey over the eastern wall promising a clear dawn. Castle guards and hostlers hurried between pools of flickering torchlight near the gates, tightening girths and checking saddlebags as others prepared to ride. The light threw Heather's freckled face into sharp relief as she demanded, "Not to mention, why are you leaving at all? With Rose sick, you'll be needed!"

Willow turned on her heel to face her younger sister, looking seriously into Heather's cloudy blue eyes. "We have no idea what happened up there, or who's responsible." She pulled Heather closer by the elbow, lowering her voice so no one else would overhear. "If I go upstairs and tell Rose any of this, it might send her somewhere no one can reach. We need clear information, and someone to represent the Crown." She clenched her teeth. "And if Erven's behind this too, I'm planning on punching him myself."

"You might have to take your turn," Tora announced as she approached. The healer had traded her work apron for trousers and tunic, and her shoulder belt pulled tightly under the weight of a slingstone pouch and hunting knife. "I don't care what his motivations are; this crosses the line."

"Agreed." Willow squeezed her sister's hand. "You can handle things while I'm gone." She glanced up at the tower. "Take care of Rose."

Heather nodded, responsibility erasing the mischief from her face. "I will. Take care of yourself, Old Thing."

THEY MADE good time up to Hollow, the path to the Shona base now grown into a proper trail. The lake had thawed in the center, a small pool of open water rippling in the wind coming down the pass. Around the shore, piles of weather-sculpted boulders guarded a cluster of snug log buildings, an expansion from the original Shona camp. As they approached, sentries heralded their arrival with shrill whistles. Willow swung down from her horse just as Annika emerged from the tunnels leading to the outpost's namesake subterranean room. The lanky Hollow commander smiled tightly as she saw Willow and the squad of guardsmen. "Thank you for coming so fast."

Willow met her with a firm handclasp—somehow, a hug didn't seem appropriate under the circumstances. "We came as soon as we could. What happened?"

"We still aren't sure," Annika said. Wind blew strands of her choppy hair around her face as she explained, "Lins made it here about midnight, and we sent word as fast as we could. All we know is that a mixed group of highlanders attacked Whitecaps sometime yesterday."

"Arielle left some of her patrol up there, right?"

Annika nodded. "Ansel and a handful of others. Tait went that way as soon as Lins arrived. The attackers were mostly in Aubron and Thinar colors, but some had patterns she didn't recognize."

"It matches what Arielle said, about what clans are actually at Hold Aubron right now." Willow wondered if she ought to pry any further, but was saved from asking as Tora joined them.

"What about Erven?"

Annika's shoulders stiffened under her tunic. "No one saw him, if that's what you mean. If he'd been there, they wouldn't have let him get away." She turned away as some of the other Shona appeared with laden packs. "Whitecaps doesn't have long term shelter for horses. You'll have to get there on foot."

By evening, Willow was glad she'd been putting effort towards improving her physical condition. Her shins and feet ached by the time the sunlight faded from the peaks above them. As they started moving again after a break, she squinted to see a white quartz cliff face looming from the darkness.

"Whitecaps was named after those," Tora told her, gesturing at the cliffs. "We're getting close. Are you ready?"

Willow eased her shoulders under her pack straps, knowing what the healer was really asking. "I saw the aftermath of the battle at the ridge. I won't panic if I see blood." She sighed. "This does feel different, though."

Ahead in the darkness, a whistle sounded. Someone answered from the front of their group, the swooping call ringing between the rocks. Within a few minutes, the lights of Whitecaps resolved in the distance, far too many torches for the time of day glowing around the smoldering shells of several buildings. Willow could barely make out the glint of javelin points and hurrying figures around the outpost, but even from a distance she could sense the chaos.

"Tora!" Tait ran across the bloodied snow, his unruly hair disheveled around his ears. He skidded to a halt and hugged Tora around the shoulders. "I'm so glad you're here. We put all the wounded in the main hall." He pointed at the only stone building in the outpost. It had escaped major damage, the stones marred by soot and the front door dangling crazily from one hinge. "Do you think you can—"

"I'll take care of it." Tora slid out of his arm and hurried towards the building.

"Spread out and reinforce the line around the outpost," the guard captain told his men. "Send the sentries in for a respite if you can. Further orders will be forthcoming."

As the men began dispersing, the captain clasped hands with Tait. "What happened here, Commander?"

Tait shook his head. "They were extra vigilant the day or so after we left, but people have to rest at some point. The day they returned to their usual patrol schedule, they were attacked from two sides."

The captain spat into the snow. "Bastards."

"I got here this morning. They were still trying to put out the fires, then." Tait gestured for them to gather in the circle of light cast by a torch stuck in the snow. "Survivors say the highlanders weren't interested in plunder, or even in killing everyone." He shifted from foot to foot, visibly perturbed as he added, "They took the flag from the main building and left one with that tower crossed by wings."

Willow frowned. "That's not settling a vendetta, that's making a different kind of statement." She surveyed the torchlit clearing, acutely aware of dozens of tasks needing to be done. "Rose needs accurate information before she decides how to respond." *There's no way I'm telling them she's taken ill.* "But that can wait another day." She yawned, her body reminding her how long it had been since she'd slept. "Did the kitchen survive? I can talk to everyone tomorrow, but I'd rather be useful now."

Tait gratefully pointed her towards one of the buildings, where Willow threw herself into clearing debris, stoking a fire, and digging through crates of ruined supplies. Her insides quaking with exhaustion, she tossed together ingredients for stew in one pot and oats in another.

As she cleared space for her blanket in a corner, she mulled over what the commanders had told her. *The attackers were here for sport, or to send a message. If they'd wanted to wipe out the outpost, they could've. I'd give a lot to know who gave the order, and who they were trying to send a message to.* Pulling the blanket over her shoulders, Willow leaned her head back against the sack of cracked oats and fell asleep, not even hearing the unrest as Whitecaps continued to smolder.

A HANDFUL of days after the council with the Crown's envoys, a delegation came from Hold Eskel to settle details of the upcoming moot. Erven spent two days in meetings, emerging only briefly for meals and to sleep. The Hold Eskel representatives were cordial, but he suspected they would still side with Rose at the moot.

It doesn't matter. It won't take much to win the majority to our side.

After the delegation left, he gratefully returned to the activities that had become routine. It had been weeks since the last major storm, and the mood about the Hold was one of optimism. While snow still lay in packed areas along the paths and in shadows, the air held a warmer note, and the first lambs of spring were making their plaintive cries heard down in the folds. His side ached as he navigated the twisting paths through the houses to the blacksmiths' shop. *That's strange.* He popped his head out from under the awning to look at the peaks. *I don't see any clouds, and there's no wind.*

Shaking the thought out of his head, he went back to pumping the bellows as the smith heated a bar of iron for beating into a sickle. Strangely, the exercise didn't help work the cramp out of his side, and after a while he took a rest as the smith took over the bellows.

The iron was heating nicely when Erven heard the bells clanging. After months of hearing them at regular intervals, they were as familiar to him as the signal drums back home. "What's going on?" he asked, as one of the apprentices went past with a bag of scrap.

"Raiding party's returned, is my guess." The lad's words were almost lost in the clatter of metal as he set down the bag, and Erven had to ask him to repeat himself.

"What raiding party?"

The smith frowned as he pulled on the bellows, sending a shower of sparks spiraling out of the forge. "They left a handful of days ago, I guess. While you were in conference with them from Hold Eskel."

A gnawing feeling crept in as Erven asked, "Do you know where they were raiding?"

The smith paused to stir the coals. When he finally

answered, the answer sent a sickening chill through Erven's stomach. "I'm not sure, but someone mentioned intruders coming in from the lowlands." He stopped to look up at Erven. "Are you all right, Sir?"

Erven stammered some kind of answer, fleeing the forge before anyone else thought to ask him more questions. As he made for the Hold, he caught sight of the first members of the raiding party passing the earth walls. All his suspicions were confirmed at the sight of one man, gleefully waving a navy-blue flag over his head. Even from the top of Hold Aubron, Erven could make out a flash of gold and red from the emblazoned star and roses.

He stepped back from the edge of the terrace, his heart pounding. Rounding a corner into the courtyard just before the Hold, he almost crashed into Torvald. The fear and anger from the last few months came together in a heartbeat. Before the Holdmaster could react, Erven had pinned him against the outbuilding wall, forearm across the man's throat and hunting knife poised.

"What did you do!?"

He would never forget the look Torvald gave him—fearlessness and contempt all mixed into one poisonous stare. "The Shona were becoming a problem. They would've attacked the moment we let our guard down." He coughed before adding, "And *you* needed a reminder of how far our hand can reach."

Erven's hand trembled around the knife hilt as he moved the blade to touch Torvald's throat. "I should kill you right now. Your life isn't worth any of theirs, but it'll be a start."

"Kill me, then." Torvald gasped. "Your friends will be next."

With a growl, Erven stepped back, sending Torvald

sprawling. "You're not always going to have them to hold over me." He couldn't stop his voice from shaking as he added, "And trust me—when I take the throne, I'll make sure you'll regret this as long as you live."

He turned to leave, but a final jab from Torvald stopped him in his tracks. "It's interesting how emotional you are about those who once trusted you. It makes me wonder how you'll react when it's time to decide your rival's fate." The man's voice had regained its usual mocking tone as he said, "It's just as well you've severed all ties, otherwise it'll be terrible when you have to kill her yourself."

The blood drained out of Erven's face. After an eternity, he was able to breathe again. *He's right. They've been planning this all along, and I've been too stupid to see it.* With supreme effort, he forced the fear out of his voice. "That's where you're wrong." He faced Torvald, matching the other man's scornful look with an icy one of his own. "The Shona are my clan. Brielle Thinar isn't. When the time comes, you can be assured I'll make the right decision."

He walked away, keeping his face studiously neutral until he'd turned the corner. Once out of sight, he sprinted for his quarters as fast as he could. The door slamming behind him brought some clarity back to his mind, and he sank to the floor.

"Mate?" Merald's voice came through the door. "What's going on?"

"I'm all right," Erven called. "I'm just getting my things for practice. I'll be there in a moment."

Once he heard Merald's footsteps receding from the door, he sat up, scrubbing tears from his face. *He still doesn't know.* Standing slowly, he collected his practice sword from his new weapon rack. *How could I have let things get this far out of control?*

It took him another ten minutes to compose himself and assemble the rest of his practice gear. Finally, Erven made his way through the village. The news of the attack on Whitecaps was spreading, and he felt the eyes of everyone on him as he walked down through the terraces. *If they wanted a sign that I'd completely left behind my old loyalties, they've gotten it. They'll never know it wasn't my idea.* The stares unnerved him, and it was a struggle to walk calmly across the open ground to the practice arena.

Merald and Cedric had already arrived, their highland guards leaving as he entered. As soon as he came in, Cedric turned and walked out of the room, his face stormy. Merald was not nearly as stoic.

"Whitecaps?! You ordered them to attack the Shona?"

Erven dropped his armful of gear, putting his hands out as Merald grabbed a practice sword. "I know you won't believe me, but I didn't. I didn't know anything about it, I swear!" He jumped to the side as Merald swung the sword at his head. "Mate, stop!"

"I trusted you!" Merald swung again, tripping him as he tried to dodge.

A stab of pain went through Erven's bad wrist as he fell. He rolled away, tangling his feet in Merald's to send his friend thudding to the ground as well. Getting to a crouch, he dove on Merald. "Listen, man! It wasn't me!"

Merald elbowed him in the side, and the impact sent white stars through his vision. Before he could clear his head, he was on his back, Merald's knee planted firmly on his stomach. "Stop! Stop and listen to me!"

"No, you listen to me." Merald was breathing raggedly,

his voice breaking. "When I met you, you were willing to pay any price in order to protect the people you love. What happened?!"

"I'm telling you, the attack wasn't my idea!" Erven fought to keep his voice under control.

"Somehow, I just don't believe you." Merald grabbed the practice sword and held it reversed, the pommel poised for a crushing blow.

"You'll have to trust me!" Erven raised an arm to block. Even wearing his arm guards, he knew it would be useless if Merald managed to get a good hit in. "I've given up everything I valued—my reputation, my pride, my *loyalty*—just so the people I care about wouldn't get hurt!"

The sword quivered in Merald's hand. "I don't know or care how they got inside your head. I *do* know nothing you've said or done in the last two weeks has sounded anything like you."

"And don't you think it's hurt me the worst?" Erven hissed. "I made a *mistake*, and now we have to undo it if there's any chance for her to survive."

"Her?" Confusion laced Merald's voice. "Your sister?"

"Rose." He was relieved to see hesitation in his friend's face as he explained. "I thought I could stop the highlands from exploding in her face. But I found out today they won't be satisfied with her abdication. If they're looking to put me on the throne by right of combat, she has to die—"

"—and you have to kill her." Merald slid off to kneel beside him, dropping the sword in the dust. "I don't know how I didn't see it earlier."

"Torvald couldn't resist an opportunity to twist the knife." Erven pushed himself up on his elbows, wincing as his side throbbed. "He'll regret that."

"We've got to stop them," Merald said.

"We have to try, at least." Erven sat up, his muscles quivering. "But even if we do, she'll never trust me again." He scuffed his sleeve across his eyes. "If she knows what's best for her throne, she'll banish or execute me."

"Well, whatever we do, we need to do it soon." Merald gave him a hand up. "Today. Tomorrow. Whenever there's a moment they aren't looking." He grimaced and rubbed his side.

"You too?" Erven gingerly moved his wrist. "Mine's been hurting too. There's a storm coming."

"It's been calm for weeks," Merald said. "You think?"

Erven nodded, certain now. "Like Violet says, old injuries don't lie." He looked out the door. "We need to catch Cedric. They'll be drinking hard tonight, and we're not going to have a better opportunity."

23
SHEEPKILLER STORM

That evening, Erven disappeared into his quarters at the earliest opportunity. He didn't even need to lie to the other Holdmasters—every leader in the coalition had heard about his shattered reaction to the Whitecaps attack. As he began packing his things into his haversack, he felt the building quiver under a sudden gust of wind. His side twinged again. *I was right.* He remembered a previous conversation with one of the shepherds, who'd talked at length about the dangers of late-winter storms. *A Sheepkiller.*

Another shudder went through the building as Erven finished stuffing his pack with renewed urgency. He shucked off the tunic he'd been wearing, frowning at the sight of the Hold Aubron colors before replacing it with the charcoal-grey one he'd been wearing the day they left the castle. Doing up the clasps on his jacket, he hurriedly donned his armor and sword belt and fastened his cloak and hood over all. *Now for the difficult part.*

Erven stepped out into the hall, tipping a casual salute

to the guard in front of Merald and Cedric's room. "Another storm coming?"

"It sounds that way, Sir." The guard looked wistfully down the hall. "That'll put a damper on the celebration, I guess."

"I'm sure," Erven agreed. "I was about to go down there, myself. Would you like me to bring back anything for you? Hot drink, maybe?"

The guard's shoulders straightened, and he smiled. "Thanks, Sir! That's kind of you."

"Don't mention it." Erven gave a wave as he left through the storm room. By now his feet knew every path and alleyway as he hurried to the square. Twilight was beginning to fade into a dark sky, the gathering clouds illuminated from below by the crackling bonfire. Sounds of revelry filled his ears as he approached, and he stopped to gather his composure.

"Commander, you've decided to join us!" The head of Hold Aubron had clearly been drinking for some time already. "Here's to successful raids and a long reign!"

Erven forced a smile onto his face. "I couldn't stay away."

As the local ringleaders welcomed him into their circle, Erven shivered under his jacket. The whirl of gaiety caught him up as countless highlanders invited him to join them for a drink, a dance, a song, or a story. As cider switched to mead and the tales grew more and more elaborate, Erven kept an eye to the skies.

I need to get the others, so we can be away.

Finally, someone began relating a well-beloved highland tale. Those not occupied in their cups sat listening enthusiastically. Erven sidled around the circle until he'd reached the far side, the bonfire blocking Torvald's view of him. Grabbing a flask of cider, he hurried back up the hill towards the barracks. A gust of wind followed him inside, the first flakes of snow swirling in his wake as he greeted the guard.

"Told you I'd remember you!" Erven cheerfully said. "It's a pity you can't join the rest of us out there."

"Aye, but orders is orders," the man said, with a longing look towards the door. "Once we knew there'd be a celebration, we drew for it. I lost." He shrugged philosophically.

"Well, I brought you this." Erven held out the cider. "At least it's something."

"That's decent of you, Sir. Thank you." The guard set his club down, and Erven seized his opportunity. He swung the jug as hard as he could against the side of the man's head, pottery breaking with a smell of apples, hawthorn, and honey as the man crumpled to the floor. Erven dropped the shards of the jar, careful not to cut his hands. The door opened to reveal Merald and Cedric, already dressed in winter gear.

"Ready?" Erven asked.

Merald buttoned his jacket to his chin. "We're ready. What's your plan?"

Erven gestured towards the corridor. "We've got to get to the armory. That's where they keep skis and poles." He stepped back into the hall, pulling the unconscious guard into his room. He winced at the man's shallow breathing, hoping he hadn't done so much damage as to kill him. "And we need to hurry. It's already starting to snow."

They retrieved Erven's pack, hurrying through the dark terraces and down stairs until the glow of the forges shone in the distance. Erven pointed through the gloom. "There."

They stopped in the shelter of the awning, the whickering of horses stabled nearby barely audible over the rising wind. Erven slid the bolt back on the storeroom at the side of the blacksmithing complex and stepped inside. The forge fires and light from the cloudy sky barely reached past the threshold. "Careful you don't trip over anything in here."

"Think we can risk a light?" Merald asked.

"Better make it a small one. I think there's a lamp... Ah." Erven struck a spark to the lamp sitting on a shelf beside the door. Closing the door against the light, the three of them surveyed the racks of skis, poles, snowshoes, and other cold-weather items, stowed safely for when the inhabitants of Hold Aubron set out on trading or hunting missions.

Cedric frowned at the racks of gear. "No armor or weapons. Is there another room?"

"Through there." Erven pointed at the door on the other side of the shed.

"How long till they notice we're gone?" Merald asked as he swung his pack onto his shoulders.

"I'm hoping it'll be a bit." Erven ran his hand down one of the skis, wishing they were in better condition. "They know I was upset with the attack, but I don't know how long it'll take them to realize I'm neither in my room or at the bonfire."

"Or before someone finds the guard you knocked out." Merald knelt to gather a set of skis under his arm.

Cedric reappeared through the back door, wearing his own armor and carrying two sheathed swords. "Found our things. I can't imagine why they didn't just redistribute them to their own men."

"Ummm..." Merald pointed at Cedric's chest, where the star surrounded by roses appeared on his armor.

"Ah." Cedric shrugged, handing over one of the swords. "Better take that. You got skis?"

"We're ready." Erven blew out the lamp and opened the door, letting in a blast of cold air. Between snow and reflected light, they could make out the earthen wall, and the sturdy gate blocking their way to the forest beyond.

With muttered conversation here and there, they quietly made their way through the gate to the edge of the pinewoods. Once safe in the trees, they put on the skis and began gliding down the trail. Within minutes of leaving Hold Aubron, the snow began in earnest, making all of them stop frequently to brush off their shoulders and packs.

After some hours, they came out of the forest to stand at the head of a valley, pines giving way to aspens at the edges of a winding creek. Erven thought the valley was one they had traversed on their way up to Hold Aubron, more than two months previous. To his relief, the game trails made for fast travel, and they found themselves at the bottom of the valley much quicker than he had been expecting.

As he halted once more to catch his breath, Erven noticed Merald had dropped farther behind him and Cedric.

"We'll need to stop for his sake," Cedric remarked in his deep voice. "He can't keep up this pace for much longer."

"I can hear you," Merald said. With a swish of skis, he glided down to them. "I can keep up."

"No one's saying you can't," Erven reassured him. "We just don't want to drive you into the snow."

"I'll be fine." Merald glowered at him through the darkness. "Once the Holdmasters figure out we're gone, they'll be after us like wolves on an injured deer."

"All right, we'll keep going for a bit longer," Erven

agreed. "Then we'll stop." He brushed melting snow off his hood. "I'll be needing a rest by then, too."

They stopped just as the sky began to lighten. Too exhausted to make a fire, they dug through a drift to the hollow under a giant spruce tree and clustered together for warmth. Merald immediately fell asleep, his eyes flickering behind closed lids.

Erven unwound his scarf and shook the snow and ice crystals from it. Cedric did likewise, both of them trying to keep their movements from disturbing Merald.

"How long do you think we can safely rest?" Cedric doffed his hat and shook it out. "If I make my guess right, we can't stay in one place for too long."

"They'll know we're gone by now," Erven confirmed. He pulled his knees to his chest and leaned against the tree trunk, wrapping his cloak tightly. "I don't think we can spare more than an hour. Just long enough for you to nap."

"You're sure?" Cedric asked. "I was going to offer to take the watch, if you wanted to sleep. We've been stuck in our room for days with plenty of time to nap."

Erven laughed half-heartedly. "Thanks. Wake me if anything happens, or once it's full daylight."

At Cedric's acknowledgement, Erven curled tighter into his cloak and huddled against Merald. Between cold feet, growling stomach, and worry about what they'd walk into at Whitecaps, he doubted sleep would come easily. He'd resigned himself to just resting when exhaustion hit him like a tidal wave, and he knew nothing more until being shaken awake by Cedric.

In the half-light that passed for daytime during the storm, they shared a handful of the hard biscuits that Erven had managed to scrounge from the supplies in the armory.

Merald eyed the snow with interest. "Water would've helped get this down. I suppose eating snow's out of the question, though."

Erven hoped the cracking in his mouth had been the food, not a tooth. "Sorry. If we get farther ahead with this next run, maybe we can build a fire farther down the mountain."

"Suits me fine." Cedric had wolfed his portion and was getting his gear in order. "Let's get moving again. I'd like to get properly warm."

The next day fell into a blur, as they pushed themselves to the point of exhaustion before finding a spot to hide. After a rest period in which one of them kept watch while the other two slept, they shared food and pressed on once more, sharpening their eyes for a glimpse of the quartz cliffs above Whitecaps.

Erven had lost track of how many times they'd repeated the pattern of ski, rest, ski when a blast of wind slammed into them. They were navigating down a steep slope, and the momentary gust sent him careening into Cedric. Both of them tumbled into an ungraceful downhill skid, skis and poles tangled beyond easy recovery. Finally, a snow-covered thicket of currant bushes broke their slide, mere feet from a heap of jagged boulders.

Swearing miserably and on the verge of tears, Erven yanked his boots from their bindings and struggled upright. Cedric, likewise, had freed his feet and was untangling himself from his poles. Shaking snow from his clothing, Erven could hear Merald laughing somewhere above them. The thought of how ridiculous they must look struck him, and he couldn't help but join in.

"All right, we look silly," he laughed, retrieving scattered equipment from across the snow. "Just don't tell any of the men. They'll never respect me again if they knew I couldn't keep my feet."

"Not a sound from me," Merald promised. "Not a single word."

Cedric brushed snow from his hair and pulled his hat back down to his eyebrows. "I don't suppose we can stop now, can we?" He began wriggling his boot back into the bindings on his ski. "It's getting close to nightfall."

"Let's," Erven agreed. "We're only going to keep running into each other and getting hurt, the longer we stay at this." He squinted through the driving snow to point out a rock outcropping at the foot of the slope. "Let's make for those rocks."

The wind swirled around the edges of the formation, leaving a space where the snow had banked up in the mouth of an overhang. Leaving their skis, they cast around the nearby spruce and pine trees for dead inner branches, building a tiny fire in the small space. After many attempts, their patience was rewarded. A tongue of flame flickered into life, catching in the few dry pine needles they'd been able to scrounge. Erven glanced at the sky as they carefully added more fuel. "I suppose this wind *is* of some use. No one will see the smoke before it gets blown away."

The others nodded wordlessly, holding their reddened hands out to the fire. Erven joined them, looking at Merald with concern. Their pace had been hard even for him, and he wondered how much longer Merald would be able to keep it up. "I think we'd better make this a longer rest."

Cedric leaned against the rocks. Beyond, the snow whirled past. "It's a good spot, if you think it's safe."

Erven pulled off his gloves and flexed his hands, prickles

of warmth speeding up his arm. "I wonder if the Holdmasters had a hard time assembling a patrol to follow us." He gave the others a wry grin. "With the amount they were drinking, it would've been hard to recall which end of the ski is supposed to point downhill."

"I hope so." Merald fed another branch into the fire, now burning warmly enough to feel against their faces. "I just want to get back to my family, so the priest can speak the words over us. Anneli's been without parents for far too long."

"I want a bath," Cedric commented, shifting so he could sit on an edge of his cloak. "Bath and a hot meal, and daytime guard duty with no storms." He raised an eyebrow at Erven. "What about you?"

"I just wish I could've seen my sister one last time," Erven admitted. "Between the Shona and Rose, I'm expecting to be killed the moment I show my face."

Both of the others shook their heads. "We're not going to let that happen," Cedric protested. "Besides, she's not going to order something like that."

"If she lets me live, she's making sure her authority will be questioned for the rest of her rule." He looked out at the swirling snow, not wanting to meet his friends' eyes. "The Holdmasters have some twisted ideas, but they were right about some things. According to the people, it's only ever going to be her or me."

"Unless you're ruling at her side." Merald flicked a piece of bark into the fire, his expression lending gravity to his tone. "There's no better way to put those rumors to rest."

The idea was so absurd that Erven couldn't help but laugh. "No. Rose wouldn't even consider it."

"Would *you*?"

He wasn't sure if it was just the fire making his face warm. "Maybe, if things had been different." His mind drifted towards that thought, tempting him to envision a world that would never exist now. He shook his head fiercely, driving the image away. "Now, I can't even let myself *think* of it as a possibility."

"I'll lay you odds," Merald said, raising an eyebrow at him. "If she hasn't thought of it, Arielle has."

Erven rolled his eyes. "Fine. You have your bet. I still say it's not likely." He eyed Cedric's pack. "Better get out whatever food we have left. And let's melt some snow. My teeth don't want to go head-to-head with those biscuits again."

24
RETURNING TO LIFE

Rose didn't know how many days and nights she drifted through fevered nightmares. Once or twice, she awoke enough to see Arielle's concerned face, catching brief snippets of worried conversations before delirium dragged her down again.

Worthless. Her foster mother's favorite taunt resounded in her mind. *That girl is worthless.*

"I'm not worthless!"

She fell to her knees on the tower roof, stars opening overhead in an endless dance. Scarves of beautiful light drifted between the stars, their dazzling colors capturing sunset, sunrise, and laughter all at once. She got to her feet in wonder, staring up into the sky.

"You know, there are plenty of people in this life who will hate you."

Erven's voice came from behind her, and she turned to see him standing in the door to the stairwell, the expression on his face heartbreakingly sympathetic.

"What are you doing here?" she stammered, feet taking her unbidden towards the edge of the parapet. "Stay back!"

Panic flashed across Erven's face as a gust of wind caught her. The stars filled her vision as she fell, a scream ripping out of her throat.

A hand clamped around her wrist.

Erven pulled her back onto the tower, his voice firm. "Rose, you're strong enough to face them. Don't add your own hatred to theirs."

"Rose?"

The stars dissolved into the curtains around her bed, Arielle appearing in her field of view. Lines of concern and relief etched the healer's face as she asked, "Can you hear me?"

Rose's voice came out a raw-throated croak. "I think so." She pushed herself to her elbow to see around her room. Fire crackled in the hearth, and the air was filled with medicinal smells. "How long have I been asleep?"

"It's been days." Arielle sat on the bed next to her and laid a gentle hand against her forehead. "Your fever's gone down, though."

"You were yelling at things we couldn't see." Rose hadn't realized Heather was in the room until she appeared around the curtains to sit next to Arielle. Her friend's sweater was pushed to her elbows, and her curls tumbled in disarray around a faded pink scarf. "You had us scared for a wee bit."

"Where's Willow?"

Heather and Arielle exchanged a wary glance. "She's... out," Heather said at last. "Taking care of things, like."

"Oh." Rose slumped back against her sweat-soaked pillow, wondering what else had happened. "The highlands?"

"It's better if you rest now," Arielle said. She drew a curtain halfway across the bed as Heather got up reluctantly. "There'll be time later to talk. I'm just glad you're back with us, dear one."

OVER THE NEXT TWO DAYS, the fever waned enough for Rose to sit up in bed for longer periods. Her chest burned like fire as a cough set in, keeping her awake for hours at night. One night, the coughing was enough to wake Arielle, who only sighed and swung the kettle over the fire before wrapping Rose's shawl tighter around her shoulders.

"I'm sorry," Rose said once she'd caught her breath. "I know you're tired."

"It's all right. We were expecting something like this would happen, even if you weren't." Arielle brushed Rose's hair back from her forehead. "You've carried a heavy burden this winter."

The thought made Rose slump back against her pillow. "I keep thinking I should be used to it by now."

Arielle made a sympathetic noise. "The responsibilities of the crown reach into every part of your life, and you're never the same afterwards." The healer laughed softly as she stirred up the fire. "Your mother always said her crown felt heaviest when she *wasn't* wearing it."

Rose coughed again, her shoulders shaking under the strain. Once the fit had passed, she asked, "I thought my father was the king."

"He was..." Arielle's voice faded into memory. After a long moment, she straightened from the fire and came to sit on the end of Rose's bed. "Your father was the heir to the throne, but his ties to his clan ran deep. The Thinar proposed marriage between him and your mother, to settle a feud that was tearing the highlands apart. She felt the weight of his crown long before they married." Arielle ran her hands thoughtfully over the covers, smoothing out wrinkles as she said, "Your father had the aspen leaf made—it was the symbol of our house, just like the star was of his—and sent to her as a betrothal gift." Arielle chuckled. "It stayed in her box until their wedding day. She had spirit, and I'm glad your father recognized it. Once she put it on—once she chose him, like he'd chosen her—she didn't take it off until your christening day."

Rose flattened a hand against her collarbone. She could just barely feel the edges of the aspen leaf pendant under her shift. "I wish I could have known her like you did. When I think of my parents, I feel so much closer to her than to my father."

"I notice you stopped wearing his necklace," Arielle said softly.

"Yes. A while ago." Rose looked uncomfortably at the tiny box sitting next to her circlet. Inside, her father's gold star necklace lay curled in a fabric nest. She cleared her throat. "He seemed so distant. And once I found out what the Thinar clan thought of our family—" She stopped, looking at her lap as heat crept up her face.

"Your father did everything he could to protect the people he loved," Arielle said resolutely. "There's no better marker of a true king than that. Those that claim he was a failure don't understand that real power lies in saving lives, not taking them." The older woman cupped Rose's cheek in a work-roughened palm. "And those who claim your bloodline is weak don't know you. You've proved everyone wrong time and time over, by doing all the things you believed you couldn't."

Rose finally fell back asleep after a cup of tea. Her dreams remained peaceful, Arielle's last reassurance seeping through her mind. "Your parents loved each other and their people. Whatever path you choose, you'll have made them proud."

WILLOW WIPED charcoal dust away from her face as she straightened up from a box of parsnips and onions. Their arrival just before the storm had been fortuitous, even if the extra manpower strained the sleeping quarters to the maximum. During the storm, they'd still made progress towards repairs; progress that now could proceed rapidly as the wind abated.

Gathering up the hem of her tunic to contain the vegetables, Willow picked up a wooden bowl with her other hand and set everything on the narrow work table. Out in the storm room, a door slammed, then slammed again as the wind rattled it in the frame. Carina, the outpost commander, banged the inner door behind her as she peeled an icy mask from her face.

"How are things in here?"

"Practically summery," Willow answered as she began chopping the vegetables. Between the storm, feeding everyone, and interviewing as many of the Shona as she could, she felt like she hadn't slept in days. Even in the hours she managed to snatch, her mind replayed the previous day's conversations, troubles, and worries until she awoke to begin again. "Are we able to move between buildings again?"

"Tait and the others just finished clearing the paths." Carina picked up the end of a parsnip and took a bite. "I told them to build the snow up into a bulwark." She shook her head, her good eye calculating. "I don't think anyone will attack again, but if they do…"

"They'll find about twice as many fighters here as they were expecting." Willow dumped the chopped vegetables into the pot over the fire. "But something tells me they won't. Whatever message they meant to send has been very effectively communicated." She thumped the knife onto her chopping board. "I'll finish talking with everyone today, and we'll get out of your sleeping quarters as soon as we can."

"Take your time," Carina said around the last bite of her snack. "We'll survive tight quarters for another few days. I just stopped in to tell you I'm taking the patrol this morning." She brushed melting ice from her scarf. "I know Tait and Ansel do a good job, but I want to keep my good eye on my own woods."

Willow frowned as the outside door rattled again. "It's still storming. Even if it *is* dying out, you're still going to patrol?"

"We got caught off guard once," Carina said grimly, the scar across her face catching the firelight as she left the kitchen. "I'm not willing to let it happen again."

THEY MUST HAVE MISSED the quartz cliffs, Erven thought. On their last rest, they'd eaten the last of their food, huddled miserably in a scruffy aspen thicket. As they staggered up again for another push down the mountain, Erven hoped they hadn't overshot Whitecaps. *Or worse,* he thought as he wriggled freezing fingers in snow-caked gloves. *What if we've gone the wrong way altogether?* He glanced back at Merald, his friend's movements growing more dogged with each passing hour. *If we don't find more permanent shelter and food soon, we'll be in serious trouble.*

Not for the first time, the thought crossed his mind of striking out to find Whitecaps on his own. As another blast of wind struck, forcing him to dig in his poles to keep his balance, he once again decided against it. *We stand a better chance of surviving if we stay together.*

A sound pierced through his cold-numbed mind. The others heard it as well, stopping and drawing instinctively closer to each other.

"What was that?" Merald asked over the wind.

Erven hadn't expected how warm he would feel at that sound. "A signal!" With numb fingers, he fumbled in his jacket for the string on which he kept his carved-bone whistle. Fishing it to his lips, he drew a deep breath and blew the Shona signal for 'help'. Over and over, he blew the signal, straining his ears between each blast for a response.

Before the snow could accumulate further on their shoulders and hoods, they all heard the responding call. "That way!" Cedric shouted, pointing down the mountainside.

They pushed in the direction of the signal with renewed energy, shouting greetings as the Whitecaps patrol appeared out of the snow. Erven's relief mixed with fear as one of them shouted in alarm and readied a sling. He dropped his poles and threw his hands out where they could be seen. "Don't! We're friends!"

"Don't touch your weapons!" A voice he recognized as

Carina's cut through the dying wind. "Commander, drop the sword."

With stiff hands, Erven unbuckled his sword belt and passed it back to Cedric. The Shona moved forward warily, their eyes stern over masks and scarves as they surrounded the three of them. Erven kept his hands out as Carina approached, belt knife poised to attack. "What are you doing here? You know what's happened, right?"

Time to start putting things to rights. "I heard. But you're going to have to believe me when I say they acted without my knowledge."

Cedric looked up from tightening the bindings on his boot. Beside him, Merald had sunk to his knees in the snow. "We need to keep moving. They're coming after us."

"What?" Carina exclaimed. Her head snapped up to examine the mountainside behind them. "How many?"

"We don't know how many, or how close behind us they are." Erven winced as he thought of the guard he'd wounded. "But they'll be angry."

Carina's good eye narrowed over her scarf as she surveyed the three of them. "The outpost's less than an hour away. Can you make it?"

Erven looked over at Merald and Cedric. Knowing he was under discussion, Merald raised his head defiantly. "I'll be fine." He dug his poles into the snow. "I want to get out of this wind."

"Good enough. Help them, you lot. Let's get moving." As the patrol helped Merald to his feet, Carina turned back to Erven. "Commander, I'm not letting you into the outpost unless it's as a prisoner."

He blinked, startled. "They'll be coming after us any time, and you're worried about that?"

"A week ago, I'd have rejoiced that you were back, and safe." Bitter distrust filled her voice as she held up her hunting knife. "Now, I'm torn between hearing your story and putting this through your throat right now. If it weren't for the fact that the Holdmasters are slipperier than oil on glass, we wouldn't even have given you a chance to surrender."

"There's more to the story than you realize, but I can't expect you to listen." Erven's heart sank as the last of the patrol disappeared into the valley below. *There's nothing stopping her from killing me right now.* He took the risk of lowering his hands. "Whatever you decide to do, just promise me you'll warn the queen."

"Warn her?"

"The Holdmasters aren't interested in just removing her from the throne." Erven kept his eyes locked on Carina's as he said, "They wanted me to kill her. Now that I've left them, I don't know what they might do. You're within your rights to kill me after what I've done, but please make sure she's warned."

"That sounds more like the person I trust." Carina's stern voice weakened, and she slid the knife back into its sheath. Tears welled up in her eyes, and she unexpectedly clapped him on the shoulder. "We've got to get you back. For your own safety, though, we'd best let everyone see you're not a threat."

"At least let me get downhill with my hands free." He picked up his ski poles. "I'll only slow us down if I'm falling all over the mountainside."

They rapidly caught up to the rest of the patrol before making their way into the valley guarded by the quartz cliffs. At the bottom of the hill, Carina stopped him. "It's time."

Erven held his hands out to Carina, glad that his gloves tempered the feeling of rope around his wrists as she pulled the knots tight.

"I'm sorry," she whispered.

"It's not your fault."

Carina sniffed hard and wiped her eyes before putting a hand firmly around his upper arm. Word had spread ahead of them, and Erven felt the pressure of many eyes as Carina stopped him in the clearing. Men sat astride the ridgepoles of one of the smaller buildings, hammers echoing across the outpost as they worked to secure a temporary roof above the scorched walls. His anger mixed with guilt as he recognized the newcomers as castle guardsmen. *Rose knows, then. Carina's probably disobeying orders, leaving me alive.*

His confrontation with Rose's allies came faster than expected, as a person with blonde hair and a large apron marched out of one of the earth-banked buildings. He'd seen Willow angry before, but the fury in her movements made him take a surprised step back.

"You bastard!"

The slap rattled his jaw and set him off balance enough that Carina had to brace his shoulder. He barely had time to gather his wits before Willow was yelling in his face. "D'you have any idea of what we've been going through trying t'clean up your mess?" She slapped him again, hard enough that it sent tears to his eyes. "Rose hasn't been sleeping because of you! Did you even *think* of what this would do to her?!"

"All right, that's enough," Carina ordered, putting a hand out to stop Willow from hitting him again.

"No, she has a point." He blinked back the tears. "I deserve it."

"Frogs and toads, yes you do." Willow's fierce hug was more unexpected than the slap had been as she confessed, "We've been so worried about you." Her stormy eyes filled with tears as she let go of him. "Please don't tell me I have to go back to Rose and tell her you're her enemy."

"He's been trying to keep her safe this whole time," Cedric said, hefting skis and poles off his shoulder and leaning them against a sawhorse. "Don't be too hard on him."

"It was difficult for all of us." Merald was leaning against one of the trees, lines of exhaustion etching his face as he pulled his scarf down. "You have no idea..." His voice faded off as a spasm of pain crossed his face.

Erven yanked his shoulder free from Carina. He caught Merald on bound wrists just as his friend lost his balance.

"Easy, Mate. I've got you." He looked back over his shoulder at Willow and Carina. "We can debate my actions for hours, but he needs rest and maybe a healer." He nodded his thanks as Cedric hurried over to take Merald's weight on a broad shoulder. "I don't want his wife to kill me after I promised I'd keep him safe."

"Lucky that Rose sent healers with us." Willow nodded towards the stone building. "And one healer in particular is going to be relieved to see you." She smiled at Merald.

"Tora? She's here?" Merald revived some as Cedric began helping him towards the stone building.

"Here and busy, yes. They weren't interested in a slaughter, but it was still bloody." Willow crossed her arms over the apron, and Erven was briefly reminded of her tactician father. "So, your allies?"

"Not my allies," Erven insisted. "Not that anyone'll believe me."

"Allies or not, do they know you're here?"

One of the ropes had slid onto his skin when he caught Merald. Erven twisted his wrist, grimacing at the feeling of rough nettle fibers. "They'll know I've left by now. Like I told Carina, they'll be close behind us. And they'll be angry."

"There'll be the kraken to pay," Willow said. "Assuming you're really back for good."

The question rang in the clearing, and he was aware of everyone watching them. The other Shona's hands had gone to their weapons when he'd pulled away from Carina, but otherwise they'd been content to watch with suspicion. More than one face looked conflicted as he took a deep breath and settled his shoulders.

"I'm back."

MERALD BARELY NOTICED the continuing cold as Cedric helped him up the steps of the Whitecaps building. Voices came from inside, unfamiliar tones mixing with a voice that sang to him of hearth and home. He could almost ignore the throbbing in his side and the dizziness sweeping his head as he caught the familiar crisp cadence of Tora's 'business' voice.

"—See about getting the woodpiles renewed again." Tora emerged into the storm room with another Shona healer, her dark hair tucked messily under a cap and sleeves pushed to her elbows. Her hurried steps faltered as she saw him. "Merald."

Merald shook off Cedric's helping hand as she rushed to him, the two of them colliding in a frantic embrace.

"You're safe!" she cried into his shoulder. "You're safe! How did—" She pulled her head back to look first at him, then past him towards the courtyard. "Is Erven with you? Did he have anything to do with this?"

"Don't be too hard on him." Merald tipped her chin up to kiss her gently. "He saved our lives."

"I'd argue, but you're here." Tora hugged him again, her arms tightening suddenly as a wash of dizziness overcame his vision and made him stagger. Her voice filled with worry as his head cleared. "Are you hurt?"

"Not hurt," Merald managed to reassure her as Cedric steadied him again. "Just tired."

Somehow, Tora and Cedric ushered him back into the hall, filled with the voices of healers and smells of medicines and smoke. Once sitting on the edge of a makeshift bed, the pain he'd been holding at an unsteady arm's length came rushing back, and he collapsed back onto the cot.

Cedric's voice came from a far distance. "Will he be all right?"

Tora's hand lay comfortingly across his forehead as she answered, "He's pushed himself too hard. He needs to rest."

"I'll tell Erven. I'm just glad he made it back here." Cedric's hand brushed Merald's arm. "Rest, Mate. Let us handle things from here."

The rest of the infirmary sounds faded as Merald fell asleep, his last conscious memory the sound of Tora's voice.

"Sleep, my love. I've got you."

WILLOW RETURNED TO HER COOKING, throwing her frustration into messily butchering the rabbits retrieved from the trap lines. Dumping the carcasses into her stockpot, she began mixing dumpling dough, all the while feeling her headache increase. "You really need to get some sleep, Old Thing," she said to herself as the last chunk of dough landed in the stew. "You're going to do something you'll regret if you don't."

Making sure the fire was burning warm enough to keep the stock simmering, Willow settled against the rapidly slimming sack of oats to close her eyes briefly. She awoke to shouts and whistles, and the sounds of running feet outside. Muttering a word that would have made Violet blush, she staggered up from her nap, pushing hair back into her bun and wondering how late it was. She was just untying her apron when the storm door crashed open.

"Patrol's back," Carina said. She pulled her hood back, revealing armor under her cloak. "There's a highland force coming this way."

"Frogs," Willow cursed. She dropped the apron on the table and swung the stew away from the fire. "Where do you want me?"

"Go help Tora barricade the infirmary. Do whatever you can to stop them from getting to the wounded." Carina tugged the straps holding her shoulder armor, her good eye wide and frightened. "And pray they don't get that far."

Willow grabbed her bag and followed Carina out of the kitchen. As the outer door closed behind her, she saw the sky was thick with clouds, and growing darker by the second. The guards she'd brought from the castle were streaming out of the living quarters, buckling armor and undoing the catches on sword hilts. Outside the main building, several archers carefully unfurled bowstrings and checked quivers. As Willow was about to go in, a sudden thought caught at her mind. "Carina!"

The commander turned around. "What?"

Her heartbeat pounding in her throat, Willow raced back down the steps to ask, "Erven. Where is he?"

Carina's forehead wrinkled. "In one of the barracks. Last I checked, he and Cedric were both sound asleep. You think I should get him?"

Willow shivered as a gust of wind rippled the temporary canvas roofs on the buildings. "Sleeping or not, he needs to be out here. If he's on their side, they might back off if they see him. But if he's for us, we need him." Both women jumped as a horn sounded on the mountainside overhead, sending a shock through Willow's bones.

"Get inside," Carina ordered. "I'll find him."

25
RETALIATION

Erven had fallen into a dreamless sleep immediately after changing into dry clothes. Despite his exhaustion, he jolted to his feet as Tait burst into the room. "What's going on?"

Tait seized him in a bear hug, saying, "Cedric told us everything. I'm so sorry I doubted you." Letting him go, the younger man asked, "Are you fit enough to fight?"

Shouts from outside pierced through his sleep-fogged mind. *They're already here.* "How many?"

Tait handed him his sword. "Patrol just tumbled in. There're almost a hundred of them, coming this way fast." He stopped with a hand on the doorframe, sudden caution furrowing his brow under the fringe of his hair. "You're not —"

"I'm coming." Erven picked up his jacket and jammed his arms through the sleeves. "Don't worry. They crossed the line when they decided hurting my family was a good idea."

A crooked smile crossed Tait's face. "You have no idea

how good it is to hear that. Meet us up by the top trap line once you're ready."

The door banged behind Tait as the younger man left. Erven's fingers were stiff, and his muscles even stiffer as he did up the buckles on his armor, hauling his sword belt over his head. He briefly considered the importance of a hood before a muffled horn call pierced through the earthen walls. *They're coming for me. I'm not going to hide.*

Tugging the laces on his bracers tight, he emerged from the barracks just as Carina came running from the main building, her hair standing up in cowlicks around her hairline. "Good, you're here."

"I can't say I blame you for worrying." Erven slid his sword belt into a better spot on his shoulder. "Where are Merald and Cedric?"

Worry flickered across Carina's face. "Cedric's with Tait and the others. Merald's—Merald's still sleeping." She sighed. "He had a fever, and Tora said he's beyond exhausted."

Erven shook his head, apprehension twisting in his stomach. "I hope this wasn't too much for him, but we really had no choice." He looked up at the ridge over Whitecaps. "Tait asked me to help reinforce up by the top trap line."

"Follow his lead," Carina ordered. "And remind them that the mountains still have teeth."

Erven smiled. It was a phrase that had seen them through a number of raids in previous years. "Don't worry. My teeth are still sharp." He saluted her and hurried towards the trail leading out of Whitecaps, boots crunching on the snow left by the sheepkiller storm.

Tait met him in the pines near the top of the ridge. "They'll have to come down this way." He motioned to a pair of archers, obscured in their cloaks atop a rock over-looking the trail. "We'll see how many they can pick off."

Erven was about to answer when a whistle cut through the wind. The Shona defenders fell quiet, peering through the growing twilight for the first signs of their opponents. Suddenly, his eye caught a flash of green and yellow through the trees. "On the left! There!"

He drew his sword as the archers loosed overhead. The arrows hissed through the trees. A man shouted in the distance, and another horn called from somewhere beyond. Suddenly, the rocks that had provided cover felt looming, and a sixth sense made him wheel to see running figures breaking onto the path towards the outpost.

"Behind us!"

Tait swore as they readied their swords and ran to engage. In the darkness below the ridge, Erven didn't recognize the first highlander he downed, but the voices all sounded familiar after the months at Hold Aubron. The next man managed to get inside his guard, landing a blow with a club on his upraised arm guard. Pain lanced up his arm as he stumbled back in the snow, fear lending his next slash extra strength. The highlander tumbled backwards down the slope as Erven scrambled to his feet. Below them, he could hear yells from the outpost as the archers began choosing targets.

"There're still wounded in the outpost," he yelled to Tait. "We've got to pull back."

Tait freed his sword from a corpse with a growl. "Signal it, then! Hell's teeth, man, don't ask me!"

Ducking behind a tree, Erven fished his whistle from under his jacket. Drawing a deep breath, he blew the signal for 'retreat' three times. All over the mountainside, the defenders disengaged or slew their attackers and took off running back towards Whitecaps. Within seconds, Erven had vaulted over the snow wall surrounding the clearing. His muscles protested as he landed, reminding him just how little time he'd had to rest.

"Hold your ground here!" he shouted, gesturing along the snowbank. "Don't let them reach the wounded." The castle guards responded first, crouching behind the bank and readying their weapons. A flurry of conflicted looks went among the Shona before several of them sheathed swords and pulled out slings, taking cover behind the trees and around the buildings.

Tait joined him at the center of the embankment, both of them watching the treeline while they caught their breath. Hastily lit torches cast their shadows long and black in front of them, flickering back and forth with each puff of wind. As the highlanders emerged from the trees and into the pool of light, Shona slingstones and arrows downed man after man. Those that made it to the edge of the outpost met their match in the snowbank defenders, as dozens of men slumped unconscious or dead just outside the outpost boundary.

Erven estimated the invading force had been whittled down to less than a third of their original number when a handful of enemies burst from the darkness. After sending a man backwards over the snowbank, Erven stepped back between Tait and Cedric. Lines of blood traced down Tait's face from a cut somewhere high in his hairline, and Cedric looked as exhausted as Erven felt.

"Signal everyone to press forward." Erven eyed the highlanders, noticing several with frightened expressions as they engaged the castle guards. "If they want to run, let them."

Tait wiped blood from his eye before pulling out his whistle. "I think one of their leaders is back there somewhere."

"I know." Erven wiped his sword against the snowbank, leaving a bloody smear on the trampled snow. "I'm going after him."

"I'm right behind you." Cedric said, catching his breath.

Erven vaulted over the snowbank and ran into the darkness under the trees. Behind him, Tait's signal sounded across the outpost, echoing eerily from the surrounding mountains. The defenders pressed forward with a roar, sending many of their attackers running.

Erven blinked hard in the darkness, straining his eyes for a glimpse of the highland leader. In the hubbub of shouted orders and battle cries, he caught sight of one of the Hold Aubron leaders. The man was standing just inside the tree-line, trying unsuccessfully to rally his panicking men.

Time for us to send a message back. Erven crashed through a snow-covered bush to hurtle into the man, knocking him back towards Whitecaps. The Aubron leader cursed and attacked with a snarl. Erven smashed the sword aside, knocking it from the man's hands and sending it to land several feet away in the snow. Before the highlander could react further, Cedric crashed into him, throwing him backwards to the ground. As the rest of the defenders reached them, Erven planted a foot on the man's chest.

"I have a message for your masters." Erven rested his sword blade an inch away from the man's throat. "You sent out the call to moot, and we'll be there. If you try to back down now, the entire highlands will see your true cowardly colors." He bent down, locking eyes with the highlander. "And no tricks. Let the people decide without your poisonous intervention. But hear this—" He gestured at the Shona surrounding them, voice going deathly cold. "These people are my clan. If you *dare* attack them again, I swear I'll destroy that tower of yours so completely that no single stone stands on top of another." He removed his sword and stepped back, letting the man scramble away. "Now, get out of Shona territory."

As the remaining highlanders retreated through the trees, Erven raised his voice to the defenders. "Get them out of here."

Most of the Shona began scattering into the trees, followed by the castle guards. Tait came over and thumped his shoulder. "Well said, mate." He gestured back towards Whitecaps. "We'd better check over the ones down there for survivors."

As Erven followed Tait back down the hill and began checking the dead highlanders, the exhaustion from before returned. By the time they were finished dealing the mercy strike to those highlanders too badly wounded to live, his muscles were shaking, and his head spun when he stood or moved too rapidly.

"You need a rest," Cedric commented as he steadied himself against a tree.

"So do you," Erven retorted, hurriedly standing upright. "I can't rest yet." He gestured at the Shona working alongside the castle men. Though busy, a few of them had paused to exchange words or clap him on the shoulder as he passed. "They're more open to me being back, but if they see me relaxing while there's still work to be done..."

"You *both* need a rest." Tait had visited the healers inside the main building. A bandage circled his head, making his dark hair stand on end around the edges. He lit one of the torches he'd been carrying, sticking it into the snow beside a guttering one before straightening with a groan. "*I need a rest, and I didn't just spend three days running and fighting for my life.*" He raised an eyebrow at Erven. "You do make a habit of that, though. If I recall, you only gave yourself a few days to recover after being beat half to death."

Erven snorted. "All right, it's a bad habit." He blinked hard, a roaring noise filling his ears. "You're right. I—I need to sleep. Badly."

"Go sleep, then." Tait waved him towards the barracks. "We'll finish cleaning up."

Erven felt like he was moving through deep water as he unbuckled his armor in the sleeping quarters, setting it next to his bedding to be cleaned properly. The dizziness started again, making his vision swim as he sat at the edge of the sleeping platform. He barely had time to get his boots off and pull his feet onto the platform before foggy blackness claimed him.

THE SICKNESS HAD LEFT Rose feeling as shaky and weak as a newborn lamb. A full ten days after first taking ill, she finally returned to her office. While a small part of her resented Arielle's keeping the news of the Whitecaps attack from her, she couldn't deny that Heather had done admirably in keeping up with the chaos. Reports from the Shona indicated that no further incursions had come from the highlands, and she hoped Willow would take it as a reason to return home soon. *We never properly made up. I hope she's not still angry at me.*

By the time she had finished responding to letters,

following up on small issues around the castle, and composing an edict to allow the Watchmen more resources to pursue the ruffians who'd targeted the Sea Wanderers, Rose found herself wishing she'd taken another day or two to resume work slowly. She locked her box and slipped the key under her dress, fingers tangling in her necklace. With a sigh, she pulled the aspen pendant out and smoothed the chain over her collarbone.

The aspen is a symbol of my mother's house, and the star is the symbol of my father's. These weren't just christening gifts, they're the legacy of a marriage that ended in sacrifice. They had no idea what would happen the night they sent me away. She mused on the thought as she wandered down the tower steps. *The man they entrusted me with could've delivered me straight to their enemies.* Her footsteps faltered on the last turn of the stairwell. *I can't imagine the type of trust that must've taken.*

The hum of castle life carried on around her as she directed her steps to the chapel. Inside, it was dark and quiet, a single lamp burning behind the altar. Like at the Sea Wanderer embassy, the columns holding the roof were intricately carved. Simple benches lined either side of the sanctuary, nestled between the columns and facing the altar. Rose sank down on the front bench, propping her elbows on her knees and examining the altar. The burnished wood frame bore the marks of years of loving care, even as the block of roughly hewn stone inside remained unaltered by time.

Almighty, I'm at my heart's end. Rose closed her eyes, the peace of the place seeping into her tired mind. *I'm trying to lead these people the right way, but it's so hard when I can't find the confidence that I'm doing the right thing.*

"It's peaceful here, isn't it?"

The voice made her jump in the stillness, opening her eyes to see Arielle walking up the aisle behind her. The healer was carrying a wreath of pine boughs, which she set on the altar.

"I'm sorry, I thought no one was here," Rose immediately apologized.

"It's all right. I know you usually find solace on top of the tower, but this is where I come." Arielle sat on the bench across from her, arranging her skirts neatly around her feet. "When I feel things slipping from my grasp—don't laugh, they do." She raised an eyebrow at Rose, who did her best to erase the smile from her face. "I come here, and bring my trouble before the Almighty."

"I've spent more time here recently," Rose said, turning her face back towards the altar. "Mostly asking if he made a mistake, letting me be born."

Arielle didn't answer for a long time. Finally, just as Rose thought the healer hadn't heard her, Arielle said, "The Almighty doesn't make mistakes. He knew Illyn would need you specifically to lead her—the daughter of two strong houses who values life and decency after decades of occupation and infighting."

"Birth or not, I can't do this." Rose muttered. "Just as I think I can, I fail miserably."

"Your father didn't rule on his own." Arielle's voice was sympathetic but firm as she reminded Rose, "He had your mother and the clans behind him." She looked at the floor sadly. "It's not his fault they abandoned us."

"And there's the problem." Rose crossed her arms over her middle. "My father's allies abandoned him, but I keep pushing everyone away. I apologized to Willow before I got sick, but she's still up at Whitecaps, and I just know it's because she's still angry at me. She'd never be away this long if she weren't." She fixed her gaze stubbornly on the lamp burning behind the altar.

"Well, there's another explanation," Arielle said. Something in her voice made Rose turn and look properly at her advisor. "We've just had word from Hollow. Willow's there with the rest of the men."

"That's wonderful, I suppose." Rose clasped her hands in her lap. "But why hasn't she just come straight home?"

Arielle's words fell into the peaceful chapel like raindrops onto dusty ground. "She's not alone. There's been another attack on Whitecaps." Rose had barely enough time to take in the statement before Arielle added, "Apparently, the Holdmasters didn't take well to their puppet king deserting them."

Rose buried her face in her hands. Her voice squeaked. "He's safe?"

"As safe as can be." Arielle moved to stand behind Rose, gentle hands warm against her shoulders. "Merald's ill, and still at Whitecaps with Tora, but Cedric's with Erven and the others. And from what Willow says, Erven fought hard to keep the highland forces from the outpost." She squeezed Rose's shoulders. "They're waiting at Hollow until you give the word for them to return."

Rose turned to look up at Arielle. "I don't know if I should." She tried to keep the panic out of her voice. "Strictly speaking, I should be ordering the Shona to kill him right now."

Arielle's shoulders stiffened. "I think you need to hear his story before you make any decision like that." She regained her composure and stepped back, gesturing at the altar. "I'll let you be for now. Take some time and pray on it."

As the sound of Arielle's footsteps faded, Rose stepped forward to examine the altar. *She left a wreath.*

It was a pine wreath, just like the ones she'd learned to make. Heart-shaped ivy leaves twined through the evergreen sprigs. Old woodcraft lessons made their way back through her mind, and her eyes prickled as she understood the symbolism. *It's a gratitude offering.*

Rose sank to her knees and rested her head on the rough stone of the altar. Her whisper was so faint it barely carried to her own ears. "Thank you for keeping him safe." Her voice grew hoarse under tears she refused to let fall. "I trust You. Please, help me to make the right decisions." After letting the words sink into the stillness, she gathered her skirts and stood, leaving the wreath on the altar.

Less than an hour later, a rider emerged from the castle gates, following the road towards the mountains. Rose watched him disappear into the woods before leaving the parapet. *Things are set in motion. I only hope it was the right thing to do.*

26

BITTERSWEET HOMECOMING

Their ride from Hollow to the castle had been tense and quiet, each person wrapped in their own thoughts and fears. Erven had become a better rider over the last two years, but he still preferred to trust his own feet for the journey back and forth from Hollow. As the tower came into sight, he shifted in the saddle uncomfortably.

"Don't be afraid," Willow said from his right. "I don't know what will happen, but I know Rose. She's had a rough time of it, but her heart's still good."

Erven didn't bother correcting Willow as to the source of his discomfort. The castle rose before them as they emerged from the forest, sounds of daily life faintly filtering through the trees. On their left, the sea glimmered under the late morning sun.

A drum sounded somewhere behind the walls. Counting the guards on the wall, he calculated their numbers had doubled since the last time he'd been home. *Is that normal now, or is it because they're nervous about me?* With a waved signal from the guard captain, the group slowed their horses to a walk just outside the gates. Crossing under the gatehouse, Erven looked up through the murder holes to see the tense faces of several guards. He was suddenly glad he'd given Tait his sword. *If they're nervous, seeing me carrying a weapon would do nothing to reassure them.*

The horses knew the way to the stables. As they increased their pace across the courtyard, another drum sounded. Erven twisted in his saddle, looking back as the ironclad gates swung closed. He locked eyes with Tait, just swinging down from his saddle. "What's going on?"

Tait's gaze flickered from guards, to gates, and back again. "I don't know. They're probably making sure we weren't followed."

Or making sure that I don't have an escape route. Erven dismounted, patting his horse's shoulder gratefully. "Thanks for not dumping me in the snow, old fellow."

"Commander?"

It was a guard captain, his face stern as he approached at the head of a squad of three. The rope in the hands of one of them confirmed Erven's suspicions. Humiliation swept over him in a dizzying flood. *You can't have expected anything different,* he told himself as he looked around for someone to take his horse. *Even if they know about the second attack, they have no reason to believe me.*

He barely noticed Tait and the others handing their horses off to the hostlers and leaving the stable as the guards bound his hands behind his back. Unlike Carina, they weren't careful to keep the rope off his skin. Tears pricked at his eyes, and he fiercely blinked them back before anyone saw.

"This way." One of the men began leading him towards

the courtyard. Sunlight stung his eyes as he looked up at the tower, catching a glimpse of someone in a red dress standing at the battlements. *She knows I'm here.*

He dragged his attention from the tower as the guard captain opened the storm door of the chapel. "Where are you taking me?"

"You're to wait here," the man explained, prodding him inside. "Guards will be on every entrance. Don't do anything stupid."

Erven nodded silently, waiting for his eyes to adjust as the door closed behind him. A few lamps flickered farther inside the chapel, but the entryway remained dark. Clothing rustled in the gloom, and relief washed over him as he recognized Arielle's voice.

"You're home."

The rope around his wrists fell away. Eyes finally adjusted, he turned to see Commander Ricar standing behind him. "Sorry about the theatrics." The man sounded uneasy, and Erven couldn't blame him. "Her Majesty wanted you out of sight as fast as possible."

"It's all right," Erven automatically answered. He hurried over to Arielle, catching her up in a tight hug. "I'm home." Something cracked inside him, and he buried his face in her shoulder, voice choking with tears long held back. "I'm so sorry," he sobbed. "I didn't have any other choice! They would've killed them all if I hadn't done it!"

"Easy, now," Arielle said soothingly. She rubbed the back of Erven's head like she had when he was small. "You did the right thing."

"Take some time," Commander Ricar said before stepping out the door. "I'll go see what's to be done now."

Erven took a shuddering breath as Arielle released him,

reaching up to wipe his tears with the edge of her sleeve. "I'm glad you're safe." Her hand paused against his cheek, and she laughed briefly. "You have no idea how relieved I was to see you make that fist."

His own laugh felt tight in his chest. "It was the only way I could think of to get your attention. If Rose had sent anyone else, it wouldn't have worked."

"It did what it needed to," Arielle reassured him. "It made me stop and question everything we'd heard."

"Aye, and once Rose learned there was some kind of hope, she was so relieved she took ill," Heather said as she came in, Tait at her side.

"What?"

Heather genuflected towards the altar before leaning against one of the columns. Although he'd known all along that she was Rose's age, the new maturity in her voice rammed it home. "She's been through it, mate. I think the worst was when we saw the seal with the tower crossed by wings. We didn't think she'd ever doubt *us*, but it was touch and go for a bit. Does it really surprise you that she'd get sick after all that?"

"I suppose not." Erven sank down on one of the benches. "I wasn't expecting her to let me come back at all. You're saying she's not angry?"

"Oh, she was." Arielle's skirts rustled as she sat next to him. "Confused, certainly. I'd even say... Well, never mind. I'm sure she'll tell you."

"All right..." He looked uncomfortably at the floor. "What now, then? I'm assuming no one wants me anywhere near her right now."

"I'm afraid so," Heather said. "Willow's gone to talk to

her, and you *won't* like whatever solution they come up with. For what it's worth—not that anyone asked—" She winked, making Tait snort with laughter. "I think you're the safest person for her to be around at the moment. And once she gets over her nerves, I think she'll want to see you."

"We'll wait here with you," Tait said. "Until it's time."

Rose leaned against the closed tower door. *He's back. He's really back.* She closed her eyes against the sudden rush of emotion. *I shouldn't be this happy. There are still so many questions I don't have the answers to.*

She opened her eyes and rapidly composed herself at the sound of someone else coming up the tower steps. To her immense relief, Willow's blonde head popped around the corner. "Hallo dear!" She bounded up the last steps to envelop Rose in a strong hug. "I've missed you."

"I've missed you too," Rose said, grateful that her words weren't tempered with dishonesty. "Heather's lovely, but she's just not you."

"I'm sure my office is a wreck, knowing my dearest sister's working habits," Willow said as she released Rose. "We made good time back from Hollow. I think your idea of keeping horses there is definitely something we should keep doing. It made the journey so much shorter."

"That's nice..." Rose let the words trail off as she started down the steps. "How was—"

"He's fine." Willow's boots clattered against the stone. "I think he's scared, but that's all."

"Scared? Erven doesn't get scared—well." Rose bit her lip. "I suppose I'd be scared too, if I were in his boots."

Shaking off the thought, she announced, "I need to talk to him."

"Yes," Willow agreed. "If you're going to regain any kind of working relationship with him, you *do* need to sort things out. That's why I'm here." She brushed past Rose, opening the door at the bottom of the stairwell. "I have an idea of how you can talk with him *and* stay safe yourself, just in case he tries something really stupid."

Rose followed Willow into the corridor leading to her room. "You've been with him this whole week... Do you think he's safe?"

Willow stuffed her hands into her jacket pockets. "Me?" She shrugged. "I'm getting more suspicious as time goes on. After seeing him this last week, and after what he did in the skirmish at Whitecaps, I trust him. But it's like Ethan's said many times over," Willow's voice hardened. "You trust those you need to trust, but have a plan in your sleeve to kill them anyway."

The sun had dropped behind the tower. Rose clenched her hands in the folds of her skirts as she stood at the top of the steps leading into the hall. Across the courtyard, she could see Tait and Arielle, standing in a cluster with a few others near the barracks. Taking a deep breath, she looked up at the archers poised on the wall tops. Even from that distance, Rose could sense their alertness as Erven approached across the snowy courtyard. He stopped within speaking distance of the steps, far enough away that she would be able to retreat inside if he moved suddenly. "Don't worry, I'm not armed."

"And no armor either," she remarked, noticing his navy-blue uniform tunic bore no rank insignia.

"Yes." His gaze flickered to the archers. "If they want to, they'll be able to send those broadheads right through me." His expression bore only resignation as he turned back to her.

"I hope you realize how dangerous this is for me." Rose crossed her arms. "By all rights, you shouldn't even be here. It's only because of your previous history that we're even having this conversation."

"I know," he answered, caution in his eyes. "I wasn't expecting to get this far, actually. I thought you'd send a squad to collect me from Hollow, and from there directly to the dungeon."

"I'm not a tyrant," Rose said bitterly. "And I'm not so paranoid that I'll imprison someone without first hearing their side of the story." She took a few more steps towards him, wondering if the onlookers could hear them. "You were my strongest ally, but every report I've heard in the last few months says otherwise. Everyone says you've decided you're more deserving of this crown than I am." She felt something heavy attach to her next words as she spoke them. "Why should I trust you again?"

He shook his head. "I can't expect you to. I can try to explain, but there's no excuse. The Holdmasters promised that if I complied with their plans, they'd leave my men alone. Once I was in their good graces, I tried directing their plans to ensure peace. I thought they would be satisfied with simply replacing you with me, and no one would have to get hurt." He closed his eyes. "I was wrong."

"Very wrong, I'd say."

"Dangerously, treacherously wrong, yes." Erven opened his eyes, and she was taken aback to see the intensity that filled them. "I didn't realize how wrong until they let it slip that they expected me to kill you myself. They don't want a peaceful transition of power." His voice cracked. "They want you dead, Rose."

Dead.

Rose swallowed hard. Her hand curled around the signal whistle hidden in her skirt. "And you sided with them?"

"Not willingly. If I'd been alone, I'd have fought them to my last heartbeat. With the lives of so many others at stake, I couldn't." His voice lowered. "I did everything I could to stop them from shedding more innocent blood." Erven dropped to one knee in the snow and bowed his head. "I don't have any other defense to make, Your Majesty. I'm not even going to ask for mercy."

Out of the corner of her eye, Rose could see the archers ready to draw their bows. For an instant, her mind teetered between fear and trust. Finally, she brought the whistle to her lips.

ERVEN EXPECTED to hear the snap of bowstrings at any moment, heralding the imminent impact of half a dozen broadhead arrows. Then, the Shona signal 'stand down' sliced through the courtyard. He looked up in surprise to see the archers retreating from the walls. Rose's skirts rustled as she walked down the steps towards him, tucking the signal whistle back into her dress. Strength filled her eyes that hadn't been there the last time they were face to face.

"I can't fault you for trying to save lives. It's been your main concern as long as I've known you. And I can't turn my back on someone who's been so consistently loyal for years." Rose extended her hand, her ring catching the light. "This is your only chance. Prove me wrong, and there won't be mercy."

"I'll do whatever I need to, if it proves I'm worth trusting again," he promised, kissing the back of her hand. "Whatever it takes to reassure our people."

Rose tilted her head as she looked down at him, the sunlight gleaming off her hair and circlet. "It won't be easy. We're going to be dealing with rumors about this for the rest of our lives. But at least now *I* know we're on the same side." She withdrew her hand and stepped back. "Get your proper insignia back on. And armor." Something that could have been fear crossed her face. "I don't want to lose you to our own allies."

Erven got to his feet, damp patches on his trouser knees cold against his legs. "And then..."

Rose straightened her shoulders. "I want to hear the whole story, without so many listening ears." With another swish of skirts, she turned back towards the hall. Her words carried over her shoulder. "Council room, as soon as you're able."

Erven returned across the courtyard to Tait and Arielle, standing in the shadow of the barracks. Tait grinned at Erven, brushing his hair out of his eyes. "Well. I'm glad that went as well as it did."

Erven ran his hands over the plain uniform tunic. "I'm still expecting an arrow through the back any moment," he confessed. "Do you think she really would have done it?"

"I doubt it." Willow lounged against a cistern alongside Heather. Both women's faces bore nothing but relief as she reassured him. "She's too fond of you to do anything really drastic. This was my idea, by the way." A flicker of conniving appeared in her eyes. "This way, no one will be able to say she welcomed you back too easily."

"I suppose not." He dared to asked, "What now?"

"Now, you have to explain everything." She frowned. "And you might not like the questions people ask."

27
SHE'S JUST THAT STUBBORN

"All right."

Erven winced as Willow slapped a weathered parchment onto the table in front of him. Even though he was sitting in his old seat, wearing a tunic with chevrons on the shoulders, this still felt like a trial. Willow's voice was firm as she demanded, "First off, do you have *any* idea of how many horrible things have been done under this seal's authority?"

He swallowed hard at the sight of the Holdmasters' seal —the tower crossed by wings still shocked him as much now as it had the first time he'd seen it. *Brace up and tell them the truth.* "Is there any way you'd believe me if I said I didn't?"

The looks from the others weren't entirely as hostile as he'd expected. Rose sighed and tugged on her circlet. "Try."

"They took my seal soon after we were captured. I didn't even realize it was missing until after I was forced to join them." The weight of his chain mail against his shoulders steadied his nerves enough for him to insist, "I barely saw the new seal either, and they never trusted me enough to let me use it myself." He shook his head. "I have no idea what things might've been done in my name."

This was evidently the right answer. Willow and Rose exchanged a significant look across the room as Commander Ricar leaned an elbow on the table. "So, tell us, then. What *exactly* happened?"

As EXPECTED, the council meeting lasted long into the night. By the time Rose went to bed that night, her lingering tension had been tempered by exhaustion and relief. She found herself immensely grateful for Willow's unshakeable presence over the next few days—her friend's sensible, no-nonsense manner left no room for Erven's newfound skittishness. After several tense days, the ice began to thaw, and he soon sounded more like the person they all remembered. Finally, Rose felt comfortable enough to include him in the day-to-day crises, and their progress against the 'calamity list' increased significantly.

A week after Erven's return, the afternoon sun found Rose once more sitting on Mari's front stoop. "Now that he's back, what are you going to do about that moot?" the old woman asked, her fingers busy around the edge of yet another basket.

Rose swirled the water in the soaking tub. "I don't know," she confessed. "I could just ignore it, but that'll lead to the entire highlands denouncing me. But if we go and they declare him king, I'm stuck right back where I was before, and deeper." She handed Mari a new length of vine, wiping her dripping hand on her skirt. "He said he was expecting me to order his imprisonment or worse, and he had a point." She tipped her face to the clear sky, the air growing warm with the onset of spring. "It's been wonderful having him back, but taking him out of contention would have solved many things."

"Perhaps, but you let him live."

"Yes." Rose sighed, propping her chin in her hand. "I couldn't do it." She snorted. "That doesn't say much about my strength as a ruler."

Mari raised a grey eyebrow at Rose. "We do silly things, don't we, when our hearts get involved with our heads. Take them for example." As Rose shielded her eyes to look in the direction Mari had indicated, she saw Carine coming up the street with Gregor the Watchman. "He's assigned to the harbor post, yet he patrols this street every day, right about the time my widowed daughter goes to refresh the water pails." Mari's eyes twinkled with mischief as she looked back at Rose. "That makes no sense to anyone thinking with their head, but perfect sense to someone who leads with their heart."

Rose squirmed on the step. "Queens shouldn't follow their hearts."

"And by that I take it you mean a queen shouldn't have a heart at all." Mari smacked her with one of the waterlogged vines. Rose yelped as water droplets sprayed everywhere. "Now, I know you've had a nasty time of it, and there's no denying it's enough to make any sane person question everything they know. But Milady, you've spent this whole miserable season trying to make it through on head alone." She dropped the vine and seized Rose's hand. "Take it from a crone who's seen far too many wretched seasons, you'll get nowhere with this or any other problem if you rely on just your head to see you through."

"Maybe so," Rose sighed. "But when it comes to him, I still don't know how I should act. I mean, he seems just like he used to, even if he still doesn't want to talk much..."

Mari gave a short cackle. "Still fox-walking around you, is he? Bring him down here tomorrow, Milady. I'll set him straight for you."

"We're going... to tea?" Erven set down his pen and frowned at Rose, silhouetted in the door of his office with a basket on her hip.

"Tea, yes." She tossed the end of her scarf across her shoulder. "Willow's disappeared into a baking frenzy, so she can't come with like she usually would. And yes, it's an order. I want you to meet Mari."

"All right." Erven capped his inkwell and retrieved his sword from the weapon rack. "Are we walking or riding?"

"Riding," Rose said, a touch of humor in her voice. He'd forgotten she knew exactly how little he enjoyed that activity. "You'll survive."

Riding while wearing chain mail was never a pleasant activity, but Erven grudgingly admitted it was faster than walking the distance from castle to town. After greeting the artisans, warmly on Rose's part and nervously on Erven's, they set a board over an upturned crate for a table and sat down to enjoy the early spring sunlight. The packed snow of winter had turned to slush, and the tops of cobblestones appeared through the veil of water and ice. In the artisans' tiny garden, Erven caught sight of a patch of snowdrops, raising tiny white bells above a layer of dead vegetation.

Spring's here. And the moot's coming fast. He caught

himself before his thoughts went sour. *At least we still have time.*

"So, this is the young man I've heard Milady talk so much about." The older of the two basket-weavers inspected him for a long moment with eyes that had seen decades of hardship. He fought the urge to squirm under her gaze before she smiled, wrinkles softening her scrutiny. "Welcome home, son. You've had many of us worried about you."

"Thank you." He ducked his head, wondering why he felt like a small boy under the woman's eye. "It's wonderful to be home again. I wasn't sure I'd make it back."

"Don't be so quick to doubt Her Majesty, son." Mari handed him a cup of tea, her eyes crinkling around the corners. "She hides it, but she's been just as worried about you as the rest of us."

He wrapped his hands around the cup, glancing towards Rose as she sat on the stoop, circlet glittering in the sunlight. "How long have you been visiting?" he asked her. "The last I knew, you'd stopped riding because of the cold."

"Wintermorn, I think it was." Mari's daughter Carine came out of the shop with a man in a Watchman's uniform. A boy with the gangly limbs and surly expression of youth appeared by her side just long enough to look curiously at Erven before disappearing back into the house.

"Yes, Wintermorn, or just before. Heather deserted me with them." Rose laughed. "She and Willow said it was best I continue, even if I needed more guards than before."

"Thank the Almighty for that." Erven stayed standing beside their makeshift table, reluctant to sit down. *She's been coming here for months. Anyone who wanted to find her would know exactly where to look. Willow's idea this may have been, but I don't think she meant her to get this predictable.*

He looked up the street, somewhat reassured by the positions the guardsmen had taken up. As Rose and Mari began talking animatedly about Rose's last weaving lesson, something in the Watchman's posture caught Erven's eye. Despite being deep in conversation with Carine, the man had also stayed standing, his eyes constantly scanning the street and rooftops. Their eyes briefly met, and the exchange confirmed the Watchman was just as uneasy as he was.

I'll have to talk to her once we get back. Erven leaned against the garden fence, watching Rose's expression as she talked with her friends. *I'm still glad she decided to do this. She's been so alone these last few months; it's good for her to have had someone she could talk to.*

After an hour, most of the tea was gone. Erven had relaxed enough to sit on an upturned bucket a few feet away from Rose, idly listening to her and Mari's conversation. Carine's son hunkered in the doorway, desire for inclusion evidently winning out over suspicion. At the other side of the stoop, the Watchman kissed Carine's cheek and handed her his empty cup before making his farewells. "I've been away from the post for long enough."

"Good watch, Gregor." Rose shaded her eyes to look up at him. "Thank you for joining us!"

"Afternoon, Milady." The Watchman nodded to Erven. "Sir."

"Stay safe." Erven returned the man's salute.

As the Watchman walked away, the boy sitting in the doorway straightened up suddenly, gaze tracking on the rooftops across the street. "Milady?"

The note in the boy's voice sent a hidden sense tingling

through the back of Erven's skull. His fear crystalized in an instant, as a hooded archer appeared from around a chimney, bow drawn, to sight on Rose.

"Milady, duck!"

The boy's shrill treble echoed in Erven's ears as he threw himself sideways off the bucket. Catching the end of the board they'd been using as a table, he flicked it in the air as hard as he could. Rose yelped as the board flew up, her cry mixing with yells from the guardsmen. The yelp turned to a startled scream as Erven grabbed her ankle, yanking her flat onto the slushy cobblestones. The arrow met the board mid-flight, both falling to the stones with a crack as Erven rolled to his feet. "Get inside, quick!"

Rose scrambled backward and into the shop, pulling the others after her.

Down the street, Gregor turned at the shouts, alarm painting his face as he ran back. "What happened?"

"Archer," Erven shouted. Something struck his back, the impact making him gasp with shock and pain. Something ripped at the back of his shoulder, the arrow clattering to the ground as he ducked behind the fence. Throbbing pain spread across his shoulder blade as he peered up at the rooftops. A tense moment later, he sighed with defeat. "They're gone."

"Commotion scared them off, I s'pose." The Watchman was craning his neck as well, looking up at the chimneys before turning his attention to the street once more. "I knew sommat like this'd happen eventually, but she's just that stubborn."

"It runs in her family... her aunt's the same way," Erven answered, waving the guardsmen over. "Get the horses! Hurry!" His eyes barely leaving the rooftops, Erven climbed back over the fence and rapped on the door, calling, "Milady, they're gone. We need to get away from here."

By the time Rose appeared, her face dead white and tense, the two guardsmen were already mounted and had drawn their weapons. Erven boosted Rose into the saddle before clambering into his own, admonishing, "Ride as fast as you can, no matter what happens. Don't slow down, don't turn around, and whatever you do, don't stop."

The horses' hooves clattered on the cobblestones as they broke into a canter. Erven grimly clung to his reins as Rose and the guardsmen's horses rapidly outpaced his, flying up the road towards the castle. Slowing his horse as he entered the gates, he dismounted with a stagger. Tossing his reins to a hostler, he hurried over to Rose's horse.

"Rose."

Some of her color had come back, but she sat as if frozen in the saddle. Wisps of hair had come loose from her braid, sticking to her forehead as she took a shuddering breath. "I'm all right." Working her foot free from her stirrups, she slid off the horse, staggering into him. "I'm all right."

Before he knew it, his arms were around her. "You're safe. Don't be afraid."

He hadn't expected tears, and none came, but he could feel Rose shaking. "Y-you saved my life. Oh!" She tensed and looked up at him, sudden panic appearing in her face. "The second arrow! I heard you get hit—are you hurt?"

He flexed his shoulder, wincing as something stung. "It's not that bad. It's just as well I decided to wear the mail."

"I'll get a healer," Rose automatically said, pulling away from him.

"Don't." He twisted his head to see a rip in his tunic. "I'll go see Arielle about it later."

"Everyone will want to know what happened," Rose said bleakly. "I'd better go explain."

Erven stopped her with a hand on her shoulder. "The guards can explain. I'd rather you calm down, first." He shivered as adrenaline worked its way out of his limbs. "Actually, I think we *both* need to calm down."

They took refuge in the chapel, Rose curling up on one of the benches before the altar. Erven stayed close to the door, his nerves still on fire after their breakneck flight. As the minutes passed, the peace of the place began to sink into his bones. Sinking to one knee, he rested his forearms on the bench in front of him.

Our enemies have always wanted us dead, but now they're targeting her directly. He lowered his head to his arms, feeling as if a glow was spreading from the altar. *I can't do this alone. If she's going to be safe, it'll only be with Your protection.*

No answer came from the altar or to his ears, but Erven's heart settled in the silence. Now that he was sitting still, he could tell his injuries were slight. *I don't think it'll need anything more than to be cleaned. I can probably do that on my own.* Reassured, he walked up the aisle to sit next to Rose.

She quietly cleared her throat. "Which of us were they aiming for?"

"It could have been either of us." He thought back over the trajectory of the arrows and decided, "But I think it was you."

"It's just good Kit saw him..." Rose mused. "Actually, I'm surprised he said anything." She gave a short laugh. "Perhaps he's finally decided I'm worth trusting. How did *you* see him up there?"

Erven shook his head. "I was already on edge when the boy—Kit, you said?—noticed, and I just happened to see him stand up." He sighed. "For everyone's sake, it's probably best if you halt your visits for now."

"I was so enjoying the opportunity to have nice, normal conversations," Rose said. "But you're right."

Both of them jumped as the chapel door banged open. Heather stormed in, her curls bouncing wildly around her face. She made a perfunctory curtsey towards the altar before snapping, "Have *neither* of you any caution? You could've been killed." She glared at him. "It's just as well that was a hunting arrow, not a bodkin, *and* you had mail on. And after all that, you didn't even stop t'think, just got on your horses and *galloped away*." Heather put hands on hips and declared, "You should've stayed and waited for proper reinforcements. Don't you have *any idea* of how many other threats could've been out there?"

"We only had the two guards," he said defensively. "I didn't know how many other assassins there could've been, and a weaver's shop is *not* a defensible position."

"It didn't occur to you that we have more guards than just the uniformed ones?" She threw up her hands. "I thought you were clever!"

"I'm sorry, Heather, it's my fault," Rose apologized. "It happened very quickly, and Erven doesn't know about your cohort of shadows yet."

"Shadows?" Erven looked with interest at Heather. "You've been sending other guards? Disguised ones?"

"Yes, of course." Heather looked at him as if he'd grown another head. "We've done all along—oh." Her expression went from angry to thoughtful. "Well, we've done since things got more worrying. After you left. You didn't know?"

"Well, even if I'd known, it wouldn't have changed anything. We need all the help we can get." He crossed his arms, his back and shoulder aching. "I'm certain this was the Holdmasters' doing, or Torvald's, and I don't see them stopping after one failure."

AFTER REASSURING the rest of her friends and debriefing with the guards, Rose went to find Arielle. She found the healer in the compounding room, carefully decanting infused oil from one jar to the other. A pot of beeswax hung over the fire, and a row of wooden bowls stood ready to receive the finished salve.

"Did Erven come find you yet?"

"No," Arielle said, her attention only halfway on Rose. "Why? Did he get hurt again?"

"We've just come from town. There was an archer on the rooftop." Rose wrapped her arms around herself. Even hours after the incident, her limbs still felt quivery. She wondered at how level her voice remained, explaining, "He took an arrow to the back."

"Almighty..." Arielle breathed. She set down the jar with a thump. "I'm not sure who I should be more worried about, you or him."

"I'm not sure, either," Rose admitted. "It was hard to tell which of us they were targeting."

"They must be insane to attack you so close to home." Arielle's gaze sharpened. "He was hit in the back? Do you know how badly?"

"He didn't say." Rose thought back to what she had seen before Erven had departed with Heather, both of them earnestly discussing security options. "I think it was just behind his shoulder. His armor stopped most of it, but I know he was hurting."

Arielle pulled the wax pot away from the fire. "I'll go see if he'll let me help." She stopped halfway through untying her apron and asked, "How does his loyalty strike you, after this?"

Rose looked at the floor, warmth speeding through her chest. "I—well—he saved my life. And if they're willing to target him as well as me, it means they've broken ties with him as well." The warmth spread to her face as she looked up at her aunt. "And it's given me an idea of how to get around the moot's ruling once and for all."

28

HEART OVER HEAD

Amid the cheerful chaos of dinner the next night, Erven noticed Rose was missing. Leaning over to Tait, he asked, "When's the last time she ate down here with everyone?"

Tait speared a potato chunk with his knife, eyes flickering around the room as he ate. "It's been a bit. A month or so, I think." He shrugged. "I've been back and forth to Hollow so many times, I could've missed something."

"She's been on edge ever since the ambassador got potted," Heather said from farther down the table. "Only eats in her room now."

Willow snorted. "When she remembers to eat." She folded her napkin into a parcel around several slices of bread and handed them across the table to him. "Speakin' of, go give those to her? I haven't brought anything up in a while, and sometimes she forgets to ask."

Erven took the parcel, asking, "Are you sure it's a good idea?"

"You saved her life yesterday. If she's still unsure of you,

I don't know what to say." Heather stabbed a chunk of meat in her bowl. "Just *talk* to her."

"And I'm certainly not going to hold your hand up the stairs, so you might as well go." Willow waved him away before resuming her conversation with Tait.

The sounds of dinner faded behind him as he climbed the stairs. Rose's office door was locked, and no light shone from under the door. Wondering if Willow was trying to get him in trouble, he climbed the last flight of stairs to Rose's room. Knocking on the door, he called, "Willow sent me with food. May I come in?"

Greta opened the door with a cautious look on her face. "Her Majesty isn't here. Is everything all right?"

Erven handed her the wrapped-up napkin, trying not to let his sudden panic show. "I was just here to bring her something to eat. She's not in her office either."

The other maid's voice came from farther inside the room. "Have you checked the tower yet? She's been spending more time up there lately."

Relief washed over him as Greta nodded in agreement. "Aye, the tower would be a good place to find her." She smiled up at him. "I'll just get this set out for when she comes back."

"Thank you," he called as the door closed. Alone in the corridor, he settled shaky hands around his sword belt. After a moment's hesitation, he walked down the corridor and climbed the stairs to the battlements. Rose stood wrapped in her shawl, facing the sea. Against the dark sky beyond, she looked very small and lonesome.

"Rose?"

. . .

Rose's heart thumped as she heard Erven call her name. Spinning around, she clutched her shawl tighter around her shoulders. *I forgot how quietly he moves.* "You startled me!"

He took a quick step backwards, putting a hand up. "I'm sorry. I didn't mean to scare you. I just wanted to tell you that Willow sent me up with some food from dinner. I gave it to your maids."

"Thank you." She looked down at the courtyard, the torches on the wall tops flickering in the steady breeze. "Was there anything else?"

Erven's boots scraped on the stone as he joined her at the battlements. "Not really. I noticed you weren't eating with the others. When you weren't in your room either, I got worried."

"Oh..." She clasped her hands tighter around her shawl. "I haven't eaten downstairs in months. It was easier to stay away from everyone."

"I didn't realize you'd become so solitary."

Rose took a deep breath, but the words she'd meant to say came out wrong. "It's easy to become solitary when you don't know who you can trust." She looked up at him as she said it, and was mortified to see the hurt in his expression. "I —I mean... I'm sorry."

"It's all right." Erven rubbed his eyes. "I'm sorry too. I never meant to hurt you. If I'd known how badly this would go, I'd never have gone near the highlands." He bowed his head. "If the moot rules in the Holdmasters' favor, the highlands could fall into chaos. We'll have war on our hands, and it'll be all my fault."

"About that..." Rose's limbs felt quivery, and she locked her hands around each other to stop them from shaking. "I think there's only one way to make sure the moot will go in our favor."

"I know." Erven sounded exhausted and unhappy beside her. "I'll have to disappear. There'll be no other option, and the Holdmasters will have to concede defeat. You should've just ordered the Shona to stone me on sight."

"What? No! No, no, no, no, no. That's not what I meant at all!" Rose shook her head, closing her eyes against tears. "You've always been the power *behind* the crown, but you really need one of your own. The people need to see us as not rivals, but unshakeable allies." She found the courage to look up at him.

"Allies?" Comprehension dawned in his face. "You mean marriage?"

"If we're married, it won't matter which way the moot goes." She took a deep breath and calmed the shaking in her voice. "The highlanders will have to submit, because between us, we hold every claim to the throne they could possibly think of. I mean, you're right, the only other option would be for you to disappear. And—" She turned away, her voice going small. "And after yesterday, I realized I need you too much to even consider that."

The silence stretched for far too long as Rose shivered with nerves as much as cold. At last, Erven took a deep breath behind her. "Look, if we're going to do this, I need to know for certain." His hand was firm on her shoulder as he turned her to face him. "Is this just a way to stabilize things? Or is there something else?" His brow furrowed. "I can live with it either way, but—" His eyes held hers, and she was shocked to see warmth in their depths. "If you have other motivation, you need to say so. I need to know what you're feeling."

"I don't know!" Tears dripped down her cheeks, turning icy in the wind. "You've been watching my back for almost three years, even when I didn't know it needed watching. You're kind and strong and smart. Even when I thought you'd betrayed us all, you were acting in the only way possible to keep the people you cared about safe." With a sick feeling in her stomach, she admitted, "I don't even know what falling in love would feel like, but I know I don't want to do any of this without you."

"Well, then." He let go of her shoulder and stepped back, turning to look down at the sea. She wrapped her arms around herself and waited. Finally, just as Rose was certain she'd made a terrible mistake, Erven turned around. Tears sparkled in his eyes as well.

"I said I could live with it either way, and I can." He took her hand, swordsman's calluses rough against her palm. "But you have no idea how happy I am to hear that it's not *just* politics. You're the bravest woman I've ever met, and remember, Arielle's the one who raised me." Rose laughed nervously, and his smile matched hers as he continued, "If you want, I think we can make this work."

"You think so?"

Erven wiped tears away with the back of his hand. "I think so." He laughed. "I'm so relieved. After yesterday, I didn't know how I was going to keep hiding how I felt." He ducked his head to look directly into her eyes. "Is it all right to hug you?"

Rose nodded. "Please."

Erven pulled her into his arms. Rose could feel his chainmail under his uniform, and the rise and fall of his chest as she laid her cheek against his collarbone. The knots in her stomach slowly loosened, replaced by a settling feeling she could hardly identify. *Safety. And comfort. It feels like home.*

"I was so worried about you," she said into Erven's chest. "While you were gone, I kept thinking you were the person I most needed to talk to."

His voice was deep against her ear. "I missed you too. I didn't realize how much until Torvald said what he did. Then I was so angry I couldn't see straight."

She stepped out of his arms to look up at him. The stairwell light caught his eyes, filling them with blue as brilliant as the sky over the highest peaks. "Thank you for trusting me enough to come back."

Erven squeezed her hands. "It's certainly turned out better than I could've ever hoped." He frowned. "Your hands are so cold. Let's get out of this wind."

With a sheepish smile, she admitted, "I'm freezing."

"Let's go down, then." As they closed the tower door, Erven chuckled. "Merald was right. I can't wait to see their faces."

Heat crept up her cheeks. "Violet and Willow always said I was the least likely of the three of us to ever marry. I don't think any of them will expect this."

LIGHT CRACKLED around the office as Willow fed the last scraps of messages into the fire. She dusted the charcoal off a stack of slate tablets and piled them neatly at the side of her worktable. Corking the inkwell and setting it on a tray with her pens, she closed her ciphered notebook and put it away in her document box. Turning the key in the lock, she dusted off her hands and addressed her sisters, hunched over their game board in the corner of the room. "Time for bed, anyone?"

"Must we?" Clover frowned up at her. "I don't want to try and get the fire going downstairs yet. Can't you—I don't know—wait here for a bit so we can finish?"

Willow sat cross-legged on the rug before the fire, squinting to examine the board. "This doesn't look anywhere close to finished."

Heather eyed the bowl of dried plums she and Clover had been laying odds with. "I won't lie, it could go on for a bit..."

"Divide those up three ways, and just finish already," Willow laughed. "I'm tired, and I know both of you are, too."

Clover snorted. "Yes, *mum*." She dropped plums into each of her sister's hands before flicking a ship across the board. "I send a fireboat into your lines," she announced mutinously.

Heather spat a pit into her hand and lobbed it at the piece, which skittered off the board and onto the rug. "My ship had a ballista."

Willow noticed a light coming from the hallway seconds before the office door opened to admit Rose and Erven. "Evening!" She nodded towards Rose's door. "I left some things on your desk for you, but nothing that can't wait until tomorrow." She stopped, looking at the expressions on each of their faces. "Hold on, is everything all right?"

Rose's cheeks were pink, and she glanced up at Erven briefly before saying, "Yes. Well, mostly. There are still some things that need to be worked out, but..."

Willow nudged Heather's elbow. Both of her sisters looked up, making Rose's face go even pinker as Willow asked, "What's the matter, dear? Is something happening we ought t'know about?" She flicked her gaze from Rose to Erven, pieces suddenly slotting together as to what had occurred.

She knew immediately that her sisters had come to the same conclusion.

"Frogs and toads..."

Clover ceremoniously handed Willow her handful of plums, Heather following suit a moment later. "You win."

Despite her best attempts, Willow burst into laughter at Rose's shocked expression. Erven also laughed, sounding happier than he had since their return. "I told you they wouldn't be surprised."

"You said," Rose muttered. "It's one thing to say, and another thing to see it."

Heather and Clover abandoned their game to hurtle at Rose, and their combined congratulatory noises completely drowned out Rose's protests.

Willow set the plums back in the bowl, wiping sticky hands on her tunic as she stood. "All right, all right, don't maul her." Prying her sisters away from Rose, she caught her friend up in a strong hug. Looking over Rose's shoulder, she told Erven, "If you hurt her, I'll swear I'll murder you."

"Aye, an' it'll be completely justified." Heather said from behind her. "Don't underestimate us."

He shook his head, sincerity in every line of his body. "Never."

Willow stepped back to hold Rose's shoulders, looking seriously into the queen's eyes. "Are you certain this is what you want?"

Rose nodded firmly. "It'll stabilize Illyn, take power out of the Holdmasters' hands, and put to rest any assumption of us being rivals. Besides," she looked back at Erven, and

Willow's heart warmed at the sight of the fondness in her friend's eyes. "Now, no matter what calamity comes, we'll face it together."

The High Magistrate bent his head over the newly sealed contract. Finally, after moments that seemed like an eternity, he nodded briskly. "Everything is in order, Your Majesty." He carefully rolled the contract into a tube and tied it with a silk ribbon. "I'll have copies made and placed in secure locations, while the original remains with the keeper of your house."

Rose exhaled with relief as their witnesses politely clapped. The Steward sauntered over to kiss her hand, beaming up at her with a twinkle in his eyes. "Congratulations, Your Majesty. Er, sorry." He winked at Erven. "Your *Majesties*."

"On paper, I suppose." Erven ran his hands through his hair. "No crown yet."

"They do take some time to make," Rose said. "I'm having a circlet made, at least, but even that's going to be a while. We'll have to plan for an actual coronation sometime in the future."

"Well, it's time well bought. Congratulations again." The Steward bowed to both of them before leaving, every line of his face proclaiming that the news would be all over the castle by nightfall.

Heather flapped a handkerchief, blowing her nose noisily. "Sorry," she said. "It's just, *weddings*!"

"I know." Clover leaned against her sister, pulling her hat brim down and adding her own sniffling to Heather's. "They're just so, so—"

"Contrived, in this case." Willow twirled a pen between her fingers before stuffing it into her vest pocket. "And very, very necessary." She winked at Rose, who frowned back.

"Necessary or not, congratulations *are* still due to both of you." Arielle wrapped an arm around Rose's waist, kissing her temple affectionately. "I know it's not exactly how either of you would have wanted this to go, but the blessings of your friends and family still go with you."

"You're embarrassing Rose," Erven commented dryly. "Personally, I'm just pleased there'll be many copies made. I'm not convinced that a single copy wouldn't disappear if it got into the wrong hands." He gently drew her away from Arielle. "If you'll excuse us..."

"Aye, go." Willow laughed. "Take her on a long walk, or something. We'll tidy up."

Rose allowed Erven to pull her towards the walls. Once they reached the stairs, he let go of her hand to ascend ahead of her. They walked in silence for some time, nodding at the sentries' greetings and listening to the waves crashing on the rocks far below.

"Don't think my expectations have changed, just by signing that contract," Erven finally said, slowing his pace to look at her sincerely. "I meant what I said, the other night. I'll take things at your pace." He gestured up at the keep. "I've been sleeping in my office, and that's where I plan on staying."

Rose hadn't planned on speaking, but the new information startled her into asking, "Don't you have a room down in the barracks?"

Erven nodded. "Tait's been staying there while I was gone, and I didn't want to throw him out. Besides," he tapped his fingers on his sword hilt. "I didn't know how my role as the Shona commander would change, and I was going to suggest having him as my replacement."

"He would be ideal…" Rose said as they walked another length of wall. "You don't see yourself continuing to lead the Shona?"

"I don't know." Erven shifted his sword belt to a different spot over his shoulder. He'd kept wearing chain mail under his uniform, even after the chances of someone attacking him had lessened. "As I've seen since your coronation, a ruler's duties keep them too busy to do much in the field. I won't be able to lead patrols, or even keep as close an eye on the outposts as I'd like. Tait's a better fit for that role, now."

"I hadn't thought about that." Rose stopped to look down towards the sea, waves rolling into the shore in a mesmerizing pattern. "It didn't occur to me that you'd have to give up your involvement with the Shona. I'm sorry."

His hand rested briefly over hers before going back to his sword hilt. "It's all right. You've given up so much. It would be silly for me to expect anything less of myself." Erven looked back up at the tower. "Anyhow, I'm planning on staying in my office. I'm comfortable there, and it's close enough that you can find me easily."

"Thank you," Rose began walking again, unsure of what else to say. As they approached the steps once more, she said, "We have to decide how we're going to break the news to everyone at the moot. I'm sure the Holdmasters won't have expected this exactly, but they'll have something else in their pockets."

"They aren't going to give up without a fight, that's certain," Erven agreed. "Don't worry. We still have almost a month."

29
NIGHTMARES AND COMFORT

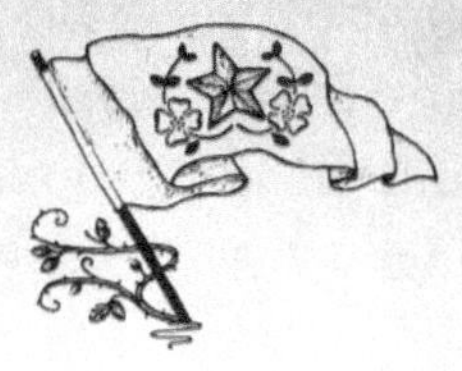

Rose's office shutters rattled under the wind—no longer a furious winter storm, but a heavy, wet thing rolling in from the sea.

"It's only rain here, but you can be sure it's snowing up at Whitecaps and beyond. I hope the Holdmasters aren't so insane as to try and travel now." Arielle had said at dinner that evening. "They said *after* the turn of spring for the moot, didn't they?"

"That's right," Erven replied, propping an elbow on the table and staring into the fire. "Once the leaves started. Besides, no one could make it up there for another few weeks, anyhow. It's still too snowy at the upper reaches."

After the hastily arranged wedding, Rose and Erven had returned to work, pausing only for meals and the occasional walk around the wall tops. Even weeks after his escape, the tower crossed by wings continued to plague their desks. Although the malcontents that had targeted the Sea Wanderers had finally been apprehended, the Watchmen still reported rumblings of further attempts against her and

Erven. As the days passed, Rose found herself anxiously pacing the office, wishing the moot could be over and done with. *At least then, there will be answers and an end to all this.*

The office fire had burned down for the second time as she slammed her document box shut. Hugging her shawl tighter, she banked down the fire and picked up her lamp. Even though she'd climbed the stairs to her rooms thousands of times, tonight the curving walls felt constrictive and looming. The flame in her little lamp flickered in the drafty stairwell, fading out with a puff of smoke as she reached her door.

Alone in the darkness, all the bad reports and threats from the last few weeks surged back in inky terror. *They tried to kill me. They almost killed him. And they won't ever stop.* Rose clamped bloodless fingers over her own mouth. Her suppressed wail sounded foreign to her ears. *My enemies only ever seem to strike where I feel safest. Why wouldn't they have reached this far?*

She stumbled back from the door and fled down the staircase, every shadow catching at her feet. Her breath catching in her chest, she ran down the corridor. A thin line of light shone from under Erven's office door, the glow bringing her feet to a halt even as panic urged her to keep running. It hadn't occurred to her that he might not have gone to bed either. Rose stood there for a long moment, closing her eyes against the fear that had driven her from her room.

It seemed he'd heard her. The door creaked as Erven opened it, the light from inside casting a glow around his head. "Rose? What's wrong?"

She didn't even realize she was shaking until she felt his arms around her. "I'm sorry. It's just been so much, and everything that's happened... I'm sorry. I didn't feel safe and —I'm so sorry." She pushed back from him. "I don't even know what I'm doing here. I'll go."

"Wait, here. I'll go with you." He slung his sword belt over his shoulder and picked up the lamp from the table, carefully shielding the flame from the draft as he stepped into the corridor.

Their shadows jumped back and forth as they went up the stairs. Erven pushed the door of her room open, glancing around before allowing her in after him. The maids had long gone to their beds in the small room across the corridor, leaving her bedchamber warm and still. He bent to stir the fire. "There. It's all right." The light steadily grew, and Rose felt her fear fade away in the warm glow.

"Thank you." She yawned, shoulders dropping in embarrassment. "I'm sorry I disturbed you. It's just—"

"Don't apologize. I don't mind." Erven looked around the room. "Do you want me to stay?" He pointed at the chairs on either side of her fireplace. "I'll just sit up until you fall asleep. If you trust me, that is."

Rose closed her hands around the edge of her shawl. "No, I trust you. I just—" She glanced at her bed, stifling another yawn. "I still don't know if I can sleep."

Erven raised a skeptical eyebrow. "You're falling asleep on your feet." He sighed and sat on the rug at the foot of the bed, his back against the footboard. "Here, sit down."

Too worn out to argue, she sat next to him, tucking her skirts around her knees. He ducked his head from under his sword belt, laying the weapon at their feet before wrapping his arm around her shoulders. "There. Now just relax and watch the fire. You'll fall asleep in no time."

Rose yawned again. "You won't—?"

His voice was gentle against her ear. "I'll stay as long as you want me to. Go to sleep."

Somehow, despite the shivers dancing up and down her spine, Rose was able to let herself relax. Soon, her head dropped to rest on Erven's shoulder, and her breathing slowed. When she next woke, she was in her bed under the covers. It was morning. The fire had burned down, and Erven was gone.

After that first night, he sat up in her room each evening until she fell asleep. Some nights, Erven also fell asleep watching the fire. Rose was grateful that no one in the flurry of moot preparations thought or cared to comment, as supplies were gathered, plans deliberated, and tents checked. Almost a week before they planned to leave for the highlands, Rose started awake at an unfamiliar noise. Grabbing for the dagger she kept under her pillow, she peered around the room.

It only took a moment of confusion before she saw that Erven had fallen asleep with his back against the door. His blanket had slid to cover his face, and by the looks of things, had triggered a nightmare. Blinking sleepiness away, Rose hurried to light a taper and hold it to the lamp. As she set the light on the table, Erven bolted awake, tearing away the blanket. One hand clamped over his left side, he sat upright with a gasp.

"Rose? Are you all right?"

"You're the one who was just fighting a blanket. I'm fine." She sat down a few feet from him. "Are *you* all right?"

"I will be." Erven took a deep breath. "I'm sorry. There's no way to tell when one of those will happen."

"Violet said something a long time ago, but I didn't realize you still had them."

"Less often, now that I'm home. But still unpredictable." Erven wiped sweat from his forehead, his breathing still uneven. They sat in silence for a long moment, as his breathing slowed and Rose's heartbeat calmed. Eventually, Erven whispered, "It's not even the wound anymore. It's the helplessness—knowing the healers' hands are only saving your life so you can die later, in as much pain as possible." Tears sparkled in his eyes. "And not knowing it's a dream until something pulls you out of it."

Rose shuddered. "I'm sorry." She shook her head. "That's a bad way to put it. I wish you didn't have to face it. Sleep should be an escape."

"Most of the time, it is." Erven reassured her. Even though he'd started sounding better, he hadn't let go of his side. "It's been better since I started falling asleep up here."

"Oh..." Rose let the word trail off into the darkness. *Just ask. He'll never offer if you don't ask.* "You know, there's nothing that says you can't sleep up here. We can move your clothes and things, and you can keep your room as just an office."

"You're sure?" Erven asked. "I don't want to push you."

Rose nodded. "It's silly to have you fall asleep on the floor every night."

He stood, pulling the blanket with him. "The floor's not bad, but, ah... it is a bit uncomfortable. Um," he looked around the room. "Do you want me to start tonight?"

Rose ordered the fluttering in her stomach to go away. "If you're all right with it, I am." She found a smile somewhere. "The contract we signed says we're allowed, anyway."

. . .

Willow had not been with the army when they'd moved encampments during the previous conflict. Heather and Clover had, and both girls took the inevitable chaos with philosophical pragmatism.

"I expected you'd be off overturning apple buckets or something, Ducky," Willow told Clover as they passed loaded saddlebags off to the hostlers. "Isn't that your and Heather's usual response to chaos—creating more of it?"

Clover blew her bangs out of her eyes. "Spare us a moment to consider that we might be growing up. Besides," she gestured at the jumble of supplies, guardsmen, and pack horses. "Compared to Hold Eskel, this is nothing."

"Well, this's only half the forces," Willow said as they walked back towards the kitchen. "Some of the Shona from Hollow are joining us."

Clover's tangled brown hair fell over her forehead again as she said, "The other clans are bringing forces of their own, right?"

"I assume so." Willow tugged her shirt straight under her tunic. "That's what worries me. If things go badly, they might just decide to wipe out all of us."

"I wouldn't worry too much about Rose," Clover said. Her hazel eyes glowed happily. "Not while Erven's near her, anyway. Greta says when she went in to stir up the fire this morning, Rose was asleep with his arm around her."

Willow chuckled. "That didn't take long." She examined her supply list, written in charcoal on a board propped against a crate. "I'm glad they have each other. We're all right, but she needed someone else to remind her that not everything has to be life and death." She smiled as Rose and Erven appeared on the hall steps. Erven bent his head to say something to Rose, who nodded before walking towards them.

"Morning, Your Majesty!" Clover gave Rose a two-fingered salute.

"Morning, Ducky." A smile crossed Rose's face, the expression more common over the last few weeks than it had been during the winter. "Getting along all right?"

Willow tucked a stray piece of hair back behind her ear. "We're almost all loaded up." She shaded her eyes, gauging the height of the sun over the walls. "We'll be ready to march by noon. If we put some bounce in our steps, we'll make Hollow by bedtime."

"Actually..." Rose was twisting the corner of her shawl. "We've been talking, and–"

"Don't tell me you're going to back down now." Willow settled her weight on one hip and crossed her arms. "We've been over this—you *need* to face them."

Rose shook her head. "No, that's not it. Erven and I are still going, and so is Arielle, but I need you to stay here."

Willow's jaw went slack. "Exactly why? You know we can't trust them from here to the door. You need people to protect you!"

"I'll have the guards. And the Shona." Rose tilted her head, warmth creeping into her businesslike voice. "And I'll have Erven."

Willow raised an eyebrow as Clover snorted.

"What?" Rose demanded.

"Nothing." Willow shook her head at Clover while fighting back her own smile. "It's all lovely protection, I'll agree, but I still don't see why you're better served with me staying behind."

Rose sank onto one of the supply crates. "You said it—

we don't trust them." She blinked hard, her eyes going glassy. "Even with our precautions, I can't guarantee any of us will come back."

Willow and Clover exchanged a single determined look before sitting either side of Rose. Clover patted Rose's knee. "You'll be back, Starshine, don't worry."

"Aye, but just in case," Rose grabbed their hands tightly. "If we don't make it back, someone will have to be ready for the worst."

"Rose—" Willow began.

"If we die, the highlands will fall into chaos and the lowlands will follow. The people here would have no one left to take care of them." A chilly note crept through Rose's voice. "If the worst happens, I want you to take the children from the Rogue School, and the others who don't have anyone to look out for them, and go back to the woods. Leave this miserable place and don't look back. Please, promise me."

Willow took a deep breath. She twisted to put an arm around Rose, gripping Clover's shoulder on the other side. "I understand."

Clover put her free hand over Willow's. "We'll take care of them."

"Thank you." Rose squeezed their hands before letting go, the sun catching in her eyes as she stood. "I'll go tell Erven. And don't worry; I plan on coming back. There's still so much to be done."

As Rose walked away, Willow and Clover looked at each other with the depth of a shared burden. "It's not really fair of her," Clover commented. "We can do it, of course, but it's not really fair to just abandon things."

Willow squeezed her sister's shoulder. "They've not

been fair to her, either. If something happens to her and Erven, I'm not going to try and patch up the country in their memory."

"That's harsh, but I think you're right." Clover sagged under Willow's touch, burying her face in her hands. "She's gone places I wish I could understand, but I can't."

"We don't have to understand everything to love someone." Willow said, smoothing Clover's hair sympathetically. "But I think you know that." A thought caught at her mind, and she had to smile despite herself. "Lady Starshine, is it?"

A smile tugged at the corners of Clover's mouth. "She's watched them for so long that she's taken on their light." She looked across the courtyard as Rose disappeared back inside the keep. "And she's needed a name that's all hers for a long time. This 'Your Majesty this', 'Your Majesty that' is getting tiresome."

"Glad to see you back, finally."

Merald set a newly packed bag down on the small table in his and Tora's room. Even with Tora's hasty departure at the news of the Whitecaps attack, there still hadn't been much to pack away for the move to the family quarters. "It's good to be back. I'm glad we'd put all that work into building up my stamina before we escaped, otherwise I don't think I'd have made it to Whitecaps."

Erven shook his head, but the set of his shoulders gave away his concern as he said, "You'd have made it. I wasn't going to leave you behind."

"Well, it laid me up for weeks, anyway. Next time you want to go off on a desperate mission deep into the highlands, you might want to count me out. I think I can be much better use to the Crown from here." Merald bent down to pick up a box from the floor, the movement pulling at his side.

"You were there when I needed someone to remind me who I really was," Erven said. "And for that reason alone, I'm glad you came. I'm just sorry it ended the way it did for you."

"It wasn't all bad," Merald conceded. "I did get back into practice with a sword. I'm pretty sure if I keep it up now, things won't have the chance to get stiff again." He smiled. "Tora said she's grateful I decided to try and work past all of it. I didn't realize how worried she'd been about me." He answered Erven's questioning noise with, "We had a lot of time to talk, at Whitecaps and on the way back here. I'm glad she came up with the others, even if it did mean she had to be away from Anneli for so long."

Erven took the bag from the table and hoisted the straps over his shoulder. "I saw them earlier. Is Anneli talking now?"

Merald's heart warmed at the memory. "When we got back, she saw me from the bathhouse steps." He laughed, "She almost sent Clover to an early grave when she ran across the courtyard in naught but her nightgown." He squinted against the sunlight as they emerged into the busy courtyard. "She calls me 'Adda, now."

"Her first word!?" Erven winked at him. "Tora's going to be disappointed."

"She's just happy we're all together, and we'll be able to adopt Anneli soon."

"Soon? Why not now?"

They'd skirted around the chaos of packing and organizing in the center of the courtyard. Merald stopped in front of a building across from the Rogue School, adjusting his hands around the box. "Tora asked if we could wait." He swallowed hard, looking down at the clothes stacked neatly inside it. "We wanted you and Rose to be our witnesses."

The bag slid from Erven's shoulder to land with a thump on the ground. "I don't know if that's so wise..."

"Why not?" Merald balanced the box awkwardly on one hip as he retrieved the bag. "There's no one else I'd rather trust more."

"No, it's not that." Erven sank down onto the steps leading into the building. "Look, you know how that time a few years ago was the only time you've seen me scared?"

Merald nodded silently, waiting for him to continue.

"Well, this," Erven waved a hand at the jumbled supplies near the kitchen doors. "This scares me more. Even with our preparations, we can't control what will happen up there. If Torvald manages to talk the majority of the clans around to his way of thinking, they might decide they'd be better off without all of us." He frowned, his hand flitting towards his sword hilt. "I'm taking Rose into a situation where both of us may die."

Merald set his armful of items down and sat next to Erven, balancing his chin on a fist. "I want to argue with you."

"Don't. You know it's a possibility." Erven's shoulders slumped. "Until now, I'd never let myself dwell on how I felt about her, but now that I could lose her, I'm terrified." He sat up straighter, turning to Merald with something bordering desperation in his voice. "Don't wait to make Anneli your daughter. I want you to still have a chance for a happy life with the people you love, even if I can't be there to see it."

Merald was on the verge of arguing when Tora and Anneli appeared from the Rogue School doorway.

"'Addaaaaaaa!!" Anneli broke away from Tora, pelting towards him with braids bouncing.

"Oh dear." Merald bolted to his feet, pausing for a moment to look back at Erven. "Will you—"

"Go on," Erven said, a smile lighting his face. "I'll be all right."

With a whoop, Merald ran over to meet Anneli's charge, sweeping her up and kissing her cheek as his ears filled with the sounds of giggles. A moment later, Tora caught up, breathless and exasperated at the toddler. In between reassuring his wife and chastising his daughter, Merald glanced back at the steps.

Erven had gone.

Rose's horse shifted beneath her, clearly sensing her rider's anticipation. As they started forward and passed through the gates, Rose turned to look back at the keep. Willow, Heather and Clover stood arm in arm at the top of the steps, Clover waving frantically. Rose could feel the fortitude in Willow's stare across the courtyard, and she held her friend's eyes as long as she could before the walls broke her line of sight. *I couldn't have left home in the care of anyone more suited.*

With a shiver, she settled herself in the saddle for the ride to Hollow. From there it would be at least a week to Hold Eskel and the moot, a week in which anything could happen. Some of the worry abated as Erven reined his horse in next to her. Her ally—*husband. I have to remember that, even if it still doesn't feel real*—had traded his emblazoned uniform tunic for Shona colors, leather armor replacing the chain mail that had saved his life a few weeks prior.

"Are we leaving the horses at Hollow this time?"

Rose looked up at the peaks beyond the treeline, trying to visualize the route that would take them past Hollow and to Hold Eskel. "We could, but that would mean we'd be walking. The pack horses have to come, anyway, and Hold Eskel has pasture and shelter." She laughed at Erven's dismayed expression. "I'm sorry, but I think we're riding the whole way."

30
PREPARING FOR BATTLE

After months of snow and storms, spring had come to the mountains. In the gullies between ridges, meltwater trickled over the rocks, leaving behind the uncurling edges of ferns and new leaves. The aspen trees stood robed in bright green infant leaves, still too small to rustle in the breeze as Rose sat wearily against a rock. Around her, the rest of the guardsmen and Shona built campfires, laid out sleeping areas, and tended the horses as part of making camp for the night.

The twilight had deepened by the time one of the sentries whistled into the darkness under the trees. Rose, who'd sat up when she'd heard the signal, relaxed as Erven approached with Tait, both men pulling hoods down as they appeared out of the darkness. They joined her and Arielle just outside of the campfire circle, Erven sitting with his back to the same rock as Rose.

"Another tribe arrived this afternoon," Tait said as he unwound a mask from over his face. "The Mori, I think. That's everyone accounted for."

Rose slid closer to Erven, pulling the edges of her cloak around herself. True to form, he'd ignored his travel weariness in order to scout ahead at Hold Eskel. "I didn't realize we'd be the last ones to arrive. I wonder how long some of them have been waiting."

"Spring moots are always tricky," Arielle said as she handed the two men bowls of dinner. "No matter how precise you are in naming the day and time, you'll always have someone who's far too early and others who can't make it down from their Holds. It's a measure of how seriously they're taking this that everyone who was summoned came."

"I feel bad for them," Rose said.

"Don't," Erven reassured her. "They knew what they were starting they saw the call to moot signed with the Holdmasters' seal." He sighed and shifted against the rock. "From the looks of things, it's evenly split. Those who are for the Holdmasters—"

"—and you," Tait interrupted with a smirk.

"I suppose they won't have mentioned to their allies that I took to the wind," Erven laughed. "They're camped on one side of the river, as far away from the Hold as possible. Everyone else is just outside the village."

"No matter where the camps are, either one of you could be the target of an attack," Arielle pointed out. "Rose is at risk of being targeted by the more revolutionary Holdmasters. And you," Arielle looked at Erven, "you're at risk of our allies trying to prove their loyalty by removing you from contention."

"I know." His voice held some of the same defeat Rose remembered from earlier as he said, "I know this was—is—

the best way to solve this, but it could still turn into a blood-bath if we take one step out of place."

Long after the others had drifted off to their beds and the fire had died down to embers, Rose stayed leaning against the rock. Erven carefully sharpened his hunting knife next to her, the repetitive noise comforting in its own way. She huddled deeper into her cloak as clouds drifted across the moon, swelled to half full over the trees.

"What's bothering you?" Erven tested the edge of the knife, muttering an exclamation and examining a nicked finger a moment later.

"You don't mind that we've done this, do you?" Rose looked up at his face, shadowed in the fading light from the fire. "Earlier, you said—"

"I said it was the best way to solve things. You said the same, that one night." Erven tucked his whetstone back into the pouch on his sword belt and sheathed the knife. "Just because it's true doesn't change how I feel."

"I still don't know *how* I feel, most days." She leaned back against the rock to look at the night sky, stars dancing in between the clouds. "I'm not sure how I'm supposed to act, and I keep thinking this might not have been something you would have chosen at all, and—ugh." Rose rubbed her forehead. "I can't help but wish things had gone differently."

Erven slid an arm around her. "If things had gone differently, and the highlands had sworn undying loyalty from the start, I would have still loved you."

Rose's breath caught in a squeak. She could feel his laugh deep in his chest as he said, "How could I not? You arrived at Hollow completely unaware of how long we'd been waiting, but when faced with the choice to run or to fight, you decided to fight for a people you didn't even know." Erven's voice subsided. "You didn't let your mind win out over your heart… not like I did."

"What are you talking about?" Rose twisted to look up at him. "Your heart for your people is what's put you with one foot in an early grave, twice!"

"Not this time. If I'd really been determined, I could have kept resisting. But there was that thought—maybe they put it there in the first place, maybe I did—that I *could* do better." His voice shook a little as he confessed. "It wasn't just for my men's sake that I gave in. I believed them."

Rose sat up straighter. "You believed them? *I* believed them! For that matter, they're right! You *can* do better than me, but I don't think any less of you because it's true." She directed his gaze up to the stars overhead. "You told me years ago not to let my own hatred of myself weigh me down. It's time you did the same."

Erven was silent for a moment, chest quietly rising and falling under his armor. Finally, he reached out to pull her back into his arms. Something thrilling shot through her chest as he pressed his lips to her temple. "I love you." Fire came back into his voice as he added, "Tomorrow, we'll go down to face them."

"Together?" Rose tipped her face up to his.

"Together."

HOLD ESKEL WAS the same as Erven remembered it—a tidy village nestled in the middle of a bowl-shaped valley, houses spreading around the Hold to peter out on the banks of a winding river. Scarcely a few weeks ago, the valley would have been covered in snow and the stream choked by ice. Now, the white blobs of sheep and new lambs could be seen grazing in a pasture to the side of the village. Almost a dozen encampments dotted the valley, banners flying prominently from the sides of tents. He laughed at the sight, causing Rose to look up and ask, "What's so funny?"

He pointed at the valley as they reached the downward slope towards the village. "There's plenty of space around the Hold, and more safety in numbers, but they'd rather space themselves as far away from each other as possible."

Rose snorted. "The more I learn, the more amazed I am that we managed to do *anything* with them two years ago."

"Two years ago, they were fed up with Lord Kuma and willing to set their pride aside to get rid of him." Erven clutched his reins as his horse stumbled on a slippery spot in the trail. Although he'd become more used to the pace and the unfamiliar strain on his muscles, he still had to suppress a curse as the horse regained its footing. "What was I saying?"

"They were tired enough of Lord Kuma that they were willing to work with us just in case we actually managed to get rid of him," Rose reminded him as her horse navigated the same slippery patch. "It's still amazing what they were willing to put up with, though."

Erven looked up at the trees, fading from evergreens to aspen as they reached the bottom of the slope. "Well, we'll find out very quickly how they feel about putting up with both of us together."

As they emerged from the trees, Erven shifted in his saddle to peer at the other camps. Even at a distance, he could make out the green and gold banner of the Aubron tribe, the navy and gold of Thinar, and a smudgy grey and black banner with the Westin emblem in white. The camps sat near each other across the valley, neighbors with several other tribes he couldn't immediately place. Turning back towards the village, he counted five more tribal flags fluttering from the Hold walls.

"It's evenly matched, if I had to guess." Arielle said, sitting enviably easily in the saddle even after the week of riding. "Not that numbers or sides matter at the moment, but it's nice to see the lay of things."

Someone in the village, or perhaps a sentry from the Hold, had seen them. Men began approaching the guards at the front of their group, exchanging words and passing the news back to those too far away to hear. A few horse lengths ahead, Rose turned back to look nervously at him. Erven guided his horse close enough to hear her ask, "What if they don't believe us? They all saw the combined seal. They're here because they think you're trying to rival me." Rose's hands went tense on her reins as she said, "There are enough of them here that not even you could fight your way free."

Erven tapped his sword hilt, trying to infuse confidence into his words. "We're not alone. We have the guards and the Shona. And don't forget Arielle," he pointed at the older woman, who had ridden to the front of the group. One of the guardsmen had fallen in alongside her, flying a banner in charcoal and rust colors from his spearpoint. An aspen leaf shone in silver thread on the patterned field. As long as he could remember, Arielle had kept the flag in a box in her room, hidden and never acknowledged during the occupation. "They'll have heard about the Brynjar tribe's return. I'll wager they don't even notice us."

He didn't think Rose had lost her worry as she exhaled slowly. "I'm glad she's decided to act in that position. Even if they disagree with her vote, they can't pretend she doesn't have the right to sit in the moot." Her eyes flicked over at a tent between the encampment and the river. "Is that where the discussions will happen?"

Erven looked as well, frowning at the sight of a canopy similar to the one they'd used as a supply tent during battle. "Probably. Let's hope it doesn't storm. Oh," Several of the faces in the crowd seemed familiar as they passed the outskirts of the camp to enter the village. "There's the Eskel chief. I'll let you do the talking."

Erven pulled back on his reins, letting the others ahead until he was close to the back of their group. The stares from the gathering highlanders grated on his nerves, and he clenched his hands hard around the reins. *They're just wondering what's going on, that's all. You'd stare too, if you were in their boots.* He resisted the urge to grab for his sword hilt. Instead, Erven straightened his shoulders under his armor, ignored the whispers and cutting looks, and followed Rose and Arielle towards the village.

Despite the warm welcome from the people of Hold Eskel, and the reassuring sight of several previously undecided tribes among her supporters, Rose breathed a sigh of relief as Erven slid the bar across the door to their room in the small public house. "I'm glad that's over."

"The first part is. The hardest part is still ahead." He looked up at the low ceiling, running hands through his hair. "And while I can't complain about the accommodations, I wish we could've stayed with the others."

"You were all right back home." Rose knelt next to the saddlebags they had brought up with them.

"Yes, but that's different." Erven shook his head, his hands dropping to his sides. "I've spent far too much time in a room like this one over the last few months."

Rose shook out one of her dresses and draped it over the foot of the bed. "You've defied them once already," she said, standing on tiptoe to kiss him. "You can face them again."

"It's that obvious?" Erven asked, his face flushing.

"Yes." Rose went back to unpacking. "I'm afraid too." She shook out another dress and held it up. The embroidered yarrow leaves and flowers around the hem caught her eye cheerfully. "That's why I brought this. I want to go into this feeling as much like myself as I can."

Morning dawned over Hold Eskel, the first sunbeams angling through campfire smoke. Erven, Tait, and Cedric paused in their exercises as a shepherd passed with his flock, on their way to pasture despite the events scheduled to occur later that morning.

Tait wiped sweat from his brow. "I think that's about all I can take." He grimaced as he pulled his tunic back over his head. "You've both gotten stronger in the last few months."

"Sparring was the only thing they'd let us do unsupervised," Cedric explained.

"And I've spent the last month wearing mail any time I was out of the keep." Erven scanned the Holdmasters' camp across the stream. Movement could be seen among the tents, and smoke drifted from their breakfast fires. "I need to get back. I left Rose asleep, and I don't want her to worry if she wakes up and finds me gone."

After bidding the others farewell, Erven climbed the stairs to his and Rose's room. The Shona guard outside saluted. "She's awake, Sir. Lady Arielle and one of the Eskel ladies are in there with her." The woman smiled. "And there've been enough giggles that it sounds like they've got all my little sisters with them."

Rose's clear laugh struck his ears as he opened the door. She sat on the edge of the bed, talking with Arielle while the highland woman twisted her glossy black hair into an intricate braid. Against her deep blue eyes, the navy fabric in her dress looked even darker, embroidered flowers and leaves standing out in brilliant pink and green hues along the neckline. Her aspen leaf necklace rested just below the hollow of her throat, delicate and silver against pale skin.

"You're gaping, my dear." Arielle said from where she leaned against the wall, going over his armor with a soft cloth. "I'll take that as a good sign."

Erven found his voice as Rose smiled at him. "You look beautiful." He looked down at his own clothes, sweaty from exercise and grimy from when Tait and Cedric had conspired to roll him into the mud. "I suppose I'd better change."

"Wash, too." Arielle handed him a stack of folded clothing. "My room, now."

Returning with damp hair and clean clothes, he found Rose and Arielle deep in conversation. Trying not to eavesdrop, he picked up his armor and ran his fingers over the embossed designs. Arielle had done a stunning job buffing the scratches out of the leather. Sliding his arms into his jacket, he did up the catches before pulling his insignia armband into place on his left arm. The diving hawk—the Shona emblem—tugged at his heart.

I need to give this to Tait. He's earned it.

He slid his head through the armor piece, cinching the

straps tight around his ribs. The leather arm guards etched with feathers had been a gift from Arielle the year he turned twenty. Tightening the laces, he flexed his wrist to make sure it was still able to move freely. Settling his sword belt over his shoulder, his hands froze in place after fastening the buckle just below his collarbone.

Battle.

He'd always put on his armor in the same way, adjusted straps to the perfect tightness, and fastened buckles in the same order before every battle he'd ever fought.

It's not that far off for today, either. Erven drummed his fingers on his sword hilt, one hand going up to the gold chain around his neck. *If we don't get this right, all of us will end up dead.*

31
THE THIRD VOICE

"It's been twenty years since our people last invoked the gathering of the moot. Brothers—and sisters—" The elder inclined his head to Arielle, who nodded graciously. "Welcome. Let us never forget that although we are many, together we are one people." The elder raised a hand to the sky. "To our unity."

"To unity," the tribes chorused.

Rose hid a grimace. *A pledge of unity, but they're here as a people divided.*

As the thought came, one of the Holdmasters took a step forward from his chair. The navy in his clothing mocked the colors in her own dress. "Brothers and sisters, you've assembled today in the name of unity." He looked around the tent, eyes taking in the two half-moons of chairs facing each other. "But as two echoes call from opposite paths, two voices call in Illyn. One calls to open our gates to those who are not our blood, and to weaken ourselves by building ties with foreign nations. This voice would have us set aside our most cherished way of life, even as Illyn grows reliant on the aid of others."

Rose was dismayed to see expressions of agreement and support on most of the faces as he continued. "In the old days, the tribes worked together to govern themselves, relying on the individual Holdmaster to determine the best course of action for his people. We can find solace once more by returning to our roots—the sanctity of the Hold, and the heart of the clan." The Holdmaster addressed his last statement to the entire moot, but Rose felt it directed straight at her. "The voice of the tribes says this—let us abolish the Crown and return to the ways of our forefathers. Only then will we see Illyn grow strong again."

Rose's heartbeat quickened. *No wonder they didn't bother pursuing Erven further. They've been one step ahead of us this whole time.*

The Holdmasters' opening statement sent the moot into a flurry of argument, counterargument, accusation, and defense. Hearing the power behind the words that had haunted her for so long, Rose had to fight the urge to shrink back into her chair. *At least the arguments inside my head are quiet.* She could only try to keep her mind wrapped around the discussion and pray for an opening as the lengthy disagreement grew into a shouting match between two men. She looked over at Erven to see her unease and fear reflected in his eyes as the elder finally called for order.

"Enough!" The man's surprisingly strong voice cut through the commotion, and the arguing slowly subsided. "This type of discussion is useless to us." He pointed at the vacated chairs and commanded, "Remove yourselves from the floor until you master your words."

Amid mutterings and pointed looks, the men sat down.

The one across from Rose muttered angrily with the men on either side of him as the leader of the Mori tribe spoke up. "Elder, may I speak?"

At the mediator's nod, he stood, quietly tucking his hands around a sword belt similar to Erven's. "To return us to the reason we've been called..." He brushed a wing of indigo-black hair out of his face as he addressed the moot. "The voice for the tribes claims abolishing the Crown will allow each tribe to make its own decisions." A ghost of humor colored his voice as he said, "As we have just witnessed, we require a mediator between us for the times when one voice speaks louder than the other. The Crown has always held that role, in hearing our disputes and mediating between us for the best outcome. While the king—or queen—" he bowed briefly towards Rose, "—had our best outcome at heart, we could see our disagreements settled with honor to all sides."

"It's impossible for one who was raised an outsider to understand our ways and mediate impartially between us." The Hold Aubron leader cast a watchful glance at the elder speaker before standing to face his opponent. "We gave Her Majesty the opportunity to demonstrate such an understanding, but that hope has proven futile."

"And what of your other attempts to satisfy our customs?"

Rose didn't see which man had asked, but she felt Erven stiffen beside her as the Holdmaster gave him a scathing look. "There *was* another who could have ruled us—a battle-tried leader whose claim on the throne satisfied every tradition. He also failed us. Our attempts to satisfy the right of succession by combat have ended, leaving us with no recourse but to abolish the Crown entirely." The man spread his hands in a gesture of futility. "Ultimately, we *would* prefer to have a strong ruler to mediate between us, but the last twenty years have demonstrated that our ruling line is only ever doomed to failure."

"The Thinar line never failed us," the leader of Hold Eskel said. Rose barely knew the man, who had not been in power during the Shona's time in his territory two years previous, but his defense steadied her heart. "When our enemies attacked, King Alaber saved his wife and daughter. When things were most dire, he resisted to the last man." He looked at Rose with eyes surrounded by the wrinkles of many hard years. "His downfall wasn't in his own weakness, but ours. Our people hid behind our tower walls, never thinking the enemies would reach us. You blame the Thinar line for Illyn's defeat, when *we* abandoned *them*." He shook his head sorrowfully. "By trying to erase that legacy, you're abandoning them again."

"Once, there may have been strength in kings," Torvald broke in, not bothering to rise from his seat. "And had Commander Erven chosen better, we would not have been driven to this course of action." Rose heard Erven's sharp intake of breath as Torvald's words cut through the air. "But to leave that power in the hands of an untried *child...*" He gave Rose a dismissive look. "Better to wipe things clean and return to the ways that stood us well in our forefathers' days."

Rose's hands tensed on her chair. *I have to say something, or I'll just be proving him right.* She started to stand, just as Arielle's hand came to rest on her arm.

"Wait," the older woman whispered.

Exhaling slowly, Rose leaned back into her chair.

"The Crown has always mediated between tribes, but

Illyn is more than just the highlands," Arielle said. All eyes turned to her, standing proudly at Rose's left. "When our enemies attacked, my people were scattered and annihilated as we ran. I lost my husband, father, and brothers in one day." Arielle's voice wavered and her eyes flicked toward Erven. "I found a new family among those left in the rubble. The Crown rules between the clans in our disputes, but also bears the task of speaking on behalf of those with no clan to protect them." Her voice strengthened with flinty resolve. "If we choose to eliminate the Crown, we will be leaving voiceless those who have suffered the most."

"Lowlanders and outsiders are not our concern," the Aubron chief said.

"You may call them outsiders," Arielle answered. "To me, they're worth more than any ancestral house. *They* deserve a voice, and I will not abandon them." She sat back down with finality, leaving a ripple of interested looks and commentary in her wake. Finally, the elder cleared his throat.

"We have heard two voices in this assembly. One speaks for the abolishment of the Crown and its power, the other for its continuation as a mediator between us." He turned back to Arielle. "You speak for a third voice, and urge us to listen."

Before fear could freeze her to her seat, Rose stood, steeling herself as every face in the moot turned to her. "*I* speak for the third voice." Mari and Carine's weary faces came to mind as she said, "I speak for those whose lives have been turned upside-down by occupation, turmoil, and loss. I speak for the boys growing up without fathers, the mothers who outlived their sons, and the widows struggling to raise their children."

She felt Erven's presence at her side as he joined her. "We abandoned our old ways for a reason. When power and justice are decided in blood, they only leave broken lives in their path. Even in regaining our freedom, we were left with those broken by our struggle. I speak for them—for those with wounds that never healed right, and who wish death had claimed them after all." Erven's voice filled with steel and stone as he turned suddenly on the Holdmasters. "And I call to *you* with the voices of those you've exiled, tortured, and killed in your pursuit of power. I can't drown those voices out, and I swear I'll never stop reminding you of them as long as I live." Erven glanced back at Rose with his jaw clenched and tears shining in the corners of his eyes.

He needs me to finish this. "We speak together for the forgotten and lost in Illyn," Rose said, her voice strengthening. "They don't need traditions steeped in blood and strife. They need someone to hear their stories, tend their hurts, and mediate between them—just like the highlands do." She turned slowly, acknowledging both sides of the moot as she said, "While our forefathers were strong, they lacked trust and cooperation after decades of infighting. When that strength was tested, Illyn crumbled. You have an opportunity to undo the mistakes our ancestors made. Don't waste it."

In the silence that followed, several of the Holdmasters' supporters looked uncomfortably at each other, as the rest of the moot leveled hostile stares in their direction. Rose swallowed nervously, just as a sarcastic voice cut the silence.

"And you, a girl with no claim or experience beyond a mistake in parentage, feel you're the best to lead us into this bright new future." Torvald's face betrayed contempt as he added, "If you're the best your house has to offer, no wonder they failed us."

The words, once the worst thing she could imagine hearing, sounded hollow and foolish to her ears. Rose gave the Holdmaster her very best icy look. "Perhaps. But I'm not alone."

Torvald's stony eyes narrowed as he looked from her to Erven.

Erven undid the clasp at the throat of his jacket, hooking a finger through the chain around his neck. "When you thought you had me in your grasp, you demanded I kill her majesty and take the throne. I refused, but there are more paths to power than shedding innocent blood." The moot went still as midwinter ice as the star pendant came to rest against his armor, gleaming gold against the burnished leather.

"It belonged to my father. He died protecting the people he loved, and planned ahead enough to save my life." Rose tipped *the gold star into his hand, chain trailing from between his fingers as she closed his hand over it. "It's my inheritance, but there's no one I'd rather wear it than you." Her eyes kindled with fiery determination. "They expected us to be rivals, but they have no idea how powerful we can be together. Our friends back home know how I feel about you—it's time everyone else did, too."*

"Between the daughter of the Thinar line and a war hero, there's no contest. There never was." Erven met the stare of his former captor with fire in his eyes. "I told you Brielle

Thinar wasn't part of my clan, and she's not. She's family, and we're much stronger together than we are apart."

Under the revelation—startling to some, a relief to others—the meeting dissolved. As the elder dismissed them with the admonition to think over what had been discussed, one of the tribal leaders who'd been previously unallied came over to speak with Erven.

"We'd heard the news, but didn't know what to believe. I came only to find out the truth." The man shifted from foot to foot as he asked, "They really did what you said? All of it, about the—"

"All of it. I didn't exaggerate." Erven rested his hand against his sword hilt, watching as the Holdmasters' supporters trailed off after them. "Her Majesty sent me and a patrol of men to try and understand why we were at odds. The Holdmasters attacked us without warning." As he spoke, he was conscious that others were listening. Raising his voice just enough so the bystanders could hear, he said, "They offered me the chance to take the throne, and I said no. They decided to torture my men instead of me, knowing it was the fastest way to ensure my cooperation. I didn't have any other choice but to act as they said."

"That explains many things," the man said. His eyes drifted to the gold star around Erven's neck. "Though I imagine a number of other things happened between then and now."

Erven allowed himself a smile. "A few things." He looked around the tent, observing that not many had left, even with the recess. "That's a story better told over drinks and around a fire. I've had enough of meeting tents for tonight."

Amid nods and handclaps, the unofficial gathering adjourned to the tent city outside the village. Before he departed, Erven caught Rose in a lull between two conversations. "Some of the undecided want to hear the whole story."

Rose nodded, clasping her hands nervously. "I think it's better if I go back to the inn. I'm certain they all know where I stand on things—it's you they're curious about. Go on." She stood on tiptoe to kiss him fleetingly. "Go set things right. I'll get to work figuring out what we need to say tomorrow."

His heart beating faster than usual, Erven departed towards the highland encampments. As the sun dipped behind the peaks and stars filled the sky, he told the story of the last few months over and over, to anyone who cared to listen. Each time, the telling grew easier. By the time the fires had died to embers, many of the curious had gone to bed, leaving him and several of the chiefs strategizing late into the night. With a sense of having done everything he could, he finally bade the others goodnight and returned to the inn.

The next two days passed similarly, as the highlanders took the opportunity of being all together to settle smaller disputes, negotiate agreements, and mend rifts. Despite the jaw-dropping conclusion of the opening statements, the elder did not reopen the discussion, and everyone retired to their camps with the question still unsettled. The Holdmasters' ringleaders stayed aloof, though their supporters continued to hold muttered dialogues around several fires throughout the encampment.

. . .

"WHAT'S WRONG?" Rose looked up from studying her notebook as Erven closed the door to their room with a deep sigh. Even though a number of undecided clan leaders had privately expressed support, she couldn't shake the foreboding that something was about to attack them from behind.

Erven leaned his sword against the corner of the bed. Undoing the buckles on his armor, he said, "There's only so many times I can go through the same story before I hate the sound of my own voice." He set the armor on top of the chest at the foot of the bed. "And having to admit over and over again that I broke my word is terrible."

Rose shut her notebook and slid it under her pillow to keep her dagger company. "Well, everyone knows the truth now, and it's up to them to decide what they want to do with it." Even though she hadn't meant it, her words came out cold.

Erven stopped in the middle of pulling off his boots. "Are you all right?"

"I'm fine."

He dropped the boots on the floor. "You're twisting your shawl again. You're upset about something."

Rose dropped the edge of her shawl with frustration. "I know the elder's giving everyone time to think before he opens up the subject again, but it feels like I'm sitting under a storm, waiting for the first thunderbolt to strike."

"I feel the same way." Erven shrugged out of his tunic, the star pendant sliding free from the neck of his shirt and dangling by its chain. "I'd like to think we've done everything we can, but it scares me too."

Rose stood up and wrapped her arms around him. "I'm afraid it's going to still come down to fighting." Tears stung her eyes. "I don't want to lose you. Not again."

"I think you need sleep." Erven slid an arm under her knees and carried her around to her side of the bed. Rose settled her head on her pillow as he reassured her, "Everything will look better in morning light."

Sliding under the blankets, Rose had to admit he was right. Once the lamp had been blown out, she rolled over to bury her head against Erven's chest. His heartbeat thumped against her ear, and his measured breathing soothed her overwrought nerves as he gently rested a hand on her back. Before she knew it, Rose had fallen asleep.

32
ASPEN AND STAR

Something rattled in the silence.

Erven jolted awake, staring into darkness as the bar on the door rattled again before dropping to the floor. He rolled out of bed just as the door opened. In the scant light from the hallway, he caught sight of several dark figures, and the reflection off a bared dagger. Erven instinctively reached for his sword before remembering setting it at the end of the bed that evening.

With a curse ringing through his mind, he grabbed his hunting knife off the bedside table and got to his feet, just as one of the figures lunged. Sudden, sharp pain blossomed across his left shoulder, sending him stumbling sideways towards the end of the bed. Erven reached desperately for his sword as something jerked around his throat and tightened. Bright spots danced through his vision and he twisted frantically, driving an elbow into the unknown assailant's ribs.

Rose screamed on the far side of the room.

Erven clawed with his free hand at the fabric cutting off

his breathing, panic setting in as his vision grew darker. A swimming sensation enveloped his head, and he dropped the knife. Somewhere outside, someone yelled. Erven's vision went black, then all noise faded into nothingness as darkness consumed him.

Sometime during the night, Rose turned to sleep on her side with one hand tucked beneath her pillow. She awoke with a start to the bar falling from the door, and Erven gasping in pain. A dark figure loomed over the bed, something glimmering in the light from outside. Rose shrieked as she rolled to the side, tumbling out of bed with her hand clenched around the dagger from under her pillow.

The man who'd been standing over her swore and toppled to the side as his feet tangled in the bedcovers. Rose steadied her hand around the dagger, Tora's instruction flashing back through her mind.

Hit them quickly and hard, or you won't get a second chance.

Rose rammed the dagger into the man's thigh, yanking it free as he roared in pain. His legs buckled, and she caught sight of his eyes in the gloom, burning with hostility as she scrambled to her feet. Across the room, Erven made a choking sound, the noise piercing through her fear and igniting cold fury.

Outside, light bloomed in the corridor, and someone shouted. Before the man could regain his feet, Rose buried her knife to the hilt in his eye. The assassin gave a strangled gasp before sliding lifeless to the floor. The other assailant abandoned Erven and bolted for the door, yelling with surprise as Cedric's sword took him through the middle.

Rose dropped the dagger and rushed around the bed as

Cedric and several of the other Shona ran in, weapons drawn. Out in the corridor, a pair of feet stuck into the doorway—their door guard, dead.

"Milady, are you all right?" Cedric demanded.

"I'm all right." Rose fell to her knees alongside Erven, lying unconscious beside the bed with his shoulder soaked in blood. "Someone find Arielle, fast!"

The floorboards rattled as one of the Shona ran out of the room. Cedric knelt beside her, a steadying hand on her shoulder. "What happened?"

"W-we were asleep. I don't know." Her hands shook as she rolled Erven to his back. Her stomach lurched at the sight of vivid marks appearing across his throat. "Please," she whispered. "Please wake up."

Erven's chest lurched, and she jumped as a fist flew past her ear. His gaze jittered around the room, terror filling his face as he pushed himself to his elbows.

"Don't get up!" Rose exclaimed. She put her hand on his uninjured shoulder, barely noticing the blood on her own fingers. "I'm all right. I'm not hurt."

Tears appeared in Erven's eyes as he sank back to the floor. No sound came from his mouth, but his lips formed her name as he reached up to touch her face. Rose covered his hand with hers and closed her eyes.

Voices filled the room as more guards arrived, demanding answers and explanations until Arielle's sharp voice cut through the chaos. "Out. Everyone, get out."

"Set up a guard around this place," Tait said from the hallway. "No one comes in, and no one else leaves." As he shouldered his way between two of the men to stand behind Rose, he ordered, "Cedric, the one they caught is downstairs. Go make sure nothing happens to him."

The guards began filtering out of the room as Arielle knelt beside Rose. "Thank the Almighty, you're alive." She looked from Rose to Erven, her face drawn with worry. "Let's get you on the bed so we can see what's wrong."

The blue in Erven's eyes had reduced to a tiny ring around wide pupils as he shook his head dizzily. His free hand tensed over his left side.

He's scared?

Suddenly, Rose understood. "We're not going to let anything happen to you. Please." She gently put her hand over the one guarding his side. "Trust me." At his reluctant nod, she looked up at Arielle. "Give us a hand?"

Erven lost consciousness again as soon as Rose pulled him upright. Tait and Arielle stepped in to help lay him back against the pillows, both making understanding noises as Rose explained, "The times he's been injured, he hasn't been able to control anything that happened. He hates feeling helpless."

"I've been there for most of it. I can't say I blame him, either." Arielle wrapped slim fingers around Erven's wrist, her face drawn with concentration. After a long moment, she gave a sigh of relief. "He'll be all right. Now," Arielle gave Rose a stern look. "Is that your blood?"

Rose looked at the front of her shift, blinking in surprise at how messy she was. "It's not mine, it's..." She pointed at the dead assassin on the other side of the room, her hands starting to shake.

"You killed him?" Tait asked, going over to check the man. He whistled in surprise as he saw the wound on the assassin's face. "Milady, you did this?"

Feeling her knees growing wobbly, Rose sat hurriedly on the edge of the bed alongside Erven. He'd regained consciousness again, and she could feel the intensity in his gaze as she explained, "I heard the board come off the door, and I saw someone standing right there." She pointed at her side of the bed. "I think I surprised him when I rolled off the bed, and he lost his balance. I grabbed the knife and—" She looked back at Erven, who still hadn't made a sound. "I heard you choking, and I suppose I lost my head." She rubbed at the blood on her hands. "I don't know how I did that."

"For everyone's sake, I'm glad you did," Arielle said. She returned her attention to Erven, who'd somehow managed to sit against the headboard. "What about you? No—don't try to talk," she warned as he opened his mouth. "You'll only frustrate yourself. Is anything hurt other than your shoulder and your throat?"

Erven shook his head, wincing as Arielle helped him out of his bloodied shirt. The healer hesitated after examining the stab wound through his shoulder, her fingers pausing on the hunter's bands around his opposite arm. Erven flinched at that touch, and Arielle's voice went hushed. "You never wanted those."

He shook his head again—fiercely this time—and pulled his arm away. Rose put a comforting hand on his leg, and he reached down to squeeze her fingers.

"Well, you got lucky this time," Arielle said, turning away briskly to soak a cloth in the water one of the men had brought up. "It went right through the muscle, but most of the bleeding's already stopped." She twisted the cloth firmly, and Rose heard a barely discernible note of anger in her voice as she said, "It wants sewing, and you'll have another scar, but you'll still be able to fight."

Erven's hand tightened around Rose's fingers as Arielle

laid the cloth over the wound in his shoulder. Rose looked away from the pain and fear in his face as Arielle suggested, "Rose, let's have you clean up. Tait?"

The Shona stood from his examination of the two assassins. "I'll be right outside."

As the door closed behind him, Rose quickly changed into a new shift and dress, sponging blood away with revulsion. *If this is what fighting is like, I never want to do it again.* Tapping on the door to call Tait back inside, she asked, "You said one of them got away?"

"He didn't get far." Tait said. He brushed his hair out of his eyes as he explained, "Some of the others were still awake. They heard the commotion and grabbed him as he came bolting through the common area. Guess regicide was a little much for his stomach."

Erven's voice came out a barely audible croak. "It is for most people."

"I told you not to talk," Arielle admonished as she wrapped bandages around his newly stitched shoulder.

"Torvald was behind this," he said with a defiant glance at Arielle. He winced and rubbed his throat. "We can't let him get away with it."

"We won't." Rose pulled her braid over her shoulder and began undoing it, her fingers steadying with the familiar task. "As soon as the sun rises, I'm calling the moot together. Targeting me is one thing." She looked at Erven again, cold fury rising. "Targeting the people I love is another. This time, they're answering directly to me."

"I'm coming with you," Erven whispered hoarsely. He pulled his shoulder away from Arielle, grimacing as he stood up. "We'll face them together."

. . .

A HORN CALLED from the top of Hold Eskel, the call to moot rebounding off the trees and across the meadow. The sun had barely risen, sending pale rays across the encampment. Rose and Erven waited impatiently in the meeting tent, standing close enough for their hands to intertwine. Erven's shoulder burned like fire under his armor, threatening to distract him from the fight he feared was coming. He tightened his hand around Rose's before letting go, grasping his sword hilt as the call to moot split the air once more.

The other representatives arrived in ones and twos, their irritation turning to confusion as they arrived to see the tent guarded by Shona.

"Milady, what's going on?" one of the men asked as he took his seat.

"Attempted regicide," Rose answered tartly. "Your questions will be answered as soon as everyone arrives." She looked over at the elder, who'd sent men to summon each of the chiefs as soon as he'd heard what had occurred. "Where are they?"

The man squinted in the direction of the Holdmasters' camp. "It would seem they're on their way, Your Majesty."

Rose set her jaw grimly, her expression matching Erven's own. He stepped back as the Holdmasters approached, far enough to keep an eye on both them and Rose. The early morning sun warmed his hand on his sword hilt as he looked across the tent to see Tait and Cedric moving into similar defensive positions.

She'll have to speak for both of us, but I can still protect her. Erven loosened the catch on his sword, carefully drawing his sword an inch or two from the scabbard. A few hours of sleep between the attack and morning had helped settle his body, but his mind still raced. He doubted Rose had slept at all.

"What is the meaning of this?" the leader of the Thinar clan demanded as the last of the Holdmasters entered the tent. "This breach of our trust and dishonorable treatment will not be tolerated—"

"Quiet." The word left Rose's lips as sharp as a sword. "You lost all tolerance in this assembly when you ordered the attack on your rulers."

The moot fell silent around them as Rose gestured sharply at the Holdmasters. "Complaining instead of offering solutions. Spreading dissension. Attacking unprovoked. Coercion, rebellion, torture, and murder. Treason!" she shouted, flinging the accusation in her clansman's face. Erven had never seen her look more beautiful than in that moment. *She's found her voice.*

"I gave you every chance to abandon this ridiculous course of action. *Every chance!*" Her eyes flashed, the fury enough to send the Thinar leader reeling a step backwards, glancing at his fellows for support. "You attacked my people, you killed my men, and you tried to kill me. I was willing to accept that you might hate me enough to want me dead, but you have gone too far." Several of the Holdmasters had deserted their leaders, slipping from behind them to the sides of the tent. She spun around, addressing the rest of the moot in one icy sweep.

"We were sleeping peacefully when armed men broke into our room and attacked us." She gestured at Erven, who lifted his chin enough for the morning light to warm the bruises across his throat. "No matter what code of honor you claim to follow, no one can deny the cowardice of sending men to kill while their victims are helpless." Heads nodded across the assembled tribal leaders, and several hands moved to weapon hilts.

Erven eyed their opponents as more men slipped from around the Holdmasters. Across the tent, Torvald pinned him with a furious look as Rose said, "The Free Holdmasters claim to have Illyn's best interest at heart, but they're interested only in power. If you side with them, you'd better hope your allies are trustworthy." Rose's voice cropped threateningly low. "If they feel endangered, they won't hesitate to turn on you who support them."

"This is outrageous," the Hold Aubron leader blustered, looking around in panic. "You have no grounds for these kinds of accusations."

At that, Erven had heard enough. His sword cleared the scabbard with a rush of steel as he closed the distance between himself and the Holdmasters. "Enough." His voice came out a painful, grating whisper. At the sound, or lack thereof, the rest of the tent went silent. "If I were you, I'd be very, very quiet."

Across the tent, clothing rustled as one of the other tribal leaders addressed the moot. "Brothers, Your Majesties," Erven blinked as the man included him in his bow, "I've heard enough." The highlander gave the few remaining Holdmasters a scornful look "Our customs respect the right of one leader to challenge another, but conspiracy and murder have never been part of our law." He bowed before Rose. "Your Majesty, we are yours to command."

Nods of acknowledgement greeted this statement, as several of the other previously undecided clan leaders also bowed in Rose's direction. The Hold Mori leader, standing shoulder-to-shoulder with Tait at the edge of the gathering, said, "Our people followed you at the first, and we'll be with you to the end." He nodded firmly to Erven. "With both of you."

Similar sentiment from the others followed, even as the Holdmasters grew more and more nervous. Finally, Rose turned her full attention back to their ringleaders. "I'm not a tyrant. I'm also not the naïve weakling you assumed me to be." She straightened her shoulders, the aspen leaf around her neck catching the light as she commanded, "Your people have spoken. I will have your sworn loyalty now, before every witness here, or you will learn how dangerous your queen really is."

Erven shifted his weight and tightened his grip around his sword hilt as the Holdmasters looked at each other with the expressions of rats caught in a trap. Finally, with a sigh of defeat, the Hold Westin leader bowed his head and took a knee. "Your Majesty." His voice carried only as a mutter. "I beg mercy."

"Well chosen. You'll have it," Rose answered sternly. "But I will not tolerate further dissension."

The other two Holdmasters reluctantly joined their comrade, the Aubron leader bowing in Erven's direction. "I'll swear to you, Sir. You showed my people kindness when none was warranted."

Erven nodded, not daring to trust his fragile voice.

Just then, the tension broke with a shriek that left Erven's ears ringing, the command carried from a signal whistle just dropping from Torvald's mouth. Before anyone had the chance to respond, Torvald's sword flashed through the air, cutting down at his former allies. Commotion exploded inside and outside the tent, as fires flared in the encampment and weapons rang out. Blood flew through the air as the Westin Holdmaster fell, the others scrambling for weapons as Erven yanked Rose behind him.

Torvald's sword clashed against an axe blade as the Thinar leader spun to hack at his unprotected legs. Erven lunged forward to intercept the blade a moment too late, and Rose's clansman fell with a deep gash through his neck. Torvald shook blood from his sword, his dark eyes targeting Rose as she stood behind Erven.

Erven's shoulder burned as he engaged, grateful for the weeks of training that had marked the time in Hold Aubron. Torvald staggered back against the onslaught of blows, the man's eyes growing frightened as Erven's sword locked against his, sending it flying. Before he could grab it, Erven kicked the blade further away, angling his sword at Torvald's throat.

"So, the king finally shows his mettle," Torvald spat. "I'm glad I was right about you."

"I'm not starting my reign this way." Erven lowered his sword, throat in agony as he forced the words out. "Leave before I change my mind."

For a moment, Torvald's stony eyes were confused as he stumbled to his feet. Then, anger broke his composed features into a snarl. He yanked a knife free from his belt and threw himself towards Erven, a yell turning into a gasp as a sword met his unarmored torso.

Rose let go of the sword hilt and stepped back in horror as Torvald collapsed. White showed all the way around the blue in her eyes as Erven motioned her back, leveling his sword in case another attack was imminent.

Torvald gasped, blood spilling between his fingers. "I was mistaken." A shudder ran through his body. "My little cousin has some spirit after all." A line of blood trailed from the corner of his mouth as he laughed bitterly, the laugh fading into a gurgle as the light left his eyes.

"Cousin?" Rose asked Arielle, trying to moderate her voice back to its usual pitch. They'd taken refuge in the tower as the rest of the highlanders and Shona worked to restore order and put out the fires set by Torvald's minions. Overhead, the sturdy beams of the Hold mocked the sense of safety absent from the last day. "I thought my family line was wiped out."

Arielle shook her head. "The royal family, yes. Your father's brother was exiled from the Thinar years before you were born. We never did know what happened to his son."

"I wish I'd known," Rose said.

Erven adamantly shook his head. The anger in his eyes reminded her of his months of matching wits with the man responsible for the Holdmasters' rebellion.

"Perhaps you're right." She leaned her head against his shoulder, the exhaustion from the last day finally making its way to her body. "The Holdmasters' resistance is finished. We won."

Callused fingers wrapped around her hand. "*You* did it, Starshine." Erven kissed the top of her head. His faint voice carried to her ears alone as the chaos outside died out. "I always knew you were strong, but now everyone knows."

33
NEW LIFE

"All right, hold still."

Rose did her best to comply as Willow tightened the laces on the back of her dress.

"Confound it, I said 'hold still', not 'stand as stiff as a sword'!"

"Sorry," Rose apologized, trying not to rumple things as Willow finished. The embroidery around the neckline and hem of her wedding dress had been the combined effort of many hands in the last two months of furious work and planning. Forget-me-nots, wild roses, violets, and daisies danced in a sage green border over dark lilac fabric, bearing many similarities to the people who'd made them—Heather's stylized and artistic, Willow's careful and precise, and Clover's exuberantly non-uniform.

Willow finally gave a satisfied sigh.

"May I move now?" Rose asked.

"Aye, go on."

"Thank you." A breeze tickled her skin as Rose turned to face her friends. Heather and Clover sat elbow to elbow on the chest under the open window, their faces gleaming with happiness and much washing.

"Beautiful, Lady Starshine." Heather slapped a polishing cloth across Clover's lap, getting up with Rose's coronation crown in her hands. The silver filigree sparkled in the light coming through the windows as Heather reached up to settle the crown on Rose's head.

"Aye, beautiful." Clover picked up a handful of sweet woodruff sprigs, tucking the delicate white blossoms around the edges of the crown.

Willow joined her sisters, holding the aspen leaf necklace. "Don't forget this." Pride filled her eyes as she clasped the necklace around Rose's neck. "You look lovely, Starshine."

Rose smiled at her friends, resplendent in their own fancy attire. "Thank you." She pressed quivering hands to her stomach. "I'm so nervous."

Heather draped an arm around Clover's shoulders. "It'll be all right. It's not like you've just met him, after all."

"It's been a long road to this day." Willow brushed a piece of woodruff from Rose's shoulder, her hand lingering a moment with a reassuring squeeze. "Don't worry. Everything will be fine."

Rose impulsively gathered all three of her friends into a hug, Clover squeaking as Heather's arm knocked her hat off her head. "What's this?" Heather gasped. "We practically have to hunt you down with a fishing net to get you to hug us."

"Didn't it occur to you that she might be growing up, just like the rest of us?" Willow admonished her sister. She settled her arm around Rose's waist on one side and

Heather's on the other. "We're only missing Violet to have things just like the old days."

The reminder sent a thread of sadness through the happy flutters in Rose's stomach. "I got a letter from her, finally. The winter was hard for them, just like it was for us." She bit her lip. "She barely found out about the wedding a little while ago."

"I wish she could be here," Clover said. "I've still got her Wintermorn gift. If things go on like this, I'll have to go back home to make sure she gets it."

"Time for that later." Willow slid out of the group embrace, tugging the sleeves of her blue-green dress down over her wrists. "No planning or plotting today, not even from me." She winked at Rose. "Today, we celebrate."

The others broke apart from the hug as Arielle came in, elegant in dark red and flushed with happiness. "Rose, dearest. It's time."

Water. New birth, new life.

Erven and Rose bowed their heads as the priest trickled a stream of crystalline water over their clasped hands. "You have sworn to protect and respect each other, to uphold the honor of your house, and to remain steadfast in times of greatest need." The priest's face wrinkled around his smile as he added, "And to all these things, you have added the promise to love, even when the storms of life cloud your minds and hearts."

Erven felt Rose's fingers tighten around his before letting go, as the priest gestured for them to face the onlookers. "Take a moment," the priest said quietly. "Remember the faces of those here, and bring them to mind when you feel the world has turned against you."

Erven took a deep breath and surveyed the crowd. The hall, opened finally after months of cold, had filled with their friends and well-wishers in a barely contained display of joy. In the throng, he recognized the basket-weavers Mari and Carine, the younger woman arm in arm with Gregor the Watchman. Arielle stood surrounded by the Shona, her eyes filled with barely contained tears of joy. Merald and Tora had their arms wrapped around each other, Merald holding their newly adopted daughter tightly with fierce pride in his face. Willow and her sisters made a bright spot in a crowd filled with people dressed in subdued colors, Clover's hat stuck with a hawk feather 'in honor of the occasion'. A similarly bright spot could be seen on the other side of the crowd, and he felt Rose inhale delightedly at the recognition of Sea Wanderer colors.

I didn't think they were coming. Willow will be pleased.

He and Rose grinned at each other before turning their attention back to the priest as he said, "As your lives are intertwined, so too are your responsibilities." Erven nodded carefully, feeling the weight of the crown against his head as the priest asked, "Do you swear to protect and uphold these people who look to you for guidance, never forsaking your duties to them as King and Queen of Illyn?"

Erven answered with Rose, "We do."

The priest nodded, solemnity barely holding ground over the joy in his face. "Join hands again, my children." As they did, he declared, "Bound in life and death to each other, in the sight of this company and the Almighty One who created us, I declare you husband and wife." As whoops and cheers rang out, the man bowed his head towards Erven. "And long live the king."

It wasn't really proper, but he couldn't resist. As applause from the onlookers filled the hall, Erven wrapped his arms around Rose and kissed her. She returned the kiss, her face pink as they broke apart. Behind him, he could hear the priest chuckling as Willow gave a war whoop and Heather whistled. "Your Majesties?" The priest gestured to the doors. "Your people await. Go in peace."

ROSE EXPECTED them to stop once they left the hall. Instead, Erven tugged her hand, hurrying her away towards the wall.

"Slow down!" she laughed, hurriedly gathering her skirts.

"Sorry." The star pendant gleamed against Erven's tunic as they reached the top of the stairs. "I wanted to get us away before everyone started coming out. Look, see?" He turned her to look back down at the courtyard, where the first people had started streaming out of the hall. "I want a minute with you all to myself."

Rose smiled up at him, the happy fluttering in her stomach calming at last. "Good idea." She didn't pull away as he hugged her from behind, one hand flat against her stomach. Neither of them said much as they watched the happy commotion down in the courtyard.

Finally, Erven commented, "I didn't expect him to add the bit about us sharing responsibilities and serving the people well. I thought that was part of the coronation litany."

"It is." She sighed. "I asked him to add it. I hope you

don't mind, but I don't think you're getting a coronation of your own."

"I did wonder why Merald brought the crown with him when he and Tait came to help me get ready." He let go of her to pull the crown—worked in gold as opposed to silver—off his head and squinted dubiously at it. "You know I was happier without one, right?"

"I know." Rose eased her own crown around her head. "You won't have to wear it often, I promise."

Erven grimaced. "I'll take your word for it. I'm happier without a coronation, too." He put the crown back on and replaced his arms around her. "This is enough ceremony for me."

Both of them laughed as a figure clad in a blue-green dress bolted out of the hall towards another person whose blond hair reflected the sunlight. Even from the wall tops, Ethan's laugh was audible as Willow crashed into his arms.

"Ah, she spotted him finally," Erven said with a soft laugh. "I noticed them during the ceremony, but I didn't know if she did."

"He never stops surprising me, how often he's able to make his way back here." Rose said as Ethan picked Willow up and spun her in a giddy circle. "I know it means she'll be leaving us someday, but I am happy for her."

"Shall we go down?" Erven let go of her waist and took her hand, his vivid blue eyes questioning. "They're all waiting."

Her hand tightened around his. "Together."

TO THE READER...

Fires of Freedom was written in the worst eight months my family has experienced to date. I didn't realize quite how bad things were until recently, now that we've come through the darkness and realized just how beautiful the light really is. Frustration and confusion, exhaustion that cuts to the bone, the urge to push away those closest to you, and this feeling of fighting a battle that never lets up... all of it bears such resemblance to the struggles Rose and Erven face in this story.

I spent months caught halfway between these two main characters. Like Erven, I found myself fighting, fighting, fighting to take care of the people I loved, not knowing or really caring how much of myself would be left by the end. And like Rose, I struggled between heart and head—knowing I desperately needed the support of those around me, but pushing away those I loved in order to shelter and protect the fragile bits of myself that I had remaining. I spent a lot of time fighting, even when giving up and surrendering to God was the best thing to do. This book was written from the bottom of a very hard season, and I don't think it was an accident that I wrote it when I did.

Maybe you can relate. Shoot, maybe you're in that same type of season now. If you are—if you're struggling in a hard time when it seems the enemies just keep coming to kick you when you're already down—Fires of Freedom is for you.

Writing this note to you makes it feel so surreal, like a half-remembered nightmare. Because here's the thing, these seasons of miserable, deepest, darkest winter don't last forever. They *do* eventually end; and let me say, being able to laugh again feels so good.

If this hits a little close to home, come tell me. I'll pray with you, cry with you, and reassure you that spring will come again.

Chin up and shoulders back, dear friend. You can do this.

-BCC

CAST OF CHARACTERS

LOWLANDERS

A country of mountains bordered by fertile plains and cold seas, Illyn was defeated twenty years ago by an army hailing out of the northern edges of the sea. Clustered in the thin strip of land between mountains and ocean, the lowland towns bore the brunt of the Illyn's long occupation. Overlooked and—in some cases—looked down on by the highlanders, the people of the lowlands have a unique understanding of what being a citizen of Illyn means.

King Alaber Thinar

Last king of the Thinar line, Rose's biological father. Killed in battle when Illyn fell, after securing the survival of his wife and daughter.

Arielle Brynjar

Castle healer and Rose's advisor. Former leader of Hold Brynjar, she keeps her background a secret from almost everyone. Raised Erven from age five onward, and knows him better than anyone else.

Brielle 'Rose' Thinar

Queen of Illyn by birth, she ascended the throne two years ago after being raised secretly in the neighboring Gaillen Woods. Since her coronation, she has grown in confidence, but still lives under the assumption that the entire burden of leadership must rest solely on her shoulders. Eighteen years old.

Carine

Widowed basket-weaver with one young son. Mari's daughter.

Cedric

A castle guardsman in his early twenties. Broad-shouldered and even-tempered, he adapted easily to the change in leadership after the warlord's defeat, and has found new friends among the Shona.

Gregor

Harbor outpost Watchman, former huntsman.

Mari

Elderly basket-weaver, mother of Mari.

Merald

Former slave and Erven's best friend, he was born and

raised in the Aubron tribe but hasn't seen his home for over a decade. At twenty years old, he is married to Tora and spends his time caring for infants in the Rogue School. After sustaining a grievous injury in battle, he has never shaken the thought that death should have claimed him.

Commander Ricar

Guard commander in the castle, overseeing most of the traditional Illyn military forces. The only officer left from the previous garrison; his knowledge of military matters makes him a welcome addition to Rose's advisors.

OUTSIDERS

While not native to Illyn, the people who assisted Rose's rise to power have remained crucial to the success of her reign. Whether from the nomadic, powerful Sea Wanderers or the mystical Gaillen Woods, Rose's most cherished allies have long since blurred the boundary between friends and family.

Clover

The embodiment of 'constructive chaos', Clover is growing into responsibility with humor and panache. A caregiver in the Rogue School, she approaches every challenge with optimism and compassion in every breath. Sixteen years old.

Ethan

Sea Wanderer Council Intelligence agent, with a crooked sense of humor and a darkly suspicious streak. Twenty-four years old.

Heather

At eighteen years old, Heather occasionally lets silliness slip away to reveal a deeply observant nature. Willow's closest confidant, she will keep a secret to the end of time, even as she adds wit and humor to every dire situation.

Tiren

Sea Wanderer boy, friend of Willow and Heather.

<u>Violet</u>

A quiet and kind healer, one of Rose's best childhood friends.

<u>Willow</u>

Older than Rose by two years, known for her dry humor and formidable will. The older sister of Heather and Clover, she keeps everyone around her grounded in reality with a no-nonsense manner and steadfast heart.

THE SHONA

Originally a group of young resistance fighters, the Shona have grown in numbers and power since the revolution. Now serving as the eyes and ears of the Crown, these elite fighters keep the peace in the foothills and beyond. Their loyalty to the queen is only matched by their loyalty to their commander, who has been known to risk his own life for their safety.

Annika

Commander of the Hollow base.

Ansel

Whitecaps Shona under Carina's command. Descended from the Mori tribe, with the physical features to match. Seventeen years old.

Arrick

Hollow Shona, nineteen years old. One of the few Shona who uses a bow as opposed to a sling, and an expert woodsman.

Carina

Whitecaps outpost commander, blind in one eye from an old injury.

Erven

Shona commander and Rose's right-hand man. Twenty-one years old. Rose's first ally in Illyn, who secured her throne by killing the previous warlord in battle. Sacrificial, kind, and understanding, he places the safety of his clan and queen above most other priorities.

Lena

Erven's sixteen-year-old adoptive sister, a trainee healer under Violet and Arielle's instruction.

Tait

Erven's second in command, and the de facto leader of the Shona when Erven is preoccupied or busy. Jittery and somewhat paranoid, he prefers to stay with something always at his back. About the same age as his commander, he has known Erven the longest among the rest of the Shona Command.

Tora

Shona healer and Merald's wife. While she remains strong-willed and compassionate, caring for the most vulnerable children in the Rogue school has smoothed some of her rough edges.

HIGHLANDERS

Notoriously obstinate and opposed to change, the highland tribes resisted Lord Kuma's attacks and retreated into their own territory. Upon Rose's appearance, most fought alongside the Shona and Sea Wanderers to liberate Illyn. In the intervening years, a movement has begun among the more traditional tribes to bring Illyn back to the old ways—succession determined in combat, and the authority of the individual Holdmaster.

The Aubron Tribe

Fierce mountain dwellers, their Hold is a terraced town set around a single stone tower. Like many other highland tribes, they uphold the ideals of honor and clan loyalty above all else.

The Brynjar Tribe

The farthest east Hold in the mountains, Hold Brynjar was razed to the ground when Illyn fell. With its people scattered, no one has raised the Brynjar Tribe's banner in almost twenty years.

The Eskel Tribe

Situated in a wide bowl-shaped valley deep in the Illyn mountains, Hold Eskel is one of the main places for multi-tribe gatherings. After sheltering Rose's mother until her death from illness, they were the first tribe to pledge loyalty to Rose as queen of Illyn.

The Mori Tribe

The Mori settled in Illyn over a century ago from the Kittai Islands. As such, they bear features similar to their ancestors—slanted eyes, tawny skin, and crow-black hair. Slow to offer allegiance, they will be loyal for eternity once it's earned.

The Thinar Tribe

Rose's ancestral tribe, their line sat on the Illyn throne for several generations before the royal family was wiped out in the invasion. While they fought on Rose's side for her parents' sake, their loyalty has since cooled.

Torvald

A mysterious survivor from the original invasion of Illyn. While his tribe is unknown, his adherence to the old traditions and relentless hatred of Rose makes him a catalyst for the Holdmasters' plans.

ACKNOWLEDGMENTS

Wow, book two!

I honestly didn't know what to expect once I got here. Crying, I suppose. Or possibly maniacal laughter, as my last two brain cells spiraled into oblivion. Theatrics aside, there are a few people, establishments, and non-corporeal entities that deserve thanks.

Thanks to the Colorado Blizzard of March 2021, which was a true joy and delight to experience. Winter isn't all bad, and I will always cherish the memories of sledding down the Nuthouse front lawn.

Bookstagram, thank you for introducing me to more talented authors, enthusiastic supporters, and new friends than I could ever list here.

Loads of appreciation to Mr. Ed Sheeran, whose song 'Perfect' came on unexpectedly in my Spotify list and hit me with the exact vibe I needed to write a very emotional engagement scene.

Extra-special thanks to the many, many people who encouraged and supported this huge leap into the unknown. In particular, my alpha readers Amy and Megan, my beta readers Julia, Michelle, Shane, Rachael, and Doug, and my sanity buddy Emmy. Your insight, comments, and sheer enthusiasm propelled me through the moments when I sat there with hands frozen by imposter syndrome, asking, "Will anyone even *care* about this story?"

Oh yes, and my family, who will probably never quite 'get' the inner workings of my head. Thank you for trying, regardless.

Lastly, sarcastically, and certainly most prominent—Tucson Fire Department and Pima Community College. Your horribly managed paramedic program created the Absolute Worst season our family has experienced to date. But yes, my thanks to you. I wouldn't have ever understood—really understood—what it is to lean exclusively on God and walk through a season of fighting on all fronts, were it not for this experience. You provided the high stakes. God provided the fire. This story is a combination of both.

Finally, Rose and Erven. You've been through hell and high water, but you've come through it holding hands and stronger together. You inspire me to reach higher and fight harder. Thank you for going on this journey with me, however far it takes us.

ABOUT THE AUTHOR

Brigitte Cromey is occasionally mistaken for an insulted tabby cat when disturbed while she's reading. In addition to hissing and sitting in bizarre postures, she loves sleep, good food, mischief, her home, and her loved ones. While navigating through this journey of life, she is constantly at war with her inner cynic, and is learning how to choose kindness first. She lives in a homely house in southern Arizona where tea, children's voices, and long naps are the order of the day.

Brigitte can be found lurking around Instagram @yarrowleafauthor, or on her website at wordsinmyblood.com

instagram.com/yarrowleafauthor